The well-bred ██████████ *sisters dream* ████████ *bridal bouquets.* **And** *now it's young Emily's turn to find the ideal mate.*

The abandoned house and land Emily Bright has claimed for her own are just what she needs to achieve her coveted independence— but the lean, rugged stranger who barges in on her one night is definitely *not* part of her plans! Emily's not about to give up her new home, no matter how much Jake Sullivan rants and raves. But while she can shut her ears to his protests, she can't stifle the warm, tingling feeling the strong, sexy loner sets off inside her.

Jake knows this is *his* land—and Emily isn't going to steal it away from him! He can wait here as long as it takes for her to grow tired of the game and leave—as long as he resists the nagging urge to hold her, to kiss those luscious lips, and to make passionate love to her. And if she still refuses to go . . . Well heck! Maybe he should just marry delectable Miss Emily Bright and be done with it!

Susan Kay Law

Marry Me

An Avon Romantic Treasure

AVON BOOKS
An Imprint of HarperCollinsPublishers

AVON BOOKS
An Imprint of HarperCollins*Publishers*
10 East 53rd Street
New York, New York 10022-5299

Copyright © 2002 by Susan Kay Law
ISBN: 0-380-81907-4
www.avonromance.com

First Avon Books paperback printing: May 2002

Avon Trademark Reg. U.S. Pat. Off. and in Other Countries, Marca Registrada, Hecho en U.S.A.
HarperCollins® is a registered trademark of HarperCollins Publishers Inc.

Printed in the U.S.A.

10 9 8 7 6 5 4 3 2 1

To Nate, on the occasion of his high school graduation

Keep safe
Go to class
Get some sleep
Have fun
Check in regularly ("Hi, Mom, I'm alive" will do)

I couldn't be prouder, or love you more.

Chapter 1

❧❧❧

Philadelphia, 1899

*T*here's a sucker born every minute . . .

    The odd thing about that was that no one who truly knew Emily Bright would ever have applied that phrase to her. For no one who spent as much time as she did with people on the extremes of human existence, in pain and grief and joy, could remain ignorant of some of mankind's essential flaws.

But she'd been born and remained a deeply optimistic person. And that cornerstone of her character, her insistence upon expecting the best in every person and situation, made her the perfect audience for the advertisement that a handsome young man thrust in her hand as she clipped down the street by the Broad Street train station. She'd sneaked off to visit Mrs. Sweeney, whom Dr. Goodale had decreed

1

was recovering nicely from a bout with pleurisy, but Emily wished to examine her one more time just to make sure.

That, and the fact that she very much wanted the information on the flyer to be true.

Free land!

It can be yours! The vast central plains of this great nation abound with plentiful game and pure, sparkling waters, soil so rich that crops spring forth before one has barely scattered seeds upon the fertile ground! And it can be yours, your own home, on your own land, due to the foresight of our government, with no more investment than your own courage and labor . . .

She stood frozen, oblivious to the stream of jostling people that eddied around her.

Home, her own home.

She'd never had one, not one of her own since she was five. Oh, she'd lived places, she and her sisters, places she'd always understood she'd have to leave eventually. Even the beautiful house she'd lived in for the last fourteen years—no one had ever allowed her to labor under the delusion it was hers. And now Norine, her sister Kate's stepdaughter, had made no secret of the fact that she was impatient to move back into the house her father had willed her.

Where would Emily and Kate go now? She'd no idea. Kate cheerfully insisted Emily shouldn't worry, all would be fine. And then she'd popped off to dinner with Floyd Ruckman, the late Dr. Goodale's old, very rich, and utterly unappealing friend.

Emily was terribly afraid that Kate had every intention of sacrificing herself on the altar of not-so-holy matrimony for Emily's sake once again. Emily had been too young to stop Kate all those years ago when she'd married Dr. Goodale. But now that Emily was fully grown and quite capable of taking care of herself, she had no intention of allowing Kate to make the same mistake again. But allowing, or not allowing, Kate to do something was never as easily accomplished as decided.

Kate had already given years of her life for Emily's sake. Emily had no doubt she would continue to do so until Emily proved it completely unnecessary. She'd wracked her brain for weeks in an attempt to figure out how to do just that, but short of marrying Mr. Ruckman herself, she'd yet to come up with a plan.

Someone plowed into her back, and she stumbled forward, reflexively clutching the precious paper.

"You're holdin' things up, missy," a man in a natty suit and handsome black bowler growled at her.

Blinking, Emily surfaced from dazzling dreams of a snug little cabin surrounded by acres of burgeoning fields and pretty orchards. Hers, all hers. "Oh. I'm terribly sorry." Around her, harried people rushed to catch the next train, shouted to hail a cab, or hurried toward the shops and businesses on the street, the ebb and flow of a great city and busy lives.

"Time to get movin'."

"Yes." She grinned so brightly the impatient gentleman couldn't help but smile back. "It certainly is."

It took her three weeks to prepare. Luckily, those three weeks had been busy ones for Kate as well, swept up in the details of settling the doctor's immense estate and of mediating between Loren and Norine, her stepchildren, who hadn't been able to divide a breast of chicken at dinner without squabbling when they were younger. Things had not improved greatly over the years.

Emily often wondered if Kate was tempted to simply step aside. There was no advantage in her standing between them; the amount of his estate that Dr. Goodale left to his second wife was a tiny sliver of his wealth. But Kate was never one to leave a project undone, and her marriage to Goodale was as much a business agreement as anything else in her life.

And so Emily had little trouble convincing Kate to allow her to journey to Colorado to visit their other sister, Anthea, and her family. Though Kate didn't approve of Emily's traveling alone, they'd made the trip several times over the years. The train to Denver was both safe and reliable, and Gabriel, Anthea's husband, always met them at the station himself. Anthea could always use a little assistance, Emily reminded Kate; their oldest son, twelve-year-old Jimmy, seemed to have inherited every one of his father's hellion tendencies.

Kate simply could not leave Philadelphia until the estate was completely settled. She must not consider it, Emily insisted. And Kate could concentrate on the numerous details more fully without Emily's presence distracting her.

Not to mention that, though she would appear in public with her petticoats hanging out before admitting it, Kate was not nearly as fond of the rustic charm and wide-open spaces of Gabriel's ranch as Emily and Anthea were. Anthea had been married for years before Kate was fully convinced that, yes, Anthea really *wanted* to live in such uncivilized conditions.

And so, three weeks and several twinges of conscience for her justifiable lies later, Emily Bright was ready to begin her grand and independent new life.

Free land, Emily soon discovered, was not nearly as cheap as one might have thought.

She'd expected the cost of the train ride that got her to Billings. The stagecoach, a dusty, bone-rattling affair, had sliced another ten dollars from her tiny hoard. She hadn't slept a wink throughout the entire ride, not only because every time she came close to nodding off the road had other ideas, but because she was also too thoroughly excited to sleep. She was nearly there! The vast, empty brown plains and low hills that rolled by outside—perhaps that one, that empty stretch right there, might be hers soon. The thought had her nearly drunk with excitement.

But she hadn't anticipated the kind land agent, who'd been so friendly and helpful, informing her that the government expected her to hand over fourteen more dollars to claim her free land.

"Fourteen?"

"Yes, miss, fourteen dollars." Imbert Longnecker stroked his handlebar mustache, of which he was, he considered, justifiably proud. They didn't get many single women out there, especially not ones as charming as this fresh young thing. The dismay on her face had him rushing to allay her fears. "But the remainder of the fee won't be due till you prove up. Eighty dollars in eight months—"

"Eighty dollars!"

"Only if you prove up on the short schedule," he assured her. "If you stay the full five years, your additional fees will be negligible."

"Five years."

"Yes." He devoutly hoped she would stay that long. "The rules are quite simple, Miss . . . ?"

"Miss Bright."

"Bright. How appropriate."

"Oh." She flushed, as if compliments were new to her and she wasn't quite sure how to take them. "Thank you."

"You'll need to plow thirty acres," he told her. "And pay the fees, and be in residence the entire time. Beyond that, the only requirements are to be an American citizen over the age of twenty-one." Her healthy color drained in an instant. "Are you all right, Miss Bright?"

"Excuse me?"

Perhaps she would faint. And then he could catch her. "A glass of water, perhaps?"

"No." White-gloved fingers desperately clutched the thick braided handle of her string bag. "My apologies. Wh-what is the next step?"

Five years, nothing. He'd be lucky if she lasted five weeks. "You choose your claim."

"We get to choose?"

"You do." Imbert was the proud veteran of two whole lotteries, and he puffed up at the opportunity of assisting someone who could truly benefit from his vast experience. "Not when the reservation first opened, of course—oh, we handed out five times as many numbers as there were claims to be had! But now, well, the excitement has moved out to the newer openings. There are at least a dozen claims to choose from." He stood up and grabbed a map. "Here. Would you allow my assistance?" He unrolled the big curl of thick paper and hummed while he considered.

Emily edged around the slab table to peer at the map. "May I?"

"Of course."

Emily could make little sense of lines gridded across the paper, tiny, neat numbers painstakingly etched in rigid order. Her stomach jittered, excitement and nerves in equal measure. Somewhere on that paper was her home; she just knew it. And once she made that final decision, there'd be no going back.

"Would you—"

"Yes?" She lifted her head to meet his eyes, and he seemed momentarily to lose his train of thought. Flushing, he ducked his head, smoothing the edges of the curling paper with the palm of his hand.

"I thought perhaps that, well, if you hadn't

selected a place already, maybe . . . perhaps you wouldn't mind a bit of advice."

"I would be most grateful for any insight you could give me."

One bony finger traced over the paper. "Maybe . . . no, not there." He inscribed an arc over a wavering line that meandered down the left edge. A river, maybe? She'd always liked the sound of water. His finger took a right turn, wandered with agonizing slowness across the bottom, as her stomach lifted into her throat. "Hmm . . . we don't have as many good ones left as I thought, I'm trying to find one that's partially improved . . ."

If she got any more excited, she thought, she was going to expire before she ever set foot on her own claim.

"There." He tapped his fingers on a square tucked into the far right corner. "Been empty a year now, maybe more. But it was first claimed in '97, should be at least partially improved. Probably even has a house, that's usually the first thing a homesteader puts up."

Her hand wavered in the air. She took a deep breath, steadied it, and placed her finger firmly on the paper. *There*. "What happened to the people who claimed it originally?"

"Who knows?" He shrugged. "We don't keep track. Sometimes they get called home. Some people are too restless to stay in one place that long. Some people find they can't live this far from the city."

She squinted, as if it could tell her something more. Straight, neat lines; thick paper discolored to mottled cream; rows of numbers; what could they tell her? A home couldn't be condensed to bare facts on a map.

"What do you think?" he asked.

The future shimmered before her, full of promise, and she need only reach out and seize it. "I'll take it."

"Here you go." Old Murphy, the locator Imbert—they were not so formal in the West, he assured her, and using his given name was not improper—had recommended to her, hauled on the reins.

"Here?" Emily, who'd been craning her neck for the past hour in anticipation, sat up even higher and spun in her seat, searching. "Where?"

Murphy climbed over the back of the seat into the wagon bed. "Right there."

"But—" The sun was almost down, sliding low and red. Which was no doubt what was making it difficult to properly make out her new home. "It's an improved claim. There's supposed to be a house."

"There is." He pitched two crates over the side and jabbed his thumb west, into the glare. "That's it."

"But . . ." She truly had not expected a house like the ones back East. She'd rolled through the plains on her way to Gabriel's ranch, marveling at some of the rustic settlements that she passed. She knew that houses were different here. Still . . . "That's not a house."

"Claim shack." He heaved her trunk over the side. "Nicer than most, at that. Could use another layer of tar paper, 'course, but that's easy enough to fix."

The wind kicked, and Emily could have sworn the structure shuddered. The land around it, flat and broad, dense with grass the color of summer, dwarfed it, made it appear no more substantial and permanent than a tissue-paper flower in the rain. It was as if the land tolerated it for the moment, and would sweep it away as soon as it had tired of its interloping presence.

"You gettin' out?" Murphy squinted up at her. "Or you want to go back? I'd just as soon you make up your mind before I unload any more of your gear."

She told herself she wasn't even tempted. What did she have to go back to? Thousands of men and women had made a success of homesteading; the newspapers trumpeted their stories regularly.

Though where all those people had gotten to was anybody's guess. There certainly was no sign of them out there.

"I'm staying." She clambered down from the seat and, for the first time, planted her feet on her own land. Give or take five years and a few legal details.

Old Murphy was as thin and resilient as the grass, and as much a part of the land. "I'll probably be back this way in a week or two. I'll stop by, see if you changed your mind by then."

"That won't be necessary." Even if it did make her feel a whole lot better.

"Do it just the same." It took him only a few moments to unload the rest of the wagon. "That'll be twenty bucks."

The figure had shocked her when Old Murphy first informed her of the fee. It cost her more to travel these last eight miles from McGyre than the train ticket from Philadelphia all the way to Billings.

She dug in her handbag, peeled off the bills, and tried not to think about how small her nest egg had become. Something would come up by the time she needed to pay the proving-up fees.

"There." Murphy pulled the last of the crates from the back of the wagon and stacked it next to her two trunks, a valise, and three boxes of supplies. "You sure that's all you need? Seems a small stash to get you through the whole winter. You wanna give me a list of dry goods? I can bring 'em back next time I'm through."

"Thank you for the offer." She breathed in; the air smelled of cedar and sage, of space and possibilities. "Life is ever so much simpler when one is not over-burdened with possessions, though, don't you think?"

He gave a neutral grunt. "Closest water's 'bout two miles straight west. It's got some soda in it; probably unsettle your bowels a bit till you get used to it."

"Two miles?" She'd expected some hardships, understood she'd miss the convenient rush of hot and cold water from the taps at Dr. Goodale's house. But it never occurred to her there wouldn't be at least a pump, as Anthea and Gabriel had.

Despite her determined cheerfulness—or perhaps because of it—some of her dismay must have leaked through, for Murphy shook his head sadly at the naiveté of impulsive girl homesteaders. "I'll leave you a barrelful. Always keep a couple in the back. And I figure you won't have much trouble sweetening some fella or 'nother into fetchin' it for you, regular-like." He winked broadly.

"I'm sure I'll manage."

"Oh, you will." He climbed back up to his seat and grabbed the reins. "Marry up right quick, that's my advice. You'll have your pick, sure shootin'. Most of the girls who come out here who aren't married aren't married for a reason, if you catch my drift. Rest are snapped up right quick. Smart thing of you, to come here to look for a husband. Surprised we don't get more of that."

"I'll keep your advice in mind," Emily said with appropriate solemnity. The last thing she intended was to save her sister from another marriage of convenience only to be forced into one herself. But Murphy seemed so earnest in his advice, she hadn't the heart to reject it out of hand.

"I'm off, then."

He drove away without looking back. Despite the fact that no one would accuse Murphy of being a scintillating conversationalist, and Emily suspected those would be fighting words should anyone try, she found herself unable to keep from watching him drive off like he was her last, best friend, her eyes tracking the back of his wagon until the settling gloom swallowed him up as he rounded over the edge of a swale.

What now? The wind rustled through the grass, whispering the question. It seemed as if there should be a thousand things to do, but she couldn't think of one.

And so she spun slowly, skimming her gaze over the land, trying to get it to settle in and take hold, trying to reconcile it with *home*. On her way to visit Anthea, neat, square little pieces of land, framed by the train windows, clicked nicely by, here and there a rustic little town, completely charming from a distance.

And even Gabriel's ranch was far less . . . intimidating than this, bounded by the enclosing mountains, crisscrossed by stock paths, tamed by cowboys.

This . . . this could never be tamed by anyone. The land wasn't as flat as it first appeared; the darkening sky exposed slight washes and bluffs, the shadows hollowing beneath, the sun glistening gold along the top of the ledges. The grass rippled and swayed, a living thing in a way the clipped lawns of Philadelphia never were. And she was alone, completely and utterly, in a way she had never been before in her entire life. She could shout, she realized, scream to the sky, and no one, not one single person, would come running.

She shivered. But it was beautiful, for all that, the way she could trace the gradations of color across the sky, gold in the west, and then pink, red, bleeding into violet where it bumped down against the ground again in the east. And there a light flickered on, so suddenly she blinked.

She couldn't judge the distance. A small light, close? A bright one, farther? But she wasn't alone after all. There were others who'd made this place their home, who'd lit a lamp and were now settling in for the evening. To supper, perhaps.

As she should be. She certainly couldn't stand out there all night.

The little shack seemed no larger as she approached it. But it wasn't as if she needed much space just for her. It'd be easier for her to maintain. She'd be . . . cozy. Who wanted to rattle around in a big echoing space like her brother-in-law's manse?

Rope as thick as her wrist trailed down from each corner. She followed the nearest one down, brushed aside the grass with her hand, and found it tied securely to a sturdy stake wedged in the ground. Just like a circus tent, she thought, and it made her smile. She tugged on the rope, found it firm. At least it wouldn't blow over in the night. That was good to know . . . though it wouldn't have occurred to her to worry about it.

The front door sagged open, hanging by a single leather hinge, and she gingerly tugged it wider, relieved when it didn't fall off in her hand. The interior was dim, the shutters closed, the fading sunlight behind her throwing her shadow tall and wavering across the wide-planked floor.

She squinted, trying to make it out. The room couldn't measure more than twelve by fourteen, intriguing shapes lurking in the shadows. The sun slipped lower, glinting off glass as it slid past—a lantern. She grabbed it off the wall, and kerosene sloshed.

Emily dashed back to her pile of supplies, congratulating herself that she'd made sure the matches were readily accessible. Curiosity had her hurrying back to the shack. The lamp balked only once before catching, light and odorous smoke wafting from it in equal measures.

But it didn't take much to illuminate the interior. A bed, a table, a couple of chairs, a tiny corner allocated for the kitchen. But for Emily, who'd lived in a mansion but who'd never truly owned much of her own, it was like having a pile of presents handed to her. They were all around her, waiting for her to unwrap and discover some wonderful thing inside. She couldn't wait.

The floor was wood. Warped and dull, studded with knots and wide gaps puttied with gray. But good firm wood, she thought fondly, tapping it with her toe, ever so much better than the dirt she'd expected. She chose to ignore the rodent droppings; she'd get rid of them, both the leavings and the creature who'd left them, soon enough.

There were two windows, the glassless openings firmly shuttered. Thin blue paper covered the walls, great sheets of it curling down from the ceiling, and it crinkled beneath her touch like wrapping paper.

She pushed on the corner of the table. Obviously homemade, it was sturdy all the same, the top sanded so smooth that she could glide her hand over it without fear of slivers. Who made this? she wondered suddenly. Nothing fancy, not the slightest bit elegant, but done with pride, the legs even, the top level, as if intended to serve a family for years.

A shelf laden with books was fastened to the wall over the bench next to the table. She lifted her lantern and tilted her head to make out the titles. James, Hardy, Stevenson, several by Twain. Even

Thoreau. A couple of ancient copies of *American Farmer* magazine. She smiled when she discovered a copy of *The Adventures of Sherlock Holmes*; Kate had read it to her when she was eleven. Grimaced when she came across *The Decline and Fall of the Roman Empire*. Try though she had, she'd never managed to slog past page twenty-five, and had finally managed to "lose" it somewhere in the depths of the clinic. Interesting that these books had meant enough to whomever had lived there to drag them all the way out when surely they'd needed lumber and flour more, but not enough for them to take the books when they left.

Whoever'd built this place, they'd surely left it fast. There were dishes in the dry sink, any water long evaporated, the bottom thick with scum. An opened tin can, empty except for the black crusting its sides, lay on the floor beside the stove.

A shadowed corner sprouted a pile of rusting tools: a hoe, a rake, a bow-handled saw. A rope bunk attached to the far wall held a pile of sheets and blankets. Clothing dangled limply on hooks. A gorgeous green silk dress trimmed with wide bands of creamy lace shimmered against the splotchy, papered walls. One good afternoon of work out there surely would have ruined it . . . a wedding dress, perhaps? Never worn again?

The rest of the clothes belonged to a man. A big one, she thought, lifting a faded blue shirt and measuring its shoulders against her outstretched arm.

What could have caused them to leave so quickly? A sudden inheritance, perhaps, that rendered these things no longer valuable. Or a family emergency, one from which they'd fully intended to return quickly but soon changed their minds.

The air simmered with memories, tangible, out of her reach. Someone else's memories.

She set the lamp on the nearest chair and lowered herself to the bed. The mattress crackled. She stretched out, enveloped in the musty smell of old, dried grass, testing it out, and found it fairly comfortable.

The activity of the past few days hit her all at once, a wave of sapping fatigue. She'd slept little on the train, too excited, afraid to miss a moment, abuzz with anticipation.

But now she was here. Home.

All her precious supplies were still stacked out where Murphy had left them. She probably should bring them in, but there was no one around to steal them. The afternoon's clear skies and mild breezes promised a lovely night. And oh, this was so comfortable. The wind was low, sloughing around the shack, a soothing sigh like a mother whispering to a child.

Just a moment, she promised herself. She'd just a rest a moment, and then she'd commence to settling in to stay.

Emily awoke to dense blackness, her heart pounding, every sense on full alert, but unable to identify exactly why. It was as if she'd been jolted awake by a terrible nightmare, but she couldn't recall a single detail. Perhaps there'd been something outside, a noise that would soon become familiar and friendly but was now shocking to ears more ac-

customed to the burble of voices and rattle of car-
riages. The lamp must have burned out on its own.

But then the door burst open. The doorway was
lightened by moonlight, thoroughly filled by a large,
and very well-defined, human form.

Chapter 2

So this was terror, Emily thought numbly. How
odd . . . though aware of her fright, she felt it
dimly, from a distance, observing more than truly
experiencing the tingling of her fingers, the tight
knot in her belly.

How strange she'd never felt it before. She'd been
sad, of course, and lonely; grieving or worried upon
occasion. Not often, and rarely for long, but those
emotions had been true and deep just the same.
She'd never been truly terrified, however, for she'd
always believed everything would work out just
fine. And it always had.

She lay flat on the bed, absolutely still, and wondered how long she could survive without breathing. Long enough, she prayed, so that the intruder
would never even realize her presence.

He moved silently into the room. There was more
light behind him, thin and pearly, spilling a rectan-

gle of moonlight on the floor. His steps were unerring, as if he could see better than she in the dimness. She kept expecting him to bump into something, the table, a trunk, but he didn't falter until he loomed over her in the bed.

"You're not sleeping," he told her.

As if a dangerous brigand cared whether he disturbed her sleep or not. Her thoughts churned, scrambling to remember which corner held the collection of tools, pondering whether the rake or the hoe might prove a more effective weapon.

"I—" She tried to speak, managed only a squeak.

"Aw, crap, don't tell me you're scared." He was as shaggy as a great bear—wild fall of hair, thick beard, immense shoulders—with a deep grumble of a voice. "You think I would've knocked on the door if I meant to strangle you in your sleep?"

Despite his looking ever so much like the sort who would do just that, he made undeniable sense. "What difference does it make if I'm asleep? Or scared, for that matter?" The first sharp bite of terror receded. Surely if this man threatened immediate danger he wouldn't simply be standing beside the bed glowering at her.

And so she took her customary approach to dealing with a difficult person.

She talked.

"Which I am, by the way. Frightened, I mean. And I was sleeping." She wondered if it would be too obvious if she yanked the covers higher around her neck. "You still haven't explained why you care if I am."

"Frightened? Because women tend to be even more unpredictable and unreasonable than usual when they're frightened, that's why. And sleeping? Because you're probably not going anywhere until you wake up."

"Going anywhere?" she repeated. Dulled by heavy sleep, her stomach still jittering with unease, she sat up—making sure the quilts were wedged firmly in her armpits—and pushed her hair out of her eyes.

"Yeah." He whacked his hand against the bed-frame so hard it nearly sent her tumbling. "Get moving."

"And where, exactly, am I moving *to*?" A nice burn of anger shoved aside the rest of her fear. If he thought she'd be traipsing off anywhere with him, well, she'd just recalled exactly where she'd left that hoe, and figured it would look mighty fine wrapped around his skull.

"How the hell should I know where you're going?" If only he wasn't so large. Plotting a clear path around him was a challenge. "Do I look like I care?"

Deranged, she concluded. Or dead drunk, though he spoke quite well for someone with a brick in his hat. "Who are you?" she ventured. It was one of the first things she'd learned from Dr. Goodale in treating patients. Learn their name, and use it often, to retain both their attention and their trust. Not that Dr. Goodale himself bothered very often, but Emily had employed it to good effect.

His head jerked toward the door. "Move."

"Sir—"

"My name doesn't matter a damn. All that matters is that this is my claim, and I want it back."

If Murphy had taken her twenty dollars and shown her to the wrong land, she was going to wrap that hoe around his neck instead. "If you'd just sit down, I'm certain we can sort through this."

"Nothing to sort through."

At a loss, she simply sat there, squinting at him through the gloom. His hair was dark and wild, blending into the night, streaming around his shoulders and into a heavy beard. All she could see was the hot glitter of his eyes when he turned his head and the moonlight caught him.

Well, if he refused to be civilized and sit down, she certainly was not going to remain on the bed any longer, craning her neck to look up at him. She swung her legs to the floor and stood, only to discover she was still forced to look up considerably.

"Mister, it's late, it's dark, and I'm tired. If you insist this is your claim, either your locator or mine made a terrible mistake." She sighed, just thinking about making the trek back to McGyre. She'd so many plans for tomorrow. "There's nothing for it, I suppose, but to return to the land office and check the numbers."

"I don't need to check any numbers. I lived in this place for six damn months and built every stick of it with my own hands. I know my own claim when I see it."

"Oh dear." Sympathy, rich and bittersweet, welled instantly. Those were his books. His shirts, hanging over her bed. "I'm so sorry. But you understand, the government recorded it as abandoned, and I paid my fee and filed on it yesterday. It's fully legal."

"Yesterday." He spat the word out. "Then you've hardly had time to become attached to the place, have you? Should be no trouble at all for you to move on."

She had to think. She knew the legalities were completely on her side. But there was legal, and there was fair.

And then there was what she could afford to do, which was something else entirely.

"It really doesn't seem wise to attempt to sort this out in the middle of the night, does it? I'm sure that, in the morning, everything will be simpler."

Impatience simmered around him. He jammed his arms over his chest, glaring at her. "Wouldn't take much for me to just haul you out of here and be done with it."

"No, it wouldn't." Charming was clearly beyond his reach, but a bare minimum of politeness shouldn't be. She could understand why he—wrongly, she reminded herself—considered this land his, but she'd never understood rudeness. "It would take a bit more for me to fetch the federal agent who deals with claim jumpers, but I imagine then I'll be done with it, too."

He just barely held himself in check. "All right then. The morning." He hooked the nearest kitchen chair and dragged it close, flopped into it, and kicked his feet up on the foot of the bed.

"You're not planning to stay *here*," she said, aghast at the idea.

His voice lightened with something that, in another man, might have been amusement. "Don't tell me you'll expire from the shock of sharing breathing space with a man for what little's left of tonight."

"I've spent the night with a man before," she said staunchly. And it wasn't even much of a lie. "Several, in fact." They'd mostly been comatose at the time, and barely capable of lifting a finger, much less anything else, but Emily didn't see why that should disqualify it.

"I'll bet."

Emily clamped down on an automatic protest. It'd be utterly foolish to allow him to spur her into ruining her own reputation just for the pleasure of calling him wrong. But his loftily superior skepticism just dared her to contradict him. And Emily had never been good at resisting a dare.

"Fine. You stay." She plopped back down on the bed. The bed that he claimed to have built, that he'd slept in for many months . . . the thought lodged itself firmly, big and brazen, at the forefront of her brain. Oh, she was going to sleep ever so well after realizing that! She'd be tempted to go ahead and hash the whole thing out right now, the late hour be damned, except that he'd be too pleased by her capitulation.

So they just sat there, her on the bed, tense, stiff-backed, hands tucked between her wedged-together knees, fervently grateful she'd fallen asleep fully dressed; him, apparently comfortably settled into what she'd considered a seriously uncomfortable chair.

"So this is what we're going to do until sunrise? Sit here and glare at each other?" she asked him.

"You can do whatever you want." The door was still open, shades of gray and moonlight washing through, but he'd pulled the chair to the side, into the shadows. She couldn't make out his borders, so he was just vague forms in the dark, denser and firmer than the gloom cloaking him, but she thought he might have shrugged.

"And you're going to . . ." She trailed off, she hoped, leadingly. And futilely, for all she received in response was silence brushed with the whispering sigh of the wind.

It went against her nature to let the conversation lie between them. She liked to prod, to ask, to learn. The most cantankerous of Dr. Goodale's patients rarely held out long against her cheerful interest. And, despite this man's *exceedingly* cantankerous nature, there was plenty to be curious about. She longed to know why he'd come there—then and now—and why he'd left. And why he'd left so much behind.

But asking would be pointless. He still hadn't even given her his name. Or asked hers.

What an interesting few days she'd had, she reflected. She'd lied to her sister, quit the city of her birth, traveled halfway across the country, chosen her new home, and been summarily delivered to the middle of nowhere. And now this, a stalemate with a stubborn stranger.

He sat with complete stillness, blending easily into the night, and she could almost pretend he wasn't there. She closed her eyes, tried to sink into the idea.

Except she could hear him breathing. Even, deep,

a steady pulsing rhythm beneath the whoosh of the wind. She found herself breathing in the same cadence, as if her lungs responded to his control rather than her own. *No, not there—not with him—breathe now . . . and now. Not then! Now!* Try as she might, she couldn't keep from falling into the pace he set; it was like purposely trying to dance off beat, when the music kept slipping into your bones and your heart and leading you into the insistent rhythm.

In . . . out. So deeply. So evenly.

Why, she thought vaguely, was she even trying to fight it?

He stayed in the shack as long as he could stand it.

It'd probably been a good thing, Jake decided, that the girl had been there when he arrived. She'd distracted him enough that the memories hadn't had a chance to whack him all at once. If they had, maybe he'd be halfway back to Chicago by now, looking for another bottle.

But then she'd fallen asleep, not five minutes after she stopped yapping. Just closed her eyes and toppled right over on the bed like she hadn't slept in weeks. Like the presence of a strange man, one who wanted her gone, didn't give her a moment's pause.

And that's when the memories arrived. So many, so fast, spinning out from every corner, crawling up from the floor, dropping down from the ceiling. Reeling out from every corner of his brain, pressing in on him until it felt like he might suffocate under them all.

And so he'd fled the pitiful excuse for a house that

he'd worked so damn hard on. He stood in front of it, hands on his hips, sucking in air like he'd just run all the way from McGyre. The air even tasted different out here. Sometimes, in Chicago, when he'd breathed in the thick, sour air, he tried to summon exactly what this air had been like and he'd never gotten it quite right. Even so, it seemed utterly familiar now, the snap of cedar and tang of sage, the sweet dust of grass, a faint tinge of animal musk.

Coming back here might have been a stupid idea. For a long time he'd believed he'd rather go anyplace on earth, no matter how dismal—and hell, too, if it came right down to it—than here. But he'd given up everything for this place, lost too much of himself here. He'd battled the urge to come back, tried to drown it, and finally gave in. He'd win something out of this place, by damn, by finally proving up the claim. Sell it or keep it, he'd decide when the time came, but he wouldn't be defeated by this cursed quarter section. He refused.

He didn't figure the girl'd be much trouble to dislodge. Her type was easy to recognize, and just as easy to dismiss; the only thing he couldn't figure was exactly what had lured her there in the first place. But then lots of people, young or foolish or both, believed the rosy propaganda spread by the government and railroads and came West without having a clue what they were getting into. He should know; he'd been one of them. And while it had been only two years ago, he'd come a good long way from *young*. *Foolish* remained to be seen. But if that term still applied to him, it wouldn't be the same kind of foolish. No more of that new and bright optimism. No longer did he believe that everything'd be all right, that he could *make* it all right.

He knew better. Oh damn, he knew better now.

Reg snuffled off to his left, dipped his head and cropped another mouthful of grass. Jake had given the gelding his head. As long as there was food nearby, the horse wouldn't wander far; it always took determined encouragement to get him moving. Jake dragged his pack from the horse's back and dropped it on a bare patch of the ground a few feet away.

He hadn't brought much with him. He didn't know whether thieves had found the place or whether all his supplies and equipment remained in the shack, and he hadn't wanted to waste his money by doubling up. It'd taken three months of unloading freighters at the docks, three hard, sweaty, nasty months to save up the little he had, and it'd take careful use to see him through the winter and pay the fees next spring. No way he was waiting the five years it'd take to prove up the cheap way.

He plopped down and nestled his head on the pack. The ground was hard and cold beneath him, but that didn't make much difference to Jake; he probably wouldn't be sleeping much anyway. It was the one thing he missed about drinking: sleep. Not that the kind of rest he'd found after downing half a barrel of whiskey was particularly restful, anyway, but at least it was some, a lot more than he'd been managing since.

The tiny shack squatted not twenty feet away, a box dropped on a wide stretch of stubbornly flat land, looking no more permanent than if he'd emptied one of the crates he unloaded at the docks and plopped it down in the middle of Montana. He'd sweated every nail he'd put into it, worried over it, tried his inexpert best, conscious every instant that it would be his and Julia's first home. But he'd had to rush because the thin-walled tent he'd temporarily pitched wouldn't suffice for long.

He'd watched Julia avidly, every time she glanced at his progress. Even more closely the first time he carried her through the door, searching for any sign of disappointment, terrified he'd find revulsion. Her expression never changed; she'd assured him she found it cozy, and that she'd enjoy living there, and that it'd be easy to keep clean. Try as he might, he'd never been able to tell if she told him the truth or not. The claim shack was a million miles from the house she'd grown up in, paled in comparison to even the meanest stables there. But Julia loved him; it was the one thing he'd never doubted. And she'd never let on if he disappointed her.

He'd disappointed himself, though, with a desperate, hollow regret he hadn't been able to shake. He'd build her a real house, he swore, a beautiful one, solid and sturdy as his love, as their future. He'd promised her, and himself, that. Even planned it, at night as they snuggled into the narrow bunk and her belly grew with their child. Two stories, big enough for a family, with a sunny kitchen and a broad porch and windows that encouraged the breeze.

Moonlight wasn't kind to the old shack. Old. He'd built it barely two years ago, but it was indis-

putably old, the roof sagging, the door loose, the tar
paper peeling like birch bark.

I'm sorry, Julia. It was as close as he ever got to a
prayer, the refrain he murmured every night, the
words he rose to every morning.

I'm so sorry.

The sound awoke her, a deep heavy rumble that
vibrated the bed, her chest. For a moment Emily
thought she was still on the train, chugging across
the countryside through the night, the car swaying
over the track.

She opened her eyes to dense and gloomy gray.
Awareness came in stages: not the train, but her new
house. And the man—oh darn! That obnoxious man.

"Sir?" Had she just plopped over and fallen
asleep while he stared at her? How embarrassing, if
not surprising. Years of being called into the clinic in
the middle of the night had taught her to fall asleep,
suddenly and deeply, when given the opportunity.

"Sir?" she tried again, a bit louder. But maybe,
blessedly, he'd slunk off after all. Maybe the fact that
the claim was legally hers had finally sunk in.
Though he hardly appeared the kind to capitulate
easily. And even less the sort who cared much about
legalities.

Still no answer; she heard nothing but the wind
and the rain and the . . .

Rain. "Shoot!" She blasted out of bed, tumbled
out of the door, and burst into the storm.

Gray hazed the sky, hinting that morning approached. The curtain of water rippled when the
wind picked up. It wasn't a violent storm, filled with

rage and destruction. Instead it was just wet, cold, and drenching, dousing the supplies she'd assumed safe in the yard.

She briefly considered grabbing a blanket to drape over her head, but there seemed no point—she was already soaked. Better to keep dry things dry.

She dashed toward her small, precious cache of supplies. And tripped right over a lump on the ground.

"Ouch!" She skidded on the slippery grass, slid right down onto her rump. Swiping her burning palms on her skirt, she rolled over, and realized in horror exactly what had tripped her.

He sat on the ground a foot from her, for all appearances comfortably settled despite the chilly rain pouring over him, one knee pulled up, his wrist resting on it.

"Oh. It's you." She swiped at the rain dripping off her eyelashes, realized it was futile. "I didn't realize you were there."

"Obviously."

"You okay?"

He stared at her so long she had to work not to shift under his regard. Finally he nodded. She waited, until it became clear he'd no intention of saying more.

"I believe I'm all right as well," she told him, making no attempt to hide the censure in her voice. After so many years with the doctor, she should be accustomed to rude men. But instead she'd never understood what a few simple manners would cost them. When she married, she'd long ago resolved, her first requirement in a husband would be impeccable politeness.

"Figured you were." He nodded in the direction of her boxes. "Best be getting your stuff in."

He said it like he'd pegged her as too stupid to drag her things in out of the rain. "I fully intend to," she said, and went to do just that.

This was going to be almost pathetically easy, Jake thought as he watched her struggle to get a good grip on a rain-slicked crate. She dropped it three times before she maneuvered it through the front door.

If there was ever a woman less cut out for the plains than Julia, it was this one. She'd sat there on her butt, a poor, pitiful kitten some heartless person had pitched out into the storm, her hair matted down around her shoulders, eyes all big and curious and wounded. The rain plastered her clothes to her, soaking down all the frills and ruffles, which made her look half the size she did dry.

She whipped back out of the house again, head down, arms pumping as she went back to her pitiful stack of supplies. Grabbing the handle of a case in both hands, she heaved and lifted it all of maybe three inches off the ground. After pondering for a second, she started backing toward the house, rear stuck out like she was wearing a bustle, even though she wasn't, dragging the case behind her.

The sky was lightening up in the east, nudging at the edges of the dark clouds. At this rate the rain'd be over by the time she got all her junk inside.

And then she stopped in her tracks, dropping the case where she stood. Hands on her skinny hips, she stared at him through the pulsating waves of water, her mouth puckered up like she was pondering something. Then, her mind made up, she headed for him with the same direct line and determined step she'd taken toward her boxes.

He planted his feet, resisting the urge to turn and run before she reached him. While he'd never claimed much knowledge of women—far from it— even he could recognize one with a plan on her mind. And he figured he wasn't going to like any scheme hatched in that pretty head.

Pretty. Now, why'd he called her that? It wasn't something he'd cared much about one way or the other, not in a long time. But she was, he realized when she took up a position a few feet in front of him with all the resolve of a general claiming the high ground. If one was partial to delicate, fine-boned, cream-skinned, huge-eyed females, and he guessed he was, considering he'd noticed and all. He'd thought he'd gotten such things out of his system once and for all. Well, he'd just have to try harder.

"I've got a proposition for you, mister . . . ?"

Mutely he returned her leading question with a glare. He didn't want to know her name, didn't want her to know his. That would imply a level of connection, however shallow. The first step toward a relationship, even just a slight one, and that was the last thing he needed.

She frowned. "Mister, then." She almost gave up at that; he saw her waver, but then she squared her shoulders, firm, sharp rounds under thin green cotton nearly black with moisture. "I've been thinking. I could use some help moving all my things inside before they float away. And it certainly can't be comfortable out here for you. So what I suggest is, you could help me lug in a few things—you look like you could take most of it in one load." She smiled at him, winsome, practically flirty, and he wondered if he looked like he could be flattered that easily. And led about by it so simply. "And then you could share the roof, just until it stops raining."

Unbelievable. If he'd wanted out of the rain, did she really think she could have kept him out? But there she stood, with her little drowned kitten face and cheerful smile—just what did she have to be so happy about, all things considered? Nearly every woman of his acquaintance would be complaining a blue streak by now, but she clearly didn't have enough sense to know when she was beat.

All in all, he figured, it'd be doing her a favor, to send her back to her nice, neat, warm life before this place did her any permanent damage.

And so he shook his head slowly.

Her smile never wavered. Maybe even widened a bit.

"Your concern is very kind, but, truly, I don't think there's much danger to my reputation out here. Who'd know? And, even if they did, well, I've been assured that some of the usual rules of propriety must bow to practicality in the West. It'd be understandable, wouldn't it? And I'm obviously in no danger from you."

The raindrops hit his skin and shattered, leaving him tingling and raw. For a man who'd spent a fair amount of time benumbed, trying his best not to feel anything, the sharp edge of sensation was brutally new.

"I like the rain."

"Oh." Her brow furrowed; not unhappy, just puzzled. "You could help me move everything inside anyway. Just to be polite."

It was a wonder she'd made it to Montana whole. It had to be pure, blind good fortune that kept her from falling prey to every confidence man, thief, and plain old rogue west of the Mississippi.

"It'd be pretty stupid of me to help you, wouldn't it, given that I'd prefer it if you lost everything and had to give up sooner rather than later. I'd have a shot at getting a crop in this year, if I could get started soon enough."

That earned him a glare, as effective as that kitten hissing at a battle-scarred old tomcat, and he almost laughed.

Almost.

"You're going to be sadly disappointed if you pin all your hopes on my giving up. I realize you don't know me, but you'd be wise to trust me when I say that I'm not the quitting kind."

"Really." Yeah, he'd bet she'd had to persevere a whole lot in her life. He wondered what had been her biggest challenge. Learning to embroider? Being forced to waltz with a partner who kept stepping on her toes? He jerked his chin in the direction of her drowning supplies. "If you'd kept moving, instead of trying to charm me into doing it for you, you might have most of that stuff inside by now."

Now, that comment she hadn't appreciated at all.

If she could have, he was sure, she'd have flounced off. Probably flounced real well under normal circumstances. But her petticoats must have soaked up a washtub of water, and so she just spun and squished off.

So he just stood in the rain and watched her scurry frantically back and forth between her cache and his house. And he wasn't one bit guilty about it.

Damn it, he wasn't.

Chapter 3

He was gone.

When Emily, refreshed by sleeping far later than she'd intended, stepped out into streaming sunlight and glistening wet grass and found no sign of her midnight visitor, there'd been a twinge of . . . something. Not disappointment, certainly. It would be foolish to be disappointed about being easily relieved of a complication, and a very uncongenial one at that. It was merely that when one had spent a fair amount of time and energy preparing for something, having it *not* happen was disconcerting.

And she had prepared.

She'd put on a lovely cream blouse and a winning smile, started a big pot of strong coffee bubbling on the little monkey stove once she'd figured out how to use it. After all, who had more experience with bad-tempered men than she? Plying them with female charm and good coffee worked wonders.

Though Gabriel, Anthea's husband, had cheerfully accused her of unfair manipulation when he caught her trying it out on one of his ranch hands, it was, in her opinion, simple good sense. Men had many advantages in the world; women must even the odds however they could.

And so, Emily consoled herself, merely the loss of an anticipated battle had her frowning when she circled the shack completely and found absolutely no sign of him. *Him.* She still didn't know his name.

Oh well, she decided, shrugging. She'd plenty to do without worrying about him.

First she spread out all her wet things, strewing them over chair backs and tabletops until the place resembled a laundry more than a home. Then she set to unpacking, humming happily, putting serious consideration into the arrangement of her things. She knew that Norine, Dr. Goodale's daughter, would dismiss her small treasures without a second glance. It didn't bother Emily a bit. There was so much pleasure in having to satisfy no one but herself. She'd always felt very much the visitor at the Goodales', perching lightly in her room without settling in. Her place had always been crystal clear.

But here . . . if she chose to paint the walls purple, leave her clothes strewn over the floor, drag the kitchen table beside the bed, no one could say her nay.

But her happiness dimmed each time she came across his personal property. Her hands, which had flown through their tasks all morning long, so quickly the rest of her had barely been able to keep up, slowed when they touched the clothes that hung limply over the bed. He'd never said "ours," only "mine," as if he'd lived there alone. But there'd obviously been a woman there.

What should she do with it all? It would be a shame to leave things unused, to waste and rot when she had need of them. But so much seemed *his* now; no longer an abstract construct, he'd taken on shape and size and ownership. How could she sleep in his bed, on his sheets, and not wonder about him? The mild curiosity she'd felt yesterday sharpened and focused to a needle point.

Finally she decided to pack up the most personal of the items in case he chose to return for them someday. She'd use the rest—the pots, the furniture, the tools—and consider them part of her claim. She needed them, and if they'd mattered to him at all, surely he would have taken them with him.

Busy as she was, noon came and went before she realized she'd forgotten to eat. But she'd made an excellent dent in her duties; it did not take long to move in, she reflected, when one did not have much to *move*. Unfortunately, she'd also begun a much more extensive list of necessary purchases than her pocketbook would bear.

Deciding to tackle the floor next, she grabbed a bucket in each fist and headed outside. And stopped dead three steps from the door.

"What are you doing?" She dropped both buckets, lifted damp-edged skirts in both hands, and ran. It didn't take long, for it couldn't have been more than thirty yards.

He didn't even look up at her shout, merely lifted

the mallet he held and slammed it down, shooting a stake deeply into the ground with one stroke. Around him were stacked boxes and bags, a coil of rope, a neatly folded pile of canvas. To the north, a horse, its coat deep red and shiny in the sun, nibbled at the lush grass and appeared no more interested in her approach than his master did.

"What are you doing?"

"Putting up a tent." He gripped the stake in one big fist and gave it a waggle. When it stayed firm, he nodded and rose.

She'd known he was big. His shirts would have covered her twice over, and last night he'd had to duck to come through the door. Still, knowing it in a vague, general way was very different from coming up against an immovable man, as big as life. It was difficult to go toe to toe with someone when your nose was level with his chest, a very broad chest covered in worn and stained cotton.

"I thought you left."

"I did." He paced off three long steps. "Now I'm back."

"But—" She scanned all the boxes that littered the site and wondered how the poor horse had managed to carry everything. "You can't put all that here!"

"Really?" he asked mildly, as if she'd just commented on the fine weather.

"Yes, really." Her temper threatened to spike, and she held on to it with effort. She truly was sympathetic to his plight. But it would be much easier to remain so if he didn't persist in being so, well, rude about the whole thing. "I understand this must be difficult for you, but surely you understood the terms of homesteading when you filed. When you left, you must have known it would likely be claimed by the time you returned."

"Never planned to come back." And then he jerked, his arm halting in mid-swing before dropping to his side, as if he hadn't intended to say that and the words caught him by surprise.

"I see." His hair, shaggy, dark, hung low to his shoulders; an equally wild beard covered the rest of his face, making it nearly impossible to read his expression. Only a glimpse of his eyes gave anything away, dark as his hair, deeply guarded. More like a wounded bear than an angry one.

He dragged over a pine crate and pried off the top, revealing neat rows of cans that gleamed dully in the sun. "Understood the rules just fine." He straightened, speared her with a glare. "Do I look like I couldn't understand what I signed my name to?"

Perhaps that had occurred to her. Maybe. "Do I look like the sort of woman who'd make hasty assumptions about others based on incomplete information?"

"Yeah, you do." And then, before she could protest, "Also looks like you're too slick to admit it."

"Now who's making assumptions?"

"Me," he admitted, completely unconcerned with her accusation. He kicked at the roll of canvas, unfurling the creamy material against the rich deep green of the prairie grass.

Around them the land, which seemed so flat and monotonous at first glance, seethed with life. Blue-bells and anemones popped open across it, drifts of color veiling the green. A hawk swooped low and wheeled back up, swift and sure.

She could see why he found it hard to give up. But there was plenty of land here, great stretches of it, surely enough for both of them. She couldn't afford to go looking for another place. But even if she left, he was still going to have to pay the fees again and could do it as easily on another claim as on this one.

"I understand this must be difficult for you—"

"You keep sayin' that." His voice flattened, hard and flinty as shale. "You don't know anything about what it must be for me. Not one damn thing."

"Nevertheless, we're going to have to discuss our . . . predicament. This is obviously unacceptable."

"What's to discuss? Soon as you give up, I'm moving in." He heaved the canvas over the frame he'd constructed and bent to tie the ropes around the stakes he'd buried. "That's all either one of us needs to know."

Emily was famous for her patience, her cheerful good nature. The worst tantrums of Dr. Goodale's most difficult patients never fazed her. And yet, when he bent over his work, ignoring her and leaving her with a view of the back of his head, his thick, tangled hair, blue shirt torn open and fraying over a powerful shoulder, she'd never been so tempted to battle to the end.

"This is my land, whether you want to acknowledge it or not. You're going to have to pack this all up and take it back to where you got it."

"Yeah? You gonna put me over your shoulder and throw me off?"

"You can't simply camp here and wait for me to fail!"

"Can't I?" He sat back on his heels and looked up at her, shadowy eyes glinting with what, in any other man, might have been amusement. "Watch me."

After she'd marched back to the shack, her skirts swishing furiously around what he was sure were skinny little bird legs, she didn't poke her nose out for almost an hour. Once or twice he thought he caught a flutter of movement in the window, at which point he threw himself into theatrically arranging his meager camp. It wasn't long on comfort, but he'd slept in far worse. And he wasn't planning to live in the tent for long.

And then she came back, crossing that thirty yards like Napoleon taking the battlefield, arms pumping, head high. She'd gussied up some, had on a frothy little hat with a white feather that dipped low and drew attention to her eyes, a shiny blue blouse that made her skin look like cream, and gloves so white they reflected the sun.

He mentally trimmed the time he figured he'd have to wait for her to go running back to wherever she'd sprouted. She'd last until wash day, maybe, the first time she had to lug and heat enough water to try and stay that fresh and neat.

This one didn't really think he'd be susceptible to a prettied-up female, did she? That he'd take one look at her all dressed up for battle and say: *Oh sure, ma'am, keep it. Whatever you want.*

Not to mention that if charming him out of his claim was what she had in mind, she'd do better to see if she couldn't manage a friendlier expression. She looked more like someone on her way to clean an outhouse than flatter a man out of his land.

He'd no idea what brought her to Montana. Told himself he didn't care, refused to be the slightest bit interested in her story. But still . . . she wasn't the usual type to come there—a sturdy farm girl, a determined widow. Probably just caught by some stray whim, he decided, trying to avoid the suitor Daddy picked out for her.

"I'm leaving," she began.

"So soon?" he interrupted. "Thanks for cleaning up the place for me, by the way. Looks good."

"Not permanently!" Heat flashed into her cheeks. Her fingers flexed in those pristine white gloves, as if she wished she could wrap them around his neck. "I have some"— she hesitated delicately—"business to attend to."

"Nice of you to keep me informed. Right neighborly of you."

"I'll be back this evening. Tomorrow, at the very latest."

He waited.

"I came to inform you that my absence is merely temporary. I am not, I repeat"—she glared at him, as if by doing so she could bore the words right into his thick skull—"*not* quitting the place permanently."

"Understood you the first time."

"Well, in our brief acquaintance, I have discovered the necessity of being absolutely precise in my explanations. Therefore I am also informing you that it would be a *very* bad action on your part to simply take up residence in my absence."

Now there was an idea. Not that he had any legal right to do so, but forcing her to try to pry him out might be worth the trouble. "Would I do that?"

"As of this point, I do not believe I have tested the limits of what you *would* do." Her feather dropped into her eye, and she huffed it away. "However, I do believe that the government has recently taken a more active interest in prosecuting claim jumpers. While I freely admit to my own inability to remove you bodily myself, I expect federal agents might be somewhat more successful."

He hadn't meant to watch her leave. No reason to waste any more time on her than necessary. Still, he found himself looking after her, watching her feather bob gallantly with each step, her small figure disappear and reappear as she strode over swells and back down into draws. The grass waved as high as her thighs, but it didn't slow her a bit, her pace steadily urgent, heading off into the emptiness until the sun's glare swallowed her up.

Maybe he should follow her. The thought jerked his head back—now where the hell had that come from? If there was ever a person less equipped to go chasing off alone into the middle of nowhere, he couldn't imagine it. She was liable to wander around in circles until her feet fell off.

And wouldn't it be downright dumb of him, halting his work to make sure she was safe and sound? It was broad daylight, and the weather promised to be fine for some time. They'd never had much problem with rattlesnakes in this section of the state, the coyotes stayed away from people most of the time, and the Indians were safely tucked behind reservation fences. Plus he'd noticed when he rode out here that there were a lot more claim shacks scattered around than when he'd left—she couldn't go more than a mile or two without stumbling onto one. She'd be fine. And really, wouldn't a night spent cold and lonely and lost be just what she needed to send her skittering back East? Hell, he'd drive her to the train himself.

And, later that evening, after he'd pried open a tin of beans and wolfed them down cold, when he took Reg out for a long ride just before sunset, he assured himself he did it only for the entertainment.

She didn't return until the next morning after all, and she brought a man back with her.

A skinny man with a gait like a turkey, all trussed up in a fancy gray suit, who drove her home in a nifty little buggy pulled by a handsome gray gelding Jake couldn't help but envy. He handed her down—pretty manners, this one; leave it to her to find the one man in Montana exactly like all the ones she'd left back East.

She shot Jake one glance—simmering with triumph that he could detect even all the way over there—before they disappeared into the shack. Before long a tendril of smoke curled out of the pipe, drifting against the flawless blue sky. Making him lunch, no doubt. Wasn't taking her any time at all to show off her culinary skills.

But it explained why she'd come there. Husband hunting—yeah, that made sense. Maybe she'd gotten herself good and compromised back home and been shipped where women were scarce enough that men couldn't be quite so picky about details of a bride's past.

Well, she was a fine enough looking woman, if you liked them pale and little and proper. She should snag some poor sucker in no time—the sooner, the better, as far as Jake was concerned. Though he'd have to check into whether the guy had a claim of his own or planned on hitching on to hers. Didn't look like he'd be much trouble to scare off if it came to that.

Jake plopped onto the chair he'd arranged specifically to provide a perfect view of her front door, grabbed the first book of the stack he'd picked up in McGyre, and settled in to wait. He'd let them nibble—she looked like she'd nibble—their meal in peace, he decided charitably, before he went poking around to see what was up.

Turned out he didn't have to poke at all. Three chapters later the pair of them headed straight for him, her gloved hand tucked proprietarily in the crook of the suit's arm.

Jake tucked his finger in his book to hold his place. She was looking quite pleased with herself, but the guy appeared a little pale around the edges. He wondered if she'd somehow talked the poor fellow into throwing Jake bodily off the land; he hoped she'd made it well worth his while, considering the bruises the poor sap was likely to earn in the process.

The guy didn't look any more impressive up close; his neck couldn't have been bigger than Jake's wrist, his skin darn near as pale as hers. It was downright insulting that she considered this lowly specimen a fair match for him.

The guy shot her an uncertain look. She smiled sweetly at him, patted his arm in encouragement, and Jake could practically see the man grow half a foot, puffing up in her admiration. It really was not a credit to his sex, Jake thought in disgust, that they were so easily manipulated by a woman's smile. Even though it really was a fine specimen of a smile, one that seemed to generate its own sunshine. The effect had to be calculated, but it looked as genuine as if it'd sprung generously from a warm heart.

"I'm Imbert Longnecker." The man cleared his throat. "The land agent for this district."

Jake lifted a deliberate brow. "Yeah?"

"Emily here . . . ah"—he cleared his throat, plunged on—"Miss Bright, well, it seems as if there's some disagreement over the ownership of this land. But I assure you the legalities are indisputable. I recorded Miss Bright's claim myself and there can be no question of her clear title."

"Well, now, *that* place you're standing, right over there, that's hers all right. Least it will be, if she manages to stick it out." He let that comment hang long enough to imply he considered that outcome extremely doubtful. "But this, right here, this is on the Blevinses' side of the line."

"What?" Miss Bright—what a name, he wondered if she'd picked it herself—dropped the besotted fool's arm as if it burned her.

"Yup." Jake pointed toward the shack. "You see, Mr. Longnecker, *I* built that place. I put it all the way over here, almost to the property line, because it was closer to the nearest stream that way. Figured on saving myself some carrying until we got a well drilled. But this"—he tapped the ground with his foot—"this here belongs to Joe Blevins. Paid him five bucks to let me camp here for as long as I wanted. I figure I'm a good three feet this side of the property line."

"I—" Longnecker looked down at Miss Bright, whose mouth was open in surprise, bright flags of color high on her cheeks as if she'd painted them there. "You won't mind if I check my maps, make a few calculations, do you?" he asked, patting her hand consolingly, trying to salvage the role of hero as best he could.

"Be my guest." Poor sap. Miss Bright didn't strike him as the sort who'd make playing hero worth a man's while. Best old Imbert there was going to get out of the deal was a slice of homemade pie—and she was too thin-hipped to be much of a cook.

The two of them trotted back to the buggy. He dug around awhile, dragged out a whole sheaf of papers and maps, and proceeded to study them. Miss Bright stood on her tiptoes and craned her neck over his shoulder, as if she might discover something the land agent would miss, ensuring a decision in her favor.

Then again, he thought, frowning, if she kept cuddling up against Longnecker like that the agent might side with her anyway. Jake knew damn well he was on the right side of the line; he'd checked it a half-dozen times to be sure.

Well, if they tried to claim otherwise, they'd get more than they bargained for in him. Maybe he'd even enjoy the fight. There'd been a time when he had—or the young man he'd been then had; that man seemed more a stranger than Longnecker now.

He got bored watching them dither over the maps, returned to his book, and sped through another two chapters before the agent climbed back on his buggy and snapped the reins over his horse. He slumped on the seat, and even his jaunty black hat seemed to droop lower than when he'd arrived.

It was most uncharitable of Jake to be so amused by the man's predicament. Hell, it wasn't as if he hadn't done a dumb thing or two in his time for wanting a woman. He should have more sympathy.

But it wouldn't keep him from prodding Miss Bright a bit. He ambled toward where she stood waving after the departing buggy with what, in his opinion, was overdone enthusiasm.

She broke off flapping and met him halfway.

"You did that on purpose."

"Did what?" He tucked his thumbs in his pockets and shifted his weight to one hip.

"You could have told me. Could have explained that you weren't on my land and saved me dragging Mr. Longnecker all the way out here."

"Somehow I don't think he minded. Besides, it didn't come up. Hardly my fault that you assumed I'd engaged in an illegal activity, Miss Bright."

"Very well. A life lesson well learned. From now on I'll assume nothing, Mr. Sullivan. But in the interests of fair play, I'll give you a friendly warning to do the same."

"Nobody's called me Mr. Sullivan in a long time. Jake'll do." He frowned. "How'd you find out?"

She winced, as if caught snitching from the cookie jar. "It's written in some of your books." Without the hat, her brown hair gleamed in the sun, reflecting like still water. "Speaking of which, I should get those back to you. I'll go pack them up, bring them over to—"

"It's not necessary."

"I don't mind."

"No point in it. I'll just have to move them back in when I do. Might as well leave them there for now. I've got enough to hold me for a week or two."

She glared as if she thought the look would make him cower. Amusing, and he hadn't been amused in such a long time it would almost be worth keeping her around for a while. "I'm not giving up." And then she left him, with a flip of her skirts, a toss of hair, leaving a sweet drift of soap and lavender water in her wake.

"We'll see," he murmured, very nearly smiling.

Chapter 4

Dear Kate . . .

So much for the easy part. From this point the letter got considerably more difficult. However, she simply couldn't put it off much longer. She truly did not want Kate to worry—though in all honesty, Kate would worry no matter what Emily wrote. But how to blunt it a little . . . she'd given a lot of serious consideration to the matter and had yet to come up with a good solution.

But for Kate to receive a routine letter from Anthea and thus discover not only that Emily hadn't shown up there but that Anthea didn't expect her would naturally cause worrying of truly epic proportions. Emily hoped her letter would scale it back to Kate's ordinary, everyday worrying.

First, Kate, before you go any further you must promise me you will read this entire letter through without panicking. No, not yet! Stop here. Promise me.

Now then . . . no, no, uncross your fingers. Every word before you make up your mind.

I'm not in Colorado. But I am perfectly safe and comfortable—there's no bandit holding a gun to my head forcing me to write this, no wild Indians hammering at my door. I am absolutely, positively, not only safe but exactly where I want to be. Truthfully, the utter lack of high adventure thus far has me slightly disappointed.

There now, breathe. It'll be all right. It is all right, though perhaps not what you would have chosen for me. Well, I know what you would have chosen for me, but I decided it was about time for me to do the choosing.

I'm in Montana. Yes, Montana, on my very own claim, in my very own house, snug as a bug, excited over this new stage in my life . . . in our lives. This homesteading is the simplest thing: choose a claim, pay a few dollars, sit tight until the land is yours, and then sell it for a tidy profit. Really, I don't know why everyone doesn't do it.

Sit right back down now, Kate. I mean it! I know you're halfway to booking a ticket here but really, there is no need. I'm perfectly safe. My claim came complete with a furnished house—yes, my luck is holding well. My neighbors are congenial, the landscape astoundingly scenic. But this place is a tad rustic for your tastes. You know that has never bothered me, I like things simple. But you would go stark mad in a week. There's no place to shop, there's no

*one to draw you a bath, and I'm too busy settling in
to entertain you. Give me a few months and I'll welcome you happily, but please, give me those few
months.*

*Until then . . . dearest sister, you are free! I know,
I know, you have always claimed that caring for me
all these years was more for your sake than mine,
that the sacrifice was none at all. I even mostly believe you. But now, with the doctor's death and my
new endeavor it is time for you to have one of your
own! Have a glorious affair, take a fabulous trip,
break those dozens of hearts you know you could.
I'm grown now, though you are loath to admit it,
and you are still young enough to enjoy a great adventure of your own. Find it, my dear. Find it.*

Montana stoked up the heat. Summer blasted
away the last, soft vestiges of spring. The grass lost
its fresh hue, the earth its soft give. It hardly rained
in the ten days Emily had been in Montana, and she
was weary enough of hauling buckets of water from
the creek that she was getting mighty frugal with the
stuff. She hoped to heavens her letter would dis-
suade Kate from coming; just the thought of Kate
without plenty of water made her shudder.

She'd propped open the front door and peeled the
flap back from the window, hoping for a friendly
stray breeze. Even the stingiest fire notched the temperature up, but one could be content with cheese
and stale crackers for supper for only so long.

The air was marginally cooler by the door, and
she leaned against the frame. Almost immediately *he*

looked up, his gaze simmering across the space between them for a long moment before he returned his attention to his book.

He slouched in his chair, which she still expected to shatter beneath his bulk the next time he sat down. The charred remains of the fire that he almost never lit darkened the ground. A burst of wind sent the doorway to his tent flapping.

He read with furious concentration, shoulders hunched, eyes hidden beneath the wild fringe of his hair. Once in a while she'd see him erupt from his chair and spring across the land at a breakneck pace, as if he couldn't contain his energy any longer and had to release it in one wild surge. He'd return, sometimes hours later, panting, throw himself down on the bare ground, and fall into a sleep that seemed little more restful than his run.

But mostly he was just there, relentlessly, impatiently waiting. And unfailingly, as soon as she glanced out the window to see if he was still there, he'd lift his gaze as if somehow alerted to her attention.

At first it infuriated her. Then it annoyed her. Now he was simply there, as much a part of the landscape as the shivering grass and the stunted box elders atop the next rise.

As she watched, he balanced his book on his knee, reached over, and grabbed a can out of a nearby crate. Without even looking to see what he'd unearthed, he pried off the lid. He tipped his head back, shook something from the can into his mouth, and chewed while he read.

Emily frowned. That was no way to have dinner.

It had to be exceedingly unhealthful to subsist on tinned food. Not to mention that a man of that size surely required more fuel than most. And Emily believed that proper digestion required both attention to one's meal and congenial atmosphere and companions. Mr. Sullivan failed on all counts.

She reminded herself firmly that it was not her problem. Rather, she should hope that starvation drove him to the nearest city and away from her.

In any case, her own supper must be nearly done. Heat boiled from the tiny oven when she cranked open the door, carrying the warm scent of biscuits.

Perfect. It had taken her a few days to get the hang of cooking on the thing, but really, it was a shame there was no one around to admire her skill.

She'd planned to finish the biscuits over the next couple of days, but they really were best warm. And the pot of stew, made from the rabbit the Blevinses, her new neighbors, had brought her when they came to visit on Sunday, was far more than she could finish in the next few days.

She grabbed a tin plate, plopped a hefty ladle of stew in the middle, rimmed the edge with a half dozen biscuits, and headed out before she could change her mind.

He glanced up again the instant she stepped out the door, and she felt the focused intensity of his regard. No emotion, not even curiosity, revealed itself on his face. But then he could have been smiling like a child at Christmas behind that great bush of a beard and she couldn't tell.

"Here," she said when she gained his side, thrusting the plate at him.

For a long moment she thought he might ignore her completely. Finally he set the book aside. "What's this?"

"I made too much. Thought you might like some."

His gaze slid up to her. His eyes were so dark they were almost black, handsomely shaped, with lashes as thick as his hair. It was all she could do not to shift under his wary inspection, and she forced her smile wider.

"Why?" he asked.

"It's no more complicated than I told you." At least she didn't think it was, and she didn't want him prodding her into looking any deeper. "You're a suspicious sort, aren't you?"

"Maybe I am." A trait he'd learned well and painfully, Jake thought.

He half expected her to take her peace offering and dash on home. Hell, he would have; he'd deliberately been a far sight less than friendly. She'd have to be desperate for company to find his desirable.

But she didn't seem desperate about anything. More like unnaturally cheerful. She sang—badly—as she fetched water. She whistled as she attempted to tack the loose tar paper back on the walls, even when it took three tries. And, always, she smiled, the same sunshiny smile she bestowed on him right now.

Her permanent and extreme cheerfulness had to be the oddest form of mental deformity he'd ever run across. There was no other explanation for it.

Accepting the plate seemed a bigger surrender than it should, softening their uncompromising antagonism. He really should show her on her way. Make her understand that he couldn't be bribed by something as cheap as biscuits. But damn, they smelled good, and he was getting awful tired of cold beans.

So he grabbed the plate and figured he owed her something back. "You been busy. Lots of visitors."

She blinked in surprise. "Was that a conversational gambit?"

"Hey, miracles happen sometimes."

Her smile dimmed a bare fraction. He figured it had to go away once in a while, but this was as close to solemn as he'd ever seen her. "Do you believe in them?"

Had he ever believed in miracles? The concept was as foreign to him as flying to the moon, the word he'd mouthed a meaningless combination of random letters. "No."

How'd she do that? he wondered. Make her smile brighten while her eyes went soft and sad with sympathy?

"Did you ever?" she asked.

"I can't recall."

"But—"

"You're not the sort to leave something well enough alone, are you?"

She laughed then, rich and raucous. How odd that there was nothing at all ladylike about Emily Bright's laugh. "No. You'd do well to take note of that, too." She gestured at the plate. "You should eat. Before it gets cold."

"Eat right in front of you, when you're not? That wouldn't be too polite of me, would it?"

She plopped her fists on her hips, tried to scowl at him. "You're not trying to get out of tasting it, are you? I didn't poison it, I swear."

He picked up the biscuit, tore into it, and nearly groaned aloud in pleasure. "It's good," he said in outrageous understatement. "When you give up homesteading, you can get a job as a cook, no problem."

Her eyes narrowed.

"If you're trying to look threatening," he told her, "you're failing miserably."

She squinted further before giving up with a laugh. "I know. It's a curse; try as I might, I look as innocuous as a kitten."

"You just *look* harmless?"

"Only look. I've got nasty claws, and don't you forget it."

"Uh-huh." He popped the rest of the biscuit in his mouth. "Heck, *I'll* hire you, if everything you make is as good as this." Now why hadn't he shooed her on her merry way by now? he wondered. He was not given to small talk. Not given to talk, period, when you got right down to it. Even if he were, she wouldn't be the one he'd be small-talking with. "But for all I know you're running a restaurant already, for all the people trotting in and out."

"Hmm." Speculation lit her eyes.

"Oh no you don't," he said warningly.

"Thanks for the suggestion. I was getting worried about scaring up enough cash before I proved up."

It should have infuriated him. But hell, who could take her seriously? Playing frontier girl might be all fun and games right now, but the instant winter grabbed hold, she'd be begging to get out of Montana. And if it didn't happen that way, well, he'd just have to give her a nudge.

"But I doubt very much you'll be able to run a restaurant with an obviously dangerous maniac capering outside your front door," he warned her, but there was no heat behind it.

"Hasn't stopped the neighbors from coming over so far," she replied lightly. Teasing him. The concept was strange enough to stun him for a moment. "That was the Blevinses on Sunday. You know them of course. I like her very much; she reminds me a bit of my sister Anthea."

He started on the stew, half listening to her bright chatter. Whyever she thought that he wanted to hear all about her visitors, he'd no idea. Still, he didn't want her grabbing her food and running off with it. Listening to her babble was a small price to pay for those biscuits.

"Joe seemed inordinately fond of my chess pie," she said slyly, "maybe even more than five dollars' fond."

"Joe? There's not a chance he's giving up a cent and you know it."

Jesus. Now she was beaming at him with delight, as if immensely proud of his pathetic banter. He'd have to remember not to give her any encouragement, because she clearly took the slightest bit and ran with it.

"And I had Mr. Biskup over on Sunday, too. You do know him; he's been here since before you came."

"Yeah, I know him." Vaguely. Skinny old duffer

with a beard down to his waist. At all hours of the day and night, he bounced around on the back of a nag that looked even older than he was, canvas packs piled high behind him like a lumpy throne. They'd passed perhaps three words between them the six months Jake had lived there before.

"He showed me several of his sketches. They're quite remarkable. But then I imagine you know that."

"Sketches?" he asked without thinking.

"You didn't know he was an artist?" She looked as shocked as if he'd up and confessed a penchant for rolling in the mud. Obviously the idea of living next to somebody for more than a day and not knowing all about them was abhorrent to her. He should be grateful she'd spared him that long.

Maybe, he thought bleakly, if they'd had company as often as she did, formed friendships there, Julia wouldn't have felt so alone.

Ruthlessly he pushed the memory away. He'd wallowed in what-ifs for a long time and it hadn't helped one bit. He'd come back there because it was time to·try another way. He'd put this place to rest one way or the other.

He glanced up to find her studying him, her mouth and eyes sober, as even he already knew they seldom were. "He mentioned you."

"Did he," Jake said flatly, hoping it'd be warning enough.

"He said you came with your wife then. Where is she?" Emily asked. And there, thought Emily, was all the emotion he never allowed to surface. Grief, oceans of it, deep, dark, turbulent, welling up from where it lived inside him, fresh as if born yesterday, old as if it'd been there forever.

He thrust the plate at her. "Thanks for the food. I'm done."

There might as well have been "No Trespassing" signs posted all around him. It was not the sort of thing that Emily generally let stop her if she considered it beneficial to forge ahead. One of the first things William Goodale taught her was the usefulness of lancing wounds. But Mr. Sullivan was not a patient who'd put himself voluntarily in her care. And she had to remember she certainly did not know him well enough to make such judgments about him.

She glimpsed a flash of white in the unruly thicket of his beard, as if he'd bared his teeth in a snarl. Really, did he think she'd be scared off so easily?

She looked down at the half-eaten plate of food, his fingers, strong and dark, curled around the bent metal edge. His sleeve was rolled up and his wrists were thick and powerful-looking. But where the wind blew his limp blue shirt against his torso he was thinner than he appeared at first glance. Still strong, but as if he'd lost some of the sturdy weight he usually carried.

"You keep it," she murmured. "I'd consider it a favor if I didn't have to waste it."

She turned and walked away, forcing herself not to look back and see whether he finished her food or dumped it on the ground.

* * *

Emily awoke late, fuzzy light leaking through her eyelids before she even opened them, her mind just as dull. She'd slept poorly and now found herself staring at the ghostly shapes of Mr. Sullivan's wife's dresses, hanging limply over the foot of the bed. She should've packed them away by now but it had seemed a violation to touch things that so clearly belonged to another. He'd abandoned them as surely as he'd abandoned the claim, and she'd used his pots and tools without a qualm. But clothes seemed so much more personal.

She slipped her feet into her boots, didn't bother to fasten them up, and clumped to the door. She paused for a moment before yanking it open. One of the more disconcerting effects of having Mr. Sullivan camp a few yards from her front door was that she couldn't discreetly slip out back. Thus far he'd shown no inclination to politely pretend not to see. She didn't expect last night had changed that. If anything, he'd probably make it all the more embarrassingly obvious he knew where she headed.

Emily did not have the same reticence about private matters that most young women did. Dr. Goodale had been brutally clear right from the start, when she'd first expressed an interest in assisting him with his patients, that he would not be inconvenienced by trying to shield her virginal sensibilities. Kate had objected briefly, contending that, at twelve, Emily was far too young to be exposed to such things. And then, as always, she'd meekly bowed to Dr. Goodale as she never did to anyone else.

But Emily's usual unconcern with matters others found mortifying did not extend to Mr. Sullivan's possessing intimate knowledge of when she needed to relieve herself, and so she usually tried to rise before he'd stirred from his tent. Today it was far too late. She mentally steeled herself for his smirk—how she knew he was smirking behind that infernal beard, she wasn't sure, but she had no doubt.

She opened the door and sunlight streamed through.

Sometime in the night he'd returned her plate. It nestled in an emerald tuft of long grass just to the right of the door. He must have even washed it; the tin glinted dully. And square in the middle rested a handful of crimson poppies.

Her gaze whipped to his bedraggled camp. He sat in his usual spot, one booted foot resting on a knee, a book wedged in the V. She waited for him to look at her, as he always did, but this time his attention remained firmly on the page.

Carefully she scooped up the bouquet. The stems were ragged, as if they'd been torn instead of cut; the colors, extravagant. She lifted them to her nose, and the scent was strong and sweet, a dozen times more concentrated than flowers grown in more sheltered conditions, and her head went light.

With the fragrance, she told herself. Only with the fragrance.

Chapter 5

He should have known better.

Jake's life had been jammed with incontrovertible evidence that giving into temptation—at least for him—was the first step toward absolute disaster.

And yet he'd done it anyway. It seemed a small thing, to give her the flowers. He'd nearly squashed a clump of them on his evening run and had grabbed a bunch out of sheer, mindless impulse. It seemed the least he could do, after she'd trotted over bearing supper, the best he'd eaten in a very long time.

But now she seemed to consider him a friend. She stepped outside, waved cheerfully in his direction, and kept flapping until he flicked a finger in acknowledgment just to get her to stop. It was the barest of salutes, but she beamed at him like a mother witnessing her toddler's first step.

It wouldn't do. They couldn't be friends. He didn't have friends, period. Didn't even want them. And most of all, he couldn't be friends with *her*. That way lay certain disaster; he was surer of it than he'd ever been of anything.

She was as slender as a willow slip, and when the wind gusted, blowing her dress against her, he half expected her to sway before it, curving gracefully low to the ground like the grass.

Summer had sunk deeply into Montana, searing the tips of the grass, and now the late afternoon sunlight caught those tips, gold over green. The same sunlight caught her hair, washed gold over the warm brown as well.

She moved out into the yard, and he noticed the hoe she held in her hand. The thing was almost as tall as she was, and he wondered what she had planned now. It was too late in the season to plant much of a garden; winter came too early here. Probably she didn't know that, though.

He'd spent so much time in the chair facing her front door that the seat had practically molded to his butt. Figuring this new development might be worth his full attention, he tipped his open book against his belly and laced his fingers over it.

She was walking with her head down in concentration, as if looking for something, crisscrossing the space. Finally she glanced back and forth between her spot and the shack, as if checking her position, and lifted the hoe high over her head.

Metal glinted in the sunlight. She put all her slight weight into it and swung down in a wicked arc.

The hoe bit, sliced into the hard earth, and caught.

She, however, kept right on moving, pitching right down with a yelp.

He came half out of his chair. But she popped right back up, glaring at the hoe as if to intimidate it into cooperation. She whacked dust off her skirts and grabbed the tool again.

He forced himself to plop back down. Obviously she wasn't hurt. And really, what had he planned to do? *Help* her?

Her second stroke went slightly better; she only ended up on her knees that time. And instead of a yelp, she burst out with a word he'd have sworn didn't reside in Emily Bright's vocabulary.

He figured she'd last fifteen minutes at the task. Half an hour at the outside.

Six hours later, they were both still there. Oh, she'd managed to shear the prairie grass off a plot of ground the size of a bathtub. At that rate, she'd have a space big enough for a pumpkin patch by the first of September.

He wasn't sure whether to admire her perseverance or pity her sheer stupidity.

His stomach rumbled, for she'd worked right through suppertime, and he couldn't quite bring himself to sit there stuffing himself while she grubbed away.

Although she hadn't, the sun had quit an hour ago. Now she was a pale wraith in the rising moonlight, an industrious ghost with her skirts fluttering around her ankles.

An exhausted ghost. You needn't have spent the last two weeks watching her to recognize the signs. She no longer dragged the hoe above her waist. Her hair had come undone hours ago and drooped around shoulders that sagged just as visibly.

What the hell was she doing? It had ceased to amuse him about an hour in. Now it annoyed him. He wanted her gone; he didn't want her dead.

She dragged the hoe up one more time. And then she wavered, unsteady as a drunk after a week-long binge, and collapsed.

He waited for her to spring back up as she'd done a dozen times already. But she lay still, her small figure almost lost in the high grass.

He jumped up so fast the chair toppled and he sprinted over to her. He dropped to his knees. Her face was turned away from him, her eyes closed. He lay his fingers against her neck, groped for a heartbeat while his breath snagged in his throat.

He found her pulse, surprisingly strong and steady. Blowing out a breath, he sat back on his heels.

Okay. Alive, then. Just fainted dead away. What now?

A week ago—a day ago—his first instinct would surely have been just to retreat to his own camp. She'd come to soon enough, and finding herself lying outside on the remnants of a truly pitiful excuse for an afternoon's work might make her finally recognize what foolishness she'd embarked on.

For some reason he'd rather not examine right now, he couldn't do that. But damned if he was going to take care of her.

None too gently he nudged her in the shoulder. "Wake up." When she didn't respond he gave her a brisk shake. "Wake up!"

Her eyes fluttered open. She blinked up at the night sky, and then her gaze slid to meet his.

"You fainted."

"I most certainly did not faint." She gave herself a shake, like a hen smoothing ruffled feathers, and sat up.

"No? What would you call it then?"

"I but took a moment to rest." She lifted her chin, and moonlight bathed her, a milky radiance that, surprisingly, suited her every bit as well as sunshine. She'd never seemed a creature of the night. "And to admire the stars. It's a lovely evening."

"Uh-huh."

"I *never* faint."

"You probably faint if a man mentions 'legs' in your presence." He didn't know why he hadn't returned to his chair already. She was obviously fine, if utterly exhausted. And he shouldn't be prodding her, not when she'd retort so predictably. Though entertainingly.

"Ha!" She dusted her hands together. "I've assisted in three amputations in the last four years, and it was my job to cart away the stump. I bet you'd turn green at the first slice."

No he wouldn't, because nothing short of chains and a stockade could keep him in the same room with a doctor set on sawing. The very idea sent acid sloshing in his stomach. "Yeah, you look like a field surgeon. Don't know why I didn't note it right off."

She pulled up her knees and tucked her arms around them, looking every bit as comfortable sitting on her rump in the middle of the prairie as she must entering a ballroom on the arm of some overbred gentleman with oiled hair and a good chunk of Daddy's money. "I've done very little fieldwork, that's true. But my brother-in-law was a doctor. Quite a famous one, when it comes right down to it, so much so that people would suffer his, well, less-than-compassionate demeanor to gain access to his skills." She smiled with more than a trace of nostalgia. "I always thought he considered it extremely inconvenient that fascinating diseases came attached to actual people. He was no fonder of me, truth be told, but once he discovered I was useful he tolerated me well enough. The patients were more tractable when I was there, and so it wasn't long before he kept me at his side even more than I would have chosen of my own accord. And that would have been a lot." There seemed no halting her chatter once she got going. And he wondered why he hadn't tried to shut her up yet. "It was fascinating, every moment of it. But I wouldn't have lasted a day were I the fainting type."

They shouldn't be having a conversation. Not that her rambling was actually a conversation. But he had little doubt she'd be working on getting him to do his fair share of the talking pretty darn soon.

He didn't want to know any more about her. Didn't want to admire her in any way. It made waiting, hoping for her to fail distasteful.

She tilted her head, studied him in a way that made him want to duck and shift away from her scrutiny. As if she might see things he needed to keep hidden.

"Are you smiling? That beard makes it hard to tell."

He nearly reached up to touch his face, checking if he was. "I don't smile," he said with a snarl, hoping against hope it would slam the topic shut, dreading his firm suspicion that it would do the exact opposite.

"Never?" He'd expected pity in her expression, steeled himself against it. Figured it would piss him off enough to catapult them back to their respective corners where they should have stayed in the first place. No matter how hard he searched, though, all he could find was bubbling curiosity. And puzzled surprise, as if she'd never conceived of such a creature. "But—"

"Come on." He got up, kept himself from extending his hand to assist her by dint of more effort than he would have liked. "You've had a long day. Last thing you need is to sit around out here talkin'. You should get some food, some rest, before you keel over again."

"I did not faint!"

Why in a merciful God's name hadn't a man been the one to take over his claim? They could have a nice, civilized brawl over the rights; he could send the fella on his way and be done with it.

"Fine. You didn't faint." Anything to get her off the ground and into the shack. "Quitting time anyway."

"Not exactly." She climbed to her feet, swayed a bit—which he knew damn well she would have denied—and reached down to gather her tools. "I'm not done."

"Oh, you're done all right." The moonlight accentuated the shadows on her face, as if the night itself had painted the deep purple hollows beneath her eyes, her cheekbones. "You're done in."

"I'm fine." She weighed the tools in her hands, decided on the shovel. She rammed it into the earth and managed to wedge it in maybe an inch. "I've a schedule, you see. I've repaired the house, and now it's time to clear the land. I figured it all out, how much I'd need to turn each day in order to be finished by my proving-up date, factoring in a reasonable amount of weather delays, and paced it all off. I have to finish the day's allotment to stay on schedule."

He stared at her, openmouthed. She truly didn't *look* insane. He'd spent weeks unloading murderously heavy cargo and he knew good and well he couldn't clear the land himself by spring. "Most people just pay someone with a team and plow to clear it for them."

"Can't afford it." She put her foot on the upper edge of the shovel, hopped up and down as if her slight weight would force it in.

"Doesn't seem to me that you'll be able to afford paying the prove-up fee then, either."

"Something'll come up by next spring," she told him.

"Then something'll come up to let you pay for the clearing."

She abandoned the shovel. It stayed where it was, blade half buried in the ground, handle sticking straight up like a signpost: "Foolish Easterner here." "I intend to be prepared either way." She bent, returning to the hoe. Slender as a reed, limned in moonlight. She'd lost weight since she'd arrived, not that she'd had much to spare. This place did that to a woman. A knowledge he lived . . . no, *survived* with, every day.

"That's it." He snatched the hoe, cocked his arm, and sent the tool hurtling into the dark night like a spear. "You're done."

"Now look what you've done." She marched in the direction in which the hoe had disappeared.

"Damn it!" He caught her in two strides. She yelped as he scooped her up, her arms flailing weakly.

"Put me down."

"Show me you've got enough energy to fight back and maybe I'll think about it."

She didn't even try, just looked up at him with big, moon-shadowed eyes. The curve of her hip pressed against his belly. The side of her breast lay softly against his chest. Her head fell back, her hair brushing against his chin on the way, and her scent rose to him, feminine, new.

Need exploded. Not want, not desire, not simple longing. *Need.* Unwanted, unsuspected, so absent from his life as to be utterly foreign to him. Something he'd never expected, never *wanted*, to feel again. Something he'd no *right* to feel again.

And so he dropped her. Right on her rump.

She yelped, lifted one hip to massage her butt, and glowered up at him.

"All right then," he said. "If you're not bright enough to know when to quit, I'm not going to force you."

"Good," she snapped. "That's what I wanted from the beginning."

"Here's what I don't understand, though." She pushed herself up, cute, bruised butt pointing skyward before she straightened, and he jammed his hands in his pockets. "You manage to charm men into doing just about everything else for you. Joe Blevins into lugging you water when he fetches his own. Longnecker into helping you choose your claim. Mr. Biskup into bringing you grouse whenever he goes hunting—didn't think I noticed that, did you? So why the hell don't you just keep playing the fragile female card and get some poor sap to do this for you, too? A few smiles, a few of those glances from beneath your lashes, and you've got a cleared field. Easy."

She stared at him, her mouth opening and closing as if she'd so many words to spew out that they'd jammed up together and she couldn't force out just one at a time.

"Or maybe that's what you're up to right now," he went on ruthlessly. "Maybe you figured on me. That's what the free dinner, the dramatic swoon were for. I'd be a challenge, right? See if you can get the guy who wants you gone to be the one to help you stay?"

Her eyes darkened, snapping with the first true anger he'd seen in her. "Is that what you think of me?"

"Maybe." Or maybe not. But now that he gave the matter some consideration, she sure did have a way of finding people to run to her assistance. Maybe it wasn't as calculated as he claimed, maybe not even conscious, but it was the end result that told the tale, wasn't it? "Yeah, I do."

Her hands fisted at her sides. Simmering anger rolled off her in waves. And hurt, which pricked in his chest though he tried his very best to ignore it.

And then, in the blink of an eye, it all disappeared when she smiled. "Thank you."

"Thanks?" he asked, effectively blindsided.

"Yes, thank you. For if I ever had any doubts about this venture," she told him, "any question about whether I'd succeed or not, you, Mr. Sullivan, just gave me so much incentive as to absolutely ensure that I will."

The sun rose early and bright, bathing the inside of Jake's white canvas tent in clean light. Jake awoke late, aroused, painfully hard, and thinking of her.

He groaned and squeezed his eyes shut while his head pounded; for a moment he forgot that he didn't drink anymore, it felt so much like he was coming off a three-day binge.

And then he remembered. *Good going, Jake old boy.* He didn't know why he ever presumed he could deal with women. His most considered plans always went awry, and last night's had hardly been considered.

He'd wanted her furious. So furious she wouldn't be tempted to trot over to visit him with sweet brown biscuits and a sweeter smile. Oh, she was mad all right, good and mad. But she wasn't going anywhere.

And the worst part was, the very first thought in his head when he'd swum up out of a restless, dark-dreamed sleep, was that he wanted her.

That was bad. Really bad. Extremely bad. Especially when added to that potent, blinding burst of need when he'd touched her.

It wasn't right. Over the past year he'd come to the conclusion that that part of himself had died with Julia. There'd been women sometimes, in the saloons he'd practically lived in, who'd made it perfectly clear that they'd be happy to help him drown his sorrows in other ways than draining a bottle—though they were right fond of that method themselves. He'd never been one bit tempted, felt nothing but vague, woozy revulsion.

It'd been right, he figured, to lose that part of himself. He deserved it. Why should he ever experience pleasure again, when Julia wouldn't? She was his wife, his heart, his love. It was only fitting that so much of him remained hers, always.

But now, unexpectedly, his physical needs had stirred. Stirred? Hell. *Erupted*. It was wrong, so damn wrong. And far too likely to happen again.

So he couldn't wait any longer. He'd do what he should have done the first day and get rid of her. Then, it had appeared easier and cheaper to wait her out. He had time.

But not any longer. For as long as she was so nearby, sleeping in the bed he'd made, the bed that he'd shared with his wife, he was in danger of doing something he'd never forgive himself for.

And he had a plenty long list of those things already.

"Here."

Emily focused blurrily on the hand Mr. Sullivan

had shoved in her direction the instant she'd stumbled out of bed to open the door.

"Is that money?"

"Yeah. Take it and go."

"Come back in an hour." Maybe then she'd be wide enough awake to make at least vague sense out of whatever nonsense had seized Mr. Sullivan.

"No." His hand slapped flat against the door, stopping it six inches before she slammed it shut. "We have to do this now."

Emily sighed in longing for the sleep that was obviously not to be hers. One more mark on the negative side of Mr. Sullivan's tally sheet, which was listing pretty heavily to port as it was. "Excuse me for not immediately understanding your intent— it's a problem I continue to have where you're concerned—but what, exactly, is this about?"

"I want to buy you out."

"Oh no."

"Yes." His tone was unequivocal, as if it had never occurred to him she would not agree to his terms. "There's enough here to pay the fees on a new claim. Plus more, for supplies to get you started."

He'd scarcely glanced at her. When she made no response, his gaze swung around, touching briefly on her face, then dropping further. Immediately he jerked it back up, focusing over her shoulder, staring into the shaded gloom of her shack as if there were something compelling there.

Reflexively her hands went to her throat. She'd been too tired to undress the night before, but she'd thumbed open the tight band of lace that constricted her neck. Emily forced her hands back down to her sides, leaving her collar unbuttoned. She would not allow him to embarrass her. She was not improperly dressed, and if her sleep-mussed state was too brazen for him, well, that was simply too bad. He was far from unimpeachable in sartorial matters.

"I don't want your money," she told him flatly. If he had made this offer in the beginning, she might have considered it. When she'd been so foolishly concerned about what had happened to the people who'd abandoned this claim for her benefit.

But not now. Not after his accusations of the previous night.

"By God, you will." He grabbed her hand and stuffed it full, forcibly bending her fingers around bills that crumpled in her hands. "You have to."

"I have to do no such thing." She yanked her hand away, and the skin burned where it had touched his. She opened her fingers and watched the money flutter to the ground, a few bills catching on spiky strands of prairie grass that sprouted at the base of the shack. "I don't have to do anything. Especially not at your ever-so-polite request."

"You won't get more," he warned her.

"I assure you, Mr. Sullivan, I am not holding out for a better deal." She was famous for controlling her temper in the most trying of circumstances. When poor Mr. Eberle, suffering greatly from a growth in his abdomen, had hurled his bowl of pea soup at her head rather than eat the spoonful she'd urged upon him, she'd merely smiled and fetched warm towels for both of them. She'd continued gently lancing frail Mrs. Kawcak's boils when the woman had rained vile invectives on her.

But Emily was finding that Mr. Sullivan shattered her cheerful serenity with unprecedented effectiveness.

"I want you gone."

"We don't always get what we want, do we?" she said through a beautifully—if she did say so herself—faked smile.

And finally he looked at her fully, messy waves of hair falling over his forehead, his eyes bleak and fierce. "I am aware of that, Miss Bright. Acutely so."

She would not sympathize with the wretch, darn it.

"I am not going anywhere, and you would do well to accustom yourself to it. Given that you *do* have the financial means to settle on another claim—something you led me to believe you lacked, by the way—you may do well to hurry up and do so. There will be no benefit in waiting for me to fail, Mr. Sullivan, and perhaps a fair amount in getting on with your future," she said, and despite herself, her voice softened at the last.

He went rigid. It was almost imperceptible, but she had trained herself to be observant of any flinch of pain in her patients. His eyes narrowed, the skin over his cheekbones drew tight, his nostrils flared.

"I offered you a fair deal. You chose not to take it." He nudged one of the dollar bills with his toe. "You remember that when you end up with nothing."

"I won't," she said, and hoped it wasn't a lie.

"Remember, or end up with nothing?"

"End up with nothing."

"Oh, but you will," he told her. And then, so quietly she almost didn't catch it, and oh, she wished she hadn't: "Everyone does, sooner or later."

Chapter 6

Emily opened the door right after breakfast to discover that the money, which they'd both stubbornly let lie in the grass, had disappeared. She wondered when Mr. Sullivan had snuck over and gathered the bills up. She had no doubt he'd done so; while he might have enjoyed the symbolism of leaving it in the dust, he wasn't stupid. Obstinate, closeminded, and short-tempered, and more complicated than he appeared on first glance, but not stupid.

However, her musings were interrupted when Mr. Biskup shuffled up on his old mare. "I've brought you a letter!" He grinned, pleased with his surprise. "I know how much newcomers always anticipate any word from home. It took some doing for me to convince the postmaster that I should be allowed to fetch it for you—no tampering with the U.S. mail, you understand—but I persevered. There are few that can hold out against my determined efforts, you know."

"Oh, I'm quite well aware of that," she assured him, even as nerves sent her stomach a-shimmying. The letter must be from Kate; no one else knew she was there. "For didn't you charm me out of a jar of my favorite apple jelly the evening we met?"

"That I did." He lurched off the back of his mount, skinny arms encased in fine but threadbare blue wool wheeling until he found his balance.

Mr. Biskup had been in Montana longer than any of them, since before the Indians had been pushed back to the reservation, when he'd come to paint a vanishing way of life and stayed to chronicle the arrival of a new one. But though his hair had grown long and gray, his garments worn, he'd never surrendered his impeccably correct dress or speech. He'd explained it that first day, when he'd ambled over and presented her with a clever little sketch of her new home that somehow made it look charming and snug without being inaccurate. Some things, he'd said, you must cling to, or risk forgetting what you are.

He bowed, deep and formally, before he finally steadied himself. Emily tried to hover close without seeming to, just in case he kept dipping down and toppled right over.

The letter he presented with a flourish.

"Thank you," she murmured. "You're too kind to me." And she'd miss him terribly, she realized suddenly, if Kate came and hauled her back to Philadelphia, for he'd never evidenced a moment's disbelief at her ability to succeed, and in that instant had won a corner of her heart. "Would you like to stay for tea?"

He studied her face thoughtfully. "Are you expecting bad news, my dear?"

"No. No, of course not."

He nodded gravely. "It has always been my policy not to pry in other's business. It is one of the reasons Montana has always suited me so well. However, that does not mean that I would not welcome the chance to assist, were I asked."

"Thank you." Impulsively she squeezed his hand, his fingers ink-stained, callused where he'd clutched a pen for so many years. "But no, there's nothing. It is simply the first I've heard from home. It makes it suddenly seem very far away."

"All right then. Thank you for the offer, but Smithie will be expecting tea himself, and I don't wish to see what he does to my place if left to his own devices too long." He pulled a paper bag from his breast pocket and popped a dried apricot in his mouth.

She waited until he rode out of sight before she carefully worked her nail under the flap. And then she dashed a glance toward Mr. Sullivan's encampment.

Some time when she wasn't watching, he'd dragged in . . . something. She couldn't decide what sort of machinery the haphazard pile of rusted metal had originally been—admittedly she wasn't all that conversant with agricultural equipment, but still. It looked like it could crush something, but animal, vegetable, or mineral, she'd no clue.

He was sitting on his rump, wrench clutched in

one grease-smeared hand, peering into its metallic guts. Making sure he had all his gear ready for duty when she gave up, she thought resentfully. If she weren't already doing this for her sake, and Kate's, she'd do it just to prove him wrong.

And then he looked up, and she wondered that the first sight of him beside her bed hadn't sent her screaming into the night. Perhaps it was lucky she'd been groggy with sleep, for if there was a more disreputable-looking man in existence, she'd never seen him. He appeared born for the back rooms of scandalous saloons, for dangerously dark alleys and business best not spoken of. Funny how she'd gotten accustomed to his threatening looks.

But she couldn't read her letter with him staring at her, and so she retreated into the dimness of the shack.

My dearest sister,

Yes, you still rate a "dearest," although you shouldn't. What on God's green earth were you thinking? Although clearly you weren't. Thinking, that is.

And that, for the moment, is all I shall say on the topic. I'm sure it will be ever so much more satisfying to speak my piece in person! And perhaps by then I will no longer be so tempted to administer all those beatings you did not receive as a child. Oh, such a delightful and obedient one you were! I should have known; nothing is ever that simple, and you must have been merely storing up all your rebelliousness for one great, grand mutiny.

But I promised, didn't I? And I shall be there soon enough, never fear. If fate is cooperative—ah, as if that would ever happen!—and the mails are unreliable—far more likely—I might have beat this letter there, and we are halfway back to Philadelphia by now. However, I do suspect that the settlement of Dr. Goodale's estate will take another two weeks, and I have promised to see it through. What a high mess those children are! And they are children, for all that Loren is two years older than I. It would have been nigh impossible to get this far without Mr. Ruckman's kind assistance, but he assures me we are nearing the end.

But never fear, I'll be there soon, and I shall fix everything. And you can begin the fall semester at Bryn Mawr just as we planned.

I am relieved that you have managed to keep yourself well enough that you were still capable of writing me a letter. Take care that you continue to do so until I arrive or what you fear hearing from me will be nothing compared to what you will.

And for God's sake, DON'T MOVE. Sit right down on the nearest chair, in the safest corner you can find, and keep yourself planted until my arrival. Not a twitch, you understand! If not, I will find you, never mind if I have to search under every rock and ford every stream in that godforsaken place. (And whyever did you have to run off to the middle of nowhere? Could you not have run off to Paris or Madrid like any sensible young girl? I am quite certain there is no one there who can trim a hat properly, never mind my hair.) But I will find you, be assured, and if you make me wander over hill and

*vale, ruining my boots, to do so you will never again
leave my side until you're safely wed. And perhaps I
will listen after all to Leola Seldomridge's endless
ravings about her exceedingly responsible nephew
and why he'd be perfect for you.*

> *With endless love and frustration,*
> *Kate*

Emily filled her cheeks and blew out a resigned
breath. Well, what had she expected? Kate had spent
twenty years of her life putting Emily's needs first—
Kate's evaluation of Emily's needs, in any case. It
would take more than a letter to change her.

But she'd been cocooned long enough. Sooner or
later every butterfly got to fly on its own, didn't it?
And Kate *had* to want a chance to stretch her own
wings, too; how could she not? She'd kept them deliberately furled for a very long time. Emily was determined to give them both that freedom.

She let her gaze trace her home. *Her home.* How
quickly it had become that. Bright curtains swung at
the windows, looped over the open crates she used
as cupboards; she'd sacrificed a skirt for those, and
they'd been worth every stitch. Purple wildflowers
bloomed in a cracked cup on the table, and the wedding ring quilt Kate had made was folded neatly, a
bright splash of color at the foot of her bed. Her
clothes hung on the wall. The dough she'd set to rise
puffed up the cloth she'd laid over the bowl on the
cold stove.

It looked like home to her. Cozy, simple, sufficient
for her needs. She liked it that way, she'd discov-

ered. Less to worry about. Less to scrub, less to take
her attention away from things that mattered. She
wondered whatever had possessed Dr. Goodale's
first wife to believe that a house the size of a hospital
was desirable.

But Kate wouldn't see it that way. Kate would
take one look, ask about the chickens that surely
were meant to roost there, and start looking about
for the real house. She'd note every crack in the
walls, every splinter that poked from the floor, every
rip in the blue insulating paper, and decide that
Emily deserved better. Hadn't she provided better,
all these years?

Oh heavens, Emily thought, *what am I going to do
now?*

Now where the hell was she going? Jake watched
as she—that was what she always was to him, *she*, as
if no other females ever turned up in his thoughts,
which was a lot more true than he preferred to dwell
on—lit out of her shack like a sprinter from the start-
ing line. For a moment he thought maybe she'd finally set the blamed thing on fire, but he saw no
smoke, not even from the chimney pipe.

Maybe she'd finally faced reality and had turned
what even he had to admit was her considerable energy into getting as far away as quickly as possible,
but that was wishful thinking on his part and he
knew it. She might not be the most practical female
he'd ever run across, but not a one of them would
flee without at least attempting to drag her dresses
with her, not unless chased by the devil himself. And
maybe not even then.

He watched her skittle across the top of a rise, heading southeast, getting smaller as she went though she wasn't much on size to begin with. The plains dwarfed her, the vast sweep of them, as if the grass might swallow her whole and she wouldn't leave a trace. It did that to people; he'd seen it, more than once. Hell, there wasn't a trace left of the Indians who'd once roamed there, though the government had rooted them out barely five years earlier.

But she—she'd disappear into it as easily as a field mouse, and make no more difference to the land. Truthfully, the sooner he pried her off his claim the better for her. Though he wouldn't count on her being all that grateful.

Suddenly she stopped and bent over, hand pressed to her side. He came half off the ground before he made himself plop his ass right back down. What'd he think he was going to do, play knight on a white charger? Surely he'd learned his lesson there, and then some.

Then she straightened. Even from that distance, sunlight glinted off her hair, a clean gleam like the beam had hit glass. It damn near took his breath away, and he hated it.

She squared those puny shoulders and took off again. Walking this time, head down, arms swinging, purpose in every step.

And he let himself hope to God—not pray, not anymore, but hope, and even that had been a long time—that she was heading off to make arrangements to leave Montana.

But then he pushed the thought firmly away. He

couldn't let what she was doing, what she chose, matter. One way or the other, he'd get what he wanted. Until then, there was the thick, gummy coating of old oil to strip, and he grabbed a cloth and bent to the task. For machines were so much easier to fix than lives.

On the long trek into town, Emily mentally rewrote and discarded thirty or forty wires before she settled on one. She filled out the form at the telegraph office, shoved it across the table to the clerk, disinterested at first, who scanned the brief message before his eyebrows shot up to his hairline and she nearly snatched it back.

She couldn't let herself question her plan. If it all fell apart, and Kate showed up anyway, well, Emily could hardly be in more trouble than she was already. Kate was as mad as she was going to get.

"That'll be a dollar," the clerk told her. She sighed and dug the coins out of her tiny string bag. She really was going to have to figure out how to make some money.

It took less than a day for her to get a response. Imbert carried the wire out to her himself—no trouble, he told her, breathless and flushed, as if he'd dashed out the instant the wire arrived. She recognized the excuse for what it was, and vowed to step carefully; his heart was more than willing to latch on to the nearest available female, and she did not wish to hurt him, not after all the help he'd been.

She tossed tea at him, and a couple of balls of leftover dough she'd fried and sugared, and turned her back to rip open the message.

ARRIVING THURSDAY. STOP.

Three words. Nothing more. Emily crushed the paper in a palm that had gone suddenly slick. She tried to convince herself that the uncommon brevity indicated Kate's newly straitened circumstances and its accompanying frugality but couldn't talk herself into even that much comfort. It was far more likely that she hadn't managed to stop shaking long enough to dictate even one more word.

"Is there something wrong?" Imbert, mouth rimmed in sugar, looked up with concern from tucking away the last bits of sweet dough. "Bad news from home?"

"No. No, of course not."

"All right, then." Shrugging, he slurped down his tea.

Hmm, she thought, tilting her head to eye him critically. Perhaps . . .

At that point, most women would have simply surrendered to the inevitable. Emily much preferred to go down struggling to the last; if there was one lesson she'd learned from Dr. Goodale, more valuable than any other, it was that as long as there was life, there was a chance. More than once they'd continued to fight long after a patient's condition seemed hopeless. Once in a great while it had paid off, and they'd saved someone all others might have let die. Even one made it worthwhile.

So she'd try, to the very last.

"Imbert."

He looked up again, so hopeful, and scrambled to his feet.

"I hope you don't mind that I use your given name."

He swallowed, head shaking vigorously from side to side. "Whatever you want," he burst out.

She smiled at him, and he beamed immediately, the tips of his ears ripening like a tomato in the sun.

He'd do whatever she asked of him. It was new to her, this kind of power over a man just because one happened to be female. Kate wielded it as comfortably as an expert marksman bore a rifle, as surely in her control.

Emily didn't like it. She didn't want his happiness on her head, couldn't use his hopeful eagerness for her own ends. It just wouldn't be fair.

"What is it?" he asked, a puppy begging for a scrap of bacon, and she felt her own hopes plummet.

"Nothing," she told him. "Nothing at all."

Reg had come up hurt. Gotten himself tangled in some mess of brush or another, earning a deep gash across his foreleg. Since the horse was barely mobile under the best of circumstances, even a scratch was enough to hobble him.

"Damn it!" Jake sprang back, not quite fast enough, and Reg's hoof nicked his shin. "That's at least three bruises, you sorry nag. Serve you right to let you fester away. You'd hardly be slower on three legs than four."

The horse snorted with a proud disdain his

bloodlines shouldn't have allowed, and Jake glowered at him. "Easy now," he said, more soothingly than he felt, and sidled carefully closer. "I'm just trying to clean it out, I'll be as gentle as a love, I promise—"

"Hello!"

The cheerful shout from behind caused Reg to jump again, out of his reach, and Jake turned his glare on the approaching woman, who deserved it even more than the horse.

"What!" he shouted, frustration getting the better of him.

Miss Bright faltered in mid-step, and her beaming smile wobbled. Only briefly, alas.

"A charmer, aren't you?" she said pleasantly. "One wonders what you're doing out here all alone. Although I suppose it's possible you wearied of the demands of the adoring throngs who no doubt flock around you in more populated areas, drawn by your charismatic personality, and so are seeking relief on the lonesome prairie."

"That must be it."

"I—" She caught sight of the horse's leg. "Oh, you poor dear!"

"Watch out! He's nasty when he's hurt, and he'll kick you—"

By then she'd recklessly dropped to her knees by Reg's injured leg, frowning in fierce concentration. "Oh no, he won't. Will you, dearie?" she whispered. Her fingers were quick and light, running down the leg, testing for more injuries, just skirting the glisten of dark blood, while Reg stood placidly, as if mesmerized. "I'm just going to see . . . yes, you have a wicked one, don't you? That must hurt terribly. We'll have you fixed up in no time."

Finished with her examination, she gave Reg a fond pat, straightened, and whirled on Jake, battle lighting her eyes.

"What were you thinking?"

"I—"

"Not so loud," she hushed him. "I don't want to frighten him again."

Christ. It was *his* lousy horse.

"He could go gangrenous in no time." Technically it might have been a whisper. But it held more fury than most people's screams. "He could have been lamed permanently. He could *die.* You have to clean out wounds like that—"

"For crying out loud, I was *trying*."

She paid him no mind, just went on with her furious instructions. "You have to clean it gently, so as not to force any foreign bits in further, and then—oh, heavens, it's much easier if I just show you."

She turned so fast her skirts snapped like a flag in the wind. "Don't spook him while I'm gone. Be *nice*, speak calmly. Let him know you're here. I'll be back in no time, sweetheart." She addressed the last to the horse before trotting off to the shack.

"Traitor. Not gelded soon enough, were you, fighting me every second but standing there like a lamb while she had her hands on you," he said, half angry, half amused. An odd mix she seemed to promote in him like no one else ever had.

She was back in an instant, a small tin in one hand, gray cloth in the other, and pushed him aside with a gently dismissive shove against his biceps: *What are you doing in my way?*

"Here we go." She knelt down beside Reg again, grass coming up to her hips. If the horse decided to kick she'd be laid out flat, and Jake's muscles twitched with the instinct to drag her from danger, or at least get between her and it. But he stayed where he was, alert and waiting, because he already knew she wouldn't listen to sense on this point. "Hold this, will you?" she said, shoving the tin in Jake's direction and letting go without waiting for his assent, as if it had never occurred to her that he wouldn't do as directed.

She cleaned the wound with an efficiency that surprised him, her hands expert, her touch magic, for Reg stayed placid and still, as if captivated by the quick flash and press of her hands over him.

"Okay, there, that's better, isn't it? Now the salve." She held out her hand and he obediently plopped the tin in her open palm. And wasn't she a managing sort, given the opportunity?

The ointment glistened in the sun, a thick layer of grease, and she was finished in no time, wiping off her slick fingers on the cloth and climbing to her feet.

"Here." She gave him back the half-empty tin. "I'm not going to bandage it now. Better it gets some air. But it should be cleaned again tonight, spread a little more on when you're done. I don't expect any problems, but if he starts limping more, or it swells up, or the wound reddens, you must call me immediately."

Curious, he lifted the ointment to his nose and

sniffed. His eyes watered immediately, the inside of his nostrils burning. "Jesus! What the hell is this?"

"You don't expect me to give away my secrets, do you?"

"You're good at that. With him." He nodded toward the horse, who'd begun lazily cropping at the grass.

"Everybody has to have a talent."

"Yeah?" He bit back the questions. How'd a frilly bit of ladyship learn to patch up a walking glue factory? But it wasn't allowed. He was not to learn any more about her, not one more thing that would make her real and interesting and anything more than an obstacle.

"So," he said into an awkward pause. "Thanks."

She'd done her duty. Proved once again why it'd be too damn heartless on his part to force her off the claim. He expected her to flounce on her way. But she just stood there, twining her fingers in front of her as if awaiting something more from him. But hell, he'd said thanks. He wasn't thankful enough to abandon the claim, if that's what she had in mind. Reg wasn't nearly useful enough for that.

She was dressed up today, he realized suddenly. Her blouse was a froth of lace and ruffles, with buttons that shone like the inside of a shell. She'd done up her hair, a pile of curls that lay in pretty waves across her ears; he'd watched a woman do her hair enough to know that carefully attractive disorder must have taken a hell of a lot of work to achieve. Her skirt was deep blue, with some kind of finish that made it glimmer like water, but she'd mussed it while she attended to Reg. There were two dark, damp ovals at her knees where she'd knelt in the grass, and a thick dark smear of grease across her left hip.

"Sorry about that." He pointed at the smear, then jerked his finger back; it seemed somehow indecent, his pointing at a part of her body, even in such an innocent way. It made his head spin. "You've ruined your skirt. Don't guess you'll want to go off to your party like that."

"Party? I'm not going anywhere."

"Not your usual wardrobe for trying to grub out another couple of yards of grass."

"Oh." She looked down at herself and laughed self-consciously. "I suppose it's not."

"So that land agent is coming out to see you again, hmm?" He should have realized; she sure looked like a woman who wanted something from a man. That skinny, weasel-faced pencil pusher was surely a goner. There was the vicious bite of . . . something . . . he refused to consider more deeply. What the hell should he care whether Miss Bright prettied herself up for Longnecker?

"No." Her cheeks colored up, like her skin had been touched by the sun. And she had been since she got there, he realized; her hair now carried streaks of gold, and the deeper tinge to her cheeks made her eyes look a brighter blue. It suited her, surprisingly well. "I just . . . missed dressing up, that's all."

She wouldn't meet his eyes. Oh, she was up to something, all right. Which was why she still stood there, rubbing a bit of skirt between her fingers, gathering her courage.

Really, did she think he was *that* easy? That she'd turn that smile on him and he'd fall as easy as Imbert, give her whatever she wanted?

And then she did smile again, fully, bright approval that beamed prettily, and he thought, okay, yeah, maybe he was a *tad* susceptible.

"I need to talk to you."

"Seems to me you're doing that already."

"Yes, well." She nodded. "I've decided to accept your offer after all. Your offer to buy me out," she clarified, and for all her lovely smile, she didn't look the slightest bit happy about it.

He nearly dropped the tin of salve. "Not that I'm not pleased about this and all"—pleased, but awfully suspicious—"but what happened to 'never give up, never surrender' and all that?"

"Sometimes one must yield the battle to win the war."

She shot a longing glance over her shoulder at the pathetic excuse for a house he'd thrown together with more hope than skill, and he decided curiosity should bow to practicality before she changed her mind again.

"That's great," he said, and wondered why he didn't sound happier. He *was* damn near delirious; he was getting exactly what he wanted. "I guess you'll want to be gone as soon as possible. I'll help you get your stuff together—"

"In that much of a hurry to get rid of me?" Wistful, but not defeated. She could be in the gutter in rags without a penny to her name and he doubted she'd be defeated. She just didn't have it in her. And then she sighed, one final expression of regret for the inevitable. "I'm afraid there are some terms to the agreement that weren't in your original offer."

Oh, he'd known he needed to be wary of her. Hadn't he warned himself of that, at least a dozen times since he'd first seen her? "Yeah?"

"Yes. Several, I'm afraid, and I'm aware they might sound a bit odd upon first inspection, but I assure you—"

"Just tell me."

"Well, you see—" She filled her cheeks with air, pretty pink balloons, and blew it out in a gust. "I find myself in need of a husband."

"So?"

"I've decided it's best that it's you."

Chapter 7

"It's only temporary," she assured him quickly.

"Well, that sure sets my mind at ease."

"And it wouldn't even have to be for very long."

"Yeah?"

"No, of course not. And we wouldn't have to—" Emily stopped, bit down on her tongue so she'd stop babbling out conditions that sounded nothing like she'd intended them. She'd known talking him into this would be a trick, and it had taken every shred of courage she could muster to blurt out her proposition. Except it was coming out all wrong, making it a wonder he was still standing there, listening. "Could you stop glowering at me? It's making me nervous."

"Is it?" he murmured, dangerously bland.

"Yes," she admitted, hoping for mercy. But he

didn't move, feet spread wide, arms jammed forbiddingly across his chest, the dark, dangerous glitter of eyes and a strong, straight jut of sun-browned nose the only features visible between his wild sprout of hair and beard.

Why had she ever thought he'd make this easy? She cast around for help until she spotted his chair. It was a topsy thing, ready to collapse into a pile of sticks beneath his weight, but he seemed fond enough of it, for all the time he spent in it.

She dragged it over and patted the seat encouragingly. "Why don't you sit down, and I'll explain everything?"

"I'm thinking maybe you should be the one sitting down."

"Oh no, I couldn't sit." And, proof of her words, she started to pace. "Please?"

He dropped down, legs and arms sprawling wide. Heavens, but he was a long one; he stuck his legs out, crossed them at the ankle, and they seemed to stretch halfway to McGyre.

"What do you want to hear?" she asked, while her skirts *swish-swished* through the grass. He could mark her agitation by the sound, restless motion that sped up as she talked. "You just want the proposal— er, proposition? Um . . ." She paused, began again— faster words, faster swishing. "I have a purely *business* proposal for you, one that will benefit us both. Do you simply want the terms, or do you want the whole story?"

"I'll take the story," he decided, surprising them both. But it was bound to be entertaining. He couldn't imagine what she'd have done that would force her into proposing to *him*, of all people. Even if she'd done so as a purely business endeavor, he thought, and found himself smiling. The grin felt odd, like trying on a coat that wasn't his but didn't fit too badly, and he let it stay.

He leaned back, suspecting it would take a while. But what was the hurry now, if he was finally going to get his claim back in the end? "Go ahead."

"I'm not sure where to begin." She reached down and plucked a blade of grass, shredding it into long green threads as she walked, as if she needed more release than the pacing afforded. "I've got a sister. Well, two of them, but only one that enters into this. Kathryn. She's older than me by a fair amount, and she's pretty much mothered me since my mother died. She's good at it."

She glanced up at that, her face earnest, as if it were important to her that he understood her sister's place in her life. The sun dipped behind her, and her hair was loose, clouds of gold-tipped silk, and he wondered what it would feel like to plunge his hands deep into that mass and grab on.

He reached out and snagged his old black hat off the top of the empty valise where he'd left it and jammed it low on his brow. "The sun," he excused himself. In truth the brim allowed him to watch her unnoticed.

"You have to understand—I don't even remember my mother; I was too young. And my father died when I was five, but he'd been grieving so much before that I barely knew him, either. My sisters were everything for me, and they made sure I never felt the slightest lack."

"Lucky for you," he said because she seemed to want a comment.

"It was!" Emily said with more than a little heat. "Except when my father died, it turned out he'd managed to grieve away every dollar he'd had, too. And it was a lot of dollars."

Emily wished she could see his eyes. Get some hint of what he was thinking, feeling. But that darned hat threw shade across his face, the shadow disappearing into his beard. As if he couldn't give her even that much, a hint of himself.

"Anyway, she worried about me. How to take care of me. I don't know . . . I was so young, everything seemed just fine to me. Oh, we had to leave our home, but I was five, what did it matter to me?"

Heavens, he could be dead asleep for all she knew. Maybe her story bored him. He didn't seem the type to be curious about other people's pasts. She thought he'd even deny much interest in his own—but if it really didn't matter to him, he wouldn't have come back here.

"Mr. Sullivan?"

"Hmm?"

"Oh. I—never mind. Well then, I imagine Kate decided the simplest way to ensure I'd have everything I needed, everything she wanted me to have, was to marry well."

"She's not the first to use that tactic."

"No, I suppose not. She's a beautiful woman. I mean, a *really* beautiful woman." She waved her hand up and down, gesturing from her own head to her toes. "Not like me, nice enough if I put some work into it."

Jesus. In another woman, he'd take that as his cue to praise her beauty. But Emily seemed completely unconcerned and went right on without giving him an opening.

Could she really not realize? He must have known prettier women in his life. But at the moment he was having a damn hard time coming up with a single one.

"She's—oh, wait till you meet her. You think you're prepared—men always do—but then you—" She shook her head, her smile fond. "Anyway, she didn't have much trouble marrying for money. And heavens, did she. And only money. I know it doesn't sound nice but it was no more romantic on his side. I don't think she even tried for a compromise, someone with reasonable prospects *and* someone she might have liked as well. No. There'd be nothing to soften it for her. Talk about a business arrangement! She got a comfortable life for both of us and Dr. Goodale got the loveliest ornament in Philadelphia for his wife."

Her motions grew jerky, her arms gesturing against her sides, her steps uneven, so at odds with her usual grace that he recognized it for the first time in its absence. Yes, she was supposed to be sure, fluid.

"She lived up to her side of the agreement—oh, how she lived up to it! I'm not—" She pressed her mouth together, the lush curve of her lips subverting into a severe line. "Kate is a strong woman in all other areas of her life. Determined. But she did every single thing he ever asked—no, not asked, told!—every last thing he commanded her without a murmur. And he commanded her a great deal."

The sun had dropped behind the tent. As she walked, she moved in and out of the shadow. In light, in dark, and light again. It fascinated him, how different she looked in each. Open and sunny and warm, then shadowed, mysterious.

"He's gone now, and I'm grown, and I thought that finally, *finally*, she'd be able to have a life of her own. Why shouldn't she? But I—she thinks I should go back to school. Is *determined* that I go. But Dr. Goodale left all of his fortune to his children. Apparently it was their agreement from the start; she'd gambled on him living awhile. And now she's seeing Mr. Ruckman, and he's even worse than the doctor. She'll do it, I just know she will, if that's what she thinks it'll take to protect me."

And then she stopped, right in the border of sun and shadow, half in, half out. "It wouldn't be fair to her. I couldn't stand it, to think that she just did it for me. *Again*. It wouldn't be fair."

"But do you want to go to school?

"Of course not. I—" She grimaced, clearly torn. "That's not true. All else being equal, I'd love it. But it's not all else equal, is it? I couldn't be happy there, knowing that she'd married Ruckman to ensure it." She shook her head. "Oh, not that I haven't been happy, all these years. Very much so. Even her being married to Dr. Goodale, for all I hated what it did to her, for me, well, he taught me so much. But it's time for me to take care of myself. She's given up fifteen years; that's plenty."

"Can't you just tell her that?"

She laughed, a short burst that dismissed his crude male thinking. "You can't *tell* Kate anything. She'll do what she thinks best no matter what I say about it. No, the only way I could think to finally set her free was to be well settled myself, no longer in need of her care."

"Maybe she doesn't want to be free."

Her head snapped up. "Then she'd just better get used to it."

"Okay." Apparently Emily was just as sure of what was right for Kate as she claimed Kate was for her.

She glared at him for a second longer before her smile broke through. It seemed her natural expression, that sunny grin, everything else a temporary aberration; her face fell easily into the lines, her teeth white and even, her lips curving up as effortlessly, inevitably, as a flower opening to the sun. "I'm sorry. I'm not angry. It just . . . matters to me, very much."

"Yeah." His father had died before he could remember him, and he'd never had brothers or sisters, but he'd worried over his mother more than she liked. "I can understand worry making you a little . . . emphatic where family is concerned."

Her smile softened with empathy. "Yes, I suppose you do."

Nope. She might be happy to spill all her secrets, but he wasn't coughing his up. To distract her he prodded: "How'd you end up here?"

"Oh! I knew the only way she'd ever stop arranging her life for my benefit was if she knew I was entrenched in a life of my own. This seemed the best opportunity."

"It did?" He looked around them, at the stark land, its promise well hidden to an unfamiliar or unimaginative eye, and the small, ugly building that he'd pretended was a home. Her rose-colored glasses must be two inches thick if she thought *this* was her best opportunity. *"Here?"*

"Of course." Her eyes shone, excitement coloring the soft curve of her cheeks. "A home of my own, on land of my own, that no one could ever take from me. I've never had that—we've never had that—a place that was just ours. I don't know if you could understand—"

"I could understand," he said flatly. He didn't want to understand. Didn't want to find this common ground with her, didn't want to know why this was more than an impulsive lark to her. But oh, that tug of wanting, needing, a place that you could call yours and no one could deny you . . . it had driven him for a long time. Maybe, in an odd way, it still did.

She beamed at him, delighted with his agreement. "There, then. I wrote her when I got here, so she wouldn't worry. I told her how well everything was going."

"And you thought she would just let it be?" He knew nothing of her sister but what she'd told him, but even he could have guessed it unlikely. Not to mention that if the situation were reversed, Emily herself would have been hog-tied before she'd have left Kate alone, something that he sort of . . . reluctantly . . . admired about her.

"I'd hoped." She made a face. "I suppose I should have known better. But hoping tends to work out well for me."

"How fortunate you are."

"Oh, I am!" she said with such fervency that no one could doubt she believed it. And yet, in the bits of her past she'd told him, she'd lost as much as most and more than some. "And, too, I was sort of counting on the fact that she'd rather have every hair on her head plucked out one by one than come out here."

"Not fond of the country, is she?"

"Goodness, no. My other sister, Anthea, lives in Colorado with her family. Kate goes to see her—of course she goes; it's her sisterly duty, and heaven knows she would never shirk that. But she drags along more luggage than a duchess, frowns the entire way there, and waves a scented handkerchief under her nose until we cross back over the Mississippi again," she said with far more fondness than exasperation. "Kate is not what one would call pioneer stock." Her gesture encompassed all of Montana. "She'll *hate* it here. Maybe she won't stay long," she added hopefully.

"But you . . . don't hate it?" She should. A woman with her air of refinement, her pretty manners and clothes: this place should have sent her screaming for home the first night.

"Oh no." She spun like a child, arms spread. "I don't hate it at all."

And he believed her. *Damn*. It'd be so much easier

if he hadn't believed her. "So that's it. She's coming, and then she'll take you home."

"Nope," she said cheerfully. "That's why I need a husband."

Husband. He'd forgotten it. Or conveniently pushed it aside while he allowed her to distract him with her story. She was easy to listen to, easy to watch while she talked. But now the word roared back, a dark, echoing refrain, throbbing painfully in his head. *Husband, husband, husband.*

He couldn't be a husband. He already was a husband.

But he wasn't, he remembered, and allowed the pain to roll over him, spear up through his gut and into his chest, to bite there, a savage throb, making no attempt to mute it because it was only what he deserved.

"You didn't forget, did you?" she went on.

"I—"

"Are you all right?" Quick as a blink, she dropped to her knees beside his chair, put her hands on each side of his head to hold it steady while she peered into his eyes. "Hmm. Hard to tell if your pupils are clear when your eyes are so dark." Her hands were impersonal, ruthlessly efficient as she examined him, brushing his forehead, probing beneath his ears. Yet he felt every point of contact, the smooth heat of her palms, the cooler, rougher pads at the tips of her fingers. Had she really no idea? It was all he could do not to grab those hands and drag them down his body. He wanted them hot and eager; the fact that she could touch him and be completely unaffected infuriated him.

She was close enough that he could smell her. Lord, was there ever such a good-smelling thing in the world as a clean woman? Not flowers, not baking bread, not perfume. *Her.*

He grabbed her wrists. So fragile; he could snap them with a squeeze.

"It's all right," she told him in a soothing voice that made him want to snarl. "If you'll just let me—"

"I'm not a horse," he snarled at her.

His tone would have warned off a thug in the meanest saloon. She didn't even flinch. "I'm even better with people than horses," she told him, coolly confident.

"I'm all right."

"You didn't look all right. You looked like you hurt, and goodness knows I've seen enough people in pain to recognize the signs. You've no fever, I grant you, but—"

"Stop." He was still holding her wrists, he realized; why hadn't he put her away from him yet? He was sure that he'd meant to. He could feel her pulse beat against his thumbs. He stayed like that for a moment, dragging air into lungs that suddenly seemed like they couldn't get enough before he jerked her hands away from him and released her. "Don't touch me again."

"I won't promise," she told him. "If I can help you, I'll do so. You're not the first who's begun by telling me to stop. But I've yet to have one who wasn't grateful to be healed, when it came right down to it."

He swore, a profane suggestion that should have

horrified any true lady should she even recognize it.

"No thank you," she said calmly, and rose to her feet, whacking dust off her skirts with complete nonchalance.

Damn it. He would *not* smile at her. He would not.

But it was hard. Oh, it was hard.

"Now then." Having beaten up a satisfactory cloud, she folded her hands before her. "Are you ready to begin negotiations?"

"Negotiations?"

He shouldn't have taken the chair when she'd offered it. It was a weak position from which to bargain. It mitigated the advantage of his height. Not to mention that no man's wits were sharp when his nose was breast-high.

He sprawled back in his chair and contrived to look relaxed. "Negotiate away."

"Kate said she was coming as soon as possible. It'd be different if she'd given me some time to get things together, but patience has never been one of Kate's finer qualities. And the truth is, as fond as I am of this place, if she sees this"—she gestured toward the claim shack—"she'll never let me stay here alone."

"Sounds good to me."

She made a face at him. "I'm aware of that. Not, however, to me. But she won't rest easy until I'm well settled, and so I decided to beat her to the punch. I told her I was married."

She said it calmly, as if her words were entirely rational. "Let me see if I understand this. You wanted your sister to stop worrying about you so you lied to her."

"It sounds bad when you say it like that."

"This is a habit of yours?"

She lifted her chin. "We've always all been willing to do whatever's necessary in order to protect each other."

"Uh-huh." Her hands had left their imprint, warm and soft, against his face, and he had the most absurd and sudden need to find out how his own would feel on her. "And you thought that telling her you were married—to someone you've known, what, a couple of weeks at the outside?—would ease her mind?"

"We have a long and successful history of precipitous marriages in our family," Emily informed him.

He stared at her, face carefully wiped clean of expression. And then he laughed, great, rusty whoops of it that bent him over at the waist and nearly toppled him out of his chair.

Emily knew she should have been insulted. He was laughing *at* her; there was no way to dress it up and pretend he was laughing *with* her. But she couldn't deny that, stated baldly, it sounded a bit . . . outlandish.

And there was his laughter. Such a sight he was, the corners of his eyes crinkling, his thin, sculpted cheeks rounding up above his beard, the sound gusting out of him as if it'd been dammed up for half his life and was just now erupting in one great rush.

She was tempted to embellish the story. See if she could amuse him some more. She doubted there'd ever been a man on earth who needed it more than he did, and being the one who gave it to him made the region of her heart go soft and warm. Oh, there was nothing she liked so much as being able to make someone feel better!

He finally quieted. Two last, small hiccups before he swiped at his eyes with the flat of his hands.

"Are you finished?" she asked.

"Maybe. Yeah, I think so." He braced his hands on his knees and leaned toward her. "Unless you want to tell me we've got three kids already, too."

"Oh heavens, no." She pretended to look appalled. "How silly do you think I am? There's only the one on the way."

"Good God!" he exploded, but then caught sight of her smile. "Oh. You're teasing."

He looked put out at that, his brow knit in confusion.

"Forgive me, Miss Bright, but I still find it hard to credit that you marrying someone you scarcely know would ease your sister's concern."

"Call it desperate measures." She sighed. "First off, convincing her not to worry is an impossibility. She'll worry. I'll be eighty years old and tottering around on a cane and she'll still be worrying. I only hoped to delay her arrival long enough to give me a chance to prove that *she* doesn't need to marry someone she doesn't wish to in order to provide me with a home."

"So you think she's going to arrive, take one look at me, figure you're in good hands, and go trotting back to Philadelphia? I'm flattered."

"As I said, desperate measures."

He blew out a breath and scrubbed a hand through the thick, unruly mass of his hair. "Up until meeting you, Miss Bright, I'd considered myself a relatively logical and intelligent man. What, exactly, do you expect to happen when your sister arrives and finds you married to me?"

"Once she sees me taken care of, she'll go back home, and she won't have to marry Mr. Ruckman. Then I'll have until spring to get things in order—there's no way she'll venture out here again until it warms up. She hardly sticks her nose out of the house when it's cold. By spring, when I'm still okay, she'll have to admit I can take reasonable care of myself and we'll both go forward from there."

"Female plotting." He shook his head while she bristled. "I assume we're not really going to be married."

"Of course not!"

"Then how—supposing you get to spring in one piece—are you going to explain what happened to your husband?"

"Oh, there are lots of possibilities. You could die tragically—at which point, of course, it would be impossible for me to remain on the claim; I'd be too heartbroken, explaining why I've had to move to another." She pressed the back of her hand to her head as if preparing to swoon.

"Yeah, *that'd* put her mind at ease about your welfare."

She frowned at him; the man had no talent for banter. "All right. We've divorced; I misjudged you, and you ran off with the local bar dancer, you heartless wretch." She tucked her tongue in her cheek. "Or maybe even with the handsome bartender. Such a shock."

He narrowed his eyes at her warningly.

She struggled not to smile. "Honestly, by then I'll probably be able to tell her the truth. Likely Mr. Ruckman will have found himself some other interest by then. And, considering I'd survived that long, even Kate will have to acknowledge that I don't require her to mother me anymore. At least not to the same degree."

"Or she'll commit you to the nearest asylum, where you clearly belong."

"You have no imagination."

"Thank God, if this is where it leads one."

"Do you know, you have the most remarkable ability to strain my sympathy?"

"And whatever gave you the idea that I wanted it?"

There was clearly no help for the man. She would do far better, she reflected, if she could ignore her natural instincts and just let him wallow in his gloom.

"So? Will you do it?"

Sound rumbled in his chest. "Why me?"

Despite her resolution, that was simply too good to pass up. "Why, your charm and sunny nature, of course. Whyever else?"

She smiled sunnily into his glower.

"Leverage, then," she admitted.

"Leverage?"

"I've something you want. I'm confident we can come to a reasonable and simple agreement."

"I'm pretty sure you got somethin' Longnecker wants, too. I'm sure he'd be rock-damn delighted to play house with you for a couple of days."

Now, that was uncalled for. "That would be . . . complicated. I'd much prefer to keep this simple."

"You'll have to give up the land, though."

"I know." She shot a longing gaze at the little shack she'd grown surprisingly fond of. "Some things can't be helped. And I'll find another."

"If you'd have handed it over when you should have, you'd have been settled by now, and all this wouldn't be necessary."

"And if you don't stop hammering about such things, I'm going to go ask Imbert after all and you can just sit over here and sulk until winter comes and you freeze in your chair."

"Aw, but that wouldn't be fair to him, remember?"

"I imagine I could make it up to him," she said in a silky voice, which earned her a quick, hard glare. "So? Will you do it?"

"Why not?" he said, with surprising good cheer.

"Oh, and not that I would ever suspect you of such designs, of course, but I think it's best that we're clear on all the details, don't you? Such as, if you should happen to, oh, get cold feet at the last minute and back out *just* as Kate arrives, I won't be leaving with her, no matter what she says. She'll hate it, but she'll stay, and we'll both be digging in for the winter."

"It never occurred to me," he said, too quickly to be convincing.

"You do ease my mind."

"Happy to be of service."

"So we're agreed?"

"The instant she gets on the train home, you're gone, too."

"Fine." She'd been completely reasonable about the entire thing. Friendly, even. And yet he had to go and make it clear that he didn't want her there one second longer than necessary.

And so she felt no compunction to make this easy on him.

She stepped back, put her hands on her hips, and eyed him as critically as Dr. Goodale had ever evaluated his prized horseflesh.

"What?"

"It's just—" She tilted her head, pursed her lips as if considering. "I described you to Kate. Or rather, I described my husband to Kate. In some detail."

"So?"

"Well . . . I took a few liberties there as well. Since I didn't think she'd ever actually meet you."

He looked toward heaven for help. "Now why doesn't that surprise me?"

"Because you're so perceptive?"

"That must be it," he added dryly. "So what'd you say about me?"

"Oh, let me see if I can remember." She pressed her forefinger to her pursed lips. "Educated, cultured, well-spoken, and well-dressed. Attentive to my every desire, of course."

He slumped back, face glum. "What else?"

"Besotted with me—that goes without saying. Prone to break into praise of my beauty regularly," she went on as he slid further down in his chair, until his head was level with the top rung of the back. "A poet. A—"

"Good God, Em!" he burst out.

"I had to make it believable that you swept me off my feet, didn't I?" she asked reasonably. *Em.* Nobody called her Em. She'd always assumed she'd hate it. But she didn't, not one bit. Odd.

"Anything else?" he asked glumly.

She looked at him, at the thick fringe of his hair drooping low, shielding his right eye, and his beard swallowing up his mouth, and she couldn't resist. "Oh, just one more thing."

His sigh of relief only got halfway out.

"You're clean-shaven, of course."

Chapter 8

Kate was to arrive tomorrow. Emily and Jake had managed to avoid each other completely for the last two days, a careful orchestration that allowed them to pretend to forget that they'd agreed to play at husband and wife. Only for a few days, Emily reminded herself frequently, and without a shred of real legal or moral ties.

But it didn't help. The idea that he was to be her husband had lodged itself under her skin, leaving her nervous, unsettled, and decidedly *not* herself.

She hoped that Kate would not recognize her tension instantly and suspect the truth. Still, a new bride could be expected to suffer a few nerves, couldn't she?

The time had come that she could no longer ignore her impending "marriage." Details must be settled between them before they could carry off this charade with any authority. And so she collected what she must, bundling it in a sheet, as well as all the courage she could muster, and headed for the squat little camp she'd done her best to ignore.

Mr. Sullivan—Jake, she amended; they'd have to get accustomed to calling each other by their given names, wouldn't they?—sat cross-legged on the ground, sorting through a pile of nuts and bolts, and didn't look up when she approached. Considering that until now he'd never failed to watch her when she stepped out her door, his inattention had to be deliberate. Perhaps this whole idea made him as uncomfortable as she. For however false it was, even pretending a marriage seemed more intimate than she'd imagined. They'd joined this charade together; it made them partners, gave them a common goal, and bound her to consider his wishes in the days ahead.

The day was warm and then some. He wore only a light shirt as he worked, and it clung damply to his back. She could see the play and swell of thick muscle as he reached for a bolt. He was powerfully built, wide shoulders, solid bone.

Dr. Goodale had been old; their patients often wasted to nothing. And the carefully chosen young men she'd sometimes flirted with were just that: young. She'd no idea of Jake's actual age, whether three years older than she or thirteen, but there was no doubt he was a man, not a boy. If she ever married in truth, she'd like a man with shoulders like Jake's; a woman could lean on them if she had to and be assured they'd bear up just fine. Not to mention that there was a certain amount of appeal in watching those muscles bunch and shift. Fascinating.

Kate would be appalled to find her so interested in a man's shoulders. And surprised. She'd only tolerated Emily's working with Dr. Goodale because she'd been convinced that there was nothing prurient whatsoever in Emily's interest. Who could be concerned with shriveled old shoulders or shrunken chests when there was a fascinating pathology to examine?

Nevertheless, she was to treat him as her husband for the next few days. A besotted young wife would be perfectly *enthralled* with her new husband's shoulders.

The sun brought up tiny glints of gold in his dark hair, the color of the rich mink Dr. Goodale had bought Kate shortly after their marriage. It had fascinated Emily; only six then, she'd buried her fingers in it, ran her hands through it over and over until Dr. Goodale had caught her at it. She'd never felt anything so soft; she wondered if his hair would feel the same. It didn't seem as if there could be anything soft on Jake Sullivan.

"What do you want?" He didn't look up, just hurled the question at her without a hint of graciousness while he squinted at the threads of another bolt.

"I thought that—" Her carefully constructed speech scrambled. "I don't know what color your eyes are." Dark, she knew. But blue, or green, or . . .

That brought his head up. "What the hell?"

"Or hardly anything else about you. I thought that we should—" Brown, she thought hazily. Deep, dark brown. She'd always thought of that as a nice warm, fuzzy sort of color. Chocolate, fur. This was darker, colder, water over dark rocks. And infinitely more intriguing. "Kate is bound to ask questions. A lot of questions. It'd be odd, don't you think, if we don't know the answers?"

He shrugged, completely unconcerned. "It's not like we've had months of courting to fill up with chatter."

"Yes, but don't you think that we'd have talked about a few things? I mean—"

"If we've only been married for such a short time and haven't had better things to do than *talk*, well, there'd be no reason for us to be rushing into marriage so fast, would there?"

"But . . . ooh!" Against her best efforts, she felt her cheeks heat, knew they must be glowing like a hurricane lamp. "But surely there'd be some opportunity. I think we should exchange the basics." Not bad, she thought. Barely a quaver in her voice; they could have been discussing the price of lumber.

"I should hope not." He sounded very sure. *Very* sure. "You don't want her thinking I just married you for the land, do you? Better I married you for your body."

She gaped; she couldn't help it. She'd thought her medical experiences had made her far more worldly than most. But it was extremely different, she'd just discovered, when it was one's own intimacies one was pondering. Even if those intimacies were imagined. And they were imagined, suddenly, in the kind of fuzzy detail that was all that her not exactly limited, but certainly impersonal, knowledge could summon. Even that was enough to soften her knees.

His beard twitched. Was he smiling at her, beneath that thicket? Laughing at her? She didn't know whether to be provoked or pleased.

"Just in case you didn't note it earlier," she began, deciding it was best to simply ignore him, "my other sister's name is Anthea. Her husband is Gabriel. Their children are Will, James, and—"

"Cripes. You're set on this, aren't you? Write down whatever you figure I need to know. I'll study like a good little boy."

"Kate'll ask questions," she warned him again.

"Afraid I won't hold up my end of the bargain?"

"I didn't mean to impugn your honorability. I simply prefer to have the bases covered, if at all possible."

"Yeah, like you did when you ran away to Montana?" he said, with just enough sneer to make her bristle. And then, "All your bases? You like baseball?"

"Yes," she admitted. "Not terribly ladylike, is it? I told everyone that I must have *some* topic to discuss with our male patients, but truly, I'd rather go to a ball game than the opera any day. You enjoy it?"

"Yeah," he said, voice warmer and less guarded than she'd ever heard it. "Used to sneak into games every chance I got when I was a kid in Chicago. Even paid a few times after they moved to the West Side Grounds. Not quite as big a thrill as sneaking in, though."

"A Colts fan?"

"You bet."

"Did you play?"

"Sure. When I was a kid. Third base, mostly, sometimes first. Always wanted to pitch, but had a tendency to find batters' heads more often than the plate."

"There, you see!" She beamed at him. "*This* is what I meant! It's exactly the sort of detail I need about you to keep Kate from getting suspicious."

"Yeah. Wouldn't want to give old Kate suspicions."

There was just enough surly edge in his voice to make Emily go back over her words to see how she'd offended him. Heavens, but men were a touchy species. "I wasn't listening *just* to glean details for Kate. I was interested, too. In fact—"

"Make me a list," he told her once again. "Just the high points. I imagine you've got all kinds of high points."

Her arms tightened around her bundle, and it gave softly. Talking to him was like walking through a marshland, never knowing when you put your foot down if it would hit safe, solid ground or sink into the morass. "I'd really prefer to discuss it. That way you can ask questions if something occurs to you."

"The list," he said, making it clear it would do her no good to argue. "I won't be asking any questions."

Oh, just write the darn list! she scolded herself. Why did she keep expending time and energy wrangling with him?

"Fine. On yours, however, I'd really like as much detail as you can manage. Kate's not the sort to take things at face value."

He gave her a hard, long look. "Tell her whatever you want. I'll go along with it."

"You want me to invent your past? Your likes, your dislikes?"

"What do I care? Make up whatever you want. You're good at that."

It stung. She tried not to let it, but it did just the same, a quick needle prick to a tender area of her pride. "I just don't want to get caught unaware, that's all. If you tell Kate something, I don't want to contradict it through my ignorance."

"Why the hell would I tell your sister any damn thing at all?"

"Kate's curious. And very good at prying things out of men that they never intended to tell her. She's bound to be extraordinarily curious about you."

"And I'm very good at keeping my mouth shut."

Yes, she knew that well. She wondered at her need to keep prodding at this topic. Oh yes, Kate must believe in her marriage. But she was afraid that there was more to it than that neatly allowable reason.

She didn't want to be interested in him, his past, his dreams. But she wondered. He looked like a farmer, strong-muscled, rough-fingered. But sometimes he spoke like a professor, smooth-voiced, careful words—and then he'd turn around and swear like a sailor. He'd homesteaded, in that bare, simple place, like a man with little money and no future other than the one he'd wrest for himself. And yet there were those books, the wide-ranging collection of a man of thought and leisure.

He returned to his work, focusing on the metallic innards she'd seen before, gears and pulleys, his head bent and shoulders hunched, ending the conversation by closing himself off from her. He seemed to want nothing more than to be left utterly alone.

But he'd had a wife.

"Another thing—"

He growled something she was glad she couldn't catch, sprang to his feet, and hurled a gear so hard it flew over his tent and disappeared on the other side of the rise.

"What *now*?" he shouted at her, loud enough to make her flinch.

"Well, *that*, for one thing. You should have risen the moment I came over. I'd never marry someone with such abysmal manners. It'd be a dead giveaway." It was a low blow and Emily knew it, but he deserved it.

"Oh, I'll mind my manners, don't you worry your little head," he said, low and dangerous.

She chose to ignore the warning. "You haven't shaved yet." She smiled into his glower. "Just a helpful suggestion. I know how committed you are to this venture. How much you'd hate it if something happened so the land doesn't get handed over to you as we planned."

"Emily . . ."

"Oh well, we'll just have to go with the 'love is blind thing.' " Then she sobered. "I brought you something." She thrust out the bundle. "I thought that you could use your clothes." She'd spent all day preparing them, washing and starching and pressing until she dared him to find a wrinkle. "I should have brought them sooner, I suppose. Everything's been in such a rush that I really hadn't thought of it until now."

He lifted his shoulders as if to say, *What do I care about clothes?*

"Anyway." She cleared her throat. "They're clean now."

"Good enough for Kate?"

"Well, Kate has unusually high standards. Good enough for me. And you, I hope. Let me know if you don't like them. If there's too much—oh, I don't know. Too much starch. Whatever."

"Oh, I will. Don't you worry, I will."

"There's—" It got harder, now. "Her . . . There are dresses. In the pile." She peeled back the sheet and pushed aside a pair of blue pants, exposing a wedge of bright green silk. Oh heavens, where were the right words when she needed them. *Were* there right words for this? "I didn't wash them. I didn't know— I didn't want to ask."

His hands, which had been reaching for the clothes, stopped in mid-air. He pulled them back, rubbed them hard down the front of his pants. She thought she detected a small tremor as he reached forward again and took the stack of clothes. He brushed his fingers over the vivid fabric, once, lightly, before lifting his eyes to meet hers.

She couldn't have said exactly how his expression had changed. Had his eyes narrowed, his mouth tightened, his brows lowered? Infinitesimal changes, certainly, that added up to grief, a deep dark welling of it, spilling up and over from that place inside him he'd contained until now. Oh, her heart hurt, just seeing it, an ache in her chest that made her rub her breastbone in a futile attempt to ease it.

"Thank you," he said, though she could tell what it cost him to say it.

"Jake." Inevitably drawn, she took a step toward him, unsure of what she meant to offer but comfort. And for that brief instant, she thought he would accept.

And then it was over. He turned away, big hands crushing the bundle of clothes she'd pressed so carefully, giving her nothing but the wall of his back.

"Tell me when your sister gets here."

Montana had never seen the likes of Mrs. Kathryn Virginia Bright Goodale. She stepped off the stage in McGyre with the carriage of a queen descending from her royal carriage. Her head dipped briefly, to ensure the safe passage of the great, curving white plumes of ostrich feathers that frothed from her soft, silk-covered toque, the rhinestone buckle glittering like diamonds.

Two old cowboys, ambling out of the nearest saloon at their usual, decrepit shuffle, stopped dead in their tracks, rheumy eyes bulging from their sockets. Across the street, Wilber Bunku came bursting out of his store to get a better look, the chicken he'd been butchering still swinging from his fist. A wolf whistle split the air, and Kathryn acknowledged its source, bending a serene smile on the thin young ruffian who leaned against the post in front of the livery.

The instant her foot hit the platform, three men appeared to offer assistance. She declined them all in such delicately flattering terms that they blushed and went away as puffed up as if she'd given one her favor. She raised the fashionable little lorgnette that she would never admit was more than an accessory and scanned the street.

"Kate!" Emily pulled the team and old buggy she'd borrowed from Joe and May Blevins to a stop, threw the brake, and vaulted off, showing enough ankle to, under normal circumstances, earn a firm rebuke from her sister. But today Kate couldn't bring herself to care. She spread her arms wide and waited for Emily to tumble into them.

"Oh! You feel good. I've missed you." She tightened her arms, then grabbed Emily by the shoulders and pushed her back to arms' length. "Here, let me look at you."

She inspected her from head to toe, prodding once to check the flesh over her ribs while Emily stood docilely and allowed it. There was no avoiding it, and she figured she owed Kate a little for worrying her so.

"Hmm. You seem healthy enough." She didn't frown; it made for unattractive lines. "A little thin, but healthy. No broken bones, and you're still on your feet."

"No oozing sores, even."

"Emily! What a thing to say." Suddenly she dug through her confection of a handbag, drew out a snowy square of linen, and dabbed at the corners of her eyes.

Emily gawked. Kate did not cry. Not ever. Guilt lumped cold and hard in her belly. "Kate, I am so very sorry if I made you worry. Truly, if there'd been any other way—there was so little time to decide, and I . . ." *I wanted to come,* she thought. *I didn't want you to marry Mr. Ruckman.* And they both seemed like weak excuses compared to the sight of her sister's damp eyes.

"Oh, for heaven's sake! There's some pollen out here that doesn't agree with me. I've been sniffling since about a hundred miles west of Chicago." She dabbed delicately at her nose and tucked the kerchief away. Then she looked pointedly at the buggy in which Emily had driven up. "So? Where's this husband of yours?"

Emily had practiced for the question a good chunk of the way into town. She didn't think her expression wavered. "Getting the place ready for you, of course."

"Hmm." Kate's usual response when she disagreed but didn't want to discuss the matter outright. She rarely used it on Emily, but she'd "hmm'd" Dr. Goodale at least a dozen times a day. "Now then, young lady—"

"Oh, Kate, not now!" She chose to ignore the "young lady." Not cowardice, but picking her battles. "I am much too happy to see you to spoil it with arguing right this minute. Let's get you some tea; the restaurant in the hotel is nearly reliable. And then we'll go back home, and you'll rest up a bit, and you'll have ever so much more energy for a lecture in the morning!"

"Hmm." She linked her arm with Emily's, strolled

in a swish of silk toward the building Emily indicated.

"You look wonderful," Emily told her. Her suit was pale, trembling gray, the color of a dove's throat, and trimmed with enough lace to dress a dining room table. The skirt was gusseted, the waist severely narrowed, and her collar swooped into a train that fluttered down her back nearly to her ankles.

She shrugged. *Of course. On to more important matters.*

"It's a beautiful suit," Emily went on. "However did you keep it so perfect on the coach?"

"Everyone must have a talent," she said, and Emily chuckled. "Excuse me?"

"I'm sorry. It's just . . . I said that very thing to Jake once."

"I see." Kate tried not to let it hurt, that Emily had memories with someone else, obviously fond memories Kate could not share. It was inevitable that she would someday. Natural, and right.

She couldn't bear to think about it.

She turned her attention instead to the street they were strolling down. Plain wood buildings listed in all directions. Had they had a competition to see who could build the ugliest structure? She'd vote for that one, with the sign that proclaimed it "The Gambler's Pride." The road could scarcely be called one, the trees were nonexistent, and she'd be persuaded to step into that unhealthy patch of grass—the only one she could see—only at gunpoint, for who knew what lurked in there?

"So. This is McGyre."

"Yes." Emily's beaming enthusiasm encompassed

it all, even the slack-jawed drunkard snoozing in the shadow of the saloon. "Isn't it great?"

Emily ever looked for the best and always found it, but McGyre must have strained even her considerable aptitude.

Kate strove for her most neutral tone. "And what was it about this place that encouraged you to settle here?"

"How could I not?" She stopped in front of a whitewashed, two-story frame building. "Here we are."

. If she breathed too hard in its direction, Kate thought, maybe it would fall over and save her from having to go in there. "Emily, it's been a long trip. I find my stomach's a bit unsettled." *Please, please, get back on the train with me and let me take you home where you belong.* "I am wildly curious to meet your young man. Let's just go on to your place, shall we?"

Unease flickered over Emily's features. Or perhaps Kate was simply looking too closely for it, a symptom of her own rampant worry.

"He is young, isn't he?"

"Oh yes. Younger than Mr. Ruckman, anyway."

Well, Kate thought, *I opened that door, didn't I?*

The ride was long, hot, dusty, and, to Kate's mind, numbingly monotonous. She managed to doze through a fair stretch, whenever Emily's merry chatter lapsed.

Oh, sporadically Kate had tried to inject more important topics. Why Emily had considered it necessary to take this wild risk. This man she'd married on so little acquaintance. *Why, oh why, did you have to*

*run away from me? You'd never seemed the slightest bit
unhappy.*

But Emily skirted the questions with ease, bubbling with tidbits of information about the territory,
pointing out the plover their passage flushed, lifting
her face to the sun and inviting freckles despite
Kate's best efforts to open a parasol over her head.

"Just because you're a married woman now
doesn't mean you can let your looks go."

"Oh, Jake doesn't mind," Emily answered with
such breezy confidence that Kate might have believed her, if she didn't have years of experience
with harder truths.

Oh, let her enjoy her newlywed glow. Later she'd
be more willing to listen to Kate's words of wisdom.
For now she'd keep her mouth shut and let Emily
wallow in it. Kate would be happy for her, refuse to
allow a foothold to the tiny little twinge of envy. For
Kate had never had that few weeks of confident
bliss.

"Here we are," Emily said, so bright with eager
pride that for the first time Kate entertained the unlikely possibility Emily had made the right choice after all.

So Kate kept her expression carefully neutral as
she surveyed the parts of the compound within
plain view. Odd that they'd spread the various
structures so far apart, for all she could see at the
moment was a declining shed and, perhaps thirty
yards away, a tent with a few crates stacked around
it. Lodging for temporary workers, she concluded.

She'd imagined that it would follow the same
arrangement that Gabriel's ranch did, where the sta-

bles, main home, bunk house, ranch house, and a variety of smaller outbuildings all clustered around a small yard.

"Oh, it's good to be home," Emily sang out and leaped down from her seat. And just when had she learned to drive a horse and buggy, anyway, even such a placid one as this? She looked like Emily, sounded like Emily, smiled like Emily. But then she kept doing things that Kate could no longer predict. It was extremely disconcerting.

"Would you like me to get the luggage down here? Or is it too far to carry?"

"Carry it where?" She went up to give the horse a fond pat. "You can leave it. Jake will bring it in when he comes. I'm not sure where he is, but—" Her brows snapped together for a brief instant, and then her smile returned. "I'm sure he'll be back soon. And what's the use of having a husband if one can't make him lug things about?"

"What indeed?" Kate managed with what she considered admirable calm. This . . . *this* was Emily's new home? She'd assumed it to be the chicken coop. Storage of winter supplies at the worst. *Her home?* After she, Kate, had given her a mansion and an education and every other advantage Emily so clearly deserved, things that would have been her birthright if their father hadn't simply folded in and given up when their mother died, she'd come to this?

"Come on, come on. Why are you still perched up there? There's nothing down on the ground that'll bite, I promise."

"Are you sure?" Kate made a show of concern—it wasn't much of a stretch, but snakes hadn't been what worried her, at least up to now—and peered over the side of the buggy. The grass was thick and high, gold-tipped emerald, and could hide any number of creatures.

"Of course I'm sure. Besides, snakes are far more afraid of you than you are of them."

"For one thing, you have no idea how terrified I am, so you cannot draw such a conclusion." Maybe she should just take up temporary residence in the buggy. It appeared to offer as much shelter as that hut, anyway, and she wouldn't have to set foot on snake-infested ground. "And for another, that's a bald-faced lie perpetrated by land speculators in order to lure softheaded, susceptible people to this godforsaken country, and you know it."

Emily laughed, and Kate's tension eased, if only a notch. Emily's merriment was a tonic, a bright and infectiously happy thing that had even worked its magic on Dr. Goodale, no small task indeed. Lord knew Kate had never been able to make him smile as Emily did. She was relieved to discover Emily's laughter, at least, had not changed.

"Come on, come down! I can't wait for you to see it."

Kate climbed down with a fair amount of reluctance, which she refused to let show. If there were snakes anywhere within a square mile, of course *she* would be the one to stumble into their nest. Or wherever it was snakes lurked when they weren't sinking their fangs into unsuspecting passersby.

"This is really intended to be temporary," Emily said cheerfully. "There's so much to be done when one first takes a claim that you just throw up a house to meet the requirements and move on to other matters. Still, it's really quite cozy. I've grown extremely fond of the place."

This time Kate had to bite down on her cheek to prevent a grimace.

"And it's nice not to have so much space to fuss over," Emily went on. "I'll almost be sorry to move into someplace else."

"And when might that be?" Kate asked in a carefully neutral tone.

"Oh heavens, I don't know. We've got to make the land a going concern first. A couple of years, maybe?"

Two years, my patootie, Kate thought. Two weeks, maybe. Two months, if Emily proved stubborn. But she'd pry her out of there before a single blizzard threatened to topple that hovel into kindling.

But it probably wouldn't be particularly helpful to mention that yet. Forewarned, forearmed, and all that rot.

Emily pushed open the door, got halfway in, and froze.

"Emily?"

She said nothing, just stood there in the tiny doorway as if her feet had gotten glued to the ground.

More alarmed now: "Emily?"

When she received no response, she hustled closer, squeezing in the sliver of space between

Emily and the doorframe, and felt splinters catch and tug the lace on her sleeve. Maybe she'd already caught that horrid new husband of hers in bed with another woman. Well, at least they were far enough from civilization that no one would hear the shot.

She peered into the gloom.

Chaos. As if a giant hand had lifted up the shack, turned it upside down, and shaken it like a Christmas globe, letting everything inside spin and tumble before setting it back down again.

The bedclothes trailed across the floor. She identified, with some effort, a shredded nest of white scraps piled just inside the doorway as having once been Emily's best petticoat. Chairs were side-turned. Long strips of colored paper had been torn from the wall, curling down like pencil shavings. Every box, every crate, every canister in the place had been upended.

Crushed crackers spread in an odd-shaped carpet beneath the table. Dried beans rivered from a side-turned crate. Partially smashed coffee beans scented the air, and flour and sugar sifted over it all like the remains of a healthy snowstorm.

"Heavens, Emily, I know you're accustomed to having a housekeeper, but don't you think—" And then Kate shrieked so loud Emily's ears buzzed long after the sound faded away. Kate pointed one elegant, shaking finger at the corner that housed the kitchen.

A small creature peered out from behind the blue flowered curtains. Fur the color of chocolate surrounded bright eyes and a twitching, flat snout.

"Smithie!" Emily scolded. "You come out of there!"

Surprisingly, he obliged, chewing frantically. The bright orange of a dried apricot peeked out from each fist.

"It's a . . . monkey?" Kate murmured, dazed.

"Oh yes." Emily sighed in resignation. Her only hope had been to put as good a face on the place as possible. And now her house resembled a zoo cage that hadn't been cleaned in weeks and her "husband" was missing. Which was maybe for the best, she thought glumly; the way her luck was running, Jake would show up looking like a mountain man who'd crawled out of his cave in the spring, having foregone baths since the snow flew.

"He's a cute creature, isn't he? But oh, what a mess." She *tsk*ed. "And I was so pleased with the decor, I—"

By now Kate, never at a loss for long, had recovered her equilibrium and bent a frown on her sister. "Oh yes. I'm sure it rivaled Goodale House before the monkey had his little party, didn't it? So spacious and sturdily built." Emily resigned herself to the inevitable. She'd avoided Kate's lecture as long as she could; there was no hope for her now. "Snakes and coyotes and other such wild creatures are bad enough, but now there are monkeys in the larder." She shuddered. "Can you imagine what vermin are in your flour? And if there's a monkey here, what else might there be? A crocodile in your well?"

"Now, that is the most *interesting* story, how he came to be here, I—"

"Emily, darling, when has distraction ever saved you? Truly, I don't know what got into you, this wild aberration of hieing off to the far reaches of the country, but enough is enough, don't you think? I won't even say I told you so, because, of course, you didn't think to *ask* me my opinion and so I did not have the opportunity to offer it. Let's just go back to Philadelphia where we belong. Norine has agreed to let us stay at Goodale House for another few months until we can settle what to do *together*. We can probably even get you enrolled for the fall term."

"And how are we paying for that fall term?"

Kate blinked at her. Emily had never questioned her about such things in the past. Perhaps if she had done so before, Emily reflected, things never would have gotten into such a tangle. But she'd always deferred to Kate's competent authority, never wanted to appear ungrateful for all her sisters had done for her.

"Now, don't you worry about that. You just leave the details up to me. Haven't we always managed just fine?"

Emily opened her mouth to protest, then shut it just as fast. What was she going to do? Accuse Kate of selling herself for Emily's future? She couldn't say that. "Aren't you forgetting something?"

"And when have you ever known me to forget something?"

"My husband. I don't think he's going to want me to go running back home, Kate. *Not*," she added hastily, "that I would want to, so don't jump on that."

"Oh. Him," Kate said with easy dismissal, as if discussing a temporary houseman rather than a spouse.

"Well now," drawled a low voice behind them, "is somebody talkin' about me?"

Chapter 9

"Jake," Emily breathed in relief and trepidation, and turned.

And then she stared. She couldn't help it.

Heavens. Oh heavens.

"Jake?" she asked, uncertain.

"I apologize for not being here when you got home." There was an awkward beat while her tongue and her brain scrambled to catch up with her eyes. And then he bent down and brushed a kiss over her temple.

The room whirled. Unthinkingly she reached up to the spot he'd kissed, sure it had to be as hot to the touch as it felt.

"I assumed you'd be staying in town to eat," he went on, easy conversation, as if they'd done this a hundred times. "Or I'd have come home earlier."

She'd never have recognized him. Never.

A mountain man, Emily? More like a prince, the kind

in fairy tales and storybooks and a young girl's gilded dreams.

He'd cut his hair. Not much, and a little shaggily, but it swept back from his forehead—high and noble, of course—and waved low against his collar. Without the shadows of that thick fall, his eyes weren't quite as dark as she'd thought, not so deeply set, bits of gold sparking here and there in the brown.

She'd assumed his chin was weak, his mouth thin. Why else be so determined to hide it? Instead his jaw was cleanly sculpted, set at a pleasing angle, and his mouth looked like it had once known how to smile easily and often. And how to kiss even better than smile.

His shirt was clean and pressed and very white against the brown of his throat, his hands. She remembered washing it for him, putting in that stiff starch, and she felt herself flush. It seemed suddenly an intimate thing, washing the clothes a man would pull over his bare skin. A wifely thing.

She'd never before seen the pants he now wore, deep gray with a simple cut. Plain clothes that, on him, looked anything but.

"You cut yourself shaving," she murmured. "Here." And then she fumbled to pull a kerchief from her handbag. She reached up and pressed it against the tiny nick on his cheek—his skin was pale there, and on his chin, where the beard had shielded it from the sun, a contrast to the skin above on his cheek. His beard had been thick, and the stubble he hadn't managed to scrape off completely left a black shadow on his jaw and pricked her fingers.

"Thank you." His hand covered hers, holding it in place. *My, my, my.* He had the nicest hands, big and warm, not the slightest bit soft, but gentle when he touched her. This—*him*—had been but a few feet from her door all this time and she hadn't realized?

But thank goodness. He would have had her spun around, and up and swindled her land before she got tired of looking at his handsome face.

"I always seem to be doing that, don't I?" he said in the quiet, private tones of a man sharing remembrances with his wife. "And this time I don't even have the excuse of you to distract me."

"Harumph."

"Oh!" Flustered—and even more so because she truly was so instead of merely acting that way for Kate's benefit; she'd forgotten completely about Kate's presence. Thank goodness she hadn't blurted out something that would alert her sister to their charade. She jerked her hand away, leaving Jake with her frilly, feminine bit of handkerchief looking completely out of place in his very masculine hands. "I'm sorry, Kate. I forgot myself for a moment."

"I could see that," she said darkly. She crossed her arms—a swish of dove-gray silk, the flutter of rare lace—and Emily could see the hem of her skirt twitch, betraying the impatient tap of her toes. When Kate was annoyed and wearing heels it sounded like a drum corps.

"Let me introduce the two of you. Kate, this is my husband. Jake. Jake Sullivan." The words sounded strange. Impossible. *Husband. Jake. Mine.*

Jake turned then, for the first time looking directly at Kate, and she had to laugh. Oh, he hid it better than most, but he gawked, wide-eyed, openmouthed.

Kate merely leaned over, placed one delicate, gloved hand beneath his chin, and pushed his jaw up. "Stop that," she snapped.

He shot a quick, apologetic glance at Emily. "I'm sorry, I didn't mean to stare, I just—" He gave up, knowing there was no excuse, and shrugged.

"Heavens, darling, don't worry about it. I've never met a man, even a newly married one, who didn't have that reaction the first time he saw Kate. It's as automatic as, and no more meaningful than, your sneezing if I blew pepper into your face."

"Thank you ever so much for that comparison," Kate said dryly.

"In fact, I'd be a bit worried about your taste if you *hadn't*, and since you married *me*, I'd just as soon not have cause to question your taste."

He recovered quickly. "Why don't you let me take care of our unwelcome visitor, and then we'll introduce ourselves properly?"

He turned and assessed the situation. "Oh, you've been a busy boy, haven't you, Smithie? Playtime's over, though. Time to go home." Over his shoulder: "Why don't the two of you wait outside?" He cast a skeptical eye toward Kate's hat. "Wouldn't want him to suddenly decide that your hair is the best nest around."

Kate needed no more urging than that. She shot out the door so fast her skirts stirred up the spilled flour into a low, dusty cloud.

They were debating just how far away was an appropriately safe distance—Emily maintained they needed to be near enough to help, should her husband require it, which she interpreted as a meager ten feet; Kate was holding out for a minimum of a half mile, which she considered scarcely sufficient—when a blaze of brown darted between them, spinning Kate around.

"You missed him," she said to Jake when he ambled up.

"He's a quick little thing. Off to ride steer, most likely. He's right fond of them, rides better'n half of the cowpokes around here, though he shies at the horses. He'll find his way home when he gets hungry."

"Bull-riding monkeys?" Kate murmured in a daze.

"Now then, Mrs. Goodale." He took her hand, kissed it with an elegant gesture that showed he'd had some practice with the niceties. "Emily has been so looking forward to your arrival."

"I'm sure she has."

"Yes. I'm delighted that you're here."

"Kate will do," she murmured, while she assessed her new brother-in-law. "*If* we're to be family."

Right up until this moment, Kate had not truly believed in his existence. He'd been no more real to her, no more likely to insert his live, breathing presence into her life, than Santa Claus. She didn't know how she'd come to that conclusion, but a part of her had truly thought that she'd simply blow and he'd disappear into the air like frosted breath, and she could take Emily home, safe and sound.

Oh, but he was a handsome one. Easy to see why

Emily's head had been turned. She wasn't so old—mature . . . well-seasoned . . . oh, there wasn't a good word for it, was there?—that she didn't still have an eye for, and appreciate, a fine specimen of a man. She did like the big, brawny ones, and he certainly had the potential for it, shoulders as wide as a barn door even though a bit narrow through the waist and hips.

But he sure had the looks, in spades. And Emily, sweet, trusting Emily, had been ripe for the fall. Kate had admittedly sheltered her, kept her away from most of the flirtations most girls her age might have had, on the theory that Emily's soft heart needed to grow up and harden a bit before being exposed to the machinations of men. But that might have been a mistake, Kate acknowledged now. It had left her with no defenses against the first handsome scoundrel she smacked into.

He moved a shade closer to Emily, put his hand at her elbow, and she jumped. But then she settled down again, even smiling up at him shyly, a hint of rose in her cheeks, and Kate wanted to whack him. *You've got no right to put your hands on her.*

But he did, didn't he? Emily had given him that right.

"Emily, how about that supper you promised me? I find my stomach's calmed down nicely, and now I'm ravenous. I'd just as soon feed it before it acts up again."

"Kate, I'm so sorry! You must be famished. Though it might take a while to get the kitchen clean enough to cook."

"Oh, let it sit for a moment. I'm much more interested in eating than waiting for you to cook something, though I'm sure it'd be wonderful. Can't you just rummage up a snack first? I'm sure we'll all work much better with something in our stomachs." She gave Jake her best smile. "And while you dig out some crackers, Jake and I will wait right here and he can tell me *all* about himself."

Emily and Jake exchanged a long look, and then spoke together.

"I really could use his help—"

"Don't you think I should be taking the buggy back—"

They both clamped their mouths shut, and neither said another word until Emily gave him a small nod.

"Nothing I'd like better," Jake said. "Though I'm sure I'd much rather hear all about you than natter on about myself. Still, we borrowed the buggy and horse from our neighbors, and I'd best get it back. Wouldn't want to take advantage of their generosity."

So the two of them didn't want her alone with Jake. Too bad. There'd be plenty of chances for her to catch him by himself.

"I'll go with you."

"No!" he said quickly. "It's a healthy walk back. Be hard on you in those skirts and shoes. Not to mention the bugs come out at twilight. I'm sure we'll have many opportunities to get acquainted." He frowned. He did a lot of that, Kate had noticed; he looked like a man who'd done some smiling in his time, but you couldn't tell it by his expressions so far. Was this a classic case of opposites attracting, then? Emily, who never stopped smiling, and this man who never started? If there was one thing she'd wished for Emily, it would be to marry a genial and good-natured man who adored her. Kate knew too well what it was like to marry a man who was none of those.

"You will be staying awhile, right?" he said with enough of an edge to have Kate suspecting he'd rather she turned around and went back home this very instant.

"Long as I'm welcome."

The nudge Emily gave his ribs was better disguised than she would have given Emily credit for.

"You're always welcome," he said, and she thought he might have choked on the words.

"Long enough to make certain my sister is well and happily settled."

He threw his arm around Emily's shoulders, a big, hearty gesture that nearly sent Emily toppling. Didn't he know to take care with her? She needed protection. Yes, he looked like he could do a fair job of fighting off bandits and wolves and whatever else was out here, but what good would it do if he didn't curb his strength with her?

"Well, then you could go home right now, 'cause you can see she already is," he said jovially. "Not that that's a hint, you understand."

"Oh, I understand."

"Then I'll leave the two of you for now. I'm sure you've got lots to talk about."

Kate missed Mrs. Birovchak. There'd been drawbacks to being married to William Goodale—plenty of them—but having an army of servants floating around to do the heavy housework, and Mrs. Birovchak to oversee them, was not one of them.

Kate prided herself on being both clear-minded and clear-sighted. She saw the good *and* bad in things, and was capable of appreciating one while ruing the other.

However, there was nothing good she'd been able to discover in this situation as of yet. It was unlikely she ever would.

She put a hand on her aching back as she pushed herself to her feet, dusting the remains of the flour barrel from her skirt. She'd changed before they'd started to clean, but even her simplest dress wasn't designed for physical labor.

"I'm done," she said. "At least for tonight." And she didn't care one bit how much was left.

"It looks better, doesn't it?" Emily opened the door and emptied a pan of sweepings into the yard. "It wasn't nearly as hard as I expected."

Not as hard as she expected? Kate looked around her, at the inadequate and dreary house; the battered, drab, and terribly insufficient furniture; and the scraps of supplies they'd salvaged. She looked at her sister, streaks of grease on her face, her clothes much worse for the wear, and she wanted to cry. *Oh damn it, Doctor*, she thought, *why couldn't you have lived just a few more years?* Then she and Emily'd be safely back in Philadelphia, giggling and shopping, plotting what she was going to bring to Bryn Mawr.

"Emily," she said, "let's go home."

Emily carefully set aside her broom and dustpan,

folding her hands over the soiled length of dish-towel she'd wrapped around her waist in lieu of an apron. "I can't."

"Of course *we* can," Kate said briskly. "We just pack up what you want to take back—there must be little enough of that—buy a ticket, get back on the train, and be gone. Nothing could be simpler."

Emily just shook her head, face set into grave, serious lines. She never looked like that, not sunshiny, happy Emily. Had this land, this marriage, already taught her that expression?

"Whyever not?" Kate waved away Emily's objections before she could voice them. "Because of your *husband*? I grant you, I can see the initial appeal, for he is very different from the men you're used to, and you've had little enough experience with them at that. Maybe that was a mistake on my part. But it's not the kind of appeal that would wear well. And you've scarcely been married long enough for it to count. No reason to cling to it just out of pure stubbornness."

"You make it sound like it was a regrettable purchase that can simply be returned to the store, not a marriage."

"More like a business contract that can be dissolved. Happens all the time."

"Why didn't you, then?"

For an instant Kate thought her heart seized, froze up like a pump in winter. "My marriage contract functioned *precisely* as it was intended to, exactly as I planned from the day I entered into it."

"But—"

"That topic is not open for discussion."

"Then neither is mine."

It was so easy to look at Emily and see the child she'd been. On the outside she'd changed very little, all big, earnest eyes and round cheeks and tiny body. "You were always the most tractable of children. When did you become so stubborn?"

"I always have been. I had a good teacher." Emily smiled as if it were a compliment instead of an insult. "It's just that we seldom disagreed, and I even more seldom found something that was worth opposing you on."

"And this is?"

"Oh yes. Every bit as much as working with Dr. Goodale was."

Deliberately, Kate let her concern show. "I miss you."

"Kate." For a moment Kate thought appealing to Emily's susceptible heart would be enough. "You'd have missed me, too, if I was off at college."

"Yes. But it's not nearly so far away. And I wouldn't have worried about you a fraction as much."

"I'll be fine."

"Emily . . ."

"That's enough for one night, Kate. There'll be plenty of time for you to scold me tomorrow, and I'm sure you'll have a lot more energy for it then." She slipped her arm around Kate's waist, the way Kate had done to her a thousand times. "For now, I don't know about you, but those crackers and cheese we had earlier aren't going to hold me all night long. And it's certainly not going to keep Jake until breakfast. How do you feel about biscuits and sausage gravy?"

Kate watched her new brother-in-law make a bed on the floor. Though *bed*, to Kate's way of thinking, was a charitable term. A thin tick stuffed, she thought, with straw or field grass or somesuch—how long after grass was picked did it take for all the insects in it to die?—laid on that hard floor, covered with a few worn blankets.

Things could be worse, she reminded herself. At least the floor was wood.

He worked quickly, silently. He was a silent man, was this Jake Sullivan. And a serious one. One might even call him gloomy. She'd done her best to charm him at dinner; on the chance that—and she was not giving up, not in any way, she just considered it prudent to have a back-up plan—Emily remained with him, she wanted to know enough about the fellow to believe that Emily was in reasonably good hands. Not as good as *her* hands, of course.

But he hadn't given her so much as a hint. Surprising; few men could resist her when she was really bent on getting something from them. He ate quickly and with complete focus, like a man who'd not always had as much as he wanted to eat, but someone had taught him a few table manners along the way, which was more than she'd dared hope for.

But every question she asked, no matter how simple or how large, no matter how pointed, he deferred to Emily. As frustrating as her inability to pry any useful details from him was, the fact that he *did* defer to Emily without any hesitation reassured her a bit. Most men took more training than that before they deferred to their wives.

They weren't easy with each other. There were none of the secret smiles, the unspoken communication common between long-married couples. Once when Emily passed behind him to fetch more coffee, she bumped his shoulder with her elbow and he jumped half out of his chair.

It seemed . . . a little off to Kate. But she couldn't discount the possibility that might be wishful thinking on her part. And truly, what did she know about how newly wedded couples acted together in those first days of marriage? Her own marriage was useless as a comparison. Perhaps it wasn't unusual for them to be a touch awkward with each other.

"Well." He got up from squatting beside the bedroll and rubbed his palms down the front of his denims. "I guess I'll—" He hooked his thumb over his shoulder, toward the door. "I'll be outside for a while. Give you ladies time to, um—" He looked to Emily for help.

"We'll let you know when it's safe to come back."

Despite his promise, Kate found herself hurrying through her toilette. After tugging on the biggest, thickest, most all-concealing nightdress she found in her luggage—which would undoubtedly have her sweating in no time, and wasn't that attractive?— she gave her hair the cursory brushing and refrained from smearing on her night cream for fear he'd come back unexpectedly. She promised herself she'd do better tomorrow night. She had to protect her looks, the way a singer might protect her voice or a seamstress her hands.

Emily's nightgown was every bit as voluminous as Kate's, swallowing up her small figure, her face pink from a fresh scrubbing and her hair tied up in a blue ribbon.

"You look exactly as you used to when you'd come to my room frightened by a storm. Remember?"

"Of course. You were always dead asleep until I came and woke you. How is it the thunder never disturbed you but my first step into your room did? I tried so hard to be quiet."

"Thunder didn't scare me." *And you always did. Or rather, the thought I might not be enough for you, might not do right for you; that terrified me from the moment Mother died.*

Emily poked her head out the door. "Jake? We're done. You can come back now."

He ducked his head, his hair damp and deeply waved, came into the room, and took it over, his presence overwhelming. He thumbed open the first button on his shirt, then looked at them and let his hands fall. He shrugged, turned for the makeshift bed on the floor, and Kate made her decision.

"I thought that was my bed."

His eyebrows shot up to his hairline. "I assumed—I mean, well, I figured you'd be sleeping with Emily and I'd take the floor."

"Don't be ridiculous." She'd made the decision, and now she poured it out as fast as she could before she changed her mind. They'd obviously been sharing a bed *before* her arrival. So she would swallow her instinctive protest and try her best to be adult about it. And anyway, it wasn't as if, honeymooners or no honeymooners, they were likely to *do* anything with Emily's big sister dozing only a few feet away. And if he tried she'd just have to have a sudden, very loud coughing fit, wouldn't she? "Do I look the sort to come between a man and his new bride?" She beamed a smile—not a bad one, all things considered—at Emily. *See what a good sport I'm being?* "And anyway, I have a trick back, don't I, Emily? Always better if I rest on a very firm surface."

"You do?"

"Yes, I *do*." What was the matter with her? Emily was usually much quicker to pick up on hints. And she was looking a bit peaked around the edges, her eyes wide, skin pale as it could be considering all the color she'd picked up out there. Well, it couldn't be a comfortable situation for her, poor dear, any more than it was for Kate; neither one of them had so much as peeked at the bed.

"Well, yeah, that's right considerate of you." He shuffled his feet and shot a quick, worried glance at his wife. It was rather endearing, to see this glowering, supremely contained man discomfited. And he suddenly appeared much younger than she'd taken him for; perhaps he was not all that much older than Emily after all. "But truly, Em'd be right put out with me if I made her sister sleep on the floor."

"But it'd be silly for *both* of you to sleep on the floor, while I took the bed. No, no, I insist. I'll be fine. Look!"

She plopped herself down, a *whoosh* of nightgown, and patted the blankets into smoother order. This kicked up a musty cloud of dust, and she pinched the bridge of her nose to keep from sneezing. "There, you see? Comfortable as can be. I'll be fine." She flopped backward, valiantly suppressing a wince when her spine hit hard wood scarcely cushioned by blankets that wouldn't keep a horse warm in July.

Jake stared glumly at Emily. Kate wondered about that; was he hoping Kate would offer to sleep somewhere else, so they could be alone? She was sacrificing enough here; that was truly above and beyond the call of duty. He could just rein himself in for a few days. Yes, they were newly married, but in her experience men whined far more about that particular subject than it called for.

Finally Emily lifted her shoulders and spread her hands wide. *Now what?* He frowned fiercely at her, and fierce, on Jake Sullivan, was downright intimidating.

He made a low sound. Kate imagined a waking grizzly bear emitted the very same tone. "I don't—"

Swiftly Kate rolled over, so her back was to the bed, and slammed her eyes shut. "I'm sleeping," she sang out.

She heard nothing for a long time, until a drawn-out sigh and the scuffle of feet. She opened her eyes a crack. Just before someone snuffed out the lantern, she caught a glimpse of the floor, studded with gaps and dozens of knotholes the size of a fist. Large enough for all sorts of nasty creatures to crawl through in the middle of the nigh to nibble on un- or rather, *sus*pecting ladies from Philadelphia.

She thought longingly of her bed, beautifully crisp, sunshine-scented linens over drifts of soft feathers, as her hip protested the floor. *Emily, I certainly hope you appreciate what I'm doing for you.*

Chapter 10

Emily put out the lamp because she thought it would be easier in the dark. But they'd left the window open, and the moonlight that shot through seemed aimed directly at the bed. She could see it all too clearly: flat, covered in white, and *small*. Horribly, embarrassingly small.

In Philadelphia she'd had a bed as big as a train car. Ridiculous, so much space for one little girl. She'd even wished it smaller, so she wouldn't feel swallowed up, so alone in that vast, unnecessary space.

But oh how she longed for that bed. Jake could jump up and down on his side of it and she'd never feel it on hers. On this one, however, she suspected she would feel every twitch of his toe, every turn of his head.

She sneaked a peek at him. Face turned toward the moonlight, he carefully avoided looking either at her or at the bed, the light harsh on his features. Shadows angled deep beneath his newly revealed cheekbones, cutting sharp lines where his jaw met his neck. How could she share a bed with him? She didn't even know him! The hulking, unkempt Jake who lurked in his chair in his makeshift camp she might have managed; she'd become accustomed to him, his constant, waiting presence. But this one—if she'd conjured up the image of a dream husband, he would have appeared like this. Only not so sad, so gloweringly fierce.

She heard a rustling from Kate's blankets, followed by a delicate cough. They couldn't stand by the side of the bed like sentries any longer. Kate would wonder what was the matter with them.

But she didn't even know which side of the bed he preferred. It suddenly seemed terribly important that she didn't take his side; she'd sucked him into this, far more than he'd bargained for. And as she'd never slept with someone, except a few nights as a child with one of her sisters, she shouldn't have developed a distinct preference for one side or another. But he undoubtedly had one. She'd heard that men were picky about such things.

She couldn't just ask him. Kate would hear and wonder why they'd not worked out such matters by now.

Tentatively she touched his arm. The muscles leaped and she yanked her hand back. But it got his attention. She gestured toward the bed, arching her eyebrows in question. But he just frowned. So she pantomimed as best she could, pointing to first one side, then the other.

He bowed, waving her in, a mocking twist to his mouth that might have been cruel if his eyes weren't so sad.

How insensitive she'd been. She could hardly believe it of herself. Her perceptions of others' emotions were usually so strong that she had to prepare herself before entering Dr. Goodale's waiting room. But she'd been so preoccupied with her own pressing concerns that she'd forgotten how difficult this must be for him.

This was his bed. Where he'd lain with his wife. And to lie here with another woman—even one with whom she shared nothing but a brief and practical agreement—must be almost unbearable.

"I'm sorry," she mouthed at him. Inadequate words. They usually were, all those times she'd murmured them to the grieving relatives of patients they'd been unable to help. She'd never meant them more. Wished there was more that she could do. In other circumstances, with any other man, she'd have reached out, laid a soothing palm on a shoulder, rubbed comforting circles between his shoulder blades. But he'd already made it clear he didn't want her hands on him.

Then the world lurched abruptly as he scooped her up and she gave a shriek of surprise. The rope frame creaked as he leaned over and deposited her, not very gently, on the far side of the bed.

And then he was beside her, arm looped over her, a heavy, unfamiliar weight, mouth close to her ear— very close; she could feel the moist, hot wash of his breath, the stirring of fine hairs at her nape with each exhalation. Her heart did something entirely new, a heavy beat, one in which she felt each rush and pump of blood, conscious of its working in a way she never was.

"It seemed," he whispered in her ear, intimate and stirring, "the only way to get you to move."

She rolled her head to look at him but misjudged the distance. His mouth brushed against her as she turned, a searing burn over her cheek.

He was so close. She'd never been that close to a man. How odd that it would be him. She'd never imagined it, never imagined *him*. But it felt right. How could it be anyone else?

For an instant she was certain he was going to kiss her. *Please, yes. Yes, yes.* He hadn't pulled away, just remained in place, his mouth inches, *fractions* of inches, from hers. She could look straight into his eyes, deep and dark as nightfall, lashes denser than she'd ever realized.

"I'm sorry," she whispered again.

"Shhh." He put his finger against her lips and inclined his head toward her sister. She hadn't anticipated the gesture and so he'd caught her with her mouth half open, the moist inner curve of her lips caught against his work-roughened skin. "It's all right."

And it was all right, Jake discovered in numb surprise. He'd stood there beside their bed—his and Julia's bed—and the memories and the guilt had nearly drowned him, the urge to flee so strong that he'd known he had to get it over with fast or he'd never climb into the bed with her. And so he'd just tossed her in.

But this wasn't his bed. She'd restuffed the mattress, more grass than he'd used, making it firmer beneath his hip. Her sheets were different, a finer weave, a crisper rustle when he moved. The smells were new, a different soap on the linens and on her hair.

His senses drank it in. They'd had few enough pleasant things to experience over the past years. Too many sour smells in rancid taverns, too many ugly, dirty sights at the wharves. He thought that he could stay there forever and just let himself enjoy it: the look and smell and feel of a clean and joyful woman.

She felt new in his arms. Smaller, yes, her shoulders narrower, her hips slighter. But stronger, lean rather than wasted, with flesh over her ribs, easy control and energy in her motion. Even her temperature wasn't the same; through the fabric of her nightdress—thin, soft, fuzzy-surfaced cotton—she felt warmer to him, as if she burned hotter, the same vibrant life that blazed in her eyes.

"Jake?"

And then his senses, which had been so busily gathering all those tidbits of information, finally sorted and recognized them all. *Woman*. His body reacted and he hardened so abruptly he was dizzy with it, dizzy enough that he would have dropped to the floor if he hadn't been lying down.

"Jake?" More worried this time, concern drawing her mouth into a pucker.

"Jeez, it's warm." He let her go and rolled away so quickly he stirred up a draft. What had he been thinking, to be so close, to let his arm lie across her chest where it had fallen when he'd flopped down?

Even now his arm retained the feel of her, pillowy imprints of breasts against the inside of his forearm.

But *thinking* never really entered into it, did it? If there was one truism history had proved a thousand times over, it was the harder the cock, the softer the brain.

"Here." He yanked up the covers, threw them over her so they covered her shoulders and half her face. "My wife was always colder than I was."

My wife. He used it deliberately, reminding them both, as much a wedge between them as the thick roll of quilt. He lay back down on his side, his hip on top of the edge of the blankets, so that there was no danger of him working his way under it in sleep or her rolling her way out.

For a moment he expected her to protest; she wasn't the kind to let things be. More like the type to beat things to death, to talk them over and over until a man came around to her way of thinking out of pure exhaustion. He heard the rush of air as she sucked in a full breath.

But all she said was "Good night, Jake." Sweet tones; soft, intimate words, the last thing husbands all over the country heard as they dropped off to sleep. And they hit him as hard as the desire had, left him aching in his heart as well as his groin. He'd missed that, so much, someone to wish him a gentle and healthful rest.

He closed his eyes, drifting in some floating, half-real place, the soft rhythm of her respiration in his ears, the scent of her soap in his nose. Even without those cues, he'd know there was someone in bed with him: a few degrees warmer, the mattress not dipping as deeply beneath him as when he lay alone.

Sleep was impossible. Surrendering to slumber seemed like surrendering to *her* and the pull of her presence, the pleasure of having her beside him in bed. He couldn't do it.

He had only one hope: that Emily's sister dragged her home soon, before he got used to it.

Kate couldn't believe it. She'd been so certain she'd snatch only a few moments of sleep, instead lying still and alert for any suspicious sound, especially from the bed. And that what meager rest she did catch would be restless, tainted with dreams of small, crunchy black creatures crawling up through the holes that studded the floor like Swiss cheese.

Instead she'd fallen dead asleep practically the moment she lay down. She hadn't realized how much the last few days—the last few weeks, for that matter—had sapped from her. How much being able to see with her own two eyes that Emily was alive and relatively well had released her from that horrible tension and fear.

It took a moment upon awakening to register where she was. The moment she did, she bolted upright, ignoring the protests of bones and muscles that had not appreciated her chosen bed.

It had to be early. Pale, gray light misted in, giving the small room a softer quality it sorely needed.

Emily and Jake dozed on, and Kate squelched her immediate impulse to grab the man's arm and haul him away from her sister.

They looked comfortable together in sleep in a

way they did not awake, with Emily turned on her side, Jake curled protectively around her. Her sister appeared tiny in his embrace, completely sheltered, in the tender curve to his body that Kate suspected he would never display voluntarily. He didn't strike her as a tender sort of man.

Sometimes, when she was much younger, Kate had let Emily sleep with her when the doctor was away and a storm howled. Kate pretended she allowed it for Emily's sake but knew it was as much for her own. She'd enjoyed watching her sister sleep, treasured knowing she was safe and well cared for through Kate's efforts.

She appeared scarcely older now. Oddly, while sleep softened her husband's features, made him more open, younger, easing the harsh lines of worry and care, it did the opposite to Emily. While awake she was always bright, happy, her eyes so full of life it seemed as if she was smiling even when she wasn't, in sleep the corners of her mouth often turned down, her brow furrowed. It had always been that way, as if her dreams were harsher than her reality. Or as if that was the only time she allowed darker thoughts to touch her.

Kate frowned, troubled. She'd worked so hard to ensure that Emily had never had to worry. Believed that, mostly, she'd succeeded. She'd never understood why Emily, asleep, always appeared unhappy.

And then she shrugged it off. No doubt she was reading far too much into it.

Jake shifted restlessly, dragging the quilt down around Emily's waist. He groaned, burying his face at the nape of her neck, and his hand settled, firm

and unerring, on her sister's breast, as if returning to
its customary preferred spot.

Kate saw red. Managed to wait a beat, certain
that, even in her sleep, her sister's good instincts
would take over and knock the intruding hand
away.

Damn.

Well then. Kate hurried to start the morning coffee with as much clattering and clanging as she
could create.

Softness. Soft and sweet, birds twittering, clouds
of good-smelling silk in his face, cushiony pillows
beneath his head, nice warm flesh in his hands.

Oh, his dreams were getting better. Fabulous,
even. After months of dreams that were dark and
bloody and raw, this was as close to heaven as he'd
never expected to get. So much so that he battled to
remain there, ignoring the persistent clanging in the
back of his brain.

He liked it there. Blessed his brain for finally taking pity on him and giving him pretty dreams. If
he'd had these dreams before, he'd have never
woken up.

Because it had to be a dream. Fuzzy edges, drifts
of sunny, flowery images, did not exist in his waking
world. His waking world was full of sharp edges
and cold winds and bitter memories.

But the damn banging wouldn't stop.

He swore, tried to make it go away, which only
made the sound hammer more energetically.

And then—damn it, he'd tried to avoid it—he
woke up. He sat bolt upright and swung bleary eyes

to the source of the brutal sound and found Emily's sister, gleefully slinging tin plates onto the table.

"Oh sorry, did I wake you?" she asked brightly.

Well, shit. Though he couldn't have said whether the oath was for the night before or being rudely jerked out of it. Emily blinked awake beside him, a slow, sleepy, utterly seductive stretch of her arms over her head, her back arching and hips shifting. "Oh," she said when she saw him. She stopped stretching—a shame, that—but then smiled up at him, which went straight to his gut and his blood as powerfully as the sight of her twisting upon his bed had. "Good morning."

Now here was a delicate situation. Somehow in the night he'd ended up wrapped around her. The scent of her still clouded his nostrils, and if he tried for a moment he could still feel her in his arms.

He had no doubt that Kate, glowering from the kitchen, was going to start pitching some of those dishes at his head if he didn't get away from her sister's side. It was unsettling, being in a woman's bed with one of her relatives looking on, a situation so far out of his experience he couldn't fathom the appropriate response.

And yet he could hardly just get up. Not without presenting Kate with too-visible proof of how much Emily's nearness appealed to his baser instincts. And for some reason he didn't think Kate would be too well-mannered to ensure her eyes never strayed close to that region.

"If you'll hurry and wash up," she told him, the brightness in her voice at sharp odds with the lethal warning in her narrowed eyes, "breakfast will be

ready in a moment." She pointed with her spatula.
"I found a few towels that survived that creature's
spree. I hope you don't mind my searching. I
thought it would be more convenient, put them
right there by the bed—"

He snatched the towels with the alacrity of a
starving man presented with a cinnamon bun. Holding the towel clutched—not too obviously, he devoutly hoped—in front of him, he mumbled
something about needing to go out back and dashed
for safety.

Spatula in hand, Kate stood frowning after him.
"Does he always growl like that?"

"He's not a morning person."

Kate suspected that he was not an afternoon or
night person, either.

"He's not around much, is he?"

"Huh?" Emily asked, purposely delaying.

"That husband of yours. Hard to tell you're married, considering how little time he spends hovering
around."

"He's a hardworking man."

"So he seems." Since Kate couldn't figure out
what he was doing half the time, she wasn't quite
ready to concede it was work. All right, so he'd disappeared right after breakfast with a shotgun,
turned up a few hours later and dropped a couple of
mutilated grouse at Emily's feet, and promptly disappeared again. It could have taken him all of five
minutes to shoot the poor birds for all she knew. He
could have been just strolling around, whistling,
and avoiding her very justified interest.

Emily leaned back on her heels, surveying her handiwork, and chose to ignore Kate's topic of conversation. "It looks good, doesn't it?"

One unanticipated benefit of her new arrangement with Jake was that Emily no longer felt compelled to spend her days trying to peel sod off a fraction of an acre of land. Clearing it was now Jake's problem. She was a tad concerned that *he* didn't seem in any hurry to get the ground broken, either—she would be most unhappy with him if she surrendered the land to him and he failed to prove up—but she told herself it was really not her business.

And so she felt able to indulge herself and spend her time fixing up the shack. She'd taken a stab at it in spare moments but she'd never felt able to turn her full attention to the matter before.

Kate surveyed the newly stained floorboards, which Emily had spent half the day sloshing with a mixture of water and old coffee grounds. "What was the point of this again?"

"It'll look richer with this dark color. Hide any stains. Once I buff it with a little hot linseed oil, it'll shine as pretty as the parquet in Goodale House's foyer."

"Where'd you learn to do this?"

"May Blevins told me about it. Been dying to try it ever since."

"I can't imagine how you've resisted this long."

Emily dunked her rag and dabbed carefully at a penny-sized spot that hadn't taken the stain evenly. "Sure you don't want to help me?"

"No." From her perch on the one chair Emily

hadn't dragged from the room, Kate smoothed a stray wrinkle out of her blue serge skirt. "It's not that I object to hard labor, you understand."

"Oh really?"

"I simply object to *messy* labor. Truth to tell, I really hadn't realized you'd a talent for such tasks. Not that working in the clinic was exactly clean and neat, but you've never really struck me as the domestic type, either."

Emily had never suspected she'd enjoy it, either. The pleasure she took in the task had surprised her. She'd told herself that she'd needed to present a happy front for Kate; appearing a woman bent on furnishing a pleasant home for her husband only bolstered their charade. But she had to admit the idea of leaving Jake a more comfortable home pleased her. When had that happened? A week ago she would have torn the place down before turning it over to him.

"You've no idea the hidden talents I've discovered since I came to Montana," she said.

"Please! Spare me the gory details. I haven't recovered from the sight of you plucking those grouse yet."

"They smell good, though, don't they?" Infinitely better than the simple rations she'd been fixing for herself. A man, she reflected, had more uses than she'd previously given him credit for. "Speaking of which, I'd better start on the rest of supper or the birds'll be done before the biscuits are even begun."

"So your *husband*"—there was an emphasis on the word *husband* that Emily didn't like at all—"will be home for supper?"

"Of course he'll be home for supper." *I hope.* Or Emily would be scrambling to invent an excellent reason why not.

"Where's he been all afternoon?"

Dark, bitterly fragrant water dripped back into the bucket as Emily wrung out the rag. She climbed to her feet, flipped the rag over a windowsill to dry, and poured the liquid over the ledge and onto the ground while she considered her answer. "I don't know about you and Dr. Goodale, but I do not feel it critical to know every detail of my husband's daily activities."

Hot color spiced Kate's skin. "Such a brief time married to him and you've already learned to be so snippy? It doesn't bode well, Emily."

"Maybe you never gave me reason to be snippy before." And then they stared at each other, both startled and unsettled at how quickly they'd begun verbally pricking at the other when they'd never been anything but kind before. Had this always been there, just carefully contained? Or had their world, their relationship, changed so completely without either of them noting it along the way?

"Kate, I thought I'd make a sponge cake, would you like to help? I—"

"Oh, there he is." Kate looked beyond her, out the window, and Emily turned to follow her gaze. Jake rode up on Reg, dragging some sort of sledge behind, piled with a high stack of clean, long, tied-down lumber. "What's he up to now, d'you suppose?"

Emily didn't have time to come up with an appropriately vague but informative answer before Kate went on, "Never mind, I'll ask him myself." She popped off her chair and went through her prebattle checklist: hair, clothing, a pinch of color in her cheeks.

Oh, Lordy. She couldn't unleash her sister on Jake. He might consider himself prepared, but he'd never seen Kate in action. "Hold on, just let me check the oven, and I'll come with you."

"Heavens, no need for that. I know you've got all sorts of culinary details to attend to. Wouldn't dream of interrupting." She smiled with enough glee to worry Emily all the more. "Don't fret. I'm perfectly capable of keeping your husband company for you. And I'm quite sure he's equally able to keep me entertained for a few moments."

That's exactly what worries me, Emily thought. "Kate, I don't mean to impose on you, as you *are* a guest, but I could use your help. If you wouldn't mind."

"As if I'd be of any use in a kitchen." Kate waved off the absurdity. "I'm sure you'll be ever so much more efficient without me."

"Don't be silly. I can teach you to separate eggs in no time."

"Do you know, Emily," Kate said, deceptively light, "that, if I didn't know better, I'd think that you're afraid to let me speak to your husband alone. But whyever would that be?"

"Don't be ridiculous," Emily said, even while her heart set up a worried thud.

"That's good." Kate called over her shoulder as she sailed out the door. "I can't wait to hear all about how the two of you met. Men's versions of such matters are always so vastly entertaining."

Emily resisted for all of two minutes. Then she opened the oven door so the birds wouldn't char too quickly, put aside her bowls, took up a prime eavesdropping position, and started practicing her excuses for charging in to the rescue.

The only thing that remained to be seen was how long Jake would manage to hold out.

Chapter 11

~~ ❦ ~~

Jake heard her coming. Quick light steps, the swish of exuberant, overflowing silk through grass, a cheery trill of "Hello" as she rounded the corner.

He muttered a dozen curses beneath his breath. After avoiding women for over a year he was now beset by them at every turn. He didn't run, though he was tempted, instead measuring out a length of string from the wall of the shack, marking the borders of the lean-to he planned, deliberately taking his time.

"I said hello."

"Heard you the first time."

"You didn't answer."

He sighed and straightened with his hands on his hips to survey the area he'd marked on the ground. Yeah, that looked about right. "Guess the wind's blowin' just right. Carried the words away." He shrugged. "Happens out here sometimes. But you wouldn't know about that."

"Hmm." She took up a position in the shade of the shack, just beside the window.

"Wouldn't do that if I were you."

"Do what?"

"Lean up against the house like that in that dress."

She jumped away, twisted around like a puppy chasing its tail. Black flakes of dirt and disintegrating tar paper clung to the amber silk. "Oh, would you look at that!" She whacked at the bits, leaving gray, palm-sized smears in their place, and he felt his mood improve. Nice to know that Kate wasn't always coldly perfect.

"It's a pretty dress," he allowed. Might as well make nice, he decided. "Looks good on you. Really good."

Kate was distinctly unimpressed by his compliments. "Yes, I know." She sighed and gave up on repairing her skirts. "Oh well, this would only do for another three months at most anyway. I expect the silhouette to be much narrower by next spring."

It was hard to believe this creature was Emily's sister. A few resemblances echoed the relationship: their noses had the same precise slope, and sometimes they tilted their heads at an identical angle. But other than that . . . Emily's smile was more ever-present, far less calculated. He tried to imagine this elegant and contained creature swinging her hoe in a field and found it impossible. She looked as out of place there as a perfect china doll in a jumble of broken, well-worn toy soldiers.

"Never mind. So." She walked over to the pile of lumber and inspected it. "What are you making?"

"Lean-to."

"How lovely. The . . . house is a tad small in its current state."

"You think so?" He lifted his brows at her. "Seemed plenty big to me. At least until a few days ago."

He had to hand it to her; her pleasant, interested expression didn't flicker. Well, he really hadn't thought she'd be that easy to discourage, had he? She had to have a few things in common with her sister.

He caught a flutter of movement in the window. Emily's head popped out from behind the drape of curtain, her expression fierce. She mouthed, *Be nice* at him, and just as quickly disappeared again.

"Oh, you can smile!" Kate said. "I was beginning to wonder."

"When the occasion warrants."

Kate paced off the perimeter he'd staked out. "So you're making me my very own bedroom, is that it? So very kind of you."

"You mean you won't mind sharing space with the press? That's right cooperative of you, Mrs. Goodale."

"Press?"

"Newspaper press." He pointed at the tent that, until last night, had served as his bedroom. "Got it in there temporarily, but it's rusty enough as it is, and I'd best get it inside before it sticks up permanently."

"Newspaper press," she repeated. And then added, with enough doubt in her voice to be downright unflattering, "Are you a newspaperman, Mr. Sullivan?"

As casually as he could manage, he edged over, giving himself a viewing angle into the house, to where Emily lurked behind the curtain, wondering if he'd discover shock on her face as well. But she was simply listening attentively. "I am now."

"I can see how there's a lot of call for a newspaper out here. Such a population center. And undoubtedly just brimming with news demanding to be printed."

He wondered if Kate was so skeptical of all men or if he was just the lucky one because he'd had the gall to marry her sister. For all that Emily had described Dr. Goodale as no prize, he could almost pity the poor guy. "Ever heard of a proof sheet, Mrs. Goodale?"

She appeared to give the matter due consideration. "I can't say that I have."

"Part of the requirement of homesteading is that you've got to publish proof of intent to make claim. Five bucks apiece." He indicated the infinite sweep of grasslands. "Any idea how many claims there are out there? And how little time any of those people have to trot off to the nearest newspaper office?"

He told himself he wasn't pleased by the glimmer of respect in her eyes. And he wouldn't let himself look over at Emily again to see if it was echoed there.

If he'd thought that it would end Kate's inquisition, though, he'd been highly overoptimistic. He jogged over to his old encampment to grab a shovel and she was still there when he returned, making no pretense of doing anything but waiting for him.

"So you're trained as a newspaperman?" she asked as he began digging a hole for a support post.

"No."

"I didn't think so."

"Oh?" He jammed the shovel into the ground. The Bright sisters were really motivating to have around when one was digging, he reflected. "What'd you think I was, then?"

"I'd assumed you were a farmer. Why else would you homestead?"

"Why else, indeed."

"Aren't you a farmer?"

"Not yet."

"Sort of a big gamble, isn't it? The homestead, and now printing? Shouldn't you stick to things you already know how to do?"

"I'm good at figuring things out." He tossed a spadeful of dirt in her direction, just close enough that a few specks of dirt spattered her skirt and she took a couple of quick steps backward. Not exactly mature of him, but satisfying just the same. He planted the shovel in the ground—better not to be tempted, no guarantee his throw wouldn't be a bit too strong next time—and leaned against it. "And just what do you envision me doing?"

"Oh, I don't know." She studied him. "Something that requires brute strength, I'd guess."

"I've done that, too." And damn proud of it, as proud as he was of all the good marks in philosophy he'd ever earned. It took as much out of a man, if in a different way, to support himself with his muscles as his head.

"Still, you've chosen well if you aspire to be a newspaperman. Emily's clever with words. I'm sure she'll be able to give you a hand with the articles. Her grammar and spelling are excellent. I'm sure she'd be happy to assist."

She was deliberately baiting him. Knowing that didn't help him resist rising to the bait. "I'm sure she would. But I think I'll be able to struggle through. My writing skills were good enough for my professors, so I imagine I can scribble an article or two without much trouble."

Emily came out of the house at a dead run, no doubt to rescue him from Kate's interrogation. She stopped in her tracks, ten feet behind Kate, so suddenly her hair and skirts swirled forward as if a brisk wind had come up behind her.

"Your professors?" Kate asked.

"Northwestern University. First in my class."

"You graduated from Northwestern University?"

"Didn't graduate. One semester short."

"Hmm," she said. "Why'd you quit so close to the end? Especially if you were first in your class?"

He could no more keep his gaze from fixing on Emily than he could keep the words from coming out of his mouth. "I got married."

"Married?" He heard Kate's query, dim and distant. But his eyes remained on Emily, on the rich sympathy in her eyes, the warm and sad curve of her smile. And the words, *I got married*, which would have brought him to his knees a few weeks ago, only echoed hollowly, a dull ache rather than roaring agony. "But how did you—you just met," she stammered, "how can you have quit, and come out here, I mean—" She stopped, whirled on Emily. "Did you know he had a wife?"

"Yes," Emily said softly, still looking at him, "I knew he had a wife."

"But—" She spun back, like a child's whirligig toy. "What happened to her?"

Aw, hell. Why'd he ever start this? Just to wipe the superior smirk off Kate Goodale's face? It wasn't worth it. He couldn't make those words come out of his mouth. *She died*. He couldn't say them. Never had. Was sure that, if he did, hell would crack open and claim him. The words would be irrevocably real.

And then Emily stood beside him, her small hand firmly in his. "She died," he heard her say, and she squeezed his hand, sending warmth up his arm that seeped through him, took the brutal edge off the hurt. Grateful, he looked down at her, let himself fall into the comfort she offered. "She died," he repeated, and the sky didn't open up, the earth didn't shake, the lightning didn't hit him. One more hurdle passed, the hardest one since he'd put down the whiskey bottle for the last time and taken his first sober steps out of the saloon door. A step away from Julia, he thought sadly. A step forward. A step toward . . . what?

He couldn't look away from Emily. Couldn't see anything but her face.

"But—"

"Let it rest, Kate," Emily said. "That's enough questions for one day. Let it rest."

"It's okay," he told her.

"Are you sure?" she asked, and he knew that she would have grabbed and muzzled her sister if he'd needed it. She would have done that for *him*.

"I'm sure," he said, and to prove it, he smiled at her. A real one, a grateful one, and it didn't hurt a bit.

He'd no idea how long they might have stood there like that, holding hands, holding gazes, if Kate hadn't spoken.

"We've got company," Kate said, an interruption that Jake wasn't sure if he rued or welcomed.

"Shit." Imbert Longnecker jolted toward them. He caught sight of them and waved eagerly, kicking his mount into a lurching trot.

"I take it you're not fond of this particular visitor?" Kate asked.

"I'm not fond of unexpected guests, period."

"I never would have guessed," she said dryly, but with a shade less censure than he'd noted from her before.

Good ol' Longnecker had dressed for the occasion, Jake thought sourly. Stiff white collar, baggy gray suit, sweaty brow, and all. He'd eyes for no one else but Emily as he rode up, grinning wide enough to show a slash of red gums.

"Emily," he cried and vaulted off. "I mean, Miss Bright. Forgive my impertinence and my unexpected arrival. It's been some time since I've visited, however—they're opening another three thousand acres, and the office has been inundated—and this afternoon I just up and thought, why, I must go and see how Miss Bright is faring."

"You're welcome anytime, Mr. Longnecker," Emily said with automatic courtesy. But she looked a bit queasy around the edges. "However, I must admit that this is not the most convenient time."

Well, damn, Jake thought. So much for keeping this simple and quiet.

"My sister's here visiting," she added, and, on cue, Kate swished over into his line of sight.

"How delightful!" he said, and then got his first good look at Kate.

Much to Jake's dismay, he had to give the skinny fellow credit; he hardly drooled at all, and recovered his tongue a whole lot faster than Jake would ever have figured him for.

"Why, Miss Bright, what a delight!" He took her hand and smiled warmly. "How lovely for Em— Miss Bright—the first one, that is—that you were able to join her! And I can certainly see how the two of you favor each other. I'll be processing applications from single men night and day once the word that there are two of you here gets out."

"Actually, it's Mrs. Goodale."

"Of course it is. What's that?" He cupped his hand to his ear. "Just the sound of hearts breaking all over the county, I'd wager."

"Very prettily said." She cut her eyes toward Jake. "Would that all men could claim such manners." She sighed. "I always assumed, when Emily chose a husband—"

"Husband?" What little color he had blanched from his face. "You . . . got married? To him?"

"I—" Jake felt Emily's tension, the taut vibration of her body against his. From his position behind her, he couldn't see her face, but he'd bet there was guilt written all over it. And Kate watched everything with avid interest.

"She sure did." He tightened his arm around her waist. For support, he'd intended, and for show, but he kept it there because he liked it. There really was nothing like having a woman in your arms. How'd he ever think he'd be able to go forever without it? And maybe he would have if fate hadn't dropped Emily into his life. "Aren't you going to congratulate us?"

Imbert swallowed hard. "When?"

"Recently," Emily murmured. "Very recently."

"Why didn't you tell me?"

Silence. A silence that a mind as devious as Kate's could easily read too much into.

Deliberately he dropped a kiss on the top of Emily's head. Just for their audience's benefit. But for an instant he lost himself. Her hair was warm from the sun, astoundingly soft, and smelled of flowers and soap, the scent that, he now realized, had drifted through his dreams the whole night through. "It's no secret, Longnecker." He rested his chin on the top of her head. "We've just been too busy. Running around making announcements just hasn't made it to the top of our priorities yet."

"Oh." Crestfallen, Imbert backed toward his horse, his mournful expression making it clear what he thought they'd been "too busy" at.

"There's no reason to rush off," Emily said. "You're welcome to stay for dinner. We've plenty."

"No, no," he said glumly, and hauled himself into the saddle. "I think it'd be a bit crowded."

"So." Kate clasped her hands in front of her skirt. "I hadn't realized your marriage was not yet public knowledge. How interesting."

Emily made to pull away; Jake tugged her back against him, stiff and uncertain in his embrace. And then she went limp, the line of her spine curving against his chest, her head falling back to rest against his shoulder, and for a second he forgot everything. *Everything.* Jesus, but she felt good. As if she'd been meant to be there all along, as if she had every right in the world to be there and he'd every right in the world to hold her. As if in the mere act of calling her his wife, however false it was, something inside him had latched on to the word and believed.

"Everybody who mattered knows," he said. "Emily and I know. I knew from the moment I saw her."

"Really."

"She never had a chance." Emily turned in his arms, looking up at him, her eyes soft and wide with wonder. "*I* never had a chance."

"How romantic," Kate said, but Jake barely heard her. If Emily's sister hadn't been there, he would have kissed her. Kissed her for real, for them alone, hard and long, until her mouth and his grew tender and bruised with it, until they had to stop or the kissing would inevitably turn into something more.

God, she had to go. She *had* to. It was a narrow ledge he walked, precarious slopes on either side, and he'd never had good balance. The very things he did to convince her sister, every action he took to hurry Kate on her way, were the same things that made him all the more willing to let Emily stay.

Let? Hell, much more and he'd rope and tie her before allowing her to go.

"Emily?" Kate sniffed. "How long are those birds supposed to roast?"

Emily shrieked and sprinted for the house.

Kate stayed put.

"Aren't you going to go help?" he asked.

"I'm of so little use in a kitchen, I'll be far more help out here," she said without a trace of embarrassment. And then, more kindly than he would have thought her capable of, "I'm sorry about your wife."

"Yeah." He snatched up the shovel and rammed it into the ground with such force the blade was buried to the hilt. "Yeah, I am, too."

Another night. Harder than the first, because now he knew what it felt like to hold her.

Jake stood beside the bed, hands on his hips, in a clean pair of pants and a shirt that promised to be damned uncomfortable to sleep in, but no way in hell was he stripping down in front of her sister. Or her, for that matter. Behind him was the rustle and bump of Kate settling in for the night, making it clear she was not thrilled to be sleeping on the floor, but her big-sister martyrdom wouldn't let her give in and sleep with Emily on the bed. He hadn't quite figured out why, because any fool with eyes could see that she hated the idea of his sleeping next to her sister.

Emily lay curled on her side, her back to him, a

snug little ball beneath a light, crazy-patched quilt. She'd tied her hair up, one thick horsetail, and a wash of moonlight kissed it, a glassy shimmer of silver on the pale brown. She hugged the far side of the bed, nudging up against the wall, leaving him plenty of room despite the fact that the width of the bed was better suited to snuggling than sleeping.

He'd always taken the outward side. Seemed only fitting—a man slept between his woman and whatever trouble might come through the door. But Emily put her pillows on the other end of the bed, and it felt odd to have to sleep on his right side to face the door. He'd slept alone for a long time; strange how weird it felt to climb into a bed and have a woman there. A half step out of rhythm, like coming down a staircase and not finding the tread where you expected it.

Was she asleep already? He saw the slow, rhythmic shift of her shoulders, as if her breath was steady and deep. But he doubted it. Didn't think a young and sheltered woman could so easily accustom herself to a man lying beside her and slide into sleep. Surely she pretended. Something that, watching her with Kate, he'd discovered Emily, with her innocent face and sunshine smile, was far better at than he would ever have suspected. He wondered just how much else she feigned.

He picked up the extra blanket at the foot of the bed and began to roll it up. Yeah, that had worked *so* well last night. He'd kicked it away in his sleep and had her in his arms probably before he started snoring. Whyever did he think it would make a better barrier tonight? That his arms would be any more satisfied with a pile of batting and calico when they could wrap around her? He pitched the quilt to the foot of the bed, where it landed in a useless heap.

Emily rolled to her back, her eyes wide and wondering. Maybe it would be easier if it were darker, if he couldn't see a slash of white cotton nightdress above the edge of her blanket, the slight swell of her breast. Ah, was there ever such a wondrous thing as the sight of a woman in bed? His head swam with it, then filled up with other, imagined images, of her lifting her hand to him and welcoming him home. Of her bringing her mouth to his, and him sinking into her, filling up all the lost, empty places inside him with the feel of her.

Was that so wrong? The doing of it, yes, a hundred times wrong. She was not truly his wife.

But nothing could possibly happen with Emily tonight. If he so much as put a finger wrong, no doubt Kate would rise from her bed and drag him off, screeching like a banshee. He couldn't ask for better insurance.

So why couldn't he revel in the dream? He could sleep by her. Slip his arm around her again, maybe put his nose against her neck and go to sleep breathing in her scent. Let the desire come, let his heart thump and blood rush and his head spin. It couldn't be any more than that. Would never be any more than that. But oh, how he burned to have at least that much. Only for this brief time, in this specific place . . . if he didn't take it now, he'd never have another chance. And he'd go through his whole life alone. It was no more than he deserved. No more than he'd expected.

But this was such a gift. He didn't know if he had the heart to turn it down.

And then she smiled at him. Not the blazing, easy, impersonal grin she usually wore. This one was more intimate, a touch wary, unsure, and more potent than the strongest whiskey. She peeled up the edge of the quilt, making a place for him to slide in.

Jake took a deep breath and gave in to the dream.

Chapter 12

Emily didn't move. She didn't dare. If she twitched, if she even breathed, Jake might come to his senses and pull away.

And this was too sweet, far too rare, to risk.

He'd slid in beside her, no attempt to put barriers between them, no careful distance between their bodies. He moved right up beside her, first the flat of his chest—so hard, so solid—firmly pressed against her. The heat came immediately, flooding the space. It was unnecessary, the night comfortably warm, but she loved his heat anyway, the blast of a live, male body next to hers.

And then his arm came around her waist. It nestled into the slope between her ribs and her hips and her breath snagged in her throat. His chin was at her shoulder, and she could feel his breath washing over her skin.

Oh, it was heaven, this stolen bliss. She didn't

consider herself a truly innocent woman—too many hours with the more graphic volumes in Dr. Goodale's library had given her a practical, working knowledge. But she never suspected the power of it, the seductive draw of Jake's body near hers. She hadn't earned this pleasure—he wasn't her husband, her suitor, her *anything*. It made it all the more scandalous, all the more precious for being unexpected, and because it might be snatched away at any second, never to be repeated, leaving her all the more inclined to savor every moment, each sensation.

His legs, so much longer than hers, stretched out alongside hers as she lay on her back. How could they possibly be as hard as they felt? She dared to wiggle her right leg a fraction. Nope, no give at all. If her leg was a pillow, his was fashioned from solid steel.

He was covered from neck to ankle; so was she. But his feet were bare, and he brushed one against hers. His toes kneaded the top of her foot. Drew a line up her instep, which made her foot twitch and him chuckle softly.

Goodness. *Feet.* Prosaic, ordinary, completely uninteresting feet. And the wickedness caught her completely. Made everything inside her go soft and weak, her skin feverish, her breath shallow and uneven. Heavens, she knew nothing! Nothing at all, if *feet* could do this. Anything more, she was sure, would send her flying.

And then he put his hand on her belly. Just rested it there, on the flat beneath her navel. So big it covered almost the entire space, so warm it seared her through the sturdy cotton of her nightdress.

"Shhh," he murmured, so quietly she barely heard it. And spread his fingers, so that his thumb bumped up against the lower swell of her breasts, and she arched a little, without realizing it was her intent. "Don't move." He pressed down against her midsection, keeping her in place, and his thumb moved. Back and forth, a small, modest, oh-so-wonderful motion, nudging her left breast, a slow sweep across the valley between them, then a brush against the right. More, less—she didn't know which she longed for, knew she needed *something*.

And then his little finger moved, and her hips shot up, coming off the bed. He began to pull his hand back. "No!" she said, before she stopped to think, and yanked his hand back, pressing it flat against her stomach.

Mortified, she squeezed her eyes shut. What had she done?

But then his head dipped, his mouth coming against her shoulder—not a kiss, a mere resting of his lips against her, and even through the fabric she could feel his smile.

Her embarrassment fled. So what if she had done something naive and wanton? If it could make Jake smile, she'd do it again, and a hundred times more.

She tried to puzzle it out. Logically think through whether it was wrong or not. He was not her husband. Not even a man who might someday be. But sharing this bed was so far beyond the bounds of propriety already; this hardly seemed like a larger transgression. He wasn't . . . *putting* himself inside her. She formed the words in her mind deliberately, knowing no others except a few bare clinical ones. Intercourse. Sexual relations.

Loving? Just thinking the terms caused a delicious thrumming in her, low in her belly where his hand claimed her.

But they were doing nothing of the sort. Nothing so clearly wrong. A touch, a cuddle. No worse than simply sharing the bed.

Except that it made her giddy and hot and made her think of those other things.

But it made him smile.

He spread his fingers again, drew them back together. Again. Again. And then wide, until his smallest finger brushed against the top fringe of her private hair. She knew he had to feel the springy curls beneath the cotton. His breath came harder, with a wild, ragged edge.

She held herself completely still. Oh, this *had* to be wrong, this sweet-painful ache. Wanting his finger to slip further down. Too wicked. Too impossible. Too wonderful.

He shifted closer, hard against her side, his lower leg looped around her ankle, his foot resting between her two, spreading her legs a sinful fraction. Anticipation surged, spiraling up like wildfire.

He was hard against her hip. It was . . . oh! She'd seen pictures. A few times, a quick, accidental glimpse of a patient's private areas. She was a curious woman; she'd availed herself of the information accessible to her, which she figured was far more than most women of her age and upbringing.

But it couldn't be . . . this was too large. Hard, bold against her. Nothing like that innocuous, funny little appendage in Dr. Goodale's books.

She whispered without considering her words: "I didn't expect it to be so *firm*."

She felt a burst of breath against her shoulder, his muffled laughter before he spoke low in her ear. "I didn't, either. At least not anymore."

A violent coughing fit seized Kate. Emily jumped, a guilty bolt, but Jake refused to let her go; his arms held firm, gently unbreakable.

"It's all right," he told her. "Remember?"

"Oh, I'm so sorry!" Another explosion from Kate, loud enough to detach a lung from its anchor. "Don't mind me. I can't imagine what's gotten into me. I'm just so sensitive to dust—you remember that, Emily—and down here on the floor . . . I do apologize if I woke you."

"You didn't wake us," Jake said, his voice a husky growl.

Dead silence, during which Emily's cheeks burned. "Oh." Kate cleared her throat delicately. "I'm even sorrier then."

Against Emily, Jake shook with silent laughter, and she wanted to whack him. Why'd he have to make it sound like that? Now Kate was convinced she'd interrupted them right in the middle of . . . well, *that*.

"It's all right," Emily said quickly.

"Easy for you to say," Jake whispered in her ear. His hips remained pressed against her side, and she was suddenly reminded that he hadn't . . . receded, not one bit. Despite everything, desire jolted through her, enough to make her lose the thread of the conversation momentarily. "It's not all right at all." She poked him then, in his side—heavens, but there was absolutely no give to the man—and he spoke over his shoulder to Kate. "Can I get you a drink of water?"

"Oh no, that won't be necessary—" was all she got out before the coughing seized her again. "Well, perhaps. If it wouldn't be too much of an imposition."

"That's not what I'd call it, no." Before he got to his feet, he spoke low to Emily again. "I'll be right back. Don't move."

She didn't. Not the whole time he was gone after he slammed out into the night, cup in hand. How could she?

Because she was almost—maybe—completely sure that, right before he'd let go, he'd . . . hugged her.

Kate Goodale considered herself an excellent judge of people in general and men most specifically. But she could not get a satisfactory fix on her new brother-in-law.

She tried her best to set aside her own disappointment at Emily's precipitous marriage and formulate an objective opinion. Jake did not make it easy.

For many years she'd cherished an image of the kind of husband Emily would eventually marry. Cultured, handsome, well-mannered, educated, genteel, and cheerful. If not wealthy, at least comfortably and solidly well off, and—this one went without saying—completely devoted to Emily's every wish.

Jake was . . . she didn't know what he was. Poor, but she had an inkling that wouldn't always be the case. He worked like a madman, sunrise to sunset, constructing that lean-to with fierce efficiency and putting together his press with a maximum of swearing but a minimum of time. And then, sweaty, ink-stained, as rough-looking as if he'd just wandered in from the meanest street in Philadelphia, he plopped down at the kitchen table and wrote an elegant analysis of the homestead movement for his first issue that was so convincing, bordering on poetic, that it almost made *her* want to stay.

He had more manners than he chose to use on most occasions. Cheerful—well, you could forget that one; Jake Sullivan had grouchiness refined to a high art. Unfortunately, he failed miserably at what Kate considered the most important test, which was that he would worship at her sister's feet.

Except that, once or twice, she'd caught him gazing at Emily with such raw hunger and pained longing that it made her own knees go weak. As soon as he realized she was watching he retreated into his usual scowl. But it had been there; she was sure it had been there. And that was the one thing that kept her from simply dragging Emily back to the city, which, despite Emily's protests, Kate had no doubts she could accomplish if events required.

And so she was stuck in Montana, unable to ease her fears enough to go, but without convincing evidence that would justify forcing Emily to leave. This had been, she had no doubt, the very longest week of her life.

To Kate's surprise, Emily worked nearly as hard as her husband. She didn't seem to mind a bit, while Kate felt out of place and distinctly unuseful. She was excellent at managing a staff, at planning a party for two hundred, at budgeting for a household of any size. She was utterly abysmal at washing clothes in the creek or wandering over the plains and grubbing up wild onions.

Imbert Longnecker had apparently wasted no time in spreading the word of Emily's nuptials. A parade of acquaintances—far more than Kate would have thought were squirreled away throughout the territory—trooped over to wish the perhaps-happy, perhaps-not (the jury was still out) couple well. Emily beamed. But then she always beamed. Jake groused. But then it appeared he always groused. Emily also seemed far jumpier than Kate had ever seen her, something that deeply concerned her. However, she'd never seen her as a new bride before and tried very hard not to read more into it than there was. She was aware of the fact that she'd prefer to take it as proof that something was amiss, thus giving her an excuse to pry Emily out of this marriage before it was too late. Still, she was determined to be fair.

And thus Friday found the three of them tromping over hill and vale—more like bumps and shallows—on their way to the home of May and Joe Blevins, two of those multitudinous, well-wishing neighbors, who'd insisted upon having a small dinner in their honor.

Small was the operative word. The Blevins home was no larger than Jake's, and so the only additional guest was Art Biskup.

"Here you are at last!" May rushed forward, her hands extended to greet Kate, bumping her husband with her sturdy hip to move him out of the crowded doorway. "Oh, excuse me." She laughed and wiped her hands on the strip of toweling she'd wrapped around her waist in lieu of an apron. "I was kneading the biscuits."

"No problem at all." Kate eyed the sticky bits of dough on her fingers, and after contemplating the blue silk of her skirts, she edged over to Emily and surreptitiously wiped them off on the back of Emily's dress, which was already the worse for its time in Montana.

"Hey!" Emily batted at her hand.

"It's French silk. I waited three months for its arrival." And was most unlikely to be able to replace the garment, and therefore was determined to preserve it as long as possible.

"This is my Joe," May said proudly.

Joe was as young as his wife. Neither one of them looked as if they'd been weaned long enough to be so far from home, round-faced and blond and broad-shouldered, from neighboring farm families in Illinois. Joe was the fourth son, May informed them, and so their only chance at having a farm of their own was homesteading, and they'd come out there two weeks after their wedding, and they were so happy to have another couple nearby, and wasn't it wonderful?

"Wonderful," Emily and Kate agreed.

"And you remember Mr. Biskup, don't you?"

"Sure she does." Art, who'd no intention of giving up his prime seat in the rocking chair to the new arrivals, waved from his corner. "Even if I don't make an impression, nobody ever forgets Mr. Smithie."

Mr. Smithie, comfortably settled on Art's shoulders, took one look at the clever felt-and-feather birds on Kate's hat and let out a screech that rattled the lone windowpane. "Hush now. Mind your manners." He pulled out a plump date from his bulging chest pocket and handed it to the monkey.

"Yes. I remember Smithie." As inconspicuously as possible, Kate flattened herself against the wall farthest from the unpredictable creature.

She didn't move while Emily and May went to finish the last few details of supper and the men clustered in the tiny sitting area. Jake, clearly on his best behavior, was extremely complimentary of the condition of Joe's fields, at which point the young man lit up with pride and launched into an extensive explanation of the new dry-cropping farming method he intended to employ.

When he ran out of steam, Art, who appeared to have been lulled to sleep by the discussion, sat up so quickly Smithie grabbed a fistful of hair to maintain his perch. "So. You got yourself another wife, did you, Sullivan?"

Kate edged closer, eyeing Smithie with rampant suspicion. "You knew his first wife?"

"Sure. Been here longer than anyone else, most likely. Only Indians and buffalo when I came—they were the best to paint, I can tell you. Not as good now, but I'm too old to go galloping off after new subjects. Then the cowboys and the cows. They'll all be gone, too, before much longer, I suppose." He sighed gustily. "Not that I don't *like* you all. Nice to have people to chat with. But the painting"—he shook his head sadly—"it's something to chronicle the changes, but it ain't as much of a challenge." Then he perked up. "Now you, Miss Kate, I could do something with." He narrowed his eyes.

"I might consider it," she murmured. "Now, about Jake's—"

"Haven't done a nude for a long time."

"And neither will you be anytime soon."

"Oh, I don't know." He made a square with his fingers and framed her in it, squinting. "Been a while, I'll admit, but I always did have an imagination."

"We'll see," she said smoothly. "Now, about Mr. Sullivan's wife . . ."

She ignored Jake's glower. It was natural for her to be curious about his previous life. If he didn't like it . . . well, he should have been the one to tell them about it in the first place, and from Emily's sudden alertness, almost but not quite hidden by her attention to the gravy she stirred, she knew very little herself.

"I had one of those once."

"You had what?"

"A wife." Slumping in his chair, Biskup gratefully accepted the brimming glass of Joe's special home brew.

"You did, Mr. Biskup?" Joe handed another glass to Jake and began to take his own seat.

"I'd like one of those, Mr. Blevins," Kate said.

"Huh?" He fumbled to cover his surprise and disapproval. "Uh, sure thing. I just couldn't . . . carry any more at once."

"Here. Take mine." Jake handed over his glass. "I don't drink anyway."

"You don't drink?" she asked in surprise.

"Not anymore. You taste it one too many times on the way up, it kinda loses its appeal on the way down." Then he turned to Mr. Biskup and changed the topic. "I didn't know you'd been married, Mr. Biskup," Jake said. Hoping that Mr. Biskup would be too busy nattering about his wife to speak of Jake's, Kate suspected.

"Sure. Till Luard Chandler offered me three hundred dollars for her."

Kate, who'd insisted on the drink only because Mr. Blevins hadn't offered her one, nearly choked on the first sip. "You sold your wife?"

He shrugged. "She liked Luard better'n me, anyway. Smithie only cost me ten bucks, and he's better company. Less trouble. Too fond of riding the bulls, but then, so was Myrtle." He cackled at his own joke. "Still and all, once I got rid of the first one, I didn't have much of an urge to get another. And here you are, Jake, with another one already!"

"Maybe I had better luck at picking them than you did."

"Oh, you surely did at that!" Art hooted. "Pretty as a picture, that first one, if a little delicate-looking for my taste. Could see the stars when the two of you looked at each other." He glanced guiltily at Emily. "Not that the two of you don't—oh, criminy. Didn't mean no offense, ma'am."

"None taken," Emily said serenely, bringing Jake a cup of coffee. She put her hand on his shoulder and his came up to cover hers. A touch awkwardly, Kate judged. Because it was uncomfortable to hear his first wife discussed in front of his second? Or because he truly was not as deeply in love with Emily? He would not be the first man who couldn't love his second wife as much. A new worry. She'd been so busy considering whether Jake was good enough for Emily that she'd never considered whether he could *love* her; she'd just assumed he would. Who wouldn't love Emily? But a man whose heart was completely and permanently broken . . . oh no.

"Excuse me!" May, who'd been efficiently puttering in the kitchen, suddenly bolted past Kate, hand pressed over her mouth, her usually ruddy complexion the color of diluted pea soup.

"Oh dear." Emily rushed to follow her.

From just outside the door came the sound of vile retching. Jake gulped his coffee like he wished he'd taken the whiskey after all. Art merely tugged a couple of dates out of his pocket and gave one to Smithie. He popped the other in his mouth and chewed noisily, which, coupled with the sound of retching outside, made Kate queasy enough to glare accusingly at Joe.

Joe, who'd drained the last of his drink, caught her disapproval. "What?"

"In case you'd somehow missed it, your wife is ill."

"So?" His usual pink skin flushed deeper.

"Don't you think you should go to her?"

"Why? Emily's with her." The jug was on the floor

near his chair, and he scooped it up, sloshing a hefty glug into his glass. "Not like there's anythin' I can do." He grinned proudly. "Already did my part. Now it's her turn."

"But—"

The two women returned, Emily supporting May's elbow, while May swiped at her forehead with a damp cloth. May's color had gone from green to chalky white. Better, but certainly not healthy.

"My apologies," May murmured. She lifted her arm away from Emily's support and folded her hands in front of her apron. "It seems the typical morning indisposition is determined to strike me at suppertime instead."

"A baby?" Jake set his cup carefully on the floor. "You're having a baby?"

And then she had color, a bright bloom of pink.

"Yup," her husband answered for her as he reached over to give Jake a companionable slap on his shoulder. "Beat you to it, Sullivan. Bet you five to ten it's a boy, too. Good breeding stock, my May."

Jake ignored him, kept his flat, expressionless gaze upon May. "When?"

"I—" She blanched again. "October. November, perhaps."

"She's worried about it," Joe supplied. "Don't know why. We're farm people, both of us. Seen things born a hundred times. And look at her hips! Squirt it out just like my best heifer, I'll wager. Why—"

Jake had him up against the wall before the last word faded away. His fists twisted the front of Joe's shirt into a tight ball, and despite the fact that Joe probably outweighed him by twenty pounds Joe's booted toes dangled six inches above the floor.

"You will," Jake said slowly, "never compare your wife's condition to an animal's again."

Joe was too stunned to be angry. "Hey, look, I—"

Jake shook him, making his heels thump against the wall. "You will do whatever she asks of you until her time comes. *Whatever*. Do you understand me?"

"I didn't mean anything. There's no reason for her to be afraid of havin' a baby, I—"

"Do you understand me?"

By this time Emily had gained their side. "Jake—"

"I asked you a question, Blevins."

"Yeah." For pride's sake, he'd tried taking a swing, but Jake had his elbows wide, pinning Joe's arms to the wall, and the punch had no more effect than a buzzing fly. "Yeah, I understand."

"If she wants a doctor, she gets it. If she wants to go back to Illinois, she gets it. If she wants you to *build* her a goddamn hospital before that baby comes, you'll do it."

"Whatever she wants," Joe repeated.

"And you won't make light of it again."

"I never was." He spread his hands, as wide as their position allowed. "Really, Sullivan, what the hell's gotten into you?"

"Jake." Emily touched his biceps.

Jake held Joe in that position, his chest heaving, muscles bulging with the weight of his burden, eyes hard as if anticipating Joe giving him an excuse to start swinging.

"Let him go, Jake." This time Emily wrapped her hands around his upper arm and tugged. "He'll take care of her. He promises, and so do I."

Jake turned his head in her direction, mouth compressed, cheekbones jutting sharp and brutal. "Jake," she said again, her voice so intimately soft she might have been whispering his name in bed. A shudder ran through him, and he let go, releasing Joe so fast he was unprepared and his legs nearly buckled beneath him before he found his feet.

Jake strode to the door, pausing briefly beside May, his head down. "I'm sorry," he said without looking at her. "I—" His right arm came up and then dropped back to his side, as if he'd meant to touch her but thought better of it. "Take care."

Bewildered, May nodded. "I will."

"No, I . . . take *very* good care." And then he was gone. The door slammed shut behind him, sucking in on a gust, leaving them all staring at it as if it might make some sense of what had just happened.

"Huh." Art chewed on another date, jaw working in rhythm with his monkey's. "Never used to be such a touchy fellow, least not that I can recall."

"Hmm." Kate supposed such a show of temper should worry her, but truly, she'd been on the verge of stringing up that idiot Joe herself.

Emily, who'd remained standing by the door, so lost in thought she'd appeared half asleep, suddenly came to life. "May, how are you feeling now?" she asked briskly.

"I'm better. I'm always fine for at least a few minutes after I empty out."

"Kate, stay with her for a while, will you, just to

make sure? Sorry to interrupt your dinner, May, it was a lovely thought, and we're both ever so grateful, but please don't wait for us if you're ready to eat. And in any case, I'll be over in the morning with a tonic we've found helpful."

A man in bad temper was, in Kate's experience, best left alone to stew. You could cheer him up when the edge was off, if you wanted, but there was no point in trying when his mood was running hot. "Emily, don't you think—"

But once again her sister was gone before Kate could stop her, rushing headlong into potential disaster.

Chapter 13

I t took her a while to find him.

The minutes Emily spent thrashing through hip-deep grass gave her a little too much time to wonder whether she should, indeed, be chasing after him. No doubt he'd much prefer to be left alone. And she'd certainly no *right* to go running after him. He was not her husband, something that was becoming harder to remember than it should have been. Which undoubtedly gave credence to their charade, but it had happened far too easily for her peace of mind. While she didn't feel *married* to him, exactly, nevertheless she couldn't deny that, way down deep, she felt as if she had some claim on the man. And some responsibility to him.

Which, while natural—what one acted very often was what one became, in her experience—also seemed disconcertingly dangerous. Because once he'd seen Kate on a coach, he'd shove her on the very next one.

But then she rounded a rise a few hundred yards west of the Blevinses' and found him there, standing on the top of a slight bluff, braced into the wind, solitary and lost, and she couldn't leave him alone.

She mimicked his stance beside him, hands clasped behind her, the wind hot and dry in her face, lifting her hair. Sunset bled across the horizon: red, orange, purple. Hot colors, seething, born in violence and flame.

"Beautiful."

"Yeah. Yeah, it is."

How'd he do that? Strip himself of every emotion, tamp them down and down until there was no chance of them erupting again? She was sure they were still there, somewhere deep; he didn't seem empty and dead, but so ruthlessly contained that the emotions had turned in on themselves.

The light danced over his features, brutally forged, strong. Like an ancient warrior illuminated by a bonfire's flames, when the only thing that mattered was survival.

He fascinated her. It surprised her, that. She'd never suspected she was so susceptible to physical allure. So drawn by a man's secrets, a man's pain, a man's strength. She could look at him, kissed by sunset and dusk, for hours. Forever.

It would be easy just to stay beside him and enjoy the view. Muddling in deep, dark places, in long-ago memories, always held the danger of wandering into wounds best left alone. She'd no doubt he'd fight her should she try to venture in.

But years of experience had taught her the value of lancing a wound instead of letting it fester. A brief, brilliant pain rather than a lingering, cancerous one.

She took a deep breath and plunged in. "So. There was a baby?"

He closed his eyes, swallowed hard. "Yeah. There was a baby."

Then he looked down at her. His eyes, dark as an old bruise, sought hers and held, only a few inches away. She hadn't realized she'd stood so near; he'd seemed so very far away, she realized, she'd gotten close without recognizing it. She could kiss him, lift up to her toes and press her mouth to his, and forget all this. Make *him* forget, at least for a little while. And perhaps that would be a greater kindness.

Except he surprised her. "Where do you want me to start?"

"I thought I'd have to drag it out of you, word by word."

"Me, too." Not a smile, but a sad, hard curve to his mouth. "I've *not* talked about it for a long time. Hasn't helped."

"Start wherever." There were no lines on his face, she realized in faint surprise. It seemed like his past should have left a mark somehow. She could tell where they'd etch in time, a deep bracket around his mouth, a furrow between his brow. Impulsively she touched him there, her fingers brushing against the corner of his mouth, and the tight tension there eased. "Tell me about your wife."

"Since when does a woman want to hear a man speak of another?"

"This woman does." She'd sometimes been told

by Goodale's patients that she had magic hands. It was an essential part of the healing process for her, laying her hands on an ailing joint, an aching belly. She didn't know exactly why. Perhaps the heat helped, the energy, or maybe there was simply some tactile symptom she detected through her skin that she couldn't define but nevertheless helped her diagnose ills correctly.

She'd never before hoped so much that her hands truly could heal.

Stepping closer, she slid her arms around his waist. She laid her cheek against his chest—hard, warm—and just held on. And it all sighed out of him, a gust of breath, a rush of tension, and the words came.

"I can't tell you about her without telling you about me."

Good, she thought; her curiosity would be satisfied at last. His heart thumped beneath her ear and his chest vibrated each time he spoke. A nice place to be, curled up against him. She wished it were for no other reason but the pleasure of it.

"My father delivered ice. It provided barely enough for a wife and a son, I suppose, though I don't remember much. I was only three when he died. Rushing home, went too fast around a corner, and the wagon overturned."

"So we've more in common than I knew." She tightened her arms, let her hands wander up and down, a motion that couldn't pretend to be anything but a caress, although the purpose could be debated. She could say it was only for comfort and almost believe it. "My mother died not long after I was born, my father when I was five. So young I barely knew enough to miss them."

"Yes." She was peeling the bandages off wounds he'd carefully covered, layer by layer, and Jake couldn't even say he minded. The pain was there, but kept at a low, dull ache by the feel of her body pressed lightly against his, her hands moving over his back. There was comfort in each stroke, a cool and soothing balm. And yet at the same time a simmer of desire, as healing in its own way as the comfort, holding the worst at bay. "But I still had my mother."

"And I had my sisters," she said briskly, turning away any sympathy he might have offered before it began.

"And a formidable pair they must be, from the one I've met."

"Oh no. I'll tell my secrets later. It's your turn now."

"I wasn't changing the topic on purpose," he said, startled to find it the truth. She . . . interested him, in a way little had for a very long time. Curiosity, long dormant, stirred. He let it sit for a bit, found he liked it more than he would have thought. "I'd like to know, though."

"Would you?"

"Yes."

"You sound surprised."

"I am."

"Then I'll confess that I am, too." His shirt was thin cotton, and her breath seeped through it, warm and moist against his skin. He gave in, and wrapped his arms around her so that he held her as tightly as

she held him. "It wasn't all that long ago that I figured you'd rather run from here to Billings than
have to listen to one detail of my life."

"I would have."

She slapped his back lightly in reprimand. "And
you're distracting me, wandering off the subject
again."

"You're not going to let me off the hook, are you?"
He chuckled, wondering at the ease of it.

"Yes I would." Her hands stilled. She tilted her
head back. "I would. If you really want me to."

"Too late now." Gently he pushed her head back
where it belonged. He couldn't look at her and get
through it all. He knew that much. He'd see the sympathy, the understanding in her eyes, and he'd be
lost. And suddenly it seemed important to say it all
at least once. "You're stuck."

Blessedly, sweetly, her hands took up their warm
caress again. He found himself speaking in rhythm
with them, as if they drew the words from him with
each circle they made. "My mother had to find work
then. There wasn't much. She'd no experience, no
skills. Just cleaning, and oh, she could do that!" He
smiled at the memory. "Still does, come to think of it.
Can make a floor shine like it was made out of diamonds."

"She's still alive?"

"Oh yeah. Still scrubbing floors. Says she's afraid
she'll stiffen up like an old lady if she stops, so she
keeps at it. She could run me into the ground any
day." And suddenly he missed her, with her wiry
body that barely came up to his chest but that could
still make him quake in his boots. He'd write her to-

morrow, he promised himself. "So she went to work for the Bateses."

"Rich?"

"Oh yeah. That house I struggled so much to build wouldn't be fit for his dog." He expected that admission to bite; he'd never been able to look at his claim shack without comparing it to the house in which Julia had been raised. But he'd built a house with his own hands that had stood up to two winters on the plains. It was more than most he knew in Chicago could claim.

"I know the kind," she said dryly.

"Oh?"

"Later," she promised, and he made a mental note to ask. Another similarity, it seemed. It no longer surprised him.

"I was too young to be left alone all the time, and the housekeeper was kind. She let Mother smuggle me in now and then. Even let me hang around the kitchen and 'approve' the desserts." He hadn't realized he still held good memories of Bates House. They'd been submerged for years, sunk beneath the weight of the darker ones. It felt good to take them out again to glitter and shine, the glowing pieces of a childhood that had been mostly bright. "They had a library. A huge room, with big arched windows that welcomed the sun. I'd never seen anything like it, and there was hardly ever anyone there. It became my sanctuary."

"The books," she murmured. He felt her mouth move against him, the press and brush of her lips against his cloth-covered chest, and had to struggle to hang on to a thought.

"Huh?"

"All those books. That you left in the shack. I wondered about them. About the kind of person who'd go to so much trouble to lug them out here and take such good care of them. And who'd have such a wide range of material."

"Impressed you, did I?"

"You most certainly did." He laid his cheek on the top of her head. He'd held her before, remembered her scent. But usually it had been for Kate's benefit and he'd weighed each move for its best effect. This he did for himself. Because he liked the feel of her, and for no other reason. Because it made him feel hopeful and warm and yes, maybe even a bit happy.

"I was . . . ten, I think. I rarely saw any of the family—the Bateses, that is. I'd been trained well to stay out of the way. But I was curious. Why wouldn't I be? I was in the library reading *Moby Dick* when Mr. Bates strolled in. He was *never* there during the day. Still don't know why he was then, but it was too late to run."

"Mr. Bates?" she asked.

"Yeah. Why?"

"Oh. I thought you were going to tell me about your wife."

"I'm getting there," he told her. "Story too slow for you? Want me to hurry up so you don't get bored?" he asked.

"Don't you dare. It's taken me long enough to get even a hint from you. I want to hear every single detail."

"You wondered about me?"

Her hair smelled like sunshine in a garden. The

scent had haunted him for days, a light drift here and there just out of his reach that he hadn't been able to get ahold of.

"Yes," she admitted. "I wondered. A lot."

"I'm flattered."

"You shouldn't be. I'm a curious sort, too."

"Never woulda guessed." Curious, and vibrant, and kind. And a lot of other things, he'd wager. Things he was now sorry he'd never have the time to find out about her. "Anyway, I stood there quaking in my shoes, clutching that book before me like I thought it might shield me. I figured I was out on my ass for good, and my mother, too."

"But you weren't."

"Nope. He took one look at the book, rocked back on his heels, and opined that I might as well stop pretending, there was no chance that a poor rough urchin like me could be reading such a tome."

"He didn't!" she said, indignant on his behalf.

"Oh, he did. He had opinions, had Mr. Bates. I took offense. Stupid; I should have slunk out the first chance I got. Mom needed the job, and I sure didn't need Mr. Bates on my tail. But instead I flipped open the book and started reading the first paragraph my eyes fell on. Fast as I could, spewing out the words before he could stop me, so I could *prove* that I knew how. That I wasn't just some dumb punk kid looking at the pictures."

"If you'd tried that on Dr. Goodale, you'd have made it to word two."

"Well, I made it to page three before he stopped me. Then he grabbed a copy of *Ragged Dick*, opened it to the middle, and shoved it at me. I read—was too afraid not to. He took a liking to me, I guess. I never was sure why."

Emily wondered how many questions she dared ask, how many pieces of the puzzle she'd discover tonight. The words that spilled out of him told her one thing. His body told her just as much; tenderness, strength, emotion carefully contained, all the more powerful for it.

"I didn't see him all that much. Once every few months he'd call me in and have me tell him what I was learning. He'd fire questions at me, always at least a couple I couldn't answer, and I'd better have it right by the next time or . . . well, he never told me what would happen 'or.' "

"You always had the answer by the next time?"

"Oh yes. I'd have been terrified not to. And ashamed."

He enveloped her. His arms linked around her back, his cheek resting on the top of her head, his voice pouring over her and sinking in deep. She'd never get the sound of it out again, not completely. From now on some part of her would always hold on to the memory of him giving her something she knew he'd given no one else.

"When I got old enough, he paid for my tuition."

"That was very kind of him."

"I thought so. Oh hell, I still think so, even though now I realize he educated me because he figured I'd be of use to him someday. It was still an opportunity I'd have never had otherwise."

He paused. It got harder now. Darker. And full of his own mistakes, ones that he could explain all he wanted but would still make him look like the worst kind of cad. And he didn't want her to think that of him. He shouldn't care, there was no reason to care, but there it was. He did.

"He had a daughter."

"Ah," she said lightly. "There she is at last. I was wondering if you were ever going to get to her."

"Julia. She was two years younger than me and for a long time I was only vaguely aware that she existed. I lived for those times I had Mr. Bates's full attention and really wasn't all that interested in remembering that she'd far more claim on him than I."

Emily tried to identify how his voice had changed. Deeper, perhaps. A barely there tremor beneath the words. An almost imperceptible hint that betrayed the anguish beneath the smooth recitation.

Unthinkingly, she turned her head and pressed a kiss on his chest. Hard, wide-mouthed, so shockingly blatant that had she stopped to consider she never would have done it. Hadn't realized such a thing would ever occur to her.

He went rigid. "Lord." Beneath her mouth, she felt his heartbeat pick up speed. "If you'll do that every time I make a confession, we can stand here all night and I can tell you about every cookie I stole and every swearword I spewed in my entire childhood."

His hand came up, fisted in her hair, holding her there. And then slowly he loosened his grip, by increments, and ran his hand through the full length of her hair, again and again, and she was glad she'd not pinned it all away today.

She turned her head again, resting her cheek against him. Darkness had dropped, a blue velvet curtain over the small slice of sky she could see above the lift and spread of the land. Even as she watched, one star winked on, as if the heavens had lit the eve's first candle.

"Tell me more."

"She grew up. So did I. And when I was eighteen years old—I'd just started at the university, and I was so full of it, and myself—I came out of Mr. Bates's study, took a small detour to the garden to enjoy the sun, and there she was. I know it sounds silly, and young, and . . . false, but I just saw her, and that was it for me."

"It doesn't sound silly. Not to me." It sounded enviable. And *that* was silliness indeed to wish that Jake Sullivan might have taken one look at her and fallen instantly in love.

"Well, it did to me. I told myself it was just . . . well, why *wouldn't* she draw me? She was everything I wasn't. She belonged there, and I didn't. But I wanted to. And I wanted her."

"And she felt the same way?"

"I don't know. I didn't even speak to her that day. I knew I couldn't get my mouth to work."

"She must have been lovely."

"Oh yes." And he wished, irrationally, that Emily hadn't said that so easily. That there'd been a trace of jealousy in her voice, to hear him praise another woman. He'd no idea his pride required such plumping. "Ethereal as a fairy, as if she wasn't of this earth. But that wasn't what drew me the most. It was that she looked at me like—well, I knew I could conquer the world. That she *believed* I could conquer the world. Her father was about challenge, and making me prove that I could make a place in his world. She never saw that there was a difference between us."

"She loved you right away?"

"Oh, we were friends. Or so we pretended. We talked. Met in secret, walked in the gardens, left little notes we knew would make the other laugh. We pretended it would be enough. But I always knew. I think she did, too."

His throat closed. He could stop right now. Emily wouldn't push. He'd told her enough.

But it would be unfair to quit now. Unfair to Emily to let her view him as a tragic figure, one who deserved her sympathy.

"I couldn't leave it at that. It wasn't enough for me. I couldn't *not*—oh, hell, Em. She was nineteen years old, sheltered for every one of them, and she cried when she told me there would be a baby."

Emily realized he couldn't be more than four years older than she. But he'd already lived so much more than she had. She'd seen people die, had even held the hands of a few as they slipped away. But she'd never loved with her whole heart and lost. Even her parents—she'd been too young to remember her mother, and her father had never been more than a vague, shadowy figure, patting her on the head before disappearing for days at a time. It seemed a canyon between them, him on one side, her on the other, separated by this vast and terrible experience. And yet she felt closer to him than anyone. She couldn't imagine the man he'd been before;

this experience had transformed him into the grave and solitary man she knew.

"I married her the instant I could arrange it. How could I not? She was carrying my child. I figured it would be hard. But we loved each other, and I was willing to give everything I had to take care of her and our baby. *Wanted* to do it. It never occurred to me it wouldn't be enough."

"Don't say that." She couldn't bear that he would think his best inadequate. And she had no doubt at all he'd done his best.

He fell silent. Debating whether to insist upon his guilt, she'd wager. "Go on," she urged him.

"I had to leave school, of course. Mr. Bates certainly wasn't going to continue to pay my tuition after what I'd done. Not that it mattered," he added quickly, unwilling to sound disloyal. "Northwestern only enrolls single students."

"But—" Why? she wondered. Why wouldn't he have expected support from his new father-in-law, his mentor? The sound of his heartbeat filled her head, resonated with her own. "He didn't approve?"

"Good God, Emily, of course he didn't approve!" And she knew that however harshly his father-in-law had judged him, Jake judged himself more severely. "I seduced his daughter."

"And you loved his daughter. You married his daughter."

He chose not to debate the point. "I had a family to support. I wanted to give them a home, a place of their own."

"So you came here."

"So I brought her here." She felt his chin move gently across the top of her head, as if he were taking in the view. Perhaps remembering what they'd seen when they arrived.

"She was . . . oh, I don't know why I ever thought it might suit us! She was too gentle for this place. The pregnancy was hard. Finally I swallowed my pride, took her home, and begged her parents to let her stay. They finally did, even though her father told her the day we left that if she went out the door with me she could never come back." He paused. Swallowed hard. "It was too late."

"Jake." Leaning back into his embrace, so she could judge the effect of her words, she chose them carefully. "I do have some experience here. To be precise, I've been present at the birth of thirty-seven babies."

She saw the shift of muscle in his jaw as his teeth clamped together. "Thirty-seven? You remember every one?"

"Every single one. You don't forget miracles, not even after a thousand, if you've been privileged to witness them."

A shudder ran through him.

"Most of the births have been perfect. A few have . . . not. Jake, if there's one thing you absolutely must understand, it's that if you'd never taken her one foot from her house it might not have changed anything. You brought her back to Chicago before the birth, yes?"

"I . . . what else could I do? I couldn't let her deliver out here alone. The nearest doctor's thirty miles away and he's drunk more often than sober."

"Bringing her home sooner, or not taking her here at all—it likely made no difference."

God, but he wanted to believe her. But she hadn't been there. She didn't know. "You didn't see how much it changed her. From the moment we came here. How hard it was on her, how much of her strength it sapped. I should have known. Should have realized it sooner."

"The hardest thing about medicine for me has always been the 'ifs.' You never know what might have happened had you done this differently, made another choice. Because there's no chance to try again, no opportunity to correct your mistakes. And you never even know if they *were* mistakes. Sometimes you do the absolutely right thing and bad things still happen. It could have been simple coincidence that she became ill when you arrived here."

Perhaps she was right. It didn't change his ultimate culpability. "Be that as it may, it still remains that the child was mine."

"Oh? And you forced her?"

He shoved her away. "Of course not!"

"Jake." She'd pushed too hard, Emily thought in regret. She'd wanted so badly to help him forgive himself that she'd only made things worse. He stood apart from her now, his hands on his hips, expression fierce and haunted as he stared into the last, dying flame of the sunset. "Jake." For an instant, for the first time since she'd awoken to a stranger beside her bed, she feared him. Still, she'd pressed the issue, and so she must take the risk. Her body painfully tensed, she laid her hand upon his arm, and let out a rushing breath of relief when he allowed it to stay. "I know that. And so did you. It does no one good for you to accept more than your share. And I doubt Julia would want it any more than I do."

He didn't answer. The wind mourned through the grass. Somewhere high, a hawk wheeling against the darkening sky called to an absent mate. But at last he placed his hand over hers where it rested on his forearm, then linked his fingers with hers.

It wasn't agreement. Not even a *maybe*. But it wasn't a *no*, and hope lifted her heart.

"Two days old. I haven't seen her since she was two days old. Jesus, she was so small. Hair like peach fuzz. She didn't even open her eyes to look at me." His voice broke. "Em, I don't even know what color her eyes are."

"But—but . . . your daughter?"

"Yeah. We named her Jenny. I don't even know if they still call her that."

"But I just assumed—" She'd assumed the baby had died with her mother. An unbearable tragedy, all too dreadfully common. "Your daughter's alive?"

"I . . ." His voice trailed off, a wafting of pain. "I assume she is. Christ, Em, I didn't even think of that." His fingers crushed hers painfully. So be it; if the bones broke, well, they'd heal. "I just . . . she'd be nearly fourteen months old by now. They'd tell me if she'd died, wouldn't they?"

"You'd know."

"Do you think so?"

"Yes," she said, and hoped there was enough conviction in her voice. "You'd know."

"God!" He yanked her back to him, bringing her hard up against his chest, the same position he'd shoved her from a few moments before. But this time it wasn't she who held him, and it wasn't gentle. He clutched her to him, hanging on with the desperation of a man clinging to his last hope.

She had to wait until she trusted her voice. "Where is she?"

"Bates House. Last I knew."

She could scarcely breathe. She didn't care; air seemed insignificant.

"Julia went into a coma two days after the birth. They threw me out. Had a footman club me over the head and dump me in the street. I tried—I tried everything to get back there. But I couldn't. Ended up in jail twice while I tried. He had everything on his side, all the power, all the money, all the connections." And the right, he didn't say. But Emily suspected he believed it. As much as Mr. Bates might blame Jake for Julia's death, it was no more than Jake blamed himself. "And then they draped the door in black and I knew. I walked straight into the nearest saloon and spent a year trying to drown it out."

She'd known all along he'd suffered loss. Too much mournful sorrow and raging anger fueled him for it to be anything else. But this was worse, a thousand times worse than she'd ever suspected.

And there was nothing she could do for him but hang on.

Because she'd judged that three more minutes in the same room with that idiot Joe Blevins *and* the monkey was likely to move her to physical violence against one, if not both, Kate excused herself with a delicate reference and lurched out the door.

Heavens! For all his other flaws, Blevins certainly could brew some potent liquor. Kate frowned and braced herself momentarily against the wall until she found her balance. There. Not so bad, after all. She prided herself on being able to sip a few genteel glasses of wine at dinner and keep complete control of her faculties. This couldn't be that much more difficult.

Why, it was nearly dark. Night fell so quickly here, much more so than at home. No gentle dusk, slowly deepening in a soothing drift of beautiful blue. Here night crashed down, sweeping lashes of strong color that were soon punched away by the dense, insistent black.

Where were Emily and that man? They'd been gone so long. They wouldn't have dared to leave for home without her. At least she didn't think so.

Unless, of course, Jake had become heartily sick of a chaperone interrupting his fun and had seduced Emily away for an evening of unbridled lust.

Oh, that was probably what had happened! He certainly didn't appear to be the sort of man who'd politely wait for his pleasures. And even she had to admit that his manly display of righteous anger, threatening Mr. Blevins into treating his poor, pregnant wife with due consideration, would spur a flutter in any woman's heart.

She swayed forward, deciding that it would indeed be wise to visit the necessary before demanding to be taken home. Though who would escort her there proved a dilemma. Joe deserved to spend the rest of the evening dancing attendance upon his wife, but she doubted Mr. Biskup could be persuaded to leave that disgusting creature behind.

Perhaps she'd find her own way home. She was almost sure it was . . . *that* direction. The grass was bent and bruised, as if someone had just passed that way. Undoubtedly a path.

She wished Jake were here so he'd be forced to acknowledge she was not the complete greenhorn he considered her. Triumphantly she plunged into the faint trail, feeling like an accomplished tracker.

The looming onset of night made her pause only briefly. Once night fell surely she could find her way back just by following the lamplight glinting through a window.

She found them just before sunset, the two of them standing on a slight rise, holding each other, completely limned in golden light.

She'd worried about stumbling across them locked in passion. But that—oh, that would have been easier. Simpler. So very understandable, a quick, flaming, physical connection between two young and healthy people.

But this, she realized in sinking dismay, she couldn't fight. Sex was temporary. But two people so wrapped in each other, swaying slightly as one, entirely alone on a desolate plain but sufficient together, needing no one else, wanting no one else—that was something entirely different. Something far more permanent forged of warmth and tenderness and care, two people against the world.

Before they ever noticed her presence she turned and slowly made her way back, feeling for the first time in her life utterly alone.

Chapter 14

"**N**ow." Pausing at the entrance to the Blevinses', Emily reached up and smoothed his collar, a proprietary gesture that startled them both only in retrospect because it seemed so utterly natural. "You must apologize to Joseph."

"I will not. He deserved it."

They'd walked back in starlight and silence. He'd held her hand, which they'd both pretended but neither believed was for safety's sake alone. Emily found herself reluctant to enter the house, afraid that the spell would be irretrievably broken.

"He's terrified, you know."

Jake gave a snort of disbelief. "Oh yeah, quaking in his boots. Saw that right off."

"He is. Even more afraid than she is, I think, and trying to bolster them both by pretending there's nothing to it."

"Really," he said, unconvinced.

"Absolutely. I've seen it before. I expect May to come through with flying colors, but I suspect Joe will faint before the baby crowns."

"You think you understand people so well, do you?"

"Yes," she said. "I'm very good at it, you know."

"Did you ever consider that, in refusing to ever find fault in anyone, you're being hopelessly taken in?" He gently touched her cheek. "You're going to be very disappointed someday, when someone you've given the benefit of the doubt lets you down."

She searched his face. She was still unused to him without a beard and was fascinated by the angles, by the play of light over his cheekbones and the shadowed cleft in his chin. How long would she have to stare at him, she wondered, before the jolt wore off?

"I don't think I'm going to be disappointed," she murmured. "I don't believe I'm going to be disappointed at all."

"Em." He shifted his weight, leaning closer until she couldn't take in the whole of his face at once and had to settle for his eyes, dark and rich and warm. "Em, I—"

"Oh, *there* you are!" The door flew inward. A glass gripped in one hand, Kate swayed, threatening to topple before she wisely braced herself against the doorway. The monkey crouched happily on her shoulder, maintaining his precarious station by clutching gleaming fistfuls of red-gold hair. "I thought you'd left me."

"I'm sorry, Kate," Emily said, fighting a start of guilt. Hadn't she done just that? Kate had always seemed utterly confident and in control. It had never occurred to her that Kate might need her.

"Oh, I don't know," Jake said, voice mild with amusement. "You look like you've been having fun." He pointed at the monkey with his chin; Smithie bared his teeth and chattered nastily at him.

"Now there, Smithie, play nice." Kate patted her bodice and skirts. "Now, where did I put . . . oh, there they are." She'd tucked a handful of dates in a convenient row of lace that bordered her sleeve and removed two now—one for Smithie, one for her. "I guess I have, at that." She saluted Jake with her glass. "Sorry that you don't like the stuff, Jake. The taste grows on one, it surely does. But then, that just leaves all the more for me, doesn't it?" And then she giggled, high-pitched, gratingly trill. She clapped her hands over her mouth, then glanced around as if to find the offending party.

Emily studied her sister worriedly. While Kate had never been abstemious, she'd also never been one to drown her sorrows, not even when Dr. Goodale had given her every reason to numb her life around the edges. "Forgive me, Kate, but for some reason I thought you weren't too fond of the monkey."

"Oh, he grows on you, too." She beamed woozily. "We've come to an agreement, he and I. And I must admit that I'm beginning to see Mr. Biskup's point." She reached up and chucked the monkey beneath his tiny chin. At that, the creature launched itself off her shoulder and disappeared, screeching, into the night. "Oh no!"

"It's all right," Jake said soothingly. "He's a wanderer by nature. He'll find his way back. You don't have to worry about him."

"Fickle fellow," she said gloomily. "Abandoning me like that." She fixed her gaze on Jake. "You won't abandon Emily, will you?" she said, more an order than a question, just before her eyes crossed.

"No, I won't abandon her," he assured her, and wondered why he felt guilty even though—technically—it was the truth. Nobody was abandoning anybody, he thought bleakly. They would merely reach the expected conclusion of their agreement. "Come on," he said, before any more uncomfortable topics could arise. "Let's take you home. I'm betting you'll sleep really well tonight."

By the time Kate and her sister were left alone, when Jake went outside to water his horse and "attend to matters," as he put it, Kate's boozy haze was wearing off. She should have snitched a bottle, she thought with some regret; what she had to do now would undoubtedly be easier with her senses dulled.

Emily was still staring after her husband, her eyes soft, her expression worried. He'd hardly spoken a word on the way home and had clomped out after murmuring the barest excuse.

"Emily, he's such a grump."

Emily shrugged. "He's got reason to be." Then she smiled fondly, as if Kate had just described a virtue rather than a serious, if not quite fatal, flaw. "And he's not always."

"Hmm." Oh hell. There was no hope for it. "You're really not coming home with me, are you?"

"Oh Kate." Emily grabbed both her hands and held on tight. "No, I'm not."

Kate squeezed her eyes shut.

"My dear, I'm so sorry. I shall miss—"

"Don't be silly," Kate told her briskly. She pulled her hands from Emily's and waved them in front of her eyes. "Save it for the goodbyes, will you? I don't intend to weep over this more than once, and you shan't expect me to."

"Kate—"

"Now then. About that husband of yours."

"Yes?" Emily asked warily.

"Emily, you must credit me with some expertise in these matters. I was married for many years, and while you may choose to disagree, the marriage worked as it had been contracted, and therefore I may offer you some useful advice."

"Of course."

"This may be difficult for you to hear. However, I hope you will give it due consideration."

"I always do."

"Then we would hardly be here, would we?" Kate held up a hand to stave off Emily's protests. "Never mind; that topic's been put to rest, and I will not speak of it again. However, I have given some thought to your husband's . . . somewhat difficult temperament."

"Kate, I assure you—"

"Emily, you will wait until I'm finished, please? This is difficult enough, and I know I taught you better manners." She took a deep breath. "You have made a number of excuses for his . . . tension. But it occurs to me that your lack of experience—don't look at me like that, Emily, if you do not lack experience in this one area I certainly do not want to know about it—has encouraged you to overlook one of the more likely possibilities."

This time, when she stopped to gulp another breath, Emily remained blessedly silent. "You are newly married. Your husband is by all accounts young and healthy. It is quite possible that you are not—that he is not—oh, the hell with it. Perhaps if you performed your wifely duties more frequently, and with more enthusiasm, his humor would be somewhat better."

"Kate!" she said, aghast.

"Oh, don't look at me like that. 'Tis common knowledge that men, if their . . . energies are forced to back up, have a tendency to become surly. Certainly Dr. Goodale was much more tractable after—"

"I don't want to hear this." Mortified, Emily clapped her hands over her ears. "I won't listen to this." *I won't think of this.* She'd always considered her sister's marriage cold-blooded and shallow. The merest suggestion of them . . . She shuddered.

"Emily, grow up," she snapped. "You're a married woman. It was not my choice, but now that you are, you could benefit from my experience. And my experience suggests that perhaps your young man isn't getting enough—enough—"

"All right!" Anything. She would have agreed to anything, if only to put an end to this embarrassing conversation. "I will . . . be accommodating. I promise."

"For some men, accommodating is not enough. One must be *encouraging*."

"Fine. I understand perfectly, I promise. No need to go into detail."

"Young women always *think* they know of such matters, young men being, generally, very easily encouraged. As time goes on, however, it helps to know a few tricks. For instance, one must discover how a particular man is best approached. Some men are most intrigued by mystery—not too much flesh, just a flash here and there of an ankle or a shoulder they hadn't expected to see. With others, however, it is necessary to be quite blatant, and—"

"Oh, hush! He might come back at any moment, and I could not bear for him to overhear us."

"Which is something else to consider. The words themselves are quite effective for some men, particularly somewhat crude words from an otherwise refined woman."

"Yes, yes! I understand. Kate, truly, I promise, if we have any . . . difficulties in that area, I will ask for your wise advice without hesitation. But I do believe I can muddle through all right for now. You must believe me when I say that Jake does *not* have a problem in this regard."

"I was only trying to help," Kate said, her voice low and wounded.

"I understand."

"To give you the benefit of my knowledge."

"I know." Now that the worst of the danger seemed to have passed, Emily attempted to soothe. "And I do appreciate it. And I do likewise realize what fortitude it took to raise such matters with your baby sister. It was very brave of you."

Kate was only slightly mollified. "It was."

"And the fact that you were willing to help to ... improve my marriage, when you were so set against it, means more to me than I can say."

Kate seized her hand and held on tightly. "I have only ever wished the best for you, Emily."

"I know. And I have had it, from the very beginning, for I have always had you for my sister."

Kate's lovely face crumpled. "Oh dear! You always do this to me. Which is why I could never remain angry at you for long." She blew out a breath and composed herself with admirable speed. "If I hadn't been so softhearted where you were concerned perhaps I would have been able to discipline you effectively and you would be more obedient."

"I was ever obedient."

"When it suited you," Kate agreed. "And I suspect that when you weren't, I rarely discovered it."

Emily frowned in mock affront. "Would I do that?"

"Yes. Just as I would ignore a promise when it suits me. To that end, I *do* have one more small technique to share with you. Dr. Goodale could never resist when—"

"Kate!" Emily laughed. "After you have a passionate fling with some handsome young gentleman you may come back and tell me every detail and I will listen, I promise. But I will *not* subject myself to any more intimation about you and Dr. Goodale. I swear, the mere thought of it will ensure I keep Jake at arm's length for weeks!" She heard the door open, didn't know whether to be relieved to be rescued or worried about Kate's embarrassing new unpredictability. If Kate started instructing Jake to be more attentive to her . . .

"Excuse me." Jake hovered in the doorway. "I thought you'd have changed by now. I'll just—" He hooked his thumb over his shoulder and began backing out.

"No, stay. I'd like to speak with you," Kate said. "Oh, don't look so panicked, Emily, it's not about *that*."

He looked to Emily for a hint. She shrugged.

"Uh, sure." He stepped in and let the door swing shut behind him. "What can I do for you?"

"I just wanted to let you know that I'm leaving."

"Leaving?" Emily studied Jake for some sign of happiness or a hint of disappointment. Once Kate left, their bargain would be complete. Would he be glad to get rid of her, to be left alone with his memories and his land? Or had some small part of him become accustomed to her presence?

Oh, don't be a goose, Em. The bare truth of it was, she wanted him to miss her when she was gone. Because, God help her, she would miss him.

"When?"

"In a hurry to be rid of me?" Kate asked dryly.

"No, of course not," he said quickly. "I just—" He stopped and pushed his fingers through his hair, forcing the waves into wild disarray. "I'm afraid you've caught me by surprise, Mrs. Goodale. We hadn't expected your visit to be so brief."

"Ah, well, I've things to attend to, you know. A life to plan." Her smile wobbled. "I'd like to stay until Tuesday, if you don't mind. For Emily's birthday."

"Stay as long as you like."

"Thank you." Her smile firmed. "Oh, Emily, I can't believe you're going to be nineteen! It seems as if I should still be helping you button your boots."

"Nineteen?" he repeated, shooting a speculative glance at Emily.

Emily winced. Oh, her chickens were really coming to roost now, weren't they?

"Yes, of course. Didn't she . . . how'd you get married without knowing her birth date? It must be on the license."

"Her birth date wasn't my uppermost consideration at the time." His smile was far too interested for Emily's peace of mind. "I'm glad to know it now, though. I'll have to put some thought into it."

"Yes, well . . ." Kate allowed herself a moment of worry, then plunged on. "It's occurred to me that I've taken gross advantage of the two of you, imposing my presence at such a time. From now on, I'll be sleeping in the tent."

Emily's heart gave a thump so hard she had to press her hand to her chest. "That's not necessary."

"Yes, it is." She might not like it, but it *was* necessary. "Oh, I admit I came here with every intention of interfering in your marriage." She shot Jake a sidelong look. "I won't apologize for that. I will always protect my sister, and I knew nothing of what I would find here."

"I understand. But there's no reason for you to sleep outside."

Kate arched a brow. "You do not wish to be alone with your wife?"

"Of course I do—"

"Then it's settled."

"—but I would feel grossly inconsiderate if my comfort is put in front of yours."

"You are not. And, given that I have traveled all this way, it would be remiss of me not to embrace the true Western experience. I am quite looking forward to sleeping outdoors."

"There'll be bugs," he warned her with a tinge of desperation as the thought of being left alone with Emily caused a riotous spurt of panic. And of something else, which worried him even more.

"Good. Then I won't be lonely," she said with an admirable show of bravery.

"I haven't been in the tent for days. It might leak for all I know."

"The weather looks perfectly fine to me."

Before he could think up another objection, she'd gathered an armful of blankets, a pillow, and a nightdress, and flounced out the door.

"Well." Emily couldn't look at him. To keep her hands busy, and to prevent them from shaking, she went to the kitchen and took down a bag of flour and a big, green-glazed bowl. "I apologize if that embarrassed you. She thought she was being helpful."

Jake leaned against the nearest wall and crossed his arms, watching her with intense, unsettling concentration. "Why the sudden approval?"

"I don't know that she approves, precisely. Kate's quite good, however, at giving in to the inevitable once it becomes apparent, and never looking back." She dared a glance at him; his face was unreadable, his gaze unwavering.

"And here I thought she'd succumbed to my charm."

"Oh that, too! Of course." She tried a smile; no luck.

He watched her as she pulled a small bowl from a warm spot behind the stove. "What are you doing?"

"I thought I'd get some bread started." Anything that would keep her occupied and *not* thinking about the fact that they were alone, for the whole night, a night Kate expected them to spend in wild and uproarious passion. "For breakfast," she clarified.

"I see." He hadn't moved. If he kept standing there, staring at her, she might just throw something at him. "And I'm sure that your sister will be convinced of our . . . entertainment, once she smells bread baking. I must be more creative than I thought."

"Oh." She set the bowl down and gripped her hands together to keep them still while she fought for an innocuous topic of conversation. There was none. Her thoughts kept circling around, worrisome to shameless and back again, unable to settle into a comfortable middle ground.

Silence simmered with expectation.

"Nineteen, huh?"

"Yes, well." Her voice cracked. "I've always been so . . . mature for my age that I often forget the precise figure."

"No doubt." He had a disturbing capacity for stillness; no wasted energy, no wasted effort. Nothing that would reveal his thoughts. She, on the other hand, had to work hard to keep from twitching under his heavy regard. "You must forget exceptionally well to be unable to dredge up the correct number when you filed and Longnecker asked you if you were twenty-one."

"Oh hell," she said, startling herself. "I give up. I checked before I came to assure that single women could apply, but it never occurred to me to investigate how old you had to be. Heavens, if I'm old enough to marry legally, surely I'm old enough to claim a few acres of land as my own. So there I was standing in front of Imbert, with this beautiful plot all picked out, dreams dancing around my head, and all my money spent. What else was I supposed to do? I couldn't think. I couldn't bear the idea of giving up after coming so far. So I just said yes, one little word. It didn't seem such a big lie at the time."

"Of course not," he murmured.

Caught, she sank into the nearest chair and sighed. "Oh, why should the government care? Dr. Goodale lied about his age to join the army when he was fourteen. After the War Between the States they gave him a medal and called him a hero. The government wants these territories settled, this land developed. As long as I can do it, why should they care about minor technicalities?"

"You justify better than anyone I've ever met."

"I know." Disconsolate, she dropped her elbow to the table and plopped her chin in her hand. "Though in most cases ignoring depressing details works for me, every now and then I'm unexpectedly brought up short by it."

She drummed her fingers against her cheek. Well, she'd also prided herself on her ability to get over things, rather than wallow in regrets. Time to prove it.

"I realize that you owe me nothing now. You could tell Kate the truth, and there's nothing I could do to stop you. You'd only have to tell Imbert my age and the land would be yours. Certainly I don't expect you to pay me for the sum we agreed on, but I am asking you to refrain from telling Kate what I've done. I've nothing to offer in return but my gratitude."

"I bet you could . . . encourage Longnecker to overlook your slight . . ." He paused, searching for the right word.

"My *lie*, you mean?" she suggested unflinchingly.

"Anticipation?" he offered.

"You don't really think I'd do that, do you?" The thought wounded her; surely he knew her better than that by now. But then, considering what he'd just learned of her, why wouldn't he think her capable of such a thing?

"No," he said without hesitation, and relief spread through her.

"Thank you." The darkness had deepened while they'd talked, cloaking him in shadows. She could barely make out his expression. Only his eyes, a hot, lively glitter, and the occasional gleam of his teeth as he spoke. So much mystery there; she'd learned so much about him tonight, and it only made her hungry to know more.

And she'd never know, she thought bleakly. Their days were numbered now, less than a week, and she'd never see him again. "And thank you for not giving me away to Kate immediately."

He was silent, absolutely still, as if he didn't even wish to disturb the air. Yet she *felt* him, as if she absorbed the breath he exhaled and was warmed by the heat that radiated from his body.

Finally he said, "And, as far as I'm concerned, your little exaggeration with the government is just that—between you and the government. I'll honor our original agreement."

"That's—"

"If you thank me again, I'm taking it back."

"All right. We're agreed, then." She extended her hand, and he contemplated it for a moment before enveloping it in his. He pumped it once, quick and hard, before pulling his hand away.

Damn, I knew I shouldn't have touched her, Jake thought. He was too susceptible to her now. Too aware that they were completely alone.

He couldn't believe all he'd spilled to her when she'd followed him from the Blevinses'. He'd kept the story locked away for the past year and never felt any urge to burden someone else with it. Even deep into his cups, he'd never been one to pour out his sad tale. But she—she'd drawn it all from him with just a few soft words and the warmth of her arms around him, as if she knew precisely which twig to tug to get the entire dam to come tumbling down.

It stripped him bare, left him feeling raw and tender and all-too-susceptible to her. What must she think of him now?

Unable to stand there any longer and feel the weight of her regard on him, unwilling to peer through the gloom and find unwelcome emotions in her eyes, he turned abruptly. He shoved aside a bench, snatched a pillow from the bed, and tossed it to the floor. Then he grabbed a blanket and began to wrap himself in it.

"What are you doing?" Her quiet voice floated to him through the darkness, a siren call. *This is what you don't have anymore. This is what you'll never have.*

This is what you'll miss.

"Going to bed." He snarled it, surly enough to make himself wince, but damn, if she spoke to him again . . . if she so much as touched him, he'd forget all the things that it was his sentence to remember.

He'd just gotten the scratchy wool wrapped around him when he heard the whisper of her footsteps and he froze. She stood a foot from him, her head bent. A cloud shifted outside, moonlight washing through the small window. He could see the straight, pale line of her part, the gloss of her hair streaming down and merging with the dark.

The sound of their breathing saturated the air, seeming louder than it could possibly be because he was so attuned to it. His own, heavy and ragged; he could feel his lungs dragging it in. Hers, shallow and quick, perhaps frightened. As well she should be, he thought, since just the sound of her respiration spurred the savage bite of desire.

And then she lifted her head, her eyes huge in the dark. She brought up her hand—slow, so slow, agonizing—and touched the fold of blanket where he held it against his collarbone.

"There's no reason for you to sleep on the floor."

Chapter 15

It was a struggle for him to speak. Even more so to make the words come out that he *must* say.

"There's every reason for me to sleep on the floor," he told her. "Even more reason to run out the door, sprint a few miles, and sleep where I drop. And if you don't know that, you're far more of a fool than I believed you to be."

"You're making this more complicated than it needs to be."

He narrowed his eyes at her. "And you have no idea at all what you're playing with here."

"I think I do." He hurt and Emily wanted to make it go away. Maybe not forever—she'd few illusions about that—but for a few hours, one night, yes, she'd mute it if she could. "And even if I don't, is that yours to decide?"

She stepped closer yet and slid her arms through the gap in the blanket. In the brief time it had swathed him, he'd heated the space inside, and his warmth enveloped her immediately. It held his scent as well, and she breathed in, memorizing, reveling.

Jake held himself completely rigid. Because if he moved he couldn't be sure of what he would do. If he would run, if he would push her away. Or if he would grab her and hang on, bury himself in the succor she offered and never let go.

So long. So long since he'd felt the promise of possibilities. So long since he'd let himself sink into the delight that human touch offered, allowed the fantasy of what might be to carry him away.

Her hands rested lightly against his sides. She rubbed her cheek against his chest, and his heart hammered.

"Mmm. You smell good," she whispered. "Why is that, do you suppose? Like warmth and home and a hundred good things all rolled into one."

"Em—"

"Shhh. Don't talk."

He squeezed his eyes shut, lowered his head, and breathed in. Flowers, soap, spice. Even a little smoke. *Emily.* "You smell good, too."

"Good. I'd hate to think that, when I'm standing this close, you think I stink."

He burst into laughter. He'd been dreaming of passion, and she'd been pondering odors!

"Well, that eases my worries," he said. "And here I thought you might have been attempting seduction."

"You did, did you?"

"Or at least flirtation."

She leaned her head back, her smile pleased, enticing. "And what if I am?"

"Emily." He grabbed her arms. He was almost sure he meant to push her away. But her breasts lay against his chest, soft and sweet and feminine, delicious, forbidden, and he couldn't force his arms to do what they should.

"Don't scold," she said, and pursed her lips in a way that she must know looked delectably kissable. "I didn't say which."

"Oh," he replied, sounding more disappointed than he should, given that seduction was impossible and even flirtation forbidden.

"Would it be so bad? Even the flirtation?"

"*Bad*, no." It'd be so much easier, he thought, if he could keep from looking at her. So he didn't view the pretty curve of her mouth, the fine slope of her nose. He knew her eyes, knew the way they softened in sympathy and lit up in laughter. Wanted, far too much, to see how'd they darken in passion. He'd no right to want that and even less to hope for it. "I'm sure it'd be very, very good," he continued. The rough edge to his voice would tell any woman with experience just what effect she had on him; his only hope was that Emily couldn't know. "But just as wrong."

"Why?"

"Why?" Exasperation spiked through the simmer of desire, warned him just how near the edge he was. "Em, you know why."

"Do I?" And then she lifted to her toes and kissed him. Just kissed him, mouth closed, warm lips, a simple kiss that burst upon and flooded his senses.

Sweet, so very sweet, a kiss that pretended to be nothing, portended nothing, meant nothing but *I want my mouth on yours*. And yet it dissolved good intentions, blunted worries, brushed aside all the *should*s.

He didn't move. Didn't dare. And she was inexpert, holding her mouth still, no tricks with her tongue, no lips rubbing to and fro to draw him in. It made no difference. She was enchantment enough, the delicious wonder of her lips, soft and warm, pressed against him. And the lack of motion became enticement itself, spurring him to notice details that might have been lost in the rush: the precise temperature of her mouth. The brush of her breath against his cheek. The plush velvet texture of her lips. The gentle press of her breasts against his chest.

And then—a moment of time, an eternity—she at last pulled away. Her hand rested against his chest, mostly on cotton, one fingertip in the V of his collar, one tiny point bare against his skin. It was the most arousing thing he could imagine, that little bit of her touching him. So small and innocuous, yet he flamed beneath her touch.

"There," she murmured. "Look at that. The earth didn't open wide and swallow us up. Lightning didn't strike. Nothing terrible happened at all."

Nothing terrible? It was utter disaster. For he understood with brutal truth that his life had just changed. He could not go back; he could no longer ignore that his body still lived, his passions still lived, his need for warmth and companionship and, yes, sex, was still very alive. He'd not permanently buried them as he'd assumed. And now awakened they held a sharp and cruel urgency all the more powerful for being ignored so long.

Stop. He was almost certain he meant to say it. *No more.* Surely he intended to shout it. But then she took her hands and spread the collar of his shirt, widening the V, and pressed her mouth right there, in the curve of his neck, and a groan tore from his throat of its own accord.

She slid her hands—small, sweet, healing hands—down his chest, over his ribs, letting them settle for a moment at the sides of his waist. Her mouth burned his skin, a light press. And then—ah, a miracle!—her mouth opened, warm, damp, and her tongue slid into his throat's hollow, and he had to struggle to draw in air.

"Jesus, Em."

"Hmm?" The word hummed against him, her lips vibrating.

His teeth clamped together, he had to force the words out. "You gotta stop."

"I do?" Her mouth roamed higher, below his chin, the angle of his jaw. She kissed the corner of his mouth, and his thoughts twisted and tangled so he had to work his way through them.

How could she not know? "Yes," he repeated.

"Yes?" In order to look at him she stopped kissing him, and before he thought to stop it he groaned again, this time from sheer disappointment. "You haven't given me a good reason yet."

"You know why."

"No, I don't."

Anger burned low, an anger he knew she didn't deserve, born of frustration and wanting.

"I like touching you," she said. Without warning, those hands that were resting, still and wonderful, at his waist grabbed fistfuls of cloth and yanked, pulling both his shirt and the knit one beneath it from his waistband. She kept right on going, shoving the fabric up, exposing his belly and half his chest. It left him gasping, too shocked to protest. *Not that you would have anyway*, the guilty, honest part of him whispered.

"You like it, don't you?" she asked. "And don't lie to me, Jake. I can tell you do."

"Of course I like it," he snapped. "What's that got to do with anything?"

"It should have a lot to do with it, don't you think?" Her gaze was fixed below his neck. He could see her only slightly, mysterious and seductive in the dusky gloom. "Heavens, I wish it was lighter, so I could see you." She touched him instead, her palms flat against the naked flesh she'd exposed, fingers wide, covering as much area as she could manage. He jerked, felt every muscle in his body leap to full alert, just in case she'd be heading their way next. "Oh, you feel good."

"Emily!"

"Oh, you're not going to make me stop, are you? I'm having fun. Aren't you?" It should have sounded coy. Except her voice was sensible and interested. As if there was nothing outrageous in her actions, nothing wild and out of character, nothing that threatened to roar through his world like a tornado, leaving utter destruction in its wake.

"How can you not know it's not that simple?" Her thumb had found his nipple, and she was brushing it back and forth, her face a study in fascinated concentration, and he thought his knees threatened to buckle beneath him.

"Why can't we let it be simple?" she asked seriously. "We're not . . . I'm not suggesting anything irrevocable. Just letting myself indulge my curiosity a little, and you letting yourself be . . . cherished for a few moments. It's not the end of the world. It's not even the beginning of it. It's just . . . us. For this one moment. Not even the next one, not the next second. Just let me touch you for right now."

It sounded easy when she put it like that. Utterly forgivable, outrageously tempting. Her eyebrows made a perfect arch over her eyes, the most elegant curve he'd ever seen. And since when did he notice women's eyebrows? Or the way the corners of her eyes tilted up just a fraction, which made her look happy even when she wasn't?

Helplessly caught, he said, "Jesus, you're so *pretty*."

"Pretty?" She beamed, a sudden glimpse of daybreak, completely delighted. "You think so?"

"Oh yeah," he admitted fervently. He could feel okay about saying that; if no one had told her, it was about damn time someone did, and he was glad to be the one to do it. "Prettier than morning. Prettier than the prairie the first day it blooms."

She hugged him. And he just stood there with his eyes closed and let the warmth seep into him, lighten up dark corners, ease pains that had been a part of him so long he wouldn't know what to do without them.

"Can I ask you something?" she mumbled against him.

He couldn't help but be suspicious. She was obviously more devious than he'd given her credit for or they wouldn't be in this position right now. "I guess so."

"Not exactly swinging the door wide open, are you?"

Her hands got busy again, in slow, easy strokes that brushed along his spine and flirted with his waistband. To distract himself, he told her, "I guess I'm not a wide-open kind of guy. But go ahead."

"Then I will." She licked his nipple. He yelped, jumped away.

"My Lord, Em."

"Oh," she said, sighing in disappointment. "You didn't like it?"

"*That* was your question? If you could do that?"

"Yes. Not a good idea, huh?"

"No." Not a good idea at all. It had lasted all of a second and he still felt it, thrumming through his veins, pooling low in his belly, making him so damn hard it hurt. "Where the hell did you learn that?"

"I didn't learn anything, isn't it obvious?" He'd been so hot, Emily remembered. A hard, tiny pebble against her tongue. "I'm sorry. I didn't mean to hurt you."

"Oh, don't look so sad. I can't stand it. You didn't hurt me."

"You jumped."

"Because it felt so good it damn near killed me."

"Really?"

"Really," he said, sounding most unhappy about it.

"Good." She sidled closer, slow and calculating as a stalking cat. "Then I can do it again."

"You—" The battle was easy to see, the strain in his face, the fierce struggle in his eyes. "Do it again," he ordered, voice harsh, almost cruel. Maybe it should have scared her, but instead excitement spiked.

And so she did. He shuddered when she flicked him with her tongue. Shook when she licked, flat and long and slow. Moaned when she tangled her fingers in the soft hair that covered his chest.

She'd only meant to give him some small joy. She'd thought she could make him forget for a few brief moments, this man who never allowed himself respite. She'd planned to stroke him, soothe him, give him a little peace and happiness despite himself.

But she'd underestimated the effect it would have on *her*. She loved having that big, strong body at her disposal. The discovery that one small caress from her along his ribs could make him shake intoxicated her. The taste of him fascinated her; she wanted to hold the flavor on her tongue and savor the richness.

Such a marvel. She lost track of the time she stood in the middle of that room and just touched him. She loved the feel of his chest as it expanded with each breath, contracted as he released it. She took it as a challenge to discover a soft spot on him but couldn't find one. His ribs were like iron, his belly ridged with steel.

She loved knowing that, right at that moment, he thought of nothing but her. Loved even more knowing that he'd wanted to say no and hadn't been able to. It made her feel powerful and sexual, irresistible in a way she'd never even wanted to be before.

But, finally, it wasn't enough. She tingled, in all sorts of places. Burned. *Wanted.*

She cuddled up close and rubbed her breasts against his chest. There, that was what she'd needed. It seemed like it might be even better if her own shirt was gone like his, but the pressure eased the ache for a moment until she realized it had only moved it further down.

"Em!" He kept saying her name. It burst out of him, short, hard, as if it gave him some release. And she knew he never once forgot who touched him.

Helplessly, Jake thrust his hips against her once, need surging painfully through him. "Em, you gotta stop, it's been so long, I can't—"

"Let me do this." She'd wrapped herself around him, close as her petticoats allowed. There must be lace on her cuff; he could feel it at the small of his back, scratching as her hands streaked over his skin, now greedy and searching with an expertise that she'd learned with astonishing speed.

"You don't know what you're doing," he told her, though it cost him.

"Yes, I do," she said with absolute conviction. "I know exactly what I'm doing. Exactly what I *want* to be doing."

Just a little more, he promised himself. Surely he'd stop her then. What could it hurt, just a little more? Though it *did* hurt, that sweet, joyous pain he'd denied himself for so long. He'd almost convinced himself that it wouldn't feel like this, that he'd be able to go on without it. God, what a fool he'd been! He should have known the instant he'd seen her, the first second he wanted her, that he could never go back.

For both their sakes, they couldn't continue much longer. He knew that. In thirty seconds he'd pull away. Maybe a minute, no more. And then her hands glided around his hips and hovered over the front of his pants and his breath snagged in his throat. Surely she wouldn't . . . oh, damn, he wanted her to.

He wrapped his hands around her wrists, holding her in place.

"Oh, don't stop me," she whispered. "Only this, I promise. Just for a little while. I want to know, Jake. I may never get another chance at this—"

"You'll get another chance," he said, even as the thought twisted savagely inside him.

She looked at him directly, a rare, unsmiling expression, her mouth sober and eyes glinting. "Not with you, I won't."

No. It was good she understood that. Even better if he did. And everything inside him screamed in protest at the knowledge.

Perhaps she had begun this for his sake, Emily thought. Because she wanted to give him some small respite before she left. But that plan had faded long ago, lost in a whirl and rush of this driving need. To know, to feel, to experience.

He said nothing. She could hear the air hissing in and out as he breathed, over the thunder of her own pulse in her ears. And then, a fraction so slight she barely noticed it at first, his grip on her wrists loosened.

Lightly she skimmed her hands over the front of his pants and he jerked violently in response, pressing himself into her palm. "Ooh," she breathed. "I didn't know."

He filled her hands. Hard, long, hot—she knew those words. But she'd never felt them like this, a living thing beneath her touch.

She stroked him once, felt him shudder against her. "Do you like it?"

His laugh was rueful, pained. "*Like* isn't the word for it, no."

"Is there something else I should do?"

"No," he managed. "No, you're doing fine."

So she stopped worrying if she was doing it right and let herself enjoy. He was so *different* from her. He'd dropped his head back, exposing his throat, and she sank her teeth in, right there.

"Em!"

She loved how he said that, every time she tried something new. An exclamation, rather than just her name, gasped out in wonder. For the rest of her life, when someone called her name, plain Emily, it would never sound exactly the same to her. She'd hear wonder in it. Maybe she'd intended to give him a gift, but she'd received one, too, learning of the power contained in her touch.

But she soon cursed the fabric that barred her from exploring further. His outlines were muted, her investigations constrained. There seemed nothing for it but to rid herself of such a nuisance.

She reached for his buttons. He sucked in his stomach on a sudden breath.

"Em, you can't."

"Yes, I can. I *am*. See?" Just to prove it, she popped open one button, so easily she wondered why people went around fastened up all the time when buttons were so easy to undo and there was so much of interest beneath them.

"You don't understand."

"Then tell me. You feel good." She opened another, pushed his drawers down an inch, and let her fingers dance against the small wedge of skin uncovered. There were few strands of hair, with more spring than the hair on his head, and she wondered if it were just as dark. And then she shivered, just as he had, with wicked pleasure and anticipation. "I feel good. Heavens, we're standing in the middle of the room, and I'm fastened to my chin, and you haven't lost a single piece of clothing. How much of a sin could this be?"

But it felt like a sin. A wonderful, irresistible, miraculous sin.

And then she couldn't wait anymore. Two more buttons fell open like ripened grapes from a vine and then the next one defeated her, clinging stubbornly to its hole. "Oh hell," she said, and gave up. She burrowed her hand inside his drawers, and found him at last. The fabric bound her hand close, made her grip him hard.

"Emily, *stop*, it's been so long, I—"

"No." She was far too captivated to stop. On a man like Jake, hard, rough-edged, to find skin like the finest silk—who would have thought it? On his sex, which was hard as the rest of him. Harder even. The tip was smooth but there were ridges farther down, veins that pulsed as she explored. "Let me, Jake. Let me make you feel good."

And then he grabbed her, his arms around her back, and clutched her to him so her hand was crushed between them. His hips thrust once, twice, and she felt wet heat flood her palm.

Release. That was the term, wasn't it? She understood the phenomenon vaguely. But this was *wonderful* release, as tension shuddered from him and sounds burst from his throat and he poured himself into her hand.

She wrapped her free hand around his back and held on as tightly as he. At length his shudders slowed, then finally ended. She was sorry to have it stop. She loved to feel him completely out of himself, given over to her and the pleasure she brought him.

But then he let go. He grabbed her hand and yanked it away from him, shoved her away so hard she stumbled.

Smiling, she met his gaze. Then her smile faded. His face was hard and harsh, his mouth set, his eyes blazing.

"Pleased with yourself, are you?" He began to remove his shirt, found it still fastened. He grabbed the sides in both hands and jerked. Buttons flew. One bounced off her chest, another pinged on the floor. He tore it off, grabbed her hand, and scrubbed the sticky wetness from her with the mutilated shirt.

"You couldn't listen, could you?" His cleansing was not gentle. Her skin burned by the time he'd scoured every bit of evidence from her palm.

"But I—"

He went on in a voice so savage each word cut. "I said stop, tried to tell you it had been too long since I . . . but no, you always know better, don't you?" He rubbed the soiled shirt over his lower belly, then two quick, violent swipes further down, as if he could wipe away what they'd done.

He balled the shirt up and hurled it into a dark corner like a soldier might throw a live grenade, as hard and far away as he could. With swift, jerky motions he buttoned his pants, tugged down his undershirt, and stood there before her, a different man from the half-naked, sensually compelling one he'd been two minutes ago.

"Was that your *prescription*, Dr. Bright?" he said with a nasty sneer. "You were gonna treat me with sex? Give the man an orgasm and walk away, satisfied that you'd cured him of what ailed him?"

She flinched, the words more painful than a blow. It didn't help to know that in some ways he was right. "It's not that simple."

"How's it not that simple? All for me, nothing for you, as uncomplicated and one-sided as if you'd stitched up a wound and sent me on my way when you finished your task?"

"I just wanted to make you happy," she said weakly. Her head spun, her heart pounded. It had felt so right, she thought in confusion. How had it gone so wrong?

"It's not your goddamn job to make me happy!" he shouted.

"Somebody has to," she shot back. She'd had

enough; she would not allow him to turn her good intentions into something evil. "Lord knows you'd never allow it yourself, unless somebody *made* you."

"Look at you." His gaze raked her, top to toe, his mouth twisted as if he didn't like what he saw. She could have been stripped bare and she wouldn't be nearly as uncomfortable. "Your hair is barely mussed. That's not what a woman who'd just had her first experience with a man should look like." And then his eyes met hers, a flare of heat within them—anger or passion, she didn't know. Maybe both. "By God, I won't allow it."

"Jake—"

He bent, put his shoulder against her belly, and straightened. She dangled over his shoulder like a half-full sack of grain. He spun for the bed.

"All right, Jake, you made your point. My hair's messed up now. You can put me down."

"Oh, I'll put you down." He flopped her onto the bed, quick and jarring. And then he stood there, breathing hard, his hands on his hips, staring down, and she felt a trickle of . . . not fear, precisely, but unease. Which was absurd—they'd been alone many a time, and he'd never done her a shred of harm. She knew him better than that; any damage he intended was aimed directly at himself.

But this was a different man from the one she'd become comfortable with over the past weeks. Harder. Unpredictable.

And undeniably exciting, capable of things she could only imagine.

"I'm sorry," she said.

"Are you?"

But she remembered the feel of him against her. The way he'd shaken in her arms, a storm that she, just Emily Bright, had caused. The wonder of his sex in her hand, and the way he'd shouted his release, and she knew she couldn't truly regret it. "I'm sorry that you're . . . unhappy about what happened," she temporized.

"Unhappy? Is that what you think I am?"

She started to push herself up.

"Don't move."

"But—"

In an instant—she hadn't a moment to prepare— he was upon her, full length, pressing her into the mattress, pressing the breath from her body.

"I told you not to move."

"Jake!" And then, softer, when she realized how near his mouth was to hers, how his breath reached her with each word he spoke, "Jake."

He reached down, pulled her arms over her head, and linked them, circling her wrists easily with one hand. "Are you going to move?"

She couldn't if she wanted to. And, God help her, she didn't want to. He was heavy, in a wonderful way that reminded her of all the differences between them—that he was big and hard and male, and she was none of those things.

He took her silence for assent. "Good."

Still holding her wrists, he rolled to one side. His free hand grabbed fistfuls of her clothes, rucking them up, skirts and petticoats, burying her chest, her neck, in froths of cotton, the lacy edge brushing her lips, until she was completely exposed from the waist down except for her knickers.

She bucked once, and he brought up his knee across her legs, trapping her.

"Jake, stop."

"Stop?" His voice was mild. "What an interesting word. Apparently it doesn't mean what I thought it did, for I could have sworn I used it not long ago without the effect I intended."

He was staring below her waist. There was nothing to see, she consoled herself. The outline of her legs beneath white cotton. No more than she'd see of a man in trousers.

But then, ever so slowly, he reached down and beneath her to unbutton the flap of her drawers and flipped it away. With just one finger, he nudged open the slit he'd exposed. Wider, and wider, as he circled his finger, circled but never quite touched her sex, and she nearly came off the bed.

"There," he murmured. "That's better."

Against her hip she could feel him grow again, harden and lengthen, an astonishingly rapid change. Because of me, she thought, and it excited her nearly as much as his hand hovering near her intimate parts.

"You should stop," she said, and it sounded weak even to her own ears.

"Can you really," he asked softly, "tell me you don't want me to do this?" His finger came a bit closer, tracing the edge of the opening, now and then brushing a curl, skimming a bare inch of flesh.

"I should."

"Oh, come now. You lie so prettily and easily. Lie to me now. Tell me you want me to stop."

She couldn't say the word. *Stop.* A short, choppy word, easily formed, much simpler than some of the lies she'd told, for every bit as noble a reason.

She told herself she couldn't say it because it would be unfair to Jake, who'd held himself from women for so long, to hear she didn't want him.

Except that lie rang hollow, too. For she didn't want him to leave her. She ached, she hurt, she needed.

"You've got three seconds," he warned her.

She opened her mouth. Nothing came out.

"Too late." And then he bent and put his mouth there—oh Lord, right *there*. She yelped, bolted up.

"Hush," he murmured, his mouth hovering a bare inch above her; when he spoke, his lips brushed lightly over her sex, and she shivered, all over, toe to tip.

"You *can't*," she told him, truly shocked. And unimaginably titillated.

"You've nothing to say about it, remember? You had your turn, now it's mine." He released her wrists so he could slip down further, giving him better access. "Leave your hands where they are."

It had never occurred to her to move. Her limbs were no longer under her control. Her body, her scandalized mind, he'd stolen them both for his own and played them to his will.

And then his mouth came down again, harder this time. He held himself still for a moment, giving her time to adjust to the feel of him there, scalding heat, moist softness, wicked bliss.

She couldn't see him. Her skirts and petticoats frothed around him, hiding him from view. The rest of the room was dark, and blood roared in her ears, muting the sound of her cries. It was as if all her other senses had dimmed, subverting to the sharp and crucial pleasure of the flesh.

She couldn't move. Was afraid to in case it might push him away. Might ruin this piercing delight, or might prove too much, driving her to someplace from which she might never recover.

But even in that stillness she soon felt herself pulsing up, the physical sensation growing stronger, richer, more insistent. And when his tongue joined in the play, one long slow stroke flat against her, she hurtled over the edge, into a quick, shuddering peak where her nerves showered pleasure through every corner of her body.

She was still dazed, drifting down into limp and sated relaxation, when he suddenly jerked away, yanking her skirts down to cover her. He stood by the bed, as unsmiling and intimidating as the night they'd first met.

"There. We're even," he said, the words holding a cruel edge.

His mouth was wet; it gleamed when he spoke, reflecting a small wash of moonlight. From *her*, she thought, instantly and acutely embarrassed; she could feel the dampness between her thighs.

He whipped his pillow and blanket off the bed with violence that left a breeze in its wake, tossed them on the floor, and threw himself down with careless disregard for his bones.

The silence flattened, drew into a vacuum that

seemed to swallow all sound leaving a dense, complete quiet, stripped of familiar, comforting nighttime rustles. He might not have even been in the room; though she strained for the sound, even evidence of his breathing eluded her.

It's over, she thought, and squeezed her eyes shut against the night.

It's over, and what a fool I was to believe it might ever have begun.

Chapter 16

⌢⌢⌣⌣⌢

The next three days seemed to take three years; long, grueling, joyless years.

Who'd have thought Jake would be so good at pretending? He threw himself into his role—ensuring, Emily figured, that nothing would delay Kate's departure a second longer than necessary. But he played the besotted husband so well that even she, who knew better, almost believed. Except each time he looked at her, there was nothing in his eyes. Even the anger, even the grief there when she'd met him would have seemed better now than his blank indifference.

He touched her often. Outwardly husbandly, affectionate caresses with hands that were completely cold. Touched her the same impersonal way he did the metal bars and gears of his press, a necessary contact to be neither enjoyed nor detested.

Emily knew she pretended every bit as well. Her

smile grew brighter, her conversation more lively, her glances at Jake more lingering. And if it went on one more day she was going to collapse into a screaming heap. On her birthday, a cheerless, gray day more suited to October than July, Emily plastered on a smile the size of Montana and it flickered only slightly when, beneath Kate's assessing gaze, Jake kissed her, his lips warm and firm and hateful in the utter lack of emotion behind them.

Emily counted each day until Kate's departure, certain that anything had to be better than this dreadful limbo, her nerves stretched as thin as cheap thread. But when she finally stood outside the shack with Kate in her beautiful green traveling suit and piles of luggage before her, Jake hovering silently at her back, and realized it would all soon be over, a hollow ache began in her chest that seemed to have every intention of staying around for a while.

"Are you sure you don't want us to take you on into town?" Emily asked around the lump in her throat. "It doesn't seem right to send you on your way alone."

"Oh heavens," Kate said, her emerald hat feather bobbing. "I've no intention of making a scene right there at the coach stop. I've never appeared in public with red eyes and I'm not about to start now. No, I'd rather say my goodbyes here and be done with it."

"I suppose so." For the first time Emily wondered if perhaps she should return to Philadelphia with Kate after all. Certainly there was nothing for her here except a few memories both piercingly sweet and painful at the same time. And Kate, her chin set at a brave angle, would be alone for the first time in her life.

"Promise me," Emily said. "Promise me you won't marry Mr. Ruckman just because you need someone to fuss over."

Kate frowned. "I wouldn't—" Then she sighed and gave in. "All right, I admit it. I would have married him for you, and been glad of it, too. Not to mention *right* to do it. But I won't do it just for my sake."

"Do you promise me?"

"Yes," Kate said, exasperated. "I promise."

Emily's tension eased one notch. Hardly noticeable as there was plenty left.

"Kate, what *are* you going to do?"

A shadow grayed the brilliant blue of her eyes. "Oh, I'm not sure," she said, injecting an airy note that fooled no one. "The doctor did leave me *some* small resources. It won't support me forever, but it'll keep body together for a while." She shrugged. "Perhaps I'll open a dress shop."

"If you don't fall madly in love and get married first," Emily said. "And maybe you'll even wait for Anthea and me to get there for the wedding."

"I wouldn't worry about that. I've had quite enough of marriage for one lifetime, I think."

"Oh Kate, don't say that. You should have a wild, passionate affair at the very least."

"Emily!" she exclaimed with the appropriate shock. And then "Hmm" as her expression grew thoughtful.

"Art's here," Jake said softly, nodding at the old

red farm wagon that served as Art's rolling studio. "He even took all that junk out of the back for you."

"But of course." As if knowing that one more look at her sister would start her dripping, Kate switched to pondering Art on his wagon. "Maybe I'll get myself a monkey," she mused.

"Kate, why didn't you ever leave him? I always wondered," Emily asked, figuring she might never have another opportunity. "We could have gone to stay with Gabriel and Anthea. You know we could have."

"Me, living in Colorado? Can you imagine? The barbed wire would have snagged all my stockings in no time." Then she sobered. "I made an agreement, Emily. There were no surprises. The doctor held to his half of the agreement; I was obligated to live up to mine." She touched Emily's cheek. "And, given the same circumstances, I would do it again."

"Thank you. I don't know if you realize how much I . . ." She searched for the right words. How do you thank someone who gave up fifteen years of her life for you?

"Emily, there's no thanks to be given. We are family. Always. You'd do the same for me and I well know it. It was only an accident of birth that gave me the privilege."

"Darn it." Emily grabbed her in a fierce hug that made Kate clamp her hand on the top of her head to keep from disarranging her hat. Kate wrapped her arms around her and squeezed until tears threatened.

"Let me go, now. I've spent some time on this

coiffure—who knows who might be on the train?—
and I'd be most put out if you ruined all my work."

"All right. Travel safe." She released her sister,
watching while Jake handed her formally up to the
narrow bench next to Art, where Kate fluffed her
skirts and settled herself as gracefully as if taking
her seat at the opera. Art chirruped to his old gray
mare, which leaned forward and plodded toward
town.

Emily waved. "Promise me," she shouted, "that
you'll do *exactly* what you wish for the next month,
and you won't give practicality a single thought.
One grand adventure. I insist."

"I'll think about it," Kate called behind her, waving so hard her feather whipped through the air as if
the wind blew ten times harder than it did.

"Promise!"

"I promise." The breeze caught her resigned
laughter, carried it behind her after the wagon faded
into the distance.

"Well." Emily folded her hands before her and
turned to face . . . she wasn't even sure what to call
him anymore. Were they back to Mr. Sullivan? "I'd
better pack."

Jake studied her face warily. He'd been prepared
for her to burst into tears any second. Her sister was
gone, she'd lost her gamble with him, and that
night . . . He shied away from the thought. That
night was more than he could think about at the moment for more reasons than one. But she faced him
with her eyes perfectly dry, her smile wide and
pretty. And utterly false; he knew her well enough to

discern the difference now between the ever-present smile that meant no more than one painted on a china doll and the true one, the rarer one, that started in her heart and bloomed outward.

"I'll help you pack."

"Can't wait to get rid of me?"

"That's not what I meant." Though perhaps true all the same. Better she leave while the anger at what she'd done was keen. It would make it easier, allowing him to welcome the solitude that must be his life.

One eyebrow lifted. "Didn't you?"

The corners of her mouth trembled. The motion caught his attention, tempted him to kiss her right there. He knew the feel of her now, and the taste, and despite the fact that he'd have given much for that blazing, agonizing night never to have happened, he wanted her. Even more now, though he wouldn't have thought it possible.

"All right then. Holler when you're ready."

Her words were clipped. "It won't take long."

It startled Emily to realize, as she sorted through the items, how few things she could claim as her own. So many felt like hers: the table she'd oiled and scrubbed until it gleamed, the mattress she'd restuffed, the iron skillet she'd rubbed with sand for nearly an hour before deeming it ready for her cornbread.

But they weren't hers. They belonged to another life, his life, and he undoubtedly had far more memories of them than she did. Memories of his wife, who'd owned them first, owned *him* first, body and soul, and obviously always would.

Had it been wrong of her to try and drag him back to life? She'd no more been able to leave him alone in his grief than she could pass a man bleeding in the street and not be driven to dress his wounds.

But sometimes one simply had to accept the inevitable and move on. Perhaps with regret, and certainly having learned from the experience, but it did no good to cling to things one could never change.

She bent down, grabbed the handle of a suitcase in each hand, and headed out the door, nearly colliding with Jake on the way.

"Oh. There you are."

"Couldn't wait any longer, huh?" she asked. The words had bite, but she didn't feel much like softening them.

He looked at her suitcases, the one small crate she'd already dragged outside. "Is that it? I thought you had more stuff."

"New life, light baggage." She shrugged. "Montana was hard on my wardrobe. Isn't worth dragging it along. You've quite a nice rag collection, if you want them."

"You can't chance bumping into Kate. If you want to stay a few hours—"

"No," she said, shaking her head emphatically. The thought of staying there one more minute with his anger and regret was unbearable. "No, it'll be fine."

"I won't be here."

"It'll be fine," she said again, firmly. Even if he was gone, the shack held too many memories. The sooner she put it behind her the better.

"I'll go hitch up the wagon," he said without inflection.

"No need. Joe's coming for me."

She thought she'd learned to read him by now. But the thick curve of his eyebrows shadowed his eyes, hiding any emotion; his mouth held a hard, impassive line.

Silently he reached into his pocket and pulled out a black wallet, the leather holding a dull sheen, the fold so worn the wallet had nearly torn in two. He opened it, counted out a thin stack of bills, and thrust it in her direction.

Nausea curled in her stomach and she couldn't bring herself to take the money. Though the sensible part of her knew she had very little choice and even fewer options, she couldn't look at those bills in his strong, familiar hand, a hand that had stroked her intimately only a few nights before, and not feel as if he were paying her off.

"Oh no." Jake grabbed her hand and shoved the bills into it, forcing her fingers around the money when she didn't take it of her own accord. "We made a deal. You're taking it." And there was no way in hell, Jake thought, he was going to spend the next few months worrying about whether Emily had ended up in a cat house or starving to death because he'd kicked her out of the only place she had. It was a small enough price to pay to quiet his conscience.

She grimaced at the money in her hand as if he'd just handed her a ball of horseshit. "You don't owe me anything. The land's rightfully yours and you know it."

Oh God, why wouldn't she just *go*? If they didn't get this over with he was going to end up with even more regrets than he already had, and he'd tallied a life's worth as it was.

"Christ, Em, it's not like you've been lolling around while you're here. You've cleaned up the house, and fed me more than once, and even fixed the damn stovepipe."

She smiled wryly. "And even cleared at least a whole two square yards of land."

Even now he couldn't resist her and gave her a weak smile that caused her own to break wide and beautiful. "At least."

Damn. If only she wouldn't smile. It spurred an uncomfortable mix of emotions in him, a tangled mess of desire and anger and remorse and a dozen other things he'd just as soon not examine.

A shout and the rattle of an approaching wagon rescued him. Joe stopped the wagon a good forty yards away and hollered again. "You ready to go?"

"Yes, of course." Under her breath, she added, "I don't think Joe's going to allow you within swinging distance anytime soon."

He wedged the crate against his hip with one arm before grabbing both suitcases in his other hand.

"I can manage," she said.

He ignored her. He acknowledged Joe with a brief nod when he reached the wagon, which Joe evaded by taking an extreme interest in his gelding's tail. By the time he'd loaded her luggage into the wagon bed dusted with the remnants of a load of hay, she'd avoided the awkwardness of having him hand her up by climbing in herself.

The crate had no more than tipped into place before the wagon jolted on its way.

Emily tried to keep her eyes forward. She'd never seen the good in looking backward; what was done was done. The future was all that mattered.

It wasn't her fault that the wagon hit a rut and tipped her sidewise. Wasn't her intent for the dip to force her head to swing to the side, making her glance back.

But, once she had, she was caught. Frozen, her neck at an awkward angle, gripping the hard edge of the rough board seat.

Behind him spread the land, stretching infinite and featureless to those who'd not known the place. But she knew better, and saw all the variety in bright relief, the dozens of shades of green and gold, the ripple and dip of subtle contours, the ever-shifting color of the sky.

And him, utterly alone upon it, hard-planed face and broad, rigid shoulders, as contained and forbidding as his land, the richness and reward he offered as inaccessible to the weak and timid. Despite everything, she hoped with all her heart that someday there might be a woman he'd allow close, one who'd be strong enough to share it with him.

She lifted her hand, fingers bent; not a wave, but a hopeful gesture. *Be safe, be well. Be, if not happy, at least not unhappy.*

Chapter 17

As Jake had once buried himself in alcohol he now buried himself in work. Over the next month he put out two issues of the *Register*, as he named his fledging newspaper. He finished the lean-to on the house and fashioned a more permanent stable for Reg. And spent an inordinate amount of time trying to convince himself that he'd done absolutely the right thing.

What other choice did he have? Ask her to *stay* with him? The idea was ludicrous. Emily was hardly the sort to live in sin, not to mention that her sister would have his head. No, a clean, swift cut was far better.

He'd cleared a few acres when he'd first had the land, which the prairie had wasted no time in reclaiming. But in a hollow down by a dry wash some of the corn he'd planted must have gone to seed and now studded the grass with stiff, prickly stalks.

It was worth harvesting, he decided. And if he spent one more afternoon hunched over his press, picking through tiny squares of type, he was liable to take a hammer to the whole damn thing. He didn't mind writing, but throwing type was the most tedious work ever invented, and he had a damnable tendency to spill it *just* when he neared the end.

The land was more gold than green now, the sun weaker. The air, while still warm, didn't have the potent heat of a month earlier.

A brace of quail rose in protest when he kicked his way into the first stand of corn. Got there just in time, he thought, and quickly stripped a half-dozen stalks of their ears. He moved further into the wash, near where a low, exposed bluff glinted with flecks of mica. As he bent to grab a fat ear low on a stunted stalk, he caught sight of a shape out of the corner of his eye.

He pressed his forefinger and thumb to his eyes. It was a given he would dream of her. Even forgivable; a man could only govern his dreams so much. But seeing her while he was wide awake . . . it was enough to drive a man back to drink.

But he still saw her, sitting near a low cedar, a basket at her side, frowning at the notepad in her lap.

Then she looked up. And smiled—in his memories, she was ever-smiling—and lifted her hand, the awkward, half-formed wave she'd given him as she rode away in Joe Blevins's wagon.

Here, he thought. *She's here.*

He went to her, fighting to keep his steps at an unaffected pace. But his legs kept striding out further until he was damn near running by the time he reached her, which must account for his pounding heart and the labored draw of his breath.

She rose to meet him, and now stood beside the tree, the spiky branches throwing geometric lace shadows across her face, and all he could do was look at her. The sun had kissed a bit of gold in the hair around her face, left an adorable spattering of freckles over her nose.

"This is . . ." She waved helplessly around her. "Is this your land? I hadn't realized I'd wandered so far."

"Near the border," he told her. "Hard to tell which is mine and which is Blevins's."

Emily knew she was staring, helpless and mute. Couldn't help it. In all the times she'd conjured up his face, remembering it in what she'd thought was considerable and accurate detail, she now discovered she'd vastly underestimated his impact on her. His eyes, that dark rich brown, drew her more now that she could recognize emotion in them. The beautiful curve of his mouth looked all the finer now that she knew the magic it could spin on her body. His hair had grown, low and shaggy against his rumpled collar stained with ink.

"I'll get out of your way," she murmured at last, and bent to replace her paper in the basket.

His hand on her wrist froze her, released a dozen memories that danced, naked and hot, in her brain.

"Don't go," he said. "Not yet."

She dropped her pencil and pad into the basket and straightened slowly, giving herself time to prepare. It didn't help; one glance at his face and she was lost, emotion knotting her stomach.

He flushed and yanked his hand back as if he'd just abruptly realized he'd touched her.

"You didn't grow your beard back."

Self-conscious, he scrubbed a hand over his naked chin. "Yeah, well, I think I slept through the itchy stage last time. Couldn't stand to let it go this time." He shrugged. "S'pose I'll miss it in December or so."

"I'm sorry I forced you to shave it off," she told him. "I hadn't really written that to Kate, you know. I was a mite put out with you at the time, though, and couldn't resist."

"Yeah, I figured that out about an hour after Kate got here." She hadn't thought ever to see that smile again, and her heart damn near burst at the sight of it. "Still, you got the worst of it all told, so I won't be after revenge."

"That eases my mind considerably."

"It should," he said, lowering his brows in a mock-threatening scowl.

She shivered in appropriately theatrical fear.

But the amusement couldn't hold out long, and the awkward silence remained.

"Em, I thought you'd gone."

"I know," she said gravely, abandoning any attempt at lightening things up. "I'm sorry."

He shrugged off her apology. "Why are you here?"

"I promised May. There's still no doctor, not in a day's ride, and I promised her I'd stay through the birth."

"You're staying with the Blevinses?"

"Yes."

She'd been there, a short sprint away, for weeks and he'd not had a clue. He ventured off his land only to mail the *Register* and he wasn't much given to chat with the postal clerk. It seemed odd to him now that he hadn't somehow sensed her presence, for right at this second it felt as if every nerve he possessed was on full alert and tuned her way.

God, how much worse would those last weeks have been if he'd known she was so near? His dreams had nearly incinerated him as it was.

"Why didn't you tell me?" he asked, with a pang for the realization she hadn't wanted him to know she was close.

Color touched her cheeks, and her lids swept down, eyelashes making a lush semicircle above the wash of pink.

"I didn't want to make it any harder," she admitted.

"For you or for me?"

She sighed. "I'm not sure. Both of us, I suppose."

Harder? It was hard to imagine anything harder.

"So you're staying?"

"Yes," she said, with relief at rounding to a simpler topic. "Until the child's born, I'm staying."

"That must be cozy."

She laughed. "Now that you mention it, yes, it is. Which is why I've taken to tramping about during the day, trying out the lessons I begged from Art, although I'm quite abysmal. May won't let me lift a finger because she's so grateful I agreed to stay, but sitting there while she waddles around and Joe pretends not to worry was making me crazy."

Art knew she was still there, too? Was Jake the only one who hadn't been privileged with that information? A green-toned, nasty thought about whether Imbert knew snuck in and coiled at the back of his brain like an asp. He resolutely squashed it, knowing that was unfair.

"I can imagine," he said. "So, who'd I sleep with?"

She jerked in shock. "What?"

"So you had to leave me. What story did you tell them? I'd like to know my sins so I don't accidentally deny them."

The pink veered toward crimson. "I suppose you won't believe this but . . . I told them the truth."

"They know we weren't married?"

She shook her head hard enough that her hair flew, whipping across her face. "They know everything. Well, almost everything," she added hastily.

They know we're not married. That caused an odd little pang, and he filed it away for further examination later.

A strand of hair snagged on her mouth. She reached up, tugged it away, and tucked it behind her ear. "I figured I'd go for a novel approach. The stories were harder to maintain than I expected."

"Oh, I don't know," he said mildly. "They served their purpose, didn't they? Or you've told Kate, too?"

"No, I didn't tell her. I've got to work up to this, Jake. You can't expect me to do it all at once."

That strand of hair was loose again; the breeze caught it and waved it along her jaw. For safety's sake, he tucked his hands into his pockets. "Have you heard from her?"

"No." A rare, worried frown flickered over her face. "Not that she'd know where to find me. She hasn't sent something to your place, has she?"

He shook his head. "I'll save it if she does. I promise."

"Thank you." And then, after another stretch of that pained silence, she reached for her basket. "Well, I'd better—"

"I'm sorry," he said, because he didn't know if he'd ever have another chance. "Em, I'm . . . I'm sorry," he said again, because he didn't know what else to tell her without getting all tangled up in the details.

The basket plopped at her feet. She straightened slowly, gathering herself before meeting his eyes.

"That's not necessary."

"It seems that it is," he said, somewhat bemused to discover it so. "I can't honestly say I never wanted to hurt you, 'cause I guess for a while I did." But he'd been so furious. So angry that she'd thought she could martyr herself like that, pushing for his pleasure while taking none of her own. "But I'm still sorry—"

"No. I don't want you to be sorry about it." Her hands clenched. "If you're sorry, then I'll have to be, and I *refuse* to be sorry. It happened. Good and bad, so twisted up together we can probably never sort out which was which. It's over, it happened, and I'd just as soon let it lie."

She fumbled for her basket, shoving in the pencils and the two green-tinged apples that had tipped out when she dropped it. "I have to go."

"Don't go."

"But—"

"I mean, really don't go." The words spilled out, too fast for him to ponder them, coming from somewhere beyond conscious decision. "You can come back."

"What?" The last apple dropped and rolled unnoticed into a clump of buckbrush. "You can't be serious."

"I'm—no, don't look at me like that, Em. It makes sense. There are three of you over there and the shack is smaller than mine. It can't be easy living with the Blevinses."

"I did get an inkling of how Kate felt, yes," she murmured while her head and heart spun like a tornado-born leaf.

"It wouldn't be—I'll sleep in the tent again, Em, I wouldn't mind a bit. You could have the shack to yourself." He spoke fast, trying to get it all out before she said no. "I don't mean anything . . . well." He cleared his throat, plunged on. "It'd be an arrangement, just like we had before."

"Yes, that worked out *so* well last time."

He paused for a moment and let his gaze linger over her face. "We both upheld our ends of the bargain."

"I couldn't put you out like that."

"You wouldn't. I'm not offering out of charity, Miss Bright. I could use all the help I can get. I might not have minded my own cooking before, but now that you've spoiled me, it seems that I'm not quite as skilled as I remembered."

"You have lost a little flesh," she said, sweeping

him with an assessing and disapproving gaze. "You've been working too hard."

"Which is why I need you." *Need you.* Now there was a slip of the tongue that revealed too much. "And I swear, if I have to scrub another pot, I'm going to just skip the cooking entirely."

"Now, as someone with some medical knowledge, I am compelled to inform you that that is truly not healthful."

"See?" He spread his hands. "That's my point precisely."

"So . . . you want to hire me?" she said slowly, trying it out.

"Well, yeah, sure," he said, though right until she'd said it he hadn't thought of it that way. "I can't pay you much—"

"You won't pay me *at all.*" She started to tick off her terms, finger by finger. "This is a trade in kind. Because it's so convenient, being this near to the Blevinses, and Joe's snoring is near to driving me mad. Room and board in exchange for housekeeping."

"I want pie every Friday."

"Oh you do, do you?"

"Hey, you're getting the bed."

Happiness flooded her. A dangerous happiness, given all that had come before. But she had someplace to go, and something worth doing, more than just calming May's fears. "Pie it is."

Emily had no more than agreed to come home— *Home? Jesus, what was he thinking?*—before Jake questioned his own sanity. He needed no more evidence of why this was a really bad idea than the heady bubble of . . . yes, it was something very close to happiness, which he scarcely recognized in himself. And that came with dread, for he, better than anyone, knew what happened when the happiness burst.

And really, what was he planning? He would hire her to keep house for him for the rest of his life? He couldn't afford it, didn't need it. Not to mention that having an employee that one regularly had lewd and very naked fantasies about was just asking for trouble. All he'd done was put off the inevitable.

Back to the tent, he thought, as he rapidly cleared out every trace of his habitation from the shack before Emily's return. She'd refused his offer to bring Reg and the wagon around, saying Joe would drive her over, and he didn't want her to walk in and find a pile of unwashed drawers on the chair.

He was pouring the used dishwater out the window—how the heck did she have time to wash dishes after *every* meal, anyway?—when the door opened and sunlight sliced across the floor. She hovered in the doorway, suitcase in her hand.

"Oh." He set the metal washtub on the table. "You're back."

"Like a bad penny." She shifted the suitcase to her other hand. With the sunlight behind her he couldn't see her face but there was tension in the set of her shoulders, uncertainty in her voice.

"Take care of the pennies, and the dollars will take care of themselves," he countered. "Are you coming in?"

"I . . ." She hesitated briefly. "Of course."

Well, this was awkward. How do you welcome back a woman who was very nearly your lover, sort of your friend, and now more or less your employee? The few manners his mother had drummed into him didn't seem to apply.

"Let me get the rest of your stuff," he said, and slid by her to do just that.

"Oh, please, don't go to any trouble," she said.

"I'll get it," he growled, finding her polite deference damn annoying.

"You shouldn't be waiting on me."

"I said I'd get it!"

"All right," she said, and stepped aside. "Before you go—I thought perhaps hash for supper, if you have the supplies. Or hotcakes if you'd rather, Mr. Sullivan."

"Damn it!" He stopped in the doorway, spun around, and whacked his hands flat against the doorjamb. "*Mr. Sullivan?*"

"I thought it might be . . . easier, if we attempted a rigorously professional relationship."

"No, it would not be *easier*." When she flinched at his words, he deliberately softened his tone. She hadn't looked at him like that, wary, as if she wasn't sure what he was capable of, for a very long time. He didn't like it. "Em, this isn't . . . I didn't suggest this because I had a yen to order you around." And though that wasn't entirely true, his wish to command her was confined to very specific circumstances that had little to do with housekeeping, and he'd no intention of revealing that little fancy. "I don't care what you cook. It'll still be ten times better than what I would have if you weren't here. You don't have to clear anything you do with me before you do it. You just needed a place for a while. I could use some help. It doesn't have to be any more complicated than that."

For a second he feared she would flee. "Doesn't it?"

"Not if we don't let it," he said, and commenced making himself scarce before he could make a lie of what he'd just promised.

"Hi."

"Oh." Surprised, Emily looked up from the socks she'd been darning when Jake sauntered through the door. The last week had been more like those first days after Jake had returned to Montana than the days when they'd pretended a marriage. Emily scarcely saw him. He was always working somewhere on the land, building, repairing, hauling supplies from town. He stopped only long enough to wolf down whatever she'd cooked, mumble his thanks, and disappear again. "Hi."

He sniffed. "What's that?"

"Juniper. May told me. You put a few fresh sprigs, maybe a few berries, on top of the stove when it's warm and it scents the air." She took a deep breath as well. "Smells good, doesn't it?"

"Yeah. Guess it does." He scratched his head in complete male bewilderment. Having Emily back had changed his life in more ways than he'd counted on. Oh, he'd sure looked forward to the food, which was every bit as good as he remembered. But all the other things . . . the luxury of coming home and finding his clothes washed and mended, and someone waiting with a smile. The sheer comfort, after a long day, of entering a room that smelled of lemon wax, finding a chair free of debris to drop into.

He was terrified he was getting far too used to it. And even more, he was struck with a terror so deep he couldn't stand to think about it, the knowledge that he was more than getting used to her. Wanted her around for more reasons than material comforts. *Needed* her there. She'd lodged herself in his life and his heart in a way he'd never wanted and wasn't sure he could survive, and he feared it was too late for him to keep her, and how he felt about her, safely contained in a neat, clean box. So he employed the tactic he'd been clinging to since her return: he ran, this time for the safety of his printing room.

Emily shrugged and went back to her darning. She'd resolved to keep from poking into areas he'd clearly marked to be left alone. She'd tried that once, and look what had happened. Instead she'd do the only thing she could think of to help him. By the time she left, his buttons would be sewed on so tightly they'd never pop off, his clothes as clean as if they were brand-new, and his pantry thoroughly stocked.

From the lean-to came a metallic clatter, like a box of bullets dumped on the floor, followed by a healthy streak of inventive and emphatic curses. She dropped the shirt and raced to see if he'd bruised anything that mattered.

Perched on a high stool, hands planted on his knees, Jake surveyed in disgust what looked like hundreds of tiny silver cubes scattered all over the floor.

"I pied the type again," he said. "Never happens when I've barely started, of course. And this time it wasn't only the form I was working on but the whole damn thing."

"Here, let me help." She bent over to begin. "I don't have a clue where to start."

Sighing heavily, he grabbed a side-tilted, divided wooden box off the floor and slammed it down on the small table he'd slapped together from raw boards and covered with a layer of tin. "To start, we sort."

Unlike Jake, Emily didn't mind the job. Jake had built a wide window in the outside wall and the shutters were open. Sunlight streamed in. The wind, gentle today, shuffled through carrying birdcalls that blended with the clink of type. And—okay, might as well admit it—she enjoyed working beside him, watching his concentration, the quick sure motions as he grabbed up great handfuls of spilled letters, glanced at them one by one, and hurled each at its small cubbyhole. Each throw got progressively harder, until at last one bounced out of its niche and back onto the floor.

"Shit!" Then he shot a guilty glance at Emily. "Sorry."

"Always wanted to be a newspaperman, did you?" she asked, amused by his impatience. She found sifting through the pieces and putting them into their proper places soothing, a task that could be done and put aside with a precision and confidence life rarely offered.

He laughed. *Oh, it is such a triumph to get that man to laugh!* she thought. *Easy to become addicted to the challenge and reward of it.*

"How'd you guess?" He shook his handful of type and the pieces clattered like the beads of a child's rattle. "No, I've never had much of a leanin' toward it."

"I liked your article, though," she said. "The one on flax cultivation."

His hand froze in mid-shake. "You read it?"

"Of course I read it."

"But . . . why would you need to know about flax?"

"I have no interest at all in flax. At least I didn't before I read it." She scooped up a few squares and poked through them. Two *c*'s, a *b*, and a spacer. "But you wrote it, so I read it."

When he made no further comment, she looked up to find him staring at her, his brow furrowed. Had it been so long for him then, that he'd had someone in his life who'd be interested in something he'd done just because it was *his*? So long since he'd had, well, a friend?

"Why do you do it, then? The newspaper, I mean. If you've no interest in it."

"Five bucks a proof."

"That's it?"

"Five bucks a proof times hundreds of claims is more than reason enough."

That was hard to argue with. She dropped her type into the case and rummaged a half dozen from beneath the table. "What, then?"

"What'll I do after I have the money?"

"No. You were in college, you said. What did you intend to be?"

He laid out his forms with more concentration than the task required.

"Well." She shook a couple of pieces of type like dice while she pondered. "If you don't want to tell me, I'll guess."

He swiveled on his stool, leaned back with his legs stretched in front of him, and crossed his arms. "This ought to be good."

"Let me see." She pursed her lips, tapped them with her forefinger. "Not a chef."

"No, I tried that one. They paid me not to go near the kitchen again."

"Really?" she asked before she caught the glint of humor in his eyes, and for once didn't mind her own gullibility if that was the result. "A hat designer, perhaps. You have such flair."

"Don't I?" He batted his eyelashes at her like the most practiced coquette, and her heart fluttered just as wildly. "Perhaps all is not lost in that regard. Do you suppose Kate would hire me?"

"She'd be a fool not to."

"Good to keep my options open." Was this who he'd been, before life had stripped the joy from him? His eyes alight, his smile ready? No wonder Julia had defied her father to be with him. "Try again."

"You did say Mr. Bates wished you to clerk for him. Considering your fondness for money . . . an accountant, perhaps?"

"Good God, no." He uncrossed his legs and sat up in protest. "I'd go stir mad, poring over the books and searching for lost pennies."

"Well?"

"No more guesses?"

They'd retrieved more than half the spilled type, she noticed when she bent for another handful. Then she'd have no more excuse to stay there with him. And so she made sure she had a terrible time finding the compartment for the *t*'s. "Teaching, maybe?"

"Worse and worse."

"I didn't say I thought you'd be *good* at it."

"No, I know my limitations, and I don't fancy ending up in an asylum after three days of work." He took pity on her. "I'd planned to read for the law."

"A lawyer?"

"Yeah." This time his laugh carried a bitter edge. "A guy I grew up with got arrested when we were seventeen. Theft, they said, and I suppose he might've done a fair amount in his time. But he said he didn't do it, and I believed him—no reason for him to lie to me, y'know? But they put him in prison. Mostly, I figured, 'cause he didn't have money to hire somebody decent to defend him."

"Is he still there?"

"Far as I know."

"I'm sorry."

"If there's justice to be had in this world, Em, it's gotta be found in the courts, too. I *hate* that it's reserved for those who can buy it."

In his agitation his elbow bumped his mock-up table, and they both dove for it, splaying their arms across to rescue the type they'd spent the last half hour sorting. They ended up tangled together, arms entwined, she half lying across his back.

"I'm sorry," she said quickly and sprang away, her face flaming.

Once he was sure the type was staying put, he peeled himself up slowly. "Don't be," he said. "Especially when you look so cute with your cheeks that shade of pink."

"Cute?" *Cute* wasn't really what she had in mind. Years ago, when flocks of smitten young men had descended on their house to preen for Kate, they'd tried to win Kate's favor by patting Emily on the head and pronouncing her "cute."

"Oh, don't look so put out," he said. "It's not an insult."

"That's what you think."

"Yes, that's what I think." He tapped her lightly on the nose, and she had the most unaccountable urge to nip the offending finger. "Em, you can't keep jumping every time we accidentally bump into each other."

"I don't do that," she lied. She hated that it seemed to be so easy for him, and so completely unsettling for her.

"Must be me, then."

"I'm sure it must be."

He studied her thoughtfully until she could no longer hold his gaze, which she realized too late was every bit as telling as her skittishness.

"How'd you like a job?"

"I thought I had one."

"No, a real one. Five bucks a week as my printer."

"But I've got no more idea how to run that machine than I do how to break a colt."

"I know. Which is why you're only getting five. Going rate's eight."

Jake could've whacked himself over the head for being so thick that he hadn't thought of this before. It'd swell Emily's nest egg a bit. Even better, she'd have a skill that would be in demand. There'd be hundreds of proof sheets popping up— if things worked out the way he planned, a fair number of them might even be his—and so maybe this time, after she left, he wouldn't go near crazy worrying about her. Hell, maybe he'd even keep her himself.

And now *there* was a slip of the brain that threatened to keep him up nights.

"I hate writing," she objected. "Kate used to have to bribe me with gingersnaps to get me to write to Anthea."

"I can write," he told her. "It's those dinky pieces of metal that make me crazy."

But she eyed the hulking, rusty press with open suspicion. "I don't know," she said doubtfully.

"Heck, Em, if you can deliver a baby, you surly can do this. A lot fewer hidden parts, I promise." He tried his most winning smile, surprised to find that he remembered how. "And it'll keep me from taking a mallet to this thing one day."

"What makes you think my temperament is more inclined to patience than yours?"

"You put up with me." He meant it as a joke. But his voice softened at the end, set up a warm humming in his chest. "Here," he said hastily, and yanked off his printer's apron. He dropped it over her head before she could protest, wrapped the ties around her narrow waist—three times, before the ends didn't trail on the floor—and knotted it tight. "There. Let me see."

Ink mottled the stiff canvas, which puffed out from the belt and held its own shape instead of hers. It flipped up in front where it hit the floor like a bent strip of tin.

"Kate would have a fit." Laughing, Emily lifted her hands and spun for his benefit. "What do you think?"

He opened his mouth but she beat him to it.

"If you say 'cute,' " she said warningly, "you're going to be picking up type till spring."

"I'm surprised Godey's hasn't picked up on it yet."

"You must promise," she told him, "that, if I'm terrible at it, you will fire me without a second thought."

"I will be a terrible ogre of a boss," he promised her solemnly. "You will curse me with every letter you set."

"Oh, I've no doubt about that."

Because he wanted to kiss her, he took her by the

arms, plopped her on the stool, and spun her around to face the setup table so those dancing eyes wouldn't tempt him. But then he ruined the noble gesture by standing right behind her, bracing his arms on the table on either side, and peering over her shoulder. And even he couldn't convince himself he did so because that was the easiest way to demonstrate what to do.

She caught on quick. Too quick, to his way of thinking, because he loved reaching over her shoulder to show her how to throw the lines of type into the form while the scent of her drifted up from her hair. Enjoyed how she'd turn around to ask him a question and her face would be only inches from his, and she'd startle to realize how close he was, her eyes going wide, but she wouldn't move away. Was fascinated by the lilting tune she hummed when he showed her how to whittle bits of matchsticks into the right size to wedge into the form when the lines of type weren't quite tight enough.

He demonstrated how to snip a bit of tin can and fold it when she ran out of blank type to make spaces. Her mortification at the curse that slipped out when she couldn't bend it just right delighted him to no end.

And he laughed at the fierce pride she took at hammering the wedges into the frame to lock it in place, swinging the mallet like a lumberjack with an axe.

"See? You better watch out," she said, and flexed an arm to show off her puny muscle. "I might try it on your head if you're late with my pay." She spun on the stool and rapped her knuckles lightly against his forehead. "Pop like a ripe melon, I'd wager."

"Consider me warned."

Her eyes danced, only inches from his. The curve of her mouth was exceptionally kissable—he wondered that he hadn't noticed it the first day they'd met.

He'd loved Julia with all the fierce passion and pride his young heart owned. But they'd been often self-conscious, their times together brief and stolen, so overcome with their feelings and the risk of their meeting that they'd rarely laughed. He'd certainly never felt this wondrous ease.

"Thanks, Em," he said.

"You're welcome," she said softly, as if she understood he thanked her for far more than just relieving him of a task he detested. Her breath hitched and the friendly simmer of passion that had warmed him pleasantly all afternoon abruptly burst to riotous life, like a small flame that had sizzled down a long wick and just hit dynamite.

Don't ruin it, he told himself. *Don't ruin this again, when it's working out so well.*

"So what are you going to do now?" she asked him, and—God help him—a hundred thoughts sprang to mind, wicked and sinful and hopelessly impossible. Perhaps they showed, for she suddenly spun back to the table and poked through the remaining type, mumbling about missing *p*'s.

"Em—"

"Now that I've taken over all your work, I mean,"

she said in a fluster. "What are you going to do with all your free time? Get fat and lazy?"

He sighed and reluctantly moved away. It was for the best, but that didn't mean he had to like it. "I think," he said slowly, "I'm going to build a new house."

Chapter 18

On Tuesday Jake piled the newspapers Emily had printed into the back of his wagon and headed into town to mail them. He was gone for two days, which Emily divided evenly between sleeping and trying to scrub the ink off her fingers.

Shortly after he returned, a huge load of lumber, nails, and tools was delivered and stacked neatly upon a slight rise about two hundred yards from the claim shack.

A day later a man with the build of a young bull arrived with a massive team of horses and a plow that towered over Emily. Within moments great curving slices of sod were being stripped from the land. Mice scattered, and the dark peels of earth studded with fat white grubs drew flocks of happily cackling blackbirds in his wake.

Tom—just Tom, he'd told her cheerfully—and his team plowed the required thirty acres in under two days, even with regular pauses to shovel in vast quantities of food. Watching them, remembering all the effort she'd put into trying to clear a garden plot, Emily couldn't help but laugh at her naiveté and ineptitude.

Emily managed to curb her curiosity for three days before giving in. She cut a slice of the ribbon cake she'd just baked as an excuse and slapped her best straw hat on her head.

Grass still clung to the sides of the small rise, the earth dark and rich on the top. Jake caught sight of her approach, stuck his shovel in the ground, rested his arms on it, and waited for her to arrive.

"Ah, there you are," he said. He'd rolled up his sleeves, and she admired his well-muscled forearms above his leather work gloves. The thin fabric of his white shirt was damp with sweat, and she remembered too well exactly what all that muscle felt like beneath her palms. Perhaps he'd had the right idea all along: they should spend as little time with each other as possible, avoiding temptation. "I'd wondered how long you'd hold out."

"Excuse me?"

He gestured toward the cleared ground, crisscrossed with fat twine tied to stakes in a rectangular grid. "I wondered how long it'd be before you came to see what was what. You held out longer than I expected."

"Don't be silly," she said. "I've no interest in what you're building. You just didn't eat very much lunch, and you've got to be hungry after all this digging."

"Mmm." He peered at the plate she carried. "Cake?"

"Yes."

He tugged off his gloves and tucked them in his back pocket. There was a line across his wrists, brown above, lighter below. He began to reach for the plate, then stopped, bent down, and plucked a yellow daisy that bloomed at her feet.

"Stand still," he said, and she held her breath while he reached up and tucked the flower into the ribbon of her hat. "There. Thanks for the cake."

"You like ribbon cake, I hope. I didn't ask, but—"

"I love it," he said, once he'd swallowed the first bite. "And this is particularly good. Angling for a raise, are you?"

"You're the boss." The strings delineated the future rooms, she decided. The parlor there, perhaps. A decent sized kitchen in the back. She preferred bigger ones, but—

"Front door's there." He pointed about halfway. "There'll be a porch, of course."

"I didn't ask."

"I know you didn't." He jogged over to a pile of lumber and balanced the empty plate on top. "But now that you're here, you might as well look around."

He stepped over the nearest piece of twine, then turned to help her over it. She hadn't bothered with gloves, and his hand was very warm as she lifted her skirts and stepped in. And was it her imagination that he released her hand with reluctance once she was safely on the other side?

"I staked out the rooms because I had a hard time imagining them from the drawings," he said. "Thought I could envision them better this way. Tell if they were big enough, or too big. It still looks like nothing more than dirt squares to me. I could figure out if you can play baseball on it, but a house is beyond me."

"You've gotten so far." Eyes narrowing thoughtfully, she spun slowly, envisioning walls, furniture, people.

"I had Tom loosen the first layer with his plow. Made for easy digging."

"It's going to be a big house." Far too much for just one man.

"The stairs go up right here."

"Upstairs, too?"

Silently he reached into his pocket, pulled out a piece of paper, and handed it to her.

The creases were fuzzy, as if it had lived in his pocket a long time. She unfolded it with reverent care.

The left side of the paper held a front view of the house. Not grand, but a big, wonderful family house, with plenty of windows and a columned porch that ran the entire length of the front and appeared to be made for long summer evenings and lemonade. Trees guarded the wide steps, with a child's swing hanging from the sturdiest branch.

To the right were floor plans, spare and precise drawings with the rooms neatly labeled: study, kitchen, parlor. *Baby's room.*

"You didn't draw this," she said.

For a while she thought he wouldn't answer. That he regretted trusting her with this. "How can you tell?"

"The handwriting."

"Oh." He frowned. "Sorry about that. I know my

writing's a mess, never did have a hand for it. I'll rewrite the article on—"

"Your handwriting is fine." She would never admit to him that it had taken her two hours to decipher the first two paragraphs. She'd gotten used to his scrawl, and was proud of that. "This is just different."

He came to stand behind her, looking over her shoulder at the drawing. "Julia drew it."

Carefully she refolded the paper. "It's a beautiful house."

"Yeah. It is, isn't it?" He tucked it safely back into his pocket. She'd never noticed it there when she emptied his pockets for washing and wondered if he'd carried it with him all the time, suspecting that he did.

She pondered her next words for a moment. He was ever so hard to read—except when he wanted her, she remembered. That she could see in his eyes, the set of his mouth, the tension in his features. But his face gave her no hints now.

Part of her was flattered that he'd shared this with her. A bigger part worried that he still clung to a dream that was lost long ago.

"It's a big house," she ventured carefully, "for one man."

His jaw tightened. "I—."

An agitated chatter and a tug on his pants leg stopped him. They looked down to find Smithie at his feet, teeth bared, clever fingers in a vise grip on faded denim.

"Lord, Smithie, not *now*," he said. He bent and tried to dislodge his grip but the animal wouldn't budge. "Isn't there a cow around you can bother?"

For a moment Emily regretted the interruption. They'd been edging up on something that mattered. But if it did matter, she decided, it'd be there in a few moments, a few days, or it wasn't worth what she thought anyway.

Jake gave his leg a gentle shake. Smithie clung on and shrieked in protest. Then, after looking between them, he let go and fell on the ground, eyes closed, playing dead like a well-trained dog.

"Yes, yes, you're good," Jake told him. "Now run along like a good little monkey and—"

Smithie sprang up again and howled at him, a call they'd never heard from him before, one that would have frozen Emily's blood in her veins if she'd heard it echoing across the plains on a dark night. And then the animal dropped to the ground again, unmoving.

The creature was a gifted mimic. Once when Mr. Biskup was over for supper, Smithie had watched her as she did the dishes. And then he'd scampered up, grabbed her dishtowel, and seized a clean plate from the shelf. Bemused, she'd watched as he'd scrubbed the plate and replaced it on the stack without so much as a chip.

He sprang up and, apparently giving up on the stupid male, tugged on Emily's skirts instead. He dashed off, perhaps five yards, and then looked back at them as if wondering why they weren't following.

"Something's wrong," she murmured, and started to sprint.

It was just far enough that Emily was good and

winded by the time they found him. They saw Biskup's old horse first, cropping at a tuft of sweet grass, reins trailing on the ground. And beside him on the ground, a crumpled figure like a discarded doll, lay Mr. Biskup.

Emily dropped beside him immediately, laying her head against his narrow chest. There . . . his heartbeat too thready, his breath shallow and slow, but there. Thank God.

She sat back on her heels and ran her fingers over him, neck, head, limbs. It was as if she'd been split into two parts: the friend, worried and praying, even as the part of her well-trained by the doctor examined him with quick and professional care.

She slowed as she turned his head. There was a gash at his temple, the thick, dark shine of blood matting his hair.

"What can I do?" Jake asked.

"My bag, it's in the—" And then the worry broke through her training. Her voice shook, her hands trembled. "Jake, I—"

"You'll help him," he said, and then his hands squeezed her shoulders, warm and supportive, faith and strength shining through his touch, and immediately her nerves settled and her mind cleared.

"I think it's safe to move him," she decided. "Better than trying to treat him out here."

"It's closer to our house than his," he said. *Ours.* Through her concern, she tucked the word away to ponder later. "Want to take him there?"

"Yes. The supplies are there, too. I'll stay with him until you get the wagon. But hurry."

He hesitated a second. "How about if I carry him? It'd be faster."

"All that way?"

"It's not a problem." He was as good as his word, lifting Mr. Biskup's still body as carefully as if he'd held a child, his even, strong pace covering the distance to their shack so quickly that she, after scooping up Smithie, had to trot to keep up.

"The bed?" Jake asked after shoving open the door with his foot.

"Yes," she said, and watched as he carefully laid Mr. Biskup down. The man hadn't moved the entire time. Not good, she thought. "I'll need lanterns," she instructed Jake. "As much light as possible."

She bent over and gently tugged up an eyelid. The pupils reacted sluggishly. Not dangerously so, she judged, but perhaps not normal, either.

"Jake?" she asked as she straightened.

"Yes." He came to her side immediately.

"Could you heat some water for me? And my bag's over in the—"

"I know where it is." He obeyed without question.

Luckily she could run through an examination by rote, conscious all the while of Mr. Biskup's heartbroken concentration, struggling not to reveal her concern. She'd treated patients on her own before in certain circumstances, when both they and Dr. Goodale agreed. But she'd always had the comfort of knowing the doctor's skill was there if she needed it. She missed him then, which she'd never expected to do considering how much she'd regretted her sister's years under his thumb. But she loved the medicine she'd learned. A kinder man might have tried to spare her. He'd been willing to use her, and in doing so gave her something she treasured.

"Emily?"

She shook her head. "I don't know, Jake. There's nothing obviously dangerous, but . . . I don't know."

He was an old man. She'd always believed him less fragile than he appeared at first glance, but . . . "Fell off his horse, I suppose," she said and she probed the growing bruise at his temple. There was no fluid under the skin, she decided, the first good news. "I wish I knew why." If he'd had some sort of a fit to cause his accident—well, she might be treating the immediate symptoms, and entirely missing something even more serious. She frowned.

"That horse has always been skittish," Jake said. "God only knows what set it off this time. Hit his head on a rock, did he?"

"I believe so." Jake didn't sound a bit worried. Had he so much faith in her, then?

"Guess he'll be glad of his hard head for once."

Afternoon faded into evening as she worked. There was so little she could do. She cleaned his cuts, sprinkled in finely ground black tea, and smeared them with lard mixed with beeswax and resin. Mr. Biskup's right arm twisted at a painful angle. She probed the bones, which felt fragile as a child's, but cursed her own slight frame when she couldn't straighten them herself.

"May I?" Jake asked, his hands hovering over Art's arm.

"Like this," she said, adjusting his aim slightly. He followed her directions with absolute confidence, pressing carefully until the bones moved back into place. Emily splinted it with pasteboard and cotton batting.

But through it all Mr. Biskup hadn't stirred, apparently so deeply out, even the pain of straightening his broken arm hadn't penetrated. So she elevated his head, bathing it with cold water as she plunged his feet into a hot mustard bath. And through it all Jake was there, ready to help should she but say the word, a supportive hand touching her elbow the moment she began to doubt . . . how did he know? But he unquestionably did.

Vaguely, through her concentrated concern, she had a notion that this was something new. Except for public viewing he'd rarely touched her first. She'd always been the one to touch in comfort and support. She filed the notion away for further study later, when she could give it the attention it deserved.

Evening faded into night without notice. They dragged two chairs beside the bed. Jake dropped in and out of sleep without warning, without outward sign; Emily would look over and be surprised to find his eyes open or shut, for even the comforting rhythm of his breathing never varied.

And she held vigil.

Hours later, the dark outside so deep, the clouds obscuring the sky so it was near impossible to judge the time except that it was the dead of the night, Emily wearily propped her head on her hand, still watching for some sign, *any* sign, from her comatose patient.

Though it didn't feel like it, she must have dozed, for the next thing she was conscious of was Jake's warm hand, rubbing sweetly between her shoulder blades.

"Why don't you rest?" he suggested. "I put a cot up in the lean-to."

"No." She scrubbed her palm over her face, trying to force alertness. "It's my responsibility."

"I'll watch him carefully. I'll wake you if there's the slightest change." The strokes were mesmerizing and she leaned back into them, feeling tension evaporate with each pass his fingers made over her muscles. "I promise."

"I couldn't sleep anyway."

His fingers paused a moment, then took up their magic again. "All right."

He got points for not arguing with her on this matter, she thought. She didn't know if she would have shown the same restraint. In gratitude she reached up and caught his hand on the top arch of its caress and linked her fingers with his. "I know you would keep watch as carefully as I. But I couldn't—there's no point in both of us staying up, and I'd only worry. I've held watch enough to know."

His fingers squeezed and warmth swept over her. Here was an intimacy she'd never known, in such unusual circumstances, the two of them wrapped in weary darkness, joining in their worry, trusting each other's support.

"Is he going to be okay?"

"I wish I knew."

"No change?"

"Not that I can tell." She was too tired to sigh; air just slid out of her. "Jake, there's so much I don't know. I hadn't realized."

He stood there for a moment longer. And then he pulled his chair closer to hers, sat down, and took her hand again. He held it through the rest of the night, awake or asleep, beside her all the way, and it helped. More than she would have guessed.

Near dawn—the clouds hadn't left, but the sun seeped through, turning the inside of the shack to gray—she closed gritty eyes. When she opened them, she blinked, and twice more, before it registered.

Smithie had spent the night curled against Mr. Biskup's side, holding a vigil of his own. Emily tried to bribe him away with an apple and had finally let him remain. But now he sat on Art's chest, looking straight into Art's blurry but open eyes.

She sprang to his side and felt Jake join her a second later. Placing her hand on Mr. Biskup's forehead, she found to her relief that he was cooling. Avoiding a fever, she knew, was half the battle. "How do you feel."

"Lousy."

"Good."

"Good? I really hit my head, didn't I? How's that good?"

"All things considered, you should feel lousy. If you didn't, I'd know something more was wrong." No frown had ever made her so happy.

She wouldn't be satisfied without giving him a complete examination, through which he groused all the way. And then *he* wouldn't be satisfied until Jake moved him into the lean-to—he would not, he told them, put them out of their bed. Emily's protests did no good and finally she gave in, deciding she was grateful he felt well enough to argue. Once settled on the cot, he fell immediately back asleep, a true one this time, his breath even, his heartbeat strong, Smithie snoring at his side.

Fatigue hit her at once. She stumbled back into the main room and then stood in the center, swaying, unable to decide what to do next.

"Go to bed, Emily," Jake ordered her.

"It's such a mess," she said, surveying the piles of dirty towels, pots, and the clutter of her precious medical supplies strewn across the table. And they hadn't eaten since . . . she couldn't remember.

"I can clean," he told her, taking her by the shoulders and pointing her in the direction of the bed, just in case she'd forgotten where it was. "Oh, don't look at me like that, Emily. I *can* clean; I am not Mrs. Sullivan's son for nothing. It'll be done by the time you get up, and if you don't like it, you can order me around for the rest of the day and I shall follow every instruction to the letter, I promise."

"I should make you breakfast. Or dinner. Or whatever."

"For God's sake, Em, you've been up all night."

"We have an agreement."

"And I am *not* the ogre employer you apparently think me. I will not starve, I can assure you—I *did* manage to feed myself without you for years—and if you do not get yourself to sleep I guess knocking you over the head might achieve the desired result as effectively as it did with Biskup." He said the words as lightly as he could manage, suspecting she'd fight orders he really wanted to issue tooth and nail.

He watched her lurch toward the bed. The morning sunlight did nothing to disguise her pallor. Exhaustion hollowed deep, heavy blue circles beneath her eyes, drew the impression of lines around her mouth that she was far too young to have.

"There you go," he said, as she toppled over. "Go to sleep, and it'll be to rights by the time you wake up."

"Oh, I won't be able to sleep." She stretched, arms high over her head. *Now stop that*, he told himself. *So what if she looks marvelous in bed? I'd be the ogre in truth if I wanted anything more than for her to sleep right now.* "But this does feel good."

"Of course you'll sleep."

She shook her head. "Stayed up too long, with too much stimulation. It'll take hours for me to wind down. Truth is, I could just as easily help you, for all the good it'd do me to lie here." She smiled at him but there was nothing behind it. "But I rather fancy watching you play housekeeper."

"Whatever you want," he said, figuring she'd be out by the time he walked around the table. But after he'd rinsed and wrung out the rags, emptied dirty water into the yard, and grabbed a broom to start pushing dust around on the floor, she was still awake, watching him with wide, blue-green eyes, shifting back and forth as if she couldn't find a comfortable spot.

"There's no hope for it," she said, and sat up.

"There's too much leftover energy; if I don't burn it off, I'll never be able to sleep."

"You just stay right where you are," he barked. If she burned off anything more there'd be nothing left of her.

He tossed the broom aside with a clatter and came beside the bed. And then he stood there for a moment while he reminded himself that this was for her sake before he sat down beside her.

"Jake!"

"Hush," he said. "Turn over."

"Excuse me?" She couldn't quite hide her shock, and it made him smile.

"I'm not planning to take advantage of your weakened condition."

"Oh," she said, sounding so disappointed he grinned.

"I'm just going to rub your back." He probed gingerly where her neck widened into her upper back. Her muscles had contracted completely, knotted into balls as hard as twisted rope. "Jeez, Em, you gotta relax."

"I'm trying," she said, her voice muffled against her pillow.

"Feel good?" he asked. Lord knew what had happened to her pins during the night but now her hair was loose and he brushed it aside, out of the way. Her neck was vulnerably white, barely tufted with downy hairs, and damn it, kissing her right there seemed like such a fine idea he had trouble remembering why he wasn't supposed to.

"Hmm-hmm," she mumbled.

"Relaxing?"

"Well, no."

"No?" His hands stilled. "Am I hurting you?"

"Not that, either."

Without warning she rolled onto her back. He didn't move his hands fast enough, and he brushed her upper arm, and then her breast, before he pulled them away. His whole hand tingled, just with the memory of that slight touch.

"Having you touch me, Jake—I can't imagine that I'm ever going to find that *relaxing*," she said, so honest it made him hurt. And want, and wish, and a hundred other things he'd sworn off.

"So you can't relax, you can't sleep, you can't let me rub your back . . . Em, why don't you just have a good cry and get it over with? Bet you could sleep then."

"Cry? Didn't you see? Art's fine. It was a happy ending. No reason to cry."

"Happy's as good a reason to cry as sad for most of the women I know."

She lifted her chin at being compared to "most women." "Not for me."

"What would be a good reason?"

That perplexed her. Her eyebrows furrowed, and she came about as close as he'd ever seen to frowning. "What are you talking about?"

"When your sister left—I was sure that'd do it. I was all prepared to nobly let you drip all over me. Even had a stack of kerchiefs handy. But you didn't cry."

"That doesn't mean I don't miss her."

"I didn't mean to imply that you didn't," he said. "I just wondered. Do you ever cry?"

"Of course I cry."

"When?"

"When it's appropriate," she snapped.

"And when would that be?"

"I don't know," she retorted. "I know it when it happens, though."

"Uh-huh."

"I've nothing to cry over. I'm lucky and I know it."

"Em. It doesn't diminish anything your sisters did for you if, just once in a while, you are less than perfectly happy."

"That's not it."

But it was. He was sure of it. Somehow she'd gotten it into her head—though not just her head, he realized; her bones, her soul—that if she was ever unhappy, ever worried or sad, she would seem ungrateful for all her sisters had done for her.

It couldn't be good for her, he thought, to limit her emotions in such a way. The mirror of what he'd done. He'd allowed no joy, and she'd allowed no sorrow. They'd both been wrong. Life and the heart required free rein.

Oh, damn, it might be a terrible mistake to push this. How was he supposed to know what was the right thing to do? He'd avoided messy emotions whenever possible.

But she'd pushed, he remembered. Pushed him when he'd prayed she'd stop and he couldn't be sorry for it. "And when was the last time you cried?"

"I don't know." A bit of temper showed through, overtaking the fatigue.

"Okay." He took her hand and made light, soothing circles in her palm, a nearly hypnotic rhythm. "What'd you think, when we found Art?"

"I thought he was dead."

"No . . . I mean you. What did it feel like? Is there . . . I don't know, excitement, focus, concern? To know that you've work to do? That someone's life is in your hands?"

She sighed. "I don't know. Some of each. Excitement that it would be my decisions this time, without Dr. Goodale sniping over my shoulder. Worry about the same thing. Wishing I knew more. But that only takes a fraction of a second. Then you think about what you've got to do and nothing else."

Such gentle, small hands she had. He pressed his thumb in the middle, felt her flesh yield, and ran his fingers down hers: thin, elegant, strong.

"Are you worried about May?"

"No."

"Really?"

"If there's one thing I'm well trained at, it's delivering babies. I did most of the examining of pregnant women in Dr. Goodale's practice, for that was far easier than trying to convince a woman he should have a good look up her—well, you know. Plus the doctor had little patience for sitting with a woman through labor, and half the time it was all over before he got there. And . . . okay, I'm a little scared." Her eyes flashed. "And if you so much as hint that to her, I'll kill you."

He didn't bother to dignify that with an answer. He'd worked enough on her hand that it was pliable beneath his fingers, but her shoulders remained stiff, hunched at an awkward angle, her features pinched. If he was going to rub the tension out of her, muscle by muscle, he might have her asleep by sunset. Maybe.

"What was the worst case you ever had?" he asked. "Patient? Case? What do you call it, anyway?"

"For Dr. Goodale it was a case. For me, a patient."

"So what was it?" He moved on to her wrist, and the bones felt delicate enough he might snap them with his thumb. But it would be a grave error to think her fragile. "The worst one?"

"The hardest one was an elderly man, a former butcher. He'd been referred from his own doctor, who couldn't come up with a diagnosis," she began, a brisk recitation. "He presented with symptoms of—"

"No," he interrupted. "Not the most difficult to treat. The *worst*." He left off massaging her wrist, hesitating only a moment before he brushed his fingers right over her heart. It leaped beneath the contact. "The one that you can't forget. The one image that hovers, waiting for you to close your eyes."

She sat silently, sifting through memories. "I almost said a child; they're always difficult. But that's not the one, though she had children of her own, and that made it worse. She was in her early forties, and had a cancer of the breast, and her eyes were very blue, very much like Kate's, and she—" She looked up at him, her eyes swimming. "Oh, that's not fair!"

"I know," he admitted, and scooped her into his lap. *Probably close to the same age as her mother when she died*, he thought. *And she left children behind, too.* He gently pressed her head to his chest, and the first shudder ran through her. "Go ahead," he murmured. "Go ahead."

"I don't want to," she said. But she'd already begun.

He held her while she wept in his arms. His shirt grew damp, the feel of her tears on his skin blindingly intimate. She shuddered against him. Sobbed. And he was the worst kind of bastard because, God help him, every good intention he had was blown to hell and gone.

Finally she quieted, one last hiccup and a wet snuffle. "Do you think you can sleep now?"

She leaned back. "You can't be serious."

"That was the plan." He brushed tendrils of hair away from her wet cheeks. "Not a good one, huh?"

"It wasn't a bad one," she said with a spent sigh.

"Well, well, would you look at that." Her nose was red, her eyes swollen, her face splotchy.

"Not a pretty sight, is it?" she said without a trace of concern.

"No, not pretty," he said, his voice gone unexpectedly hoarse. "Beautiful, though. Just beautiful."

"Jake."

And then, helpless to resist, he kissed her. Kissed away the tears on one cheek, and then the other. Tasted salt at the tip of her nose. Licked a drop as it ran down her jaw. A hundred kisses, a thousand kisses, one for every tear he'd pressed from her, and even more for all the ones she'd battled back in her life.

"Jake," she murmured, just before he took her mouth. There were even tears there; they'd slipped along her lips, flavored their kiss as he nudged her lips open and finally kissed her completely, deeply, without reserve or regret. Without anything but all the joy and pleasure he could give her. It seemed impossible to him that he'd kissed her intimate flesh, knew how she tasted and how she shuddered when she peaked, and he'd never kissed her like this.

At last, gulping, he had to come up for air. Drowning when he kissed her, drowning when he stopped.

"Jake? Is this . . . isn't this a cliché? Comfort sex?"

Sex. The word sizzled in his veins like wine, made his heart thunder and blood rush. To know, to *decide*, instead of merely follow an urge . . . it seemed all the more forbidden, wondrously exciting.

"It's not a cliché," he said. "It's a classic."

Chapter 19

She put her hand on his chest to steady her head and instead it only spun all the more, a wonderful drunken whirl that tempted her to jump in and let herself get drawn into the tumult.

"Jake."

"Yeah?" There was a spot beneath her ear where the skin felt like fine silk, thrummed with her pulse. He laid his mouth there, felt it vibrate against him.

"Shouldn't we"—she had to stop, gasp a breath—"talk about this?"

"No." Oh, she was sweetness itself. It called to him, filled up echoing places he hadn't even known were empty. "Don't you remember? There're better things to do with our mouths than talk."

"I do remember." She couldn't help but remember, a low, dull ache that never left. "Jake." Because it seemed the only way to stop him, she took his face in both hands. "I couldn't stand it, Jake. If you woke up tomorrow—tonight—*whatever*, if, when it was over, you were sorry again, I . . ."

"I promise you," he said with the solemnity of a vow, "that the only thing I would regret is if I left you right now."

Amazing that, after all that weeping, there were any tears left. But she felt the burn of them and battled them back by planting her mouth on his, falling into the sweeping burn of another kind.

"Oh Jesus," he said, when he came up for air. "Where'd you learn to kiss like that?"

"Beginner's luck."

"I'm not sure whether I should hope to be around when you're an expert or not." He kissed her again, just because he couldn't resist, quick and hard and breathless. "I would be your slave forever."

Talking was harder now. "Oh darn, you tumbled to my plan. Now it'll never work."

He flipped open the top button on her blouse and admired the slim wedge of skin revealed, shadows and hollows, the anticipation of more. "I'm not so sure but that it hasn't worked already."

She softened: knees, heart, mind. But still, one small corner of sanity remained. And worried. "Jake—"

"It'll be okay, Emily." Another button, a sliver of lace revealed. His mouth went dry. "We're not doing anything new so much as filling in the blanks." His eyes met hers. "We skipped a lot of steps, Em. And by damn, I'm sorry I missed them."

He dropped a kiss on the first high swell of her breast and her voice went up three notes. "What steps?"

"A lot of kissing, for one. Though we made a good start there." Which encouraged him to do it again, and again, until he pulled away with a groan. "If we keep that up, we'll never get to the rest." The third button popped free. "And we missed naked. I'm truly looking forward to filling in naked."

If there were more protests to be made, she couldn't remember them, all lost at the sound of that word. *Naked.* Maybe it should have embarrassed her. Worried her. Instead it made him her squirm on his lap, wriggling around until he clamped on her hips to hold her still. "Christ, Em. I don't want it over so fast this time, and you're pushing things along by doing that."

"But I—"

"We'll get to that, too, Em. I promise."

He blessed the clear morning light. He could see the snap of color in her eyes, the blush that stained her cheeks and spread down her throat.

He ran out of room, the buttons open all the way to where her blouse snagged into her waistband. He spread the front of her shirt wide, tucking the sides around her breasts. And then held his breath while he did the same with her shift, nudging it aside with one forefinger, exposing one curve, the side of her breasts, then one sweet pink nipple. The other, too, as lovely and tempting as the first, and he just sat there, staring, while her breasts quivered in the yellow light and she sat with her hands light on his shoulder and watched him watch her.

He bent his head, and the feel of his mouth on her breast made her jump, and then just as suddenly she went limp, sinking into the sensation.

His hair brushed soft against her when he angled his head; it gleamed, dark and healthy, against the white of her skin. Sweetness drizzled over her like warm honey; hot mouth, gentle tongue, dazzling pleasure. When he shifted to the other breast, the air cooled the wet nipple and it beaded, tight and tingling.

He tumbled her back to the bed and the world faded. Only the pleasure remained, sometimes slow and kind, stealing her breath, stealing her heart. And then sharp and piercing, leaving her gasping and shuddering and helpless against its power.

She never knew when the rest of her clothes were removed. She swam up through a fuzzy haze of joy and bursting desire to find them gone. And then his hands molded her breasts and she dove again, nearly drowning, overcome.

He reared back, raking her with hot eyes. His hair stuck out in all directions—had she done that? Her memories were distant, blurred by the spell he worked upon her. She'd wanted to know the texture, whether it would slip right through her fingers or tangle around them.

"Look at you." He pulled her arms wide, letting them arc against the dark quilts. "How many times have I dreamed of you like this?"

"You . . . dreamed of me?"

"Endlessly." He smiled, easy, sure. "And cursed myself for having missed the chance." His hands skimmed over her, quick and light. "But in all that imagining, I never pictured you as pretty as you truly are." Another stroke, this time slow enough to have her arching into his touch. "You steal my breath, Emily."

It was good to take his breath, she thought. But she wanted his heart, and she didn't know if it would ever be whole enough for him to give. A little dart of sadness stabbed through the pleasure but she refused to let it take hold.

This was what she had of him. Now.

She lifted her hand toward him, found him just out of her reach. "I'm not sure that I'm as skilled at undoing your buttons as you were at undoing mine," she said, "but I'll do my best."

Her fingers fumbled and shook. She kept getting distracted by the things she discovered along the way. Who could focus on buttons when there was a lovely stretch of neck to nuzzle? Who could worry about removing a shirt when it was already open, giving her access to a truly fascinating chest?

So he helped. Laughing, kissing, four hands less efficient than two would have been, but that only drew out the pleasure, made her hold her breath in anticipation. And then she let it out in sheer joy when at last he was naked, too, stretched full against her.

"Jake." It said nothing, just the murmuring of his name. And yet Emily felt as if it carried her heart with it. *Jake.* It was all there was to say. She wrapped her arms around his shoulders, pulling the solid bulk of him closer even though it was nigh impossible.

His sex was thick against her. She could feel it against her belly, and pressing further down, and the sweet, soft warmth that stirred and flowed between them exploded into blinding heat.

She spread her legs and tilted her hips to encourage the contact, her sensitive flesh gliding slickly against his, and she shuddered.

"Em." He reached down to hold her hips still—tight against him, but unmoving. And she thought she would go wild if he didn't free her.

He lifted his head to look into her eyes, his expression so tender she nearly wept. His kiss was gentle as morning, and for a moment she was content with it. His hips moved, a tiny pulse that sent pleasure spearing through her, curling her toes.

Unthinkingly she reached down, grabbed his rear, pulled him harder against her. Oh yes, that was better. Not enough, but better.

"Em." He sounded pained. "Em, I—"

She lifted herself against him. She had to get closer. She didn't know how, didn't even know why; instinct had taken over, a molten urgency that flowed and twisted in her belly, made her mindless with need.

Jake lay still, overwhelmed, awash in the bliss of her bare beneath him. Her skin was so fine, abloom with warmth, soft as rose petals against his. Her heart thumped against his chest, her breath sighed past his ear, and the whole of her was his, every inch of her skin pressed against his. He scarcely dared move for fear this dream would vanish like smoke.

"Please, Jake. I don't know how—*please*."

The plea in her voice broke him. Shattered every thread of restraint he owned. That he could make her feel like this clouded his vision, narrowed his world down to her. Something roused in him, an emotion so unexpected he had to let it stir and settle for a while before he could identify it.

Joy.

It had left him so long ago and so completely, he'd never thought to know it again. Never hoped. And yet it was there, in every breath she took, every sigh he drew from her, in the lift of her hips and the stroke of her hands. And because he now knew how fleeting it could be, how precious, he drew it out, let every second be complete and cherished of itself.

But then she whispered his name again, impatient, near frustration as her hips shifted restlessly.

There were borders here. Lines he couldn't cross. But they seemed distant, unimportant—what could matter but Emily?

Remember, he told himself. It would end soon. It must. But a little more . . . just a little more, to hold her, to give her back some small bit of what she'd given him.

To give her joy.

He moved his sex against her, and it slid easily over flesh that was hot, slick, soft. So soft. She fell into the rhythm, as if they'd been lovers for years, as if their bodies had accepted this moment, planned for this moment, for far longer than their minds had known.

Only a little more.

She strained against him. So beautiful; he was grateful for the light that let him see her: eyes half closed, mouth open, stunned and lovely. He could live a thousand years, see a million sights, and this one would remain.

Not enough. It wasn't enough, this simulated joining, when heaven was so near.

He levered back a fraction, positioned the tip of his sex at the entrance to her body. And let himself lean forward just a bit, torturing himself with what he couldn't have, what he wanted beyond life.

"Now, Jake. Now."

He circled his hips and her eyes flew open. "Oh Jake, I . . ."

"I'll stop before—"

Her eyes flew open, and she glared at him. "If you leave me now, I'll kill you."

Laughter exploded, a short, pained burst. "I won't."

He could do this, he told himself. Maybe even believed it. He would think only of her, give only to her, and it would be enough.

An inch . . . he could do an inch, give them both a taste of what they wanted. She cried out. And then he held himself there, the muscles in his arms shaking with the need to keep himself still because he knew even the slightest bit further would take him irrevocably past control.

"More," she demanded.

"I can't," he gasped.

"But—" Before he registered what she was about she reached down between them and took hold of him. Oh God, he was going to die, he was going to live, he couldn't—

She pulled him into her body. Cried out and

arched into him, her body closing around him as if to hold him there. And the pleasure pumped through him, a fiery heaven, and he could do nothing but drive deep and let go.

Gray light sifted through the old shack, blurring edges, coloring it with fond nostalgia. Emily awoke, disoriented, a little sore, tingling pleasantly in places that until recently she'd not given much consideration.

She couldn't remember if it was morning or evening; the light was soft and indistinct. She had a vague memory of having awakened at some point, thrown on her dress and going to check on Mr. Bishop. She found him sleeping peacefully and stumbled back to bed, ripped off her clothes and climbed back in next to Jake. It was impossible to sort through how much time had passed. Her brain spun with images, wondrous, blatantly sexual, flashes of Jake bending over her with hot eyes and ardent hands. The feel of him, urgent and thick, pressing deep inside her. What meaning did time have against that?

Moving seemed more trouble than it was worth. Jake lay flat on his back, arms over his head, and she'd wrapped herself around him. Belly cuddled up against his hip, leg thrown over his thigh, arm slung across his lower belly. Her head fit neatly against his shoulder, and it was so easy to shift a fraction and press a kiss there, his skin hot and salty on her tongue, and memories simmered, then kicked right into heat.

Smiling, she tilted her head, found his jaw with her lips. He'd grown bristles while they slept, his whiskers a rough and male abrasion. Interesting. She shifted yet again, wanting to admire him while he slumbered, and found herself looking into dark and angry eyes.

"Oh no." She sat up abruptly and pushed the tumble of hair out of her eyes. "You *promised*. You promised me you wouldn't be sorry."

"I know I did." That was what he regretted most of all and always had. All the promises he'd never been able to keep. "But I didn't know . . . I didn't think it would go that far. I'd planned to stop in time."

Her hair streamed over her shoulders and curled around her breasts. Unable to resist, he reached out and smoothed a tress aside, revealing the pretty bud of her nipple, and promises seemed irrelevant. He brushed it once with his thumb, watched it pucker up, and his mouth went dry. One afternoon in bed with her had done far more to encourage his passions than sate them.

She knocked his hand away and glared at him. Which he deserved, and she was so appealing with that fire in her eyes he almost smiled. Which would earn him more than a glare, he suspected, and rightly so.

"You thought you were going to . . . quit in the middle of things?"

"Well . . . yeah," he admitted.

"You were going to leave me like that?"

"No. I'd planned to . . ." He paused, looking for a delicate way to explain a very indelicate matter.

"Oooh." Her expression cleared. "You were going to leave *you* like that."

"No, I'm not that much of a martyr, either. But I hadn't planned to—"

"You couldn't resist me."

She looked so pleased with herself that this time he did grin. "That's about the size of it."

Her expression grew wicked, and she inspected the length of him. "Not that I recall."

He laughed. "Just wait. If you keep looking at me like that I can guarantee it."

"So I see." Eyes alight with mischief, drunk on her new power, she reached out and swept her hand down his belly. "Do you think," she asked, teasing him by circling lower, and lower, but never *quite*— "that you could resist me better now? Now that you're prepared for my—"

"Armored against your charms, you mean?" He grabbed her hand, because if she went one inch further he'd forget everything he had to say. "Not a chance." He drew her hand to his mouth, closed his eyes while he kissed it. "I've never been armored against you, Emily, and that, at least, must be obvious. But I need to talk you."

"Oh, don't look like that. Don't be serious now. You can be as serious as an undertaker later, I promise. But not now."

It tempted him. *She* tempted him, in every way and sense of the word. But if he'd learned nothing else well, he'd finally taken as truth that putting off a problem never solved anything.

Still holding her hand, he dropped them to his . . . No, not his lap, bad plan. He yanked it up higher.

"Emily," he began seriously. And then, "Stop that!" When her fingers began to wander, he flattened her hand against his chest and held it there. And then the words got all tangled up in his tongue. "Emily . . ."

Her smile softened. It must be nearly dusk; the light went rosy, and her skin glowed with it, pink and pretty, and he had to stop for a while and admire it, a lovely naked woman in his bed. A man who'd take such a sight for granted, he thought, was a man who deserved whatever misery he got.

"I didn't mean to brush you aside," she said quietly. "I just didn't want to—it was so lovely, Jake. I didn't want it to be anything else, not yet."

"Whether this is something else or not I'll leave for you to decide." He squeezed his eyes shut, then decided it was easier looking at her after all. *Just say it, Jake,* he ordered himself, while his heart knocked so hard against his ribs that it seemed in danger of knocking itself out.

He let go of her hands because his were cold, going slick with sweat.

"Jake." Gentle, she traced a finger down his jaw, a touch that had little to do with the passion that had come before and everything to do with the friendship that they'd had for far longer. "Tell me."

It came out in a rush. *"Weshouldgetmarried."*

"What?" she asked, wary, confused. "I'm not sure—"

"You heard me."

"Heard, maybe. Believed, that's something else."

There was a part of her that wanted to leap and shout with happiness, rush headlong into the future. Except that he was pale, wearing the dazed expression of a man about to face a firing squad. "Just why," she asked carefully, "do you think we should . . . do that?"

He gestured wide, encompassing the bed they'd left in a tumble of sheets and quilts. "That's obvious."

"Not to me."

His gaze drifted over her head. She wanted to tell him to look at her, *see* her. He was right beside her, naked, in the bed in which they'd just loved, and he was a hundred miles away.

Or perhaps, she thought, only a year or two away.

"I can't do it again, Emily." The words came out in a whisper, burning all the way. "I can't wait around to see if there's a child, and then rush into a wedding. I . . . I just can't."

She opened her mouth to tell him it was different, *she* was different, but realized there was no point in it. Logic had no sway against the kind of emotion that grabbed you by the throat and hung on. "Jake, you do know . . . it was only once. The odds are not that great. More than likely . . ."

His fierce gaze flew to her. "You want to take that chance?"

She was crossing unknown territory in the dark, gaping pits yawning in every direction, and she scarcely knew where to step. She was terrified of hurting him, and every choice seemed to hold the probability of doing just that. "*Want* to, no, I wouldn't say I want to." It was too hard to talk about this, about sex and babies and weddings, without touching him. She edged closer, until her hip was hard against his side, and put her hand on his chest, holding her breath until he reached up and linked his fingers with hers. Yes, she thought, this is something that, one way or the other, should be done together. "But I will, Jake."

"And what then? What if there is a child?" She deserved better, Jake thought. Deserved a man who could love her right, a man on his knees with flowers and jewelry. But it was too late for that. For both of them. "Rush into a wedding because a baby's on the way? I've *done* that, Em." And it damn near destroyed him. "I won't do it again."

"So we won't."

He frowned at her, fierce and angry. "So what then? Have the baby by *yourself*?"

"If I have to."

"No, you won't." He let go of her hand and grabbed her shoulders, gripping hard as if he wanted to shake her but instead he just held on, his fingers denting her flesh. "You will not."

"Okay, Jake," she said softly, knowing she'd dared too much. "Okay."

He yanked his hands back and saw the bright red ovals his fingers had pressed into her pale skin, and he had to look away and swallow hard before he could continue. "We can do it any way you want. If it turns out that you're . . . if it turns out that there's no baby, I'll do whatever you say. A divorce, you can blame it all on me. An annulment, even, if that's what you want. You can tell them anything necessary and I'll agree. But I have to marry you. Now, before it's too late."

This was the moment. Emily felt it in her bones, every deep and secret corner of her body, that this was when her life changed, became one or the other. She wondered if people usually knew, if the instant where your future was set on course usually came and went unnoticed, recognized only in retrospect. But this was hers.

She could follow her mind. She could follow her heart. She could follow, perhaps, the advice of her sisters—here or not, she'd no doubt what their counsel would be.

She looked at this man. Glowering, fiercely wounded. Terrified. And realized that she could think about this till she lost breath, but there'd never really been a choice. The choice had been made the day she met him and she just hadn't realized it until now.

"No, Jake, I—"

"No." It burst out of him. "Emily, there's no *no* here. That's not one of the possibilities. I—"

"That's not what I meant." She shook her head, a gesture so sharp her chin sliced an arc through the air. "I'll marry you, Jake"—relief flooded him, evaporated just as quickly when she continued—"but if I do, you have to be clear on this. There'll be no divorce, no annulment, no maybes. It'll be a marriage. Beds and babies and forever after. Everything. No option, no choices. That's it. This is your only chance to decide."

"I can't be the kind of husband you want, Em. I—"

"Did you hear me asking for declarations of ever-lasting love?" she said briskly. "Let me worry about what I deserve, okay?"

"I—" Ice speared along his nerve endings. His stomach twisted upon itself a half dozen times. His mouth was full of sawdust. "Let's go." He bounded out of the bed, grabbed her by the wrist, and hauled her after him. He was driven to hurry, unsure whether he was afraid he might change his mind . . . or she might.

"Now?"

"Yes, now." He looked wildly around him for clothes, located her petticoats beneath the table, and tossed them at her.

"But . . . but . . ." Shouldn't they sleep on it? Give him a chance to change his mind? "It must be past eight o'clock."

He shot an impatient glance out the window. "Almost nine."

"Shouldn't we . . . I don't know, go to bed, maybe?"

"We already did that."

"I meant sleep."

"You think there's a chance in hell either one of us is going to sleep now?"

She had to concede that point. "But—" He had his shirt on by now, his pants halfway up one naked leg. "Are you going to get married without your drawers on?"

"If you don't get moving, Em, you're going to get married *naked*."

Chapter 20

Despite Jake's best efforts, it took three days before they returned to the claim a married couple. First, Emily insisted on hovering over Mr. Biskup for another day and night, much to his vocal dismay. And then there were the various details to attend to, so that by the time they stood in front of a judge and mouthed a few words, a most unceremonious ceremony that took no more than five minutes, it hardly registered. How could it be that easy? For something that was supposed to be so important?

When they finally walked back through the front door, Emily's head was spinning and she was beginning to wonder if it would ever stop or just stay that way and she'd go through the rest of her days with her mind whirling like a child's kaleidoscope.

She stood just inside, her small handbag clutched in her hands, and scanned the interior. It looked exactly the same. The kitchen, neat and clean, tin plates stacked on the end of the table because there was no place else for them. She'd put a few sunflowers in a glass on the table and they'd withered in her absence, brown and drooping in a sorry curve.

They hadn't made the bed. The quilts piled at the foot, leaving the sheets white and bare and accusing.

"Okay, I got Reg put away," Jake said as he came through the door. "I think he was glad to be home."

She turned and faced him squarely. "How about you?"

"Huh?"

"Are you glad to be home?"

"Well, sure, I—" He caught her expression and winced. "Oh damn, I was supposed to carry you over the threshold, wasn't I? I forgot, I'm sorry— here, let's go outside, I'll do it now—"

"No." She shook her head. "It's not the threshold." Spinning slowly, she took in the rest—her dresses on their hooks, his collection of books high on the shelf. "It doesn't feel any different." She faced him directly. "We're married now. Shouldn't it feel different?"

Shrugging, he stepped closer. "We pretended to be married so long, I suppose it doesn't seem like much has changed."

Her husband, she thought, and waited for it to feel true. It was good to call him *hers*. But, she realized, she'd named him that for a very long time, anyway. Still . . . husband?

Maybe, she decided, *husband* wasn't a term that took hold suddenly, simply by echoing a few words and signing your names next to each other's on a license. Maybe *husband* was something that settled in, day by day, as you lived together, laughed together, building the name as you built a life.

Might as well get started.

"There's one difference," she said, and looped her arms around his neck, "from when we were pretending."

"Oh?" he said, arching his brow, trying to hide a grin. "And what would that be?"

"Forget the threshold." She jumped up and he caught her, just as she knew he would. "Carry me to bed."

Autumn did not come gently. At the end of August a violent thunderstorm rolled in from the northwest and battered everything in its path, stripping the cottonwoods, plastering grass to the earth. Strips of tar paper and shingles flew off shacks and went streaking over the land as if they weighed no more than dead leaves. Shallow washes boiled with temporary rivers.

When the storm moved on, it left cool air in its wake, and oceans of grass turned gold. The season seemed neither here nor there, a slice of time between summer and winter that was scarcely a season of its own. The waiting time, Emily mentally dubbed it. Waiting for the frost.

As she waited. Her marriage was . . . it still did not seem real to her. She wondered if it did for Jake but didn't dare ask. They got along well, she thought. Certainly they didn't argue. Which was precisely the problem, now that she considered the matter. It was artificial. They tiptoed around each other, neither one sure, both unwilling to make a misstep. As if their marriage, too, held its breath and waited to see which way the wind blew.

The second week in September, Emily sat at the table, hemming a tiny gown, when Jake entered.

His eyes dropped to the small mound of yellow flannel and he stopped cold, wearing an expression of blind panic. "Em?"

She threaded the needle into the soft cloth and set it aside. "It's for May."

"Oh." He dropped into the chair across from her. Just in time, she thought; he'd have been on the floor otherwise.

"I'm not, you know," she said.

"You're sure?"

"As of this morning." She pursed her lips and studied him. "I guess I don't have to ask how you feel about it."

"Emily." He said her name to delay his answer, trying to sort through the mix of emotion. A little disappointment, way down deep, completely buried by a tidal wave of fierce relief. "I'm not opposed to the idea of children," he said, and realized it was the truth. "Not at all. It's just that whole process of you *having* them terrifies me."

Her expression softened. "I know." She reached across the table and seized his hand. "I'm willing to wait awhile, Jake. Until you're easier with the idea. But I'm going to want them. You knew that going in."

"Yeah, I did. But I wasn't thinking that far down the road at the time," he said. "I was too busy trying to convince you to marry me."

She squeezed in reassurance. "I'm not going to die on you, Jake."

"You can promise me that?"

"I'm tempted to say yes. But you know better."

"Yeah," he said bleakly. "I know."

She told herself not to ask. How would she live with the answer, if it wasn't what she hoped? But the words came out anyway. "Are you sorry? You wouldn't have had to marry me."

She couldn't read him. His mouth was flat, his eyes shadowed. And then he smiled, lifted her hand to his mouth for a kiss. "Only," he said lightly, "if the waiting means I have to go back to sleeping in the tent."

Emily swallowed her sigh of disappointment. *Yes* would have been a hundred times worse. Instead he chose to keep it light, skating across the surface of the issue. She reminded herself she had to be patient. But she wondered if he would ever be willing to allow affection and companionship to deepen. And if it would be enough for her if he couldn't.

You knew the bargain when you entered into it, she reminded herself. There was no one else to blame.

"You won't," she said. "Kate has no idea—Dr. Goodale's funeral would have been years earlier if she had—but he was not one to edit my education. I know of a few ways to . . . well, there are several possibilities."

"Yeah?" he said, grinning so wide that she couldn't help but laugh. "Hot damn." He tried to look serious, but his eyes danced. "I'm quite certain, Em, that I'd get used to the idea of you conceiving a *lot* faster if we practice the actual conception part of it quite regularly. I'm willing to devote myself completely to the task."

"How generous of you," she said soberly, but the corners of her mouth twitched. "I'll keep that in mind."

"You do that." And then, suddenly serious, he leaned forward. "How about you? Are you sorry? You could have found someone who . . ."

Who wasn't afraid. Who had a whole heart. Who would . . . love you. She understood the words as clearly as if he'd spoken them aloud.

"Are you?"

The words were there, ready to pour out. Words that, true as they were, would only alarm him all the more. And so Emily held them back, chose the lighter way as well. "Of course not," she told him. "Would *you* want to have to admit to Kate that you lied to her?" She gave a mock-shudder. "Having to marry you is a small price to pay to avoid that."

The second week in October, Emily, elbow deep in biscuit dough, glanced out the window to see a few snowflakes spitting from steel-gray clouds that seemed to hover inches above the ground.

She flipped a clean dishtowel over the bowl, tugged off her apron, and dashed to the doorway of the lean-to.

Despite her hurry she had to pause a moment to appreciate. Jake was on his back beneath the malfunctioning press, which he claimed gave him even more trouble than she had when they first met. Grease streaked his forehead, his sleeves were rolled to his elbows—what nice, strong forearms the man had—and his jaw was set at a stubborn, this-machine-doesn't-have-a-chance angle.

"Jake." Wrench in one hand, he looked up, smiled, and her breath left in a whoosh. Funny, that she still hadn't gotten accustomed to that smile.

"Come to rescue me, did you?"

"Oh no. I'll do the printing, but keeping that monster in running order is *your* problem, Mr. Publisher."

"A man can only hope."

"Keep hoping," she advised him. And then, as lightly as she could manage, "I'm going over to the Blevinses'."

He shot a quick glance outside. "Be a good idea to wait, see if this develops into something. It's looking like we might get a good whap of winter early."

"That's why I'm going."

Carefully he crawled out and sat up, the hand holding the wrench falling against his thigh.

"Why?"

"If it gets worse . . . Jake, if May goes into labor and I can't get there, I'll have another patient, one in far worse shape than she, after Joe has a heart seizure."

He set the wrench down with more care than the task deserved. "I thought she wasn't due for a month."

"She's not."

"Then why are you going now?"

"Babies have a habit of picking the worst possible time to arrive." She watched him carefully. Maybe he'd paled a bit. Perhaps his mouth had tightened. She wondered if he'd tell her if this hurt him but even given how far they'd come, doubted that he would. "Let's just say that I've got a hunch and would rather not take any chances."

"All right." He tossed the wrench aside and stood, wiping his hands on his thighs. "Just let me wash up before we go."

"You don't have to come."

His eyes, flat and carefully unemotional, met hers. "I'm not letting you go out there alone."

"It's barely snowing now." *And it's too much to ask of you, to stand by a few feet from another woman laboring to bring forth a child. I would spare you.* "I'll be there before it really starts—*if* it really starts."

"And have me sitting home, wondering where you are, worrying if you're okay?" He walked over to her and cupped her face in his palms, tilting it up. "No, thank you."

The intensity in his eyes left her breathless. And hopeful. He had to feel something, didn't he, to look at her like that? "You would worry?"

"Of course I would worry."

"I—"

He stopped her with a kiss so sweet it made her eyes sting. "Shush," he whispered. "I'm coming along."

The moan died slowly, keening off into the night like a fading ghost. At the sound, the coffee cup slipped from Joe's hand and shattered on the floor.

Emily poked her head out from behind the blanket Jake had rigged to shield the bed from the part of the room where he and Joe waited. "Anybody bleeding?" she asked, her hair long lost to its knot, hanging limp around her shoulders. Her sleeves were rolled up to her elbows, and somewhere along the way she'd thumbed open the button at her throat and her skin glistened in the heat of the room— she'd had him stoke the stove high. He focused on that tiny wedge of tempting neck because it was a far better thing to contemplate than most of the other thoughts hovering around.

Jake stood up from where he'd been gathering the broken pieces of cup. He curled his fingers, hiding the small drop of blood on his palm where the point of a shard had pierced him. "Nope."

She studied him for a moment, and he did his best to appear unconcerned. "Everybody doing okay?"

"We're doing just fine," he said, and hoped it sounded better to her than to him. "No problems at all."

She shot a skeptical glance at Joe, flopped limply in his chair, staring aimlessly with glazed eyes.

"You men have any supper? I've really no time to make anything, but—"

"Jeez, Em, you think we're too helpless to throw together a sandwich?" The mere thought of food had his stomach roiling in protest. "Don't worry. Everything's under control out here." He cleared his throat. "How about . . . ah . . ." He jammed a finger at the blanket. "Everything okay in there?"

Her smile was brilliant. "Perfect," she said, the blanket flapping forlornly as she disappeared behind it again.

Perfect, he thought, as a brief, short shriek, abruptly cut off on a rising note, had panic surging thickly at the base of his throat.

He gathered the rest of the debris, this time with more care, and looked around frantically for someplace to stick it. Finally he dumped the shards in a pot, sloshed the spilled coffee around with a rag he pulled off the back of a kitchen chair, and called it good enough.

They'd arrived at noon, wet and chilled, the sky shedding flakes more thickly by that time. May, obviously surprised to see them, invited them to join the lunch they were just sitting down to.

Stuffed with May's excellent plum cobbler, Jake had just begun to relax when May stood up, squeaked, and looked down at the rush of fluid pouring from beneath her skirts.

Jake and Joe stood dumbly, useful as boats in the desert, while Emily efficiently mopped up the floor, tucked May into bed, and got water steaming, bustling around the men as if they were furniture.

And then time hit the wall and stuck. Oh, it must be passing; the sun had crept across the sky and slid down, but every time Jake glanced at the clock the hands hadn't budged a bit since the last time he'd checked.

"Jake," Joe finally said, his low voice filled with dread. "Is it supposed to take this long?"

How the hell should I know? "Oh yeah, sure. Emily said sometimes it takes even longer than this."

"Longer?" Joe's face bleached the color of his white shirt, crisp when they'd arrived but now limp and rumpled as if put on the moment it was pulled from the wash. "Did it . . . did it take so long with . . ."

His hands were slick and Jake rubbed them against his thighs. "Yeah." He closed his eyes briefly against the memories that charged up, clear and raw as the day they'd been born. "It's not the same, Joe."

"How do you know?"

"Emily promised." He said it with forced conviction only to ease Joe's mind. But it settled his, too; Emily might shade the truth when the situation required it, but she'd been completely confident on this point. He was sure of it.

Another cry rent the air. Joe sat bolt upright, eyes wide with terror. "Jesus, Jake! I can't—" He looked longingly toward the door, apparently on the verge of bolting through it.

"Oh no, you don't." How'd he ever believe Joe would take this lightly? Jake wondered. Another point to Emily. "If you run out now, you'll be suffering for it till the day you die."

"I wish it was me. It's got to be worse . . . the waitin' and worryin', it's got to be worse than the doin'. Doesn't it?"

Oh no, it's not, Jake thought, but in the interests of keeping Joe here, spared him that answer.

"Now see here." Jake rose from his chair and his

bones creaked, reminding him just how long he'd been hunched there, his muscles so tense they'd practically frozen in place. "I'm the last person to recommend drinking as a solution to anythin', but where the hell's that whiskey you make?"

"I—" Dazed, Joe blinked until the question took hold. "Keep it behind the woodbox."

Jake dove for the bottle, decided not to bother with a cup. He yanked out the cork and shoved it at Joe. When Joe didn't respond, Jake reached down and forced his fingers around it, then pushed it toward Joe's mouth.

Joe gulped, then shuddered. "Ahh." He gulped down a quarter of the bottle, bringing enough color into his cheeks that he no longer looked in danger of fainting at any moment.

"How about you?" Joe asked.

Jake's mouth went dry. The sharp smell of the alcohol burned his nostrils and he missed it, more sharply than ever, and the black oblivion it promised. He swallowed hard. "No," he said. "I'm all right." That might be a lie, he thought, but he sure as hell hadn't been all right when he'd been drinking, either.

Another cry, long and strained. Joe's bottle tilted in his slack grip, the pale liquid spilling out and forming a puddle right into the damp spot the coffee had left.

Ten brutally long seconds later, Joe straightened his shoulders like a man who knew there was nothing for it but to charge into battle even though he'd surely be killed. "I'm goin' in there."

Jake grabbed his arm. "Em'll call you if you're needed. She promised."

"But—"

And then there was another cry, a new one, wavering, nasal, as beautiful a thing as this earth offered.

"Jake," Joe said, stunned as a poleaxed steer. "Did you hear that?"

"Yeah." He grinned. "I heard it," he said, grabbing Joe's hand and pumping hard.

"Thanks, I—" He stopped dead, gaze glued over Jake's shoulder. Jake spun, saw Emily approaching with a smile the size of Montana, a yellow-wrapped bundle tucked carefully in the crook of her arm.

"Is that—" Joe took half a step, couldn't go any farther.

"Of course it is. What else would it be?" She beamed at him. "Congratulations."

"May, is she—" Full sentences were beyond him.

"She's wonderful. She did a beautiful job." Emily pushed back a corner of the blanket. Jake caught a glimpse of dark, wet hair, plastered against an impossibly tiny skull. "Don't you want to meet your daughter?"

"That'll be ten bucks, Blevins," Jake said, but Joe ignored him.

"My daughter," Joe whispered, with such reverence that Jake knew any preference Joe might have had for a son had disappeared the instant he'd laid eyes on this girl. Haltingly, Joe stepped closer, tucked his hands behind his back, and peered into the swirl of blanket as if terrified of what he might see. "My—"

He dropped to the floor.

Torn, Emily looked from the patient at her feet to the one in her arms.

"I'll take her."

"Jake?"

"You better check on him," Jake said, and hoped to God he wasn't going to faint, too. He felt light-headed, the blood roaring in his ears until he could barely hear her response. "I won't drop her. I promise."

"You'd better not," she said, pretending to tease while she studied him worriedly.

Carefully she transferred her precious burden to him. "Jesus. I forgot how light they are." Eyes closed, mouth open, plump cheeks curved so adorably. "Jesus."

Emily, who'd bent beside Joe, looked up, her brow knit. "He's fine. Just fainted."

"If there's ever a moment in a man's life worthy of fainting, this is it."

"I really should—"

"Attend to May," he finished when she was reluctant to do so. "Go ahead. We're fine."

"Are you sure?"

"It'll be just till he wakes up, right?" Oh, the smell of the babe rose to him, that powdery sweetness like nothing else. "Em, if we're ever going to have one of these of our own, it's probably about time I test out the idea."

She struggled to hide her concern. "All right," she said over her riotous worry and slipped behind the curtain.

She delivered the placenta, pleased to discover that May had torn only a bit—not bad for a first baby, she thought, especially one of such a healthy size for all that she'd arrived early. Despite her reassurances, Emily could now admit to herself that she'd been anxious. She had little doubt of the quality of her training but it would take her a while to get used to working so completely alone and without the comforting presence of a hospital only blocks away.

After promising an exhausted but proud May she'd return momentarily with her daughter and her husband—she hadn't mentioned Joe's little nap—she pushed aside the draped blanket.

It was a picture that would live in her mind until the day she died: Jake, crooning softly to the child, so absurdly tiny in his big arms, his face such a mixture of awe and terror that, if he hadn't owned her heart already, she'd have handed it over in that moment.

She came to stand beside him; he was too lost in his rapt fascination to notice her approach.

"Jake," she said, and put a hand on his arm.

"Isn't she beautiful?" he said, hushed as if in a cathedral.

"Beautiful," she agreed. And then, reluctantly, "May is asking for her."

"Oh. Of course." He looked up, eyes glistening.

He blinked hard. "I have to go get her, Emily. I have to go get my daughter."

Gently she touched his hair and peered over his shoulder, admiring the squawking, red-faced infant. "I know."

Chapter 21

Winter's early incursion faded as quickly as it had arrived, making way for a long, golden, fertile autumn filled with crisp days and blue skies and a hefty harvest for Joe Blevins . . . when the besotted father could tear himself away from staring into the cradle long enough to go to the fields.

The last week in October Emily returned from McGyre with the mail, and upon finding the shack empty, hurried to where the new house was rising steadily, sticks of clean, raw yellow wood blocking out the boundaries of a home to come.

It'd been a bit of a trick to convince Jake that she should be the one to take the *Register* in for distribution and pick up the mail. Part of the printer's duties, she'd informed him, but finding the little white lies that had once tripped so easily off her tongue came harder now, even though she said the words to spare him.

Hammer in hand he came to meet her, his smile uncomplicated, unfettered, and her heart swelled. Yes, there was much to be settled between them, but she could be patient. It would all work out in the end. She'd never been so sure of anything in her life.

He kissed her until the letters fluttered from her hands to the ground and she surely would have followed them if his arms hadn't held her up.

"Come on," he said. "Let me show you what I've done."

"*Now?*"

He grinned, thoroughly pleased with the reaction he'd drawn. "It won't take long. And then I'll be able to give you my full attention."

He took her by the hand and drew her into the center of the structure. "What do you think?"

"I—" It took her a moment to sort it out, translate the maze of lumber into future rooms. He'd expanded the kitchen, moved the staircase, nudged the wall of the dining room farther into the parlor. "You changed the framing."

"Yeah. Once, when we were talking about houses, you said . . . you mentioned you liked a big kitchen, and that you thought it would be clever to put it in front where you could see the comings and goings. And that you hated having to squeeze into a dining room."

"But I—" She'd always hoped. Her whole life had been fueled by it. But this . . . this was bigger than hope, all encompassing, a joyful lifting that left her light-headed, ready to float right up to the pretty blue sky. "You changed Julia's plans."

"Yeah." She looked for signs of regret. There was a shadow of sadness, yes; she knew there would always be. One could not love and lose without having the loss mark you permanently. She wouldn't even want it to disappear. It was the sum of life, loss and joy, and if you were very lucky, the balance came up bigger on the joy side.

"You didn't have to do that."

"I know I didn't have to. But I want this to be our house." He reached for her and cradled her face in his palms as if he held an object of infinite preciousness, as carefully as he'd held Joe and May's new daughter. "Julia's house still lives, in my dreams, just as it always did. But this one . . . this one is ours," he said with absolute conviction.

"Oh." She kissed him again, because sometimes words just wouldn't do.

"So," he murmured when he lifted his head. "How was town?"

"Town? It was . . ." She couldn't believe she'd forgotten. Or perhaps, deep down inside, she'd been too afraid of what was in that letter and allowed herself to "forget."

She pawed frantically through the brittle brown grass. "There!" she said and pounced on the flash of white. And then she slowed, clutching the envelope in her hand.

He stared at the white square before slowly lifting his gaze to her face. "It's from Mr. Jensen."

He put out his hand, sucked in a breath.

"Jake . . ."

"It's okay, Em. I've got to read it sooner or later, and waiting doesn't change what's inside."

She tried to mouth her usual faith in the future but the words wouldn't come. This mattered too much.

She watched his face carefully while he ripped open the envelope. The torn bits fluttered down to the ground as he scanned the two sheets of paper inside. His mouth firmed, and the rich, new life in his eyes—which she hoped she'd had something to do with—went flat and dull.

"We'll get a different lawyer," she said quickly. "Jensen, he's just one man, he doesn't know—"

"He's the best I can hire in Chicago." He crumpled the letter in his fist. "It's not that bad, Em. He said it would be hard. We knew that going in."

"But she's your *daughter*." Emily refused to believe that the courts wouldn't acknowledge the right of his claim. A child deserved to know her father, and Jake deserved his chance to be one.

"Jensen said there's no getting around the fact that I left."

"You had no choice in the matter."

"Didn't I?" he said hoarsely. "Oh, don't look at me like that. All right, I didn't have a choice. But it's my word against theirs, and Barnett Bates's word means a helluva lot more in Chicago than mine."

"There's no one there who'd vouch for your story?"

"No. No, not anymore, not with their livelihoods on the line."

"So what can we do?"

He walked over to her. "He said it'd be better if we proved up first. Finished the house. So I can show that I can offer her a real home, a stable future." He drew a line down her jaw and she trembled at the touch. "And you'll help, too. Show that I'm a responsible, happily married man."

Happily? Any other time, in any other circumstances, the word would have meant the world to her. "We'll do it, Jake. We'll get her back. I promise."

"So." He visibly boxed the subject away. "What else do you have there?"

"It's just a letter from my sister."

"Read it to me, will you?"

"Jake . . ." She didn't want to drop the subject, but he'd shut down completely, in a way he hadn't in months. She hated the barrier he put up between them. She thought she'd found her way inside.

"Your sister does entertain me," he said. "So where's Kate?"

She shook her head. "It's from Anthea."

"Ah, another one weighs in. Let's hear it."

My dearest Emily:

I bet you're all braced for the worst, aren't you? Certain you're going to get a lecture from me? But I ex-

pect that Kate has already filled that function for the both of us, and quite expertly at that.

Not to mention that I am hardly the one to talk about quick marriages to a man your sisters haven't had time to approve, am I? I can only hope that it turns out as well for you as it did for me. I have every faith that you've chosen well.

No, I'm writing to you about Kate. I'm just the slightest bit concerned about her, you see. She sent me the oddest letter, something about treasures and adventures and . . . Emily, can you think of a person less suited to an adventure than Kate? She posted it from New York, but I wired the hotel and received no answer. I'm sure she must be tucked away at some posh resort, soaking her toes, too busy fending off admirers to write to either one of us, but I'd feel more comfortable if I knew exactly where. I must have a sister to worry over, you know. Did she happen to mention her plans to you?

I'm sure it's nothing for you to fuss over, though. Fuss over that handsome man of yours instead (he simply must be handsome, I insist upon it) and be happy, my dear. Be happy.

Awaiting details and, hopefully, a visit—

> *Your devoted sister,*
> *Anthea*

December 23

The snow fell fast and thick, revenge for the mild autumn. Inside the house three pies—two mince, one dried peach—cooled on the table, while beside them three bowls of yeast dough rose high and white beneath cloths. Emily pulled a batch of nutmeg cookies from the oven, the warm, rich spice scenting the air.

She poked at the puffy dough. Needed another fifteen minutes or so, she judged. Which meant she could drink a cup of coffee and stare out at the storm without guilt.

The world swirled with white. Here and there a long piece of dried grass pierced the snow, like the few sparse, stiff hairs on Mr. Biskup's head.

Jake came out of the half-finished office where he'd been, under protest, setting type. But given a choice between throwing the next edition of the *Register* or Emily having the time to bake one more pie, he'd immediately picked the type.

"Jeez, it smells good in here." He wandered over to join her, slipping his arms around her waist, a gesture that had become utterly natural to them both. He nuzzled her neck. "Smells even better right here."

"It's really coming down. I can hardly see the stables." Smiling, she leaned back into his embrace. "If this keeps up, the Blevinses and Art won't make it here for Christmas dinner."

"You mean I'd have to eat it all?" He *tsk*ed. "Such a shame."

"You'll just have to force yourself."

"The things I do for you." He kissed her neck, her cheek, and let the simmer of desire, the promise of more to come, warm them both. "Too bad I couldn't get the house all done in time for Christmas."

Three weeks ago they'd moved into bare rooms and unfinished walls, the air sharp with the smells of sawdust and fresh paint. Emily loved every inch of it.

She turned in his arms, and her heart caught and sang. Would the day ever come, she wondered, that she would see him and not feel this? The lift, the warmth, the giddy joy? "Some things," she said softly, "are worth waiting for."

"I—" He looked over her shoulder, squinted. "What the hell's that?"

"What?" She spun, following his gaze. A dark shape, bulky and big, took form out of the snow. "A coach?"

Yes, a coach, the likes of which had never been seen in that territory, bigger than their old claim shack, glossy black sides glinting through a thick dusting of white.

"Who could possibly be out in this?" she asked.

"Must have gotten lost," he murmured. "Followed the first light they saw."

The vehicle had been mounted on skids and slid right into the yard. Four perfectly matched gray horses, their blankets a deep royal blue, pulled it, huge hooves churning the snow.

The coachman, swaddled in scarves and buffalo robes, climbed down and opened the side door. He reached inside and handed down a tiny, cloaked figure that shook off the assistance and leaped down with alacrity.

"What—" Jake's hold on her loosened and she felt his sudden, sharp alertness. And as the figure turned, took one step toward the shack, he burst into motion, sprinting out the door and into the snow.

"Mom?" Four fast steps, and then he stopped cold. "Mom?"

Emily saw the woman lift her head, and then Jake scooped her up, hugging her so her toes dangled off the ground, brushing the top of the layer of snow. Emily, who'd been a few seconds behind, finally caught up.

"Em! Em, look who's here." He set her down, but kept her hand. "This is my—"

"I know. This is your mother." Emily extended her hands in welcome and was pleased when Mrs. Sullivan took them both. She was tiny, smaller than Emily, who came up to Jake's chest on a tall day. She peered out from between a low, fuzzy cap and a big swath of fuzzy blue scarf, wrinkled and bright-eyed as a storybook elf, but her grip on Emily's hands was strong. "I'm so delighted you're here."

"As am I." Mrs. Sullivan beamed, sunshine through the swirling snow. "Though I suspect the very best Christmas present I've ever had, my dear, is you."

"But how did you—?" Flakes melted on Jake's dark cheeks, glistening droplets, and caught on his lashes. "What are you—?" He couldn't seem to get the questions out, as if there were too many to settle on any one.

"The Bateses invited me, of course."

"But—" He frowned. "They fired you. Right after Julia and I—"

"Yes," she said serenely. "But things change." She touched his cheek. "You've no coat, and there's much to talk about. Let's get inside."

"I'm not cold." Irrevocably drawn, his gaze arrowed to the massive black coach. "Emily, go ahead. I'm going to—" The words stuck in his throat when another figure, larger, wearing a huge dark greatcoat, lumbered down from the coach.

"Oh, I'm not going anywhere."

Jake didn't move. Emily thought he probably didn't even breathe.

The man, slow-moving, impressively distinguished even with snowflakes catching in his gray-streaked beard, went to Emily first.

He stabbed his beautiful mahogany cane into six inches of snow and leaned upon it. "You must be Emily," he said, and extended a broad hand. "I'm Barnett Bates."

"I'm pleased you're here."

He patted her hand and scowled. "Not sure I can say the same."

"Wait. Wait, wait, *wait!*" Jake came out of his stunned silence with a roar. "What the hell's going on?"

"We've come for . . ." He looked back at Emily. "You mean you didn't tell him? Oh, that's rich." His laugh boomed as he bent over with it, so deep only the support of his cane kept him from tumbling into a drift. "That's the best fun I've had in . . ." He sobered. "Two years or so." He was just as Jake had described him. Proud, intimidating, confident in his own opinion. But he'd come this far, Emily thought. It was enough. "Wilomene's had some trouble with a cough. Her lungs—" For a man like Barnett Bates that slight, potent pause said more than an anguished cry from another. "The doctor suggested that the Western climates might be more beneficial for her. And when we began receiving letters from your wi—" It was more than he could bring himself to do, call another woman Jake's wife. "When Emily wrote to us—"

"She *wrote* to you?" Jake broke in.

"Yes. Several times. Charming letters."

"Oh, she's charming, all right," Jake said flatly.

"She invited us to visit. Very prettily, I might add, which is more than you ever did." Snowflakes coated the black fur collar of his coat, sparkling like sugar. "When Emily mentioned that there might be several plots available here, and that in her considered opinion the air might be helpful, Wilomene and I decided the time had come to inspect it."

"We?" Jake paled. "Is . . . Mrs. Bates is here?"

"In the coach. She'll be down when the nurse gets them bundled up."

His mouth formed a word. No sound came out but Emily could read it clearly. *Them*?

He turned for the coach, made his way to it, moving like a sleepwalker through a shifting dream.

The coachman reached inside, helping down another person, as small as Mrs. Sullivan but requiring far more assistance. Swathed in cloaks that seemed to weigh down her fragile shoulders, Mrs. Bates gripped tightly to the coachman's proffered arm with both gloved hands. She stood clinging to him for a moment, waiting until she could stand on both feet before turning to face Jake.

"Hello, Jake," Mrs. Bates said.

"I—" He broke off, his attention, his whole being, focused on the slight woman climbing down from the coach with her arms full. "Em—" Hand shaking, he reached out, as if he knew she'd be there.

"I'm here," Emily said, gripped his hand, and hung on.

"God." He swallowed once. And again. "Oh God. Would you look at her, Emily? Look at her."

"I see her," she whispered. "She's beautiful." And she was, pale blond curls wafting out from beneath a snug pink cap that matched her cheeks, eyes as bright and round as blueberries.

"Jenny looks like her mother, of course," Wilomene said, imperious and proud.

"Jenny?" His head swung briefly toward Wilomene, back a second later, as if he couldn't bear not to be looking at his daughter. "You call her Jenny?"

"That's her name, isn't it?"

"Yeah. I thought maybe you'd change it, after we—"

"You thought I'd change the name my daughter gave her?"

"I didn't know." He reached out slowly, as if he couldn't take one inch nearer for granted. And then he lightly fingered one cotton-white puff of hair, as if he was afraid she might vanish if he touched more.

Jenny abruptly wailed and buried her face against her nurse's shoulders.

"She's shy when she first meets someone," Wilomene said. She clung to her pride and disapproval to the very last. But then, her gaze resting fondly on her granddaughter, she dared one step. "But she'll warm up to you quickly. And once she does, she loves with all her heart."

"Like her mother," he murmured.

"Yes. Like her mother."

"Now then." Barnett stamped over to join them. "I may be having second thoughts about all this if you're still fool enough to keep us standing around in the snow."

"Please. Go in. We'll be there in a moment," he said, and paused. "Make yourselves at home."

Barnett ushered the women in, then turned back halfway through the door. "My daughter loved you."

"I know. Almost as much as I loved her."

"Don't let her down."

Jake nodded, accepting. "I don't intend to."

Jake stared at the closed door for another full minute, stunned, as if afraid to believe his daughter was truly on the other side. And then, as slowly as if he'd aged a hundred years in the last few minutes, he turned to face his wife. His cheeks gleamed with water, his hair was powdered white, and he blinked the snowflakes off his lashes.

Bracing herself, Emily waited. And waited some more. And finally, because she'd never been good at waiting: "Are you angry?"

"Am I angry?" He stepped nearer, so she could see each individual flake as it fell and caught, a frozen star that lasted a mere second on his cheek before dissolving into a tear. "You're the one that's so good at reading people. Can't you tell?"

"I—" She had to be breathing. Her heart had to be beating. Intellectually she understood the physiology but she couldn't *feel* either one. "No. I hope, too much, and the hoping's getting in the way."

"You always were good at hoping." He shook his head. "I never was."

"That's okay. That's why you have me."

"Do I? Have you, I mean?"

There was no point in denying it. "If you want me, you do. You've known that for a long time, though."

"Yes. Yes, I guess I did," he said. "You're shivering. You're cold, let's—"

"I'm not cold." Scared and worried, but not cold. She was never cold with Jake. "Please, I can't stand it any longer, what are you thinking?"

"What the hell did you tell them that could have possibly persuaded Barnett Bates to haul himself to Montana?"

"I don't think it was anything I said," she admitted. "If anything, it was Julia. Once they got past the grief enough to remember what she would have wanted." And then the cold did hit, down to her bones. "And, too, Wilomene's health is not strong, and Barnett . . . they're not young anymore, and the last few years have been hard. Maybe they just didn't want Jenny to lose as much as they have."

"Can I do it, do you think? Do right by her?"

"Of course you can!" she cried, seizing his hand, and nearly wept in relief when he didn't pull away. "You're going to be damn wonderful at it. The best ever. I guarantee it."

"You do, do you?" he said. And then, "I love you, Em. I do. With all I am now, with everything I've learned, I love you."

And then everything began again. Her breath, her heart, her *life*.

"I didn't want to, you know. I fought it."

"I know," she said softly.

"But I never had a chance. Everything that's ever happened to me all brought me to this point, so I could love you with every cell in my body, every corner of my soul. And I'm just sorry it took so long for me to know it."

"I told you, Jake. Some things are worth waiting for."

"Yeah. That they are." Then he bent his head and kissed her, friend to friend, lover to lover, husband to wife, a vow more powerful than the one they'd taken the day they'd married. "Thanks, Em. For knowing I had it in me. And for loving me enough to see it."

"You're very welcome." She linked her arm with

his and turned for the door. The house looked beautiful, roof frosted in white, windows glowing warm and gold. A home, she thought. Yes, a home. "Let's go get to know your daughter."

Epilogue

December, 1921

December in Montana was cold. Cold enough, some said, to freeze your nose—and a few other parts polite people didn't mention—right off your body the instant you stepped outdoors.

But that didn't stop the residents of McGyre. No, they were born of heartier stock, especially when there was a celebration to be had. And so they thronged the streets, noses as bright a red as the bunting swagged from every storefront. Toes jigged to the proud, brassy marches blasted by the McGyre City Band, including, their director announced proudly, their tuba player, who'd overcome a severe mouth injury when his lips froze to the mouthpiece in order to be here.

The sky arched overhead, the kind of blue it only got when the temperature hovered well south of freezing, shining on snow as white as Mrs. Sullivan's sheets. Red, white, and blue, the people told each other happily as they thronged in the streets, swilling the hot chocolate and steaming coffee Wilber Bunku was selling from the front porch of his store. Appropriate weather, they said. A little cold wouldn't stop McGyre.

Not when they had such a momentous occasion to celebrate. Not when tiny little McGyre was sending off one of their own to Washington, D.C.

And what a distinguished senator he'd be, the ladies murmured to each other. Such a handsome figure he was, broad and tall, that dashing streak of silver in his hair, and, oh, so obviously in love with his wife! They found it so romantic that when Senator Jacob Sullivan, the famous "Proof Sheet King," resplendent in a black jacket and charcoal-striped pants, climbed out to the back platform of the train (which, they congratulated themselves smugly, they had the senator to thank for bringing to town) to address the crowds, feminine sighs rolled down the streets of McGyre like stampeding cattle.

Wilber, disgruntled because he was a Democrat, damn it, and it was his God-given responsibility to be grumpy on a day like today—not that he'd minded the business, of course—leaned over to Imbert Longnecker, his boon companion, to give his opinion on their new senator.

"I suppose it's an honor, having him come from McGyre, but you know damn well the fella wouldn't have gotten elected if we hadn't given women the right to vote."

Imbert craned his long neck to get a good view. "It's done now, Wilber. Might as well accept it."

"He's supported the women's vote from the beginning," Wilbur complained. "And you know, I think some of them voted for whoever they pleased instead of who their husbands told them to! Which was exactly why they shouldn't have gotten the vote in the first place, if you ask me."

"I don't know why a wife would ever disagree with her husband," Imbert said dryly. "Besides, think of it. The man's got five daughters! Can you imagine how little peace he would ever have had if he hadn't supported women's suffrage?" Imbert shuddered at the thought. He'd only one daughter himself, but his precious Lana could make him agree to all kinds of things he'd started out saying no to.

"It's more than that, you know. Why, he even moved all the way to Kansas for two whole years so that wife of his could attend the Women's Medical College." The thought required Wilber to finish his own coffee—spiked with the extra kick only his best customers received—in one fell gulp.

"That's enough," Imbert said sharply. "I probably would have lost my wife, and my son, too, if Emily hadn't been there when she had a hard time."

Wilber had forgotten Ellen had had such difficulties giving birth. And that Imbert had always had a fondness for Mrs. Sullivan. "Sure, and she's a fine physician, she is. Doesn't mean women should be meddling in the affairs of state."

The crowd that had gotten there early enough to get a prime spot roared. Sullivan was giving a right rousing speech, from the sound of it, though Imbert and Wilber couldn't hear a word. Didn't have to. You could always judge the success of a stump speech by watching the crowds. If they were nodding, if they laughed now and then, well, you had 'em. The words themselves didn't matter a bit.

"And that oldest girl of his, heard tell she's a lawyer. In Chicago, they say." Wilber hooted. "Now doesn't that just beat all? A girl lawyer." That called for another coffee, he decided. And maybe skip the coffee. "Ain't no daughter of mine gonna get much schoolin', I can tell you that."

"That's her right there," Imbert said, pointing at the platform. "In the back."

Wilber whistled through his teeth. "Hell, she's a pretty one, ain't she? Why'd a woman that looks like that want to waste herself in a courtroom?" Loyally, he'd tried to remain uninterested as long as he could. But, shoot, the man was his senator, wasn't he? "Who's the old lady next to her?"

"That's Sullivan's mother. And I'd watch calling her old, if I were you," Imbert said. "She'd likely tan your hide if she heard you."

"Sure." Wilber snorted. "Guess that explains a lot, though."

"And that's his former father-in-law."

"Ooo-hee, the rich one," he said in awe. "I heard o' him. Heard he owns half of Chicago, then bought out most of Montana, too. You think he bought Sullivan the election?" Though honesty compelled him to admit that Sullivan could probably have bought his own.

"I don't believe Senator Sullivan bought the election." The crowd roared. "Shhh. I want to hear."

Then, as the assembly went silent, hanging on every word, some trick of the wind carried his voice to them so that they could suddenly hear as clearly as if the man spoke right beside them.

"In conclusion," the senator said in the rich, deep tones of a natural orator, "you see before you a man as proud as a man can be, deeply honored to represent this magnificent state and its fine citizens in the capital of this great nation."

He waited patiently for the applause to die down. And then he reached back and drew forward his wife, dressed in a blue suit and red and white striped shirt for the occasion.

"His wife's still a fine-looking woman, ain't she?"

"Hush," Imbert said, scowling.

"Though I have to admit," Senator Sullivan continued, "that the *very* proudest day of my life was when this woman agreed to marry me."

Grinning, he laid his wife over his arm, bending her back, and kissed her, hard and long, full on the mouth, right in front of everybody. Giggles burst through the crowd. Two women fainted and, despite the temperature, a dozen more took to fanning themselves with their gloved hands.

"What the hell's he doing?" Wilber asked.

"If you don't know, Wilber, it's about time you learned."

"Just ain't right for a fellow to be kissing his wife like that," he complained, as Mrs. Sullivan had to clap her hand on the top of her head to keep from losing her red-feathered hat. "Not after all those years of marriage. Be giving the women ideas," he said. "It just ain't right."

Applause burst out, swelling and growing until the town rang with it. The senator came up for air, beaming, his wife flushed and flustered at his side.

"I don't know about that," Imbert said. "It looks pretty damn right to me."

Have fun in the sun this June with these sizzling romances from Avon Books!

....

AFTER THE ABDUCTION by Sabrina Jeffries
An Avon Romantic Treasure

Juliet has attended balls till she's exhausted and danced until dawn . . . but two London seasons have made one thing clear: she longs for Morgan Pryce, the dashing scoundrel who had broken her heart. Now, his twin brother, Sebastian, pursues her—but he seems so very familiar. Could Sebastian and Morgan be one and the same?

TANGLED UP IN LOVE by Hailey North
An Avon Contemporary Romance

She'd been left at the altar . . . and now she's left on the side of the road, with a broken-down car and a colicky collie. But Dr. Michael Halliday (small town vet!) is coming to the rescue of Stacey St. Cyr (big city gal). Can they enjoy this tangled, messy, sweet thing called love?

THE RAKE by Suzanne Enoch
An Avon Romance

Three determined young ladies vow to give three of London's worse rakes some lessons in love. To win a wager Viscount Dare ruined Lady Georgiana Halley—now she will use every seductive wile she has to win his heart and break it. But then he astonishes her with a proper proposal—of marriage!

THE MAIDEN WARRIOR by Mary Reed McCall
An Avon Romance

Young Gwynne was taken captive on the day she was wedded to a bold Englishman—before they could pass their wedding night together. Now, Aidan de Brice has come to reclaim her . . . and though Gwynne barely remembers the breathtaking man before her, her senses recall what her memory cannot . . .

REL 0502

Avon Romantic Treasures

*Unforgettable, enthralling love stories,
sparkling with passion and adventure
from Romance's bestselling authors*

Avon Romances—
the best in exceptional authors
and unforgettable novels!

Have you ever dreamed of writing a romance?

*And have you ever wanted
to get a romance published?*

Perhaps you have always wondered how to
become an Avon romance writer?
We are now seeking the best and brightest undiscovered
voices. We invite you to send us your query letter to
avonromance@harpercollins.com

What do you need to do?

Please send no more than two pages telling us
about your book. We'd like to know its setting—is it
contemporary or historical—and a bit about the hero,
heroine, and what happens to them.

Then, if it is right for Avon we'll ask to see part of the
manuscript. Remember, it's important that you have
material to send, in case we want to see your story quickly.

Of course, there are no guarantees of publication,
but you never know unless you try!

*We know there is new talent just waiting
to be found! Don't hesitate . . . send us
your query letter today.*

*The Editors
Avon Romance*